S0-AXD-465

GORD STARTED TO SHOUT with glee as the chain-enwrapped globe bounced and rolled across the temple floor. His gaze followed it as it weaved this way and that, then the young man's eyes widened and his delight was cut short. The globe came to a stop at the feet of a small figure, not much taller than the ball of translucent material itself, who had just stepped into the chamber. Gord recognized him at once, and spat his name under his breath as if it were a curse.

"Obmi! You dirty toad! I'll—"

The dwarf did not hear that remark, but even if he had he could not have scowled any more blackly as he looked up at Gord hanging onto the chain high above the floor. "Bolt, bring down that monkey!" he commanded, pointing toward Gord.

"Yes, lord," the wizard replied. A bolt of crackling energy shot from the spell-caster's fingertips. The purplish-blue flash of electricity hit the thick metal chain and made an eerie, fiery light play up and down its length. An aura of light surrounded Gord's form, and he fell like a stone, hitting the floor feet first and then collapsing with a dull plop, burned and unmoving.

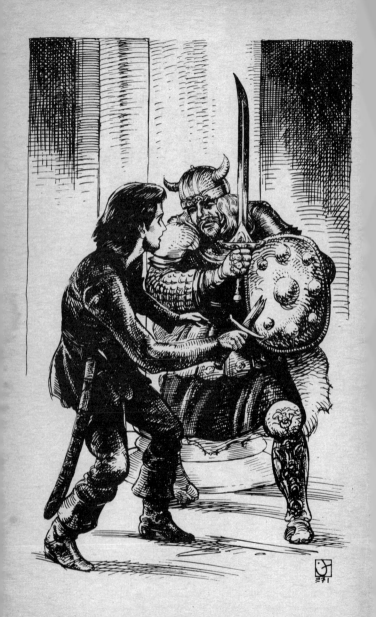

SEA OF DEATH

by Gary Gygax

**The quest for a prize that will
either save the world
— or destroy it!**

Illustrated by Jerry Tiritilli

Edited by Kim Mohan

GORD THE ROGUE™ Books

SEA OF DEATH

Copyright ©1987 Trigee Enterprises Corporation.
All rights reserved.

SEA OF DEATH takes place in the locale described in the WORLD OF GREYHAWK™ Fantasy Game Setting, which was created by Gary Gygax. Characters, towns, places, and landmarks from that product are used pursuant to license from TSR, Inc. All characters and names in this book are fictitious. Any resemblance to actual persons, living or dead, or to actual places or events, is purely coincidental.

This book is protected under the copyright laws of the United States of America. Any reproduction or other unauthorized use of the material or artwork contained herein is prohibited without the express written permission of the copyright holder.

GORD THE ROGUE is a trademark owned by Trigee Enterprises Corporation.

The New Infinities Productions logo is a trademark owned by New Infinities Productions, Inc.

WORLD OF GREYHAWK and DUNGEONS & DRAGONS are trademarks owned by TSR, Inc. The use of these terms in this product has not been approved by TSR, Inc.

The name "Ace" and the "A" logo are trademarks belonging to Charter Communications, Inc.

First Printing, June 1987
Printed in the United States of America

Distributed by the Berkley Publishing Group, 200 Madison Avenue, New York NY 10016

9 8 7 6 5 4 3 2 1

ISBN: 0-441-75676-X

New Infinities Productions, Inc.
832 Geneva St.
Lake Geneva WI 53147

Dedication

This book is dedicated to my daughters Elise, Heidi, and Cindy, because I love them! All three of them have adventured within the realms of Oerth . . . and one might possibly read this work, too.

A MAP of the western portion of the Flanaess, part of the continent of Oerik, on the planet Oerth

Key to this page:

Cities/towns

1 Bardillingham
2 City Out of Mind
3 Ghastoor
4 Hlupallu
5 Jakif
6 Karnoosh
7 Tashbul
8 Yolakand

Other features

B Barring Mtns.
C Crystalmist
   Mtns.
D Chaban River
G Grandsuel Peaks
K Lake Karnoosh
P Pennor Hills
R Ruins
T Toosmik River
Y Yolspur Tors

EKBIR

TUSMIT

JAKIF

5

T

4

BAYOMEN PLAINS

P

Y

8

YOLL

3

B

C

6

K

BARREN PLAINS

7

G

R

ASHEN DESERT

2

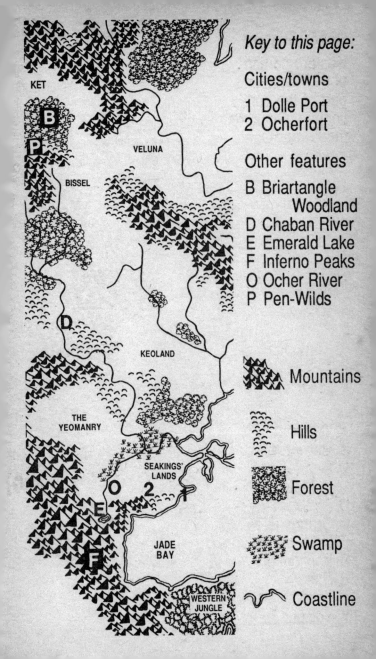

Other books by Gary Gygax

Saga of Old City

Artifact of Evil

Chapter 1

"HAIL TO GRAZ'ZT, King of the Abyss!" chorused a throng of demons in voices that chirruped, bellowed, grated, squawked, and growled.

"King Graz'zt, Conqueror of Prince Ariax!" a huge, multi-armed, snake-bodied demoness called in clarion voice. Lamia, succubi, and the menagerie of others there echoed the cry, raising a noise that would have been incomprehensible and horrifying to human or demi-human ears.

A huge, ebony figure stood receiving the adulation. His smile was charming, despite the fangs it revealed. This figure, his body seemingly carved from polished obsidian, raised a six-fingered hand. In but a moment the horde of demons fell silent, and Graz'zt spoke.

"King you proclaim me — and King I am! My recent victory over Ariax now extends our domain over fully eight planes. We rule the heart of the Abyss — and soon the rest will bow!" Pausing for a moment to allow the disparate demons to issue their noises of accolade, the newly made monarch stood with pride and delight written on his dark face as the adulation washed over him. Then his demeanor changed ever so slightly. "Enough!" he thundered, and the throng became still. The self-proclaimed king gestured toward a grotesque, hyena-headed figure on his right and spoke again.

"Honor belongs to Our Good Right Hand, Prince Yeenoghu. Cheer him as Our new Viceroy!" Graz'zt roared, motioning for the demon to stand, and again the discordant chorus sounded. He waited for the initial outburst to peak and begin subsiding, then cut off the noise and ordered Yeenoghu to sit again by lowering his hand.

"Give glory to Our Marshal, Lord Kostchtchie!" bellowed Graz'zt, raising his left hand, and a massive demon stood on the king's left as this call for recognition was made. His jaundiced skin hairless except for jutting bristles above deep-set eyes, the bandy-legged Kostchtchie leered and raised his huge iron hammer over his head.

Despite Graz'zt's command, only a faint hooting and gibbering of acclaim sounded. The squat demon was so loathsome that even the throng of lessers found it hard to voice applause. Kostchtchie seemed delighted at this, even though his round of applause, such as it was, did not last as long as Yeenoghu's had. By the time Graz'zt lowered his left hand and Kostchtchie sat again, the noise had all but died out. Graz'zt ended the silence with his next pronouncement.

"Prince Yeenoghu and Lord Marshal Kostchtchie will now accompany Me . . . elsewhere," the king said. At that, there was a babble of sound; the audience was clearly surprised. According to what he himself had announced years ago, Graz'zt was being forced by an other-worldly power to remain here in Mezzafgraduun, three hundred thirty-third layer of the Abyss, for years and even decades longer. The new king allowed the demons and assembly of creatures who served him and his associates to continue their murmuring and muttering for a short time, then spoke again.

"Silence!" he bellowed, and the crowd obeyed. "Do you doubt Me?" Graz'zt asked, and a stupid toad-demon nearby gave a short croak in response. It was a harmless gesture, for the thing simply intended to indicate its acceptance of its monarch's claim, no matter if it was true or not. But Graz'zt, incensed by what he saw as an affirmative answer to his question, raised his hand toward the offender, and a beam of black radiance shot from his palm. The demon shrieked as the bolt struck it, and its face contorted in agony. The thing's body arched, its muscles contracting so as to hurl it upward. The demon was disintegrating into a puddle of gore even before what remained of its body touched the ground again.

"Who doubts now?" said Graz'zt, and the members of the assemblage not only remained silent but fell prone in homage to their king. Graz'zt allowed a thin smile to play across his face for a moment before continuing.

"Vuron, Our Lord Steward, will rule in Our brief absence. Obey him, or face My wrath upon Our return!" At that, Graz'zt turned and departed the amphitheater, a vast, seemingly natural bowl of nacreous material, with his attendant nobles and train in tow. After the royal procession came a stream of the demonlings that were Graz'zt's subjects. Fluttering and hopping, slithering and flying, lumbering and rolling, the motley subjects raised a hideous din in Graz'zt's wake. Across and over ground resembling opals they trod and soared and crept, leaving the pearly-surfaced theater of audience to swarm across the park that surrounded that place.

Their king paid no heed to their noise or their trampling of the delicate ferns, nodding blossoms, and flowering shrubs that covered the landscape of the park. If all of Mezzafgraduun were as disconcertingly beautiful as the Royal Demesne, then this tier of the Abyss would be indeed a paradise. Translucent trunks of a luminous dove-gray hue supported luxuriant leaves of shining black, gently waving and soughing in the little breezes that played through the tops of these weird trees. Beneath the palms and cedars grew thick, soot-colored grasses and riotous profusions of tropical vegetation in shades of gray and ebony. Rainbow-hued insects and birds filled the exotic jungle. Monkeylike creatures

11

leaped around in the upper foliage, making streaks and flashes of lemon yellow and electric blue. Brightly colored deer and other smaller creatures bounded and scampered amid the black vegetation, their coats shining as if they were covered with jewels.

A vulture-demon fell upon a nest of peacocklike birds, gleefully rending and tearing adults and chicks. A baboon-demon playfully chased and beheaded several monkeys, using claws and teeth to accomplish its sport. Bloody destruction spread in a swath across the paradisiacal gardens of King Graz'zt, and the monarch smiled benevolently as he viewed the sight. "When One's subjects are frolicking in play," the handsome ruler noted to those around him, "then no other mischief is brewing."

With a slight turn of his head, Graz'zt got the attention of the tall, sticklike demon who walked several respectful paces behind him. "Lord Vuron," he said, "be sure to restock Our parks — and add some larger, noisier creatures for more sport, too — while We are gone. In fact, you may declare a Chase in Our name."

The leathery-skinned Vuron bowed in Graz'zt's direction before he responded. "You are masterful in your entertainments, mighty king," said the steward. "Your generosity and thoughtfulness will be praised by all."

"Of course," Graz'zt said in a matter-of-fact tone.

Kostchtchie, a demon accustomed to frozen wastes and frigid winds, was sweating profusely in the tropical setting of the king's domain, and his stench was clearly repugnant to many of the creatures in his vicinity, even as repulsive as they themselves were. But Graz'zt, delighted with his surroundings and his situation, showed neither any sign of being put off by Kostchtchie's odor nor any concern for his new marshal's discomfort. Surrounded by beautiful succubi and lamias, Graz'zt entered the many-porticoed, gold-bedecked sprawl of his palace. Prior to his departure, the king would be the host and guest of honor at a royal banquet to celebrate his recent triumph. The victory heralded far greater accomplishments to come, and Graz'zt reveled in his thoughts as he considered what the future would bring.

* * *

"The Ambassadors of the kings of the Tiger and Wolf tribes are awaiting your pleasure, Lord of Evil." The priest spoke these words haltingly, humility dripping from every phrase, as he addressed the withered old man who sat facing him.

"*Emperor* of Evil!" thundered the old man, his chest heaving with the effort.

High Priest Modu-Koduz, Chamberlain of his god Iuz, threw himself prone and begged for mercy, writhing in fear. After the priest had engaged in a sufficient amount of groveling, Iuz excused the error.

"You are useless and stupid, Modu-Koduz, but I must make do with the poor tools given to Me. Now, go — fetch these filthy nomads to stand and pay homage to Me. Such continual demands are wearisome, but We will bear up staunchly under them."

As the trembling chamberlain rushed to do Iuz's bidding, the form seated on the massive heap of bones and skulls that formed his throne seemed to flow and change. One minute he was a wrinkled, toothless old man; the next, he was a massive, demoniac monster — a cambion, as those of his ilk were called — with pale reddish skin and pointed fangs lining his jaws. "This form is more suitable for fools such as these barbaric horsemen," Iuz muttered to himself. The subjects of his in attendance were too far from his chair of state to hear the remark, and it was not intended for their ears — but

13

they would have certainly voiced their agreement with his statement if they had overheard.

In the past month Iuz had received homage from all the petty rulers of the Bandit Kingdoms, tribute from the Hold of Stonefist, the submission of all the chiefs who remained in the lands that once belonged to the Horned Society, and the respects of a seemingly endless stream of humanoid leaders who had come to swear fealty to Iuz as their liege lord and deity. Now, with the deputation of the wild nomad horsemen of the Tiger and Wolf tribes to the north, came the greatest triumph of all. These human savages would serve to weld Iuz's whole scheme into hard reality. The cambion chuckled happily just as the chamberlain's voice rang out from beyond the entrance to the royal chamber.

"Emperor Iuz, Lord of Pain, and soon Ruler of all Oerth!" proclaimed Modu-Koduz. The echoes of his shout still remained as the fur-draped nomad warriors entered Iuz's chamber to pay their homage. Iuz accepted the ambassadors' words of praise and gifts, bestowed presents upon them in return, and delivered his usual message, in the form of a lecture demanding their unswerving loyalty — with the admonition that the riches and favors he had granted could be taken away just as easily, and that would not be the end of the punishment visited upon anyone whose devotion was found lacking.

The ambassadors left then, and soon the vast hall was deserted except for the lowly, vaguely humanoid demons that stood permanent guard therein. Emperor Iuz had gone off to hold council with those who now considered themselves his peers, but who he vowed would soon enough be his subjects — just as surely as all the nations of Oerth would eventually bow to him.

* * *

Shape without form, illumination without light,

events occurring in timelessness. Such was the nature of the null-space brought into being by Iggwilv, or so it was perceived by those with her. Perhaps the greatest of witches, as she was known by some, actually did create this no-place, or perhaps she merely enabled herself and the others to gain access to it. The truth of this was unimportant; what did matter was that Iggwilv had provided the means by which she and the other practitioners of evil could meet.

The witch was incredibly ancient, older even than old Iuz — in fact, Iggwilv was the mother of the cambion who had designs on all of Oerth. Iggwilv's infamy reached beyond Oerth to other worlds that paralleled it and occasionally touched it for a time. Ychbilch she was called on one of these worlds, Louhi on another. No matter by what name or title she was known, she was who she was — mistress of dweomercraefting, mother of Iuz, worker of malign plots against those of Good . . . and sometimes even those of Evil. She sat at ease and in comfort now, displaying the voluptuous beauty of one of the forms she was capable of taking. Perhaps this was Iggwilv's true appearance; be that as it may, even so gorgeous a face as the one she wore now could not mask the evil that dwelled within her.

With her — and *with* is the only method of describing location in such a nullity as the place she was, for no directions existed, no places, no discernible order — were others. Iuz was here, proud and tall in his demoniac form, wearing finery and bearing his massive sword. Also here was a pulsating mound of fungi, upon and around which hopped and crawled a large toad of exceptional ugliness. The mound was none other than Zuggtmoy, Demoness Queen of Fungi — Iuz's lady, his ally . . . and his ruler? The cambion would have sneered at this last suggestion; Iggwilv would have laughed at it. Zuggtmoy would have made no comment whatsoever, for she too was what she was.

In the same non-place as these three beings came three others, absent one instant and present the next: jet-black Graz'zt, hyena-headed Yeenoghu, and disgusting Kostchtchie. Just as those who were separate from these three carried weapons and who knew what else in their arsenals, each mighty demon on the other side bore implements as well — Graz'zt his undulating-bladed sword, Yeenoghu his renowned flail, Kostchtchie his favored hammer. The gathering was a tense one at best, and a hostile one at worst, as these tokens of death so visibly demonstrated. Mutual trust among such beings as these was inconceivable, and all of them knew it.

After a series of curt introductions and acknowledgments, Graz'zt addressed Iuz directly and got right to the heart of what he assumed the conclave concerned. "The object is Mine by right, and you *will* deliver it forthwith!" said the self-proclaimed king in a thundering tone.

"I shall do nothing of the kind," Iuz shot back disdainfully.

The bandy-legged giant and the lowering, hyena-headed demon both made menacing gestures toward the cambion as he uttered this rejection. A wave of menacing thought flowed from Zuggtmoy, and a soft warning from Iggwilv checked all of them. Graz'zt frowned slightly but then smiled and spoke again.

"Son and Prince of Oerth, be not alarmed at My demand," he said in what passed for a soothing voice. "It is most reasonable. Remember that had I not assisted, you never would have come as far as you have. The object— "

"Is one which I wrested from peril with Dear Queen Zuggtmoy's aid," interjected Iggwilv. Ignoring the scowl that came over Graz'zt's countenance, the great witch added, "As mother of Iuz, I must have full right in deciding the disposition of the . . . item in question."

"That's right, dear," gurgled Zuggtmoy. "Don't

let that stupid male push you around."

"Stupid?!" roared the black demon prince, barely able to control himself.

Iggwilv was not impressed by his outburst. "It *is* stupid to ask Our offspring for a tool you *know* he needs for the little things he still must do," she pointed out.

Graz'zt gritted his fangs and said, "Your choice of the word *little* is apt indeed, Iggwilv. There is a question of whole planes at stake, and you and that amorphous pile of—"

"I'll show you just how amorphous *you* can be!" Zuggtmoy boomed as she grew in the space of two seconds into a massive fungoid shape resembling an oliphant. Even as she did so, a pool of glistening slime began to come into being, gathering at her pseudopodial extremities.

"The treaty is broken!" Yeenoghu barked in his giggling, hyenalike basso as he noted the growing mass of repulsive stuff. "Beware, King Graz'zt — the bitch is bringing in her kinsdemon, Szhublox!"

At that, Graz'zt began shouting syllables that made the air shimmer. As he did this, Iggwilv and Iuz likewise uttered rasping, throat-twisting words. Major demons, minor ones, humans, and dark elves began to pop into existence all over the null-space that had formerly been tailored for the presence of no more than the original six beings. The nullity stretched and shifted, trying to accommodate the sudden influx of new residents into its nothingness. Non-color of a different sort began to appear, running in veins and seams such as those that appear when ice begins to crack or rock develops fissures during an earthquake.

Upon seeing the effects of what she and the others had wrought, Iggwilv thought better of trying to fight. The battleground itself seemed to be in jeopardy from this venture, and if it collapsed, who knew what would happen to its occupants? "Stop! We will all be destroyed!" the witch cried out in

17

warning.

Graz'zt, realizing the same thing that Iggwilv had perceived, ordered his servants to desist, but not before Kostchtchie and Yeenoghu had each slain a pair of demonlings. In the same short span of time, Szhublox had enslimed and otherwise rudely handled several of the rampaging minions summoned by Graz'zt and his allies. Then the melee ceased. Most of the figures that had been called by the principals winked back out of the no-place, returning to wherever they came from. When the shifting and shaking of the null-space had ceased, a few of the lesser demonspawn on each side still remained. A cluster of lamias and succubi floated behind and to the sides of Graz'zt and his cohorts, and an equal-sized group of vulture-demons and toad-demons arrayed themselves in a rank behind Zuggtmoy and Iuz. Iggwilv was off to one side, seeming slightly closer to Iuz than to Graz'zt, but still arguably holding a position between the two instead of being grouped with the former.

"The presence of a few spectators does not seem to threaten the integrity of this place," Iggwilv announced sternly. The others took her at her word, accepting that she knew more of the nature of this null-space than any of them did. The witch continued, concern and sincerity evident in her tone. "But they must be spectators *only*. They are free to leave or stay, and while they stay they can see us and our actions but cannot decipher our words. This place was meant for us alone, and only we can fully communicate with one another. The others could move to attack, if anyone foolishly directs them to do so, but if a conflict breaks out and they become involved, we cannot be sure that *any* of us will persevere if this place is torn asunder!" The witch was clearly overwrought by the time she finished this lecture. For a moment or two, a strained silence enveloped the weird pocket of null-space as all those present weighed the importance of Iggwilv's words.

"Now . . . We must talk, not quarrel," Iggwilv said sweetly, regaining her composure.

"Yes, yes!" said Graz'zt with a tinge of sarcasm. "By all means let us return to our amiable parlay!" he guffawed. Then his tone turned serious again as he continued, addressing Iggwilv. "Your treacherous behavior is, as always, dear human, so monumental, your expectations so incredible, that I am most amused. Even as it was, the repulsive toad hopping about on that pile of fungus tipped the balance in your favor, four to three. Fortunately for all of you, that worthless creature is of no consequence, and I could dispatch it with a single gesture if I so chose. But now Szhublox comes — another matter altogether! Do you really think We will consent to that puddle of slime joining this conclave?"

"Your madness and lust are what bring conflict between us always," Iggwilv replied condescendingly. "The toad is obviously a niggling, just as are the harlots you enjoy surrounding yourself with. As for the Demon of Slime, I should hardly have to point out that Zuggtmoy's dear kinsman was not some agent brought to attack. Szhublox was nothing more than a late arrival."

"Your words are dung, crone of crones," Graz'zt retaliated. "We agreed to an equality of force to assure no tricks. It was to be three and three."

"Szhublox is the third," interjected Zuggtmoy, shooting forth a cloud of spores as she spoke.

Kostchtchie sneered at this remark and issued his own rejoinder. "You are too stupid to even think straight, Queen of Rot."

Zuggtmoy returned the insult by simply ignoring the demon's statement. Iggwilv spoke next, and further demeaned Kostchtchie by again addressing Graz'zt. "I am a disinterested party," she explained patiently. "How can I be else as the mother of your own beloved son? Therefore, Zuggtmoy, Szhublox, and dear Iuz are three, just as you and your two thegns make a trio."

Yeenoghu threw back his ugly head and issued a series of giggling, yowling barks to demonstrate his rage. Kostchtchie's skin took on a dark mustard color as he too flushed with rage at Iggwilv's words. He hefted his huge iron hammer and strode toward the gorgeous-looking grand witch. It was evident that he meant to destroy Iggwilv's beauty in one blow. But before he could get close enough to bring himself and his target into conflict, Graz'zt intervened.

"Stay, Marshal of the Abyss!" ordered the demon prince. "You too, Viceroy, contain thine ire! The woman speaks with hubris, but such petty insults and twisted words are to be expected. Refrain from your actions. I will handle this."

Both great demons glared at Graz'zt as he spoke, but they slowly brought their anger under control. Yeenoghu continued to snarl, baring his fangs. Kostchtchie glared, but lowered his hammer to a less threatening position.

"You and your cohorts *are* four," Graz'zt continued, "but since you and your sprat at best equal one, I shall be generous and allow your attempt to disturb the parity of this conference to stand."

Iggwilv only smiled sarcastically at the demon prince's blustering words. Iuz, however, showed that Graz'zt's statement stung him. The cambion's skin turned an angry maroon, and he retorted.

"We shall see who makes what, Graz'zt! Give Me your demonhorde now, and all Oerth will be Mine!"

Now it was the so-called king's turn to retaliate. "Give Me the Theorpart, boy, and you shall have ten thousand of my fiercest demons at your beck and call!"

"What?! How dare— "

Iuz's angry words were cut short by Graz'zt. "I am now *King!*" the great ebon demon thundered. "I dare *anything!* A dozen layers of the Abyss bow to My will, and a dozen more are tributary. Orcus cowers from Me! Mandrillagon hides rather than face Me on the battlefield! Still, Prince Lugush remains uncommitted, Eblitis and Marduk stall, and Var-Az-Hloo and his lickspittle dogs Chidun, Zomar, and Yuibiri war upon Us. Should Bulumuz and Azazel happen to make cause with them, Our advance will be checked. Then the fat sheep-head Orcus and the freakish Mandrillagon will crawl forth once more to claim power here and there. . . ." Graz'zt paused, smiled at the cambion he had sired, and then said, "Thus, dear son, your father does properly demand that you give filial obedience to Him so that He may shed His glory upon His offspring thereafter. Give Me the Theorpart!"

Drawing himself up to his own considerable height, Iuz rebutted the statements just made by the newly proclaimed king. "Know you, Graz'zt, that I am now *Emperor* of the Flanaess! True, some petty kingdoms still need to be subjugated, but the north is Mine, the west is under siege, and the heartlands will soon fall under the might of My hand. Despite such sweeping victories, the Theorpart must remain with Me. Aerdy is marshaling legions of devils, while the Scarlet Scum hides Hierarchs and recruits enemies of Iuz and the Abyss as well." Pointing an accusing finger at the huge, six-fingered demon who was his progenitor, the cambion demanded, "You will detail forces to Me, so that My conquest of Oerth can be completed in the face of My . . . *Our* enemies!"

"Bah! You blither weakling words," Graz'zt shot back with a sneer stretching his handsome, if demoniac, face. "You will give Me the Theorpart as I have ordered you to do. As a faithful vassal, dear Iuz, My son, I will furnish you with horde upon horde of My demons as soon as all of the Abyss bows to My might!"

"That will be eons from now, if ever," Iggwilv retorted smugly.

Kostchtchie grunted angrily and hefted his iron

hammer. "Lying and perverse old human bag! Bow to the will of King Graz'zt, or by All Unholy—"

"You bandy-legged bastard! My fungi will feed upon your filthy yellow flesh," Zuggtmoy said as she altered shape, and strange buds began to form on the mass of her body.

"You are wrong, toadstool!" Yeenoghu growled as he lifted his terrible flail and advanced. "I'll spread bits and spores across this no-place so that your little mushrooms will be without a head!" With this, the hyena-headed demon vented his awful giggling bark as a battle cry.

Szhublox spread forth slimy pseudopods to counter Yeenoghu's threat while Graz'zt faced off against the hard-visaged Iggwilv and livid Iuz. The lesser demons still in attendance could see what was happening. They assumed ferocious postures but held back, for they had not been commanded to take part and no actual combat had occurred. They were powerless to affect the course of events, but it was apparent to them that in a moment the null-space would become a war ground of unimaginable sort.

"It had to come to this," Graz'zt grated harshly as he raised his huge sword.

"You are at least right about *that*," Iuz snarled back, hefting his own weapon.

"Both of you, stop!"

This last came from Iggwilv, who in the space of an eye-blink had placed herself between the two rivals. Iuz was stunned at this, instantly suspecting some treachery against him on the part of his mother. Graz'zt too, a victim once of the mighty powers of this human terror, seemed surprised and disconcerted. Iggwilv's move was sufficient to make both demon and cambion pause.

"If we fight among ourselves — even if some of us survive the battle — all of our enemies profit," said the witch. "Think on it, Graz'zt: Orcus and all those in the Abyss would be jubilant. Consider, Iuz, what comfort this will give to the Hierarchs and the

Brotherhood and the others. The Hells will rejoice! Hades, Tarterus, and Gehenna will hold revels! The scum of the upper planes will vaunt, and the lordlings of Oerth's kingdoms will be reprieved. If we are to prevail, then we must cooperate. Fight now, and those who wish to oppose our ends will do so — and succeed!"

"Wise words, greatest of witches," Graz'zt said as he lowered his massive blade a little. "Yet the resolution of matters can go but one way. . . ."

"Yes," Iuz concurred, "and I shall retain what is Mine!"

As this brief conversation took place, the hostile groups had continued to glare at and threaten one another, but no actual violence occurred. "Good, good!" Iggwilv cackled gently as the commotion diminished slightly, the sound seeming exceptionally strange and gruesome coming from so lovely a throat. Then, with much more forcefulness, she added, "Both sides, cease your foolish displays!" After the antagonists had calmed down, Iggwilv spoke again.

"You are both right and wrong," she said to Graz'zt and Iuz at the same time. The demon prince glowered at this, and the cambion spat, but the witch ignored both of them and went on. "Iuz has the Theorpart, and since he is weaker than you are, dear Graz'zt, he must retain it now and forever."

Graz'zt drew in his breath to spew forth an outraged reply to this, but Iggwilv cut off his tirade before it could begin. "Wait! There is more than one Theorpart, Graz'zt, and you might have another," she said.

"You know as well as I that the dung-eating Brotherhood holds it," the demon-king grumbled. "Even I cannot wrest it from that pack of curs. Its own power and the weight of the dukes of Hell combine to stop me."

Iggwilv nodded, accepting the truth of that statement. Then, smiling, she pointed out a new fact.

"That portion of the artifact held by the Scarlet Brotherhood *is* a Theorpart, but it isn't the one I speak of. The final portion remains hidden somewhere."

Graz'zt frowned. "You expect Me to traipse off in search of *that*?" He sent forth a bellowing, booming laugh filled with mockery and derision. "I am to use My strength to chase shadows, all the while held fast in My own plane where the conjoined enemies you will no doubt encourage will be able to attack and overthrow Me? Do you think I am so gullible a fool as that, Iggwilv? For such I will have most sweet revenge, bag!"

"Consider, consider," said the witch, unimpressed as usual with the demon's outburst. "Be not so hasty, Graz'zt. What if My own dear friend and associate Queen Zuggtmoy and her brother Prince Szhublox were to become your unswerving allies?"

"Allies?"

"Upon certain conditions, of course."

Graz'zt swiveled his massive head and peered at the fungoid demon. Zuggtmoy somehow managed to convey an attitude of cooperation despite any recognizable means of doing so. The ebon-hued giant pondered this, one six-fingered hand stroking his square jaw as he reflected on what had been offered. "You guarantee me alliance and the last part of the great artifact?" he asked Iggwilv, seeking confirmation of the promise.

The witch cackled, delighted at having piqued the demon's interest. "Not just so, Graz'zt," she said. "I mentioned conditions. The alliance is under terms which are acceptable to Zuggtmoy, so should likewise be acceptable to you. The final portion of the artifact is to be awarded to the winner of . . . a contest, let us say. I have discovered the hiding place of the last Theorpart. To the first to hold it goes the prize!"

"Stop lauding yourself, once-wife, and give details of these terms and conditions you prate of,"

Graz'zt said with irritation to hide his grudging respect for and fear of this terrible human woman who could make even great demons shudder.

Iggwilv launched into the explanation of her plan. First, Graz'zt and Zuggtmoy would contest with each other, both attempting to claim the last part of the artifact from its hiding place. Then once the Theorpart was gained, regardless of which faction held it, both Graz'zt and Zuggtmoy would send their strength to aid Iuz. The Scarlet Brotherhood, even with all of its legions of devils and swarming daemons, would be unable to withstand the cambion's combined might, backed as it would be by the hordes of the Abyss and the power of two of the Theorparts — the one already at Iuz's disposal, plus the one to be sought. The portion of the artifact now held by the Brotherhood would be gained in this conflict, and would then go to whichever side did not have one, Graz'zt or Zuggtmoy.

"Thus, once-husband, you will rule all the Abyss in conjunction with Zuggtmoy," concluded Iggwilv. "King Graz'zt will hold sway over that portion you and Queen Zuggtmoy agree to, and vice versa — each of you with a Theorpart!"

"Why be so generous?" the dark demon asked suspiciously, for Iggwilv was never to be trusted.

"Self-preservation — what else?" she replied. "The three portions of the key must never be joined. When each of you have one part, neither you nor Zuggtmoy will desire to have the portion remaining with Iuz. The Abyss will be safe — and Iuz is but a reflection of it, you know. I will see to it that he conquers and reigns supreme over all Oerth. Our power, the might of the Abyss, will spread over the multiverse!"

Graz'zt turned to confer with his lieutenants at this point, and both of them gave forth exclamations of joy and merriment. Here indeed was a plan that would bring to both sides all that could be desired, they told their leader. Of course, it went

without saying at some time in the centuries to
come one of them, Graz'zt or Zuggtmoy, would
emerge as sole ruler, but time would see to that.
The black demon prince listened to his cohorts
with one ear, forming a conclusion of his own at the
same time. Then the ever-suspicious Graz'zt
brought the celebration to a halt.

"A stench like blooming flowers fills My
nostrils!" he said to Yeenoghu and Kostchtchie.
"Why does this human pit us against each other in a
contest for what she claims she knows how to get?
Why must we be opponents before we can be allies?
The bitch seeks to gull us — to have us exterminate
each other so that she can take the Theorpart for
herself!"

"Well thought, Graz'zt the Clever," Iggwilv spat,
"but you are still ignorant of certain facts. Who
spoke of knowing? Of getting? Mark you, all. It is in
my knowledge as to its location, and I am also
aware under what conditions the portion of the key
can be gained. But I cannot myself obtain it directly
— nor can any of your ilk, demonlings!"

For a change, Graz'zt absorbed the substance of
Iggwilv's response instead of reacting to her choice
of words, or the tone in which they were delivered.
"This concerns the contest," he said after a moment of deliberation.

"Yes, Graz'zt," said the witch. "The Theorpart
lies under a great dweomer which requires that it
can only be successfully sought by contesting mortals. It would be possible for one or more of us to
venture forth to gain it. But this action would invoke
the power of the dweomer, thereby bringing all of
the mighty ones of the multiverse to the spot to
contend with us for it. Then would many be destroyed, we and they alike, and Oerth would shatter
asunder under the weight of the forces centered
there.

"So, My plan is simple. Better to have family, as it
were, contending for the final portion than those

whom we must count as enemies. Am I right?"

Murmurs of agreement came from all parties in response to that. Then Graz'zt asked, "Zuggtmoy, have you a champion for this contest?"

"Of course," the fungi queen burbled. The huge, ugly toad hopped away from the mound that was Zuggtmoy, taking a place of its own next to the demoness, and suddenly changed into an evil-visaged dwarf. "Obmi, bow to King Graz'zt," commanded Zuggtmoy. The dwarf lowered his head slightly and briefly, the scowl never leaving his face. At the same time Graz'zt looked to the side, formed his mouth into a sneer, and elevated his head in an expression of haughtiness and contempt.

"And who will you have as yours then, dark one?" Iggwilv asked.

Graz'zt, after a moment of thought, gestured to a succubus somewhere distant on his right side. As she came toward the group, the demon prince uttered a string of barely audible syllables, and by the time she reached Graz'zt's side her true nature became apparent. This was no real demon but a drow, one of the evil race of dark elves of Oerth. "I present Eclavdra, My chosen representative in your contest," said Graz'zt to Iggwilv, pointedly ignoring Zuggtmoy and Obmi.

"So be it," said the witch. "Now, let us set the rules and discuss the distractions we must cause to mask the affair. It would not do to have others of unwanted sort seeking our prize."

"Others?" This word came from Graz'zt and Zuggtmoy simultaneously.

"What I have gleaned, others can also learn," Iggwilv admitted in a grudging tone. "The Hierophants, the Cabal, or that old fart Mordenkainen — not to mention the Brotherhood, Hades, or Hell's martinets."

"Just what *have* you learned, human?" Graz'zt snarled.

Iggwilv deliberately did not speak right away, to

make the point that she was volunteering information rather than giving it in response to the demon prince's demand. "The Ashen Desert hides much," she began. "The great metropolis of the empire vanished beneath the dust is now known only as the City Out of Mind. The masters of the lost empire ruled from that city, and they used the Theorpart in their final battle. It lies there now, buried beneath a blanket of dust so deep that scarcely a trace of the city can be seen from the surface."

"Why do we use such weak champions as these?" Szhublox asked in his dripping, bubbling voice.

"Only mortals, either humans or their demi-human kin, can retrieve any part of the Key-Which-Unlocks-The-Sleeper — may this never occur! This fact we know from what has transpired with the two portions already found, and from examination of the dweomer surrounding the part yet to be uncovered," said Iggwilv. "But once a part is found, the mortals discovering it may do with it what they choose. The Brotherhood holds that portion of the artifact attuned to the Abyss, and with it they would yoke us in thrall to the Slumbering One. Iuz and I hold the portion which would be able to command the Glooms of Hades, should the Theorparts be united. Somewhere in the Ashen Desert, lost within the buried City Out of Mind, rests the last portion of the key, that part commanding the Nine Hells and their dukes to slavery and obedience. All with power will sense when such a mighty thing comes into ken once again."

"I will send an army there to guard it," Iuz announced grandly.

"No!" countered Graz'zt. "I will send my demons for it, once it is held by Eclavdra!"

Zuggtmoy gave vent to an angry retort at that. "And what if that skinny bitch fails? My own servant, Obmi, will be escorted by a horde of Mine Own fiercest—"

"Contain yourselves," Iggwilv said with a flat,

forceful voice. "Should such numbers and powers assemble in the Ashen Desert, should such forces even approach it, all will be lost! Think you not that our every move is watched? Do not our adversaries have spies? Only the champions must go. Only they — or, more precisely, one of them — can return with the object."

"And to where must these champions return?" asked Graz'zt.

"Yolakand, in the land of Yoll, is favorable," Iggwilv suggested.

"Ocherfort, in the land of the Seakings, is nearer," Graz'zt said, "and less likely to be influenced by your son and puppet."

"Your son, too," cackled Iggwilv.

"Puppet? I am no puppet!" Iuz said, all but jumping up and down in his rage at Graz'zt's statement.

"Zuggtmoy, Queen of the Abyss, says that Her champion will carry the Theorpart to Yolakand," the fungoid demon burbled.

"Graz'zt, King of the Abyss, decrees that His minion, Eclavdra, will bring the final portion of the Artifact of Evil to Ocherfort in the Seakings' Lands!" countered the black demon.

Again Iggwilv intervened. "It is in all of our interests to gain the object. Can we agree that either champion can carry it to either place? Let us say that place is immaterial. Whichever of the two holds the Theorpart when either place is gained wins for his or her master — agreed?"

"Can a champion be slain?" This came from Iuz, who was more than a little irritated about being relegated to the role of an ineffectual onlooker in the matter at hand and had decided to ascertain, in a rather obvious way, whether he might be able to influence the course of events.

"Not by the other one, Iuz," Iggwilv replied forcefully. "If such were permissible, the contest would not be a true quest for the object itself, but merely a test of the ability to slay or survive. This will be a duel to the end, but not to the death. Above all, we must not lose sight of the need to gain the object for the Abyss. Of course, we do not preclude acts of violence which do not kill, and duplicity and trickery are not only possible but expected from contestants such as these."

"What of assistants?" Zuggtmoy inquired in her bubbling monotone. "If My champion is to travel a great distance to arrive at the City Out of Mind whole and sound so as to recover the object, he must have guards and servants."

After considerable debate, the demons finally agreed that two assistants could accompany each champion. Each could also hire or otherwise retain up to a dozen mercenaries or other sorts of fighters to serve as guards and escorts. Groups of such size, even if all the members of one side traveled together, were small enough to appear normal, yet strong enough to survive in the hostile wilderness and wastelands that would be crossed in their trek.

"The final stipulations are these," Iggwilv said. "The contestants will begin from Hlupallu in the Kingdom of Ket fourteen days hence. From there they will journey overland, by any means they possess or are able to procure, to the Ashen Desert and the City Out of Mind. The journey itself will be taxing, an important part of the contest and not something to be sneered at. If perchance one of the champions comes to an untimely end on the trek, the other must still locate the Theorpart and transport it back to safety. If both champions persevere through the journey to the City Out of Mind, I would not be surprised if Fate should contrive to have them both arrive at the lost metropolis at the same time. . . ." As the witch made that last remark, she allowed a thin smile to play across her face for a moment before concluding.

"And yet, even being the first to locate and hold the item is no guarantee of victory, although such possession is certainly an advantage. The contest does not end until one of the havens is reached. Simply put, whichever champion holds the Theorpart safe within Yolakand or Ocherfort gains it for Graz'zt or Zuggtmoy."

"Agreed!" the assembled demons called in chorus — all except for the cambion. If Iggwilv's plan came to fruition, Iuz stood to gain a great deal. . . . But still, he could not keep a frown from spreading across his face.

Chapter 2

"TEN MARES, TWENTY CAMELS, and her height in silver pieces!"

The cry from the Foudhi sheik seemed to go unnoticed. The beautiful, platinum-haired dancer continued to writhe sensuously in the golden light of a score of smoking lamps ringing the stage. Her skin glistened from a film of perfumed oil and perspiration, for the place was hot and her exertions strenuous despite the seeming ease with which she performed. The men in the audience gave forth quick intakes of breath, in unison, as without apparent effort she removed another of her transparent garments. It floated to the marble floor of the stage upon which her little feet moved rhythmically and her shapely body moved in complex and suggestive patterns of incredible grace and muscular control. The three-piece ensemble of musicians twittered on, playing the oddly structured melody to which she danced as the gorgeous woman kept time with finger-held cymbals of polished silver.

The crowd murmured and gasped again, almost as one. Such a response spoke far more eloquently of her performance than any words of praise could have. It was a tribute to the dancer's beauty and skill from men who had seen as many as a thousand such dances performed by an equal number of lovely females. Yet this audience of hard-bitten warriors and jaded aristocrats watched this beauty's every move and voiced their appreciation as they never had before. Gathered together this night in the wine house known as the Dar Peshdwar, one of the most popular such establishments in the city of Hlupallu, were men of both East and West. Mercenaries and merchants from Perrenland, Bissel, and Veluna rubbed elbows with soldiers and traders of Ket. Sprinkled among them were veiled and headdressed nomads from the Bayomen Plains, turbaned nobles from Jakif, Tusmit, and distant Ekbir, and dark-eyed Baklunish and gray-eyed hillmen from a dozen unknown tribes. All of these men combined to fill the large, brightly tiled, and high-ceilinged place to capacity. Nobles and their servants, ordinary men, and soldiers and guards alike seemed unable to take their rapt gazes from the woman who danced in the center of the crowded court.

This dancer was called The Pearl of Perfection. Such an appellation was not unique; some in the audience had seen that name applied to a dozen different females. But this one truly deserved the title. Men lusted for her, and the richer and more powerful of those in attendance were eager to have her. In as many minutes there were eight offers to purchase the girl, beginning with the unspectacular sum offered by the petty Foudhi sheik. The mountain of fat who owned the establishment, a Kettite of obvious Tusmite heritage named Omar, wrung his hands piteously and bowed at the one presenting this offer. He quavered his sincere regret at having to decline such a generous offer, noting that he was a thousand times a fool for being unable to accept such munificence. A hundred, two hundred, even five hundred gold pieces were not sufficient to acquire this incredible female. The air, already heavy with perfume, incense, smoke, and a score of other odors, grew heavier still with the near-palpable emotions of frustrated purchasers and the concupiscence of the entire audience as her performance neared its conclusion. Then a voice called out above the skirling pipes, twanging strings, and thumping drums of the orchestra.

"I, Kufteer, Shah of Wadlaoo, Vizier of Jakif, do offer a thousand golden dokshees — and this great pearl — for that Pearl of Ultimate Perfection!" The shah reached into a pouch at his side and pulled out a huge pearl, perfectly shaped, as large as a pigeon's egg, and glowing with a luster as fair as the dancing-girl's skin. At this sight, the others in the audience buzzed and gasped in a reaction almost as pronounced as their approval of the girl's performance.

After appearing to deliberate for only a few seconds, Omar salaamed thrice and clapped his hands loudly, causing the fat on his arms to jiggle and his gross belly to bounce. "It is done!" he said, holding out his hand to receive the pearl. The gold coin the Jakifi referred to in his offer was scarcely half as large as the eastern coin known as the orb, but the fat Kettite owner acted quickly to seal the bargain when he laid eyes on the pearl. Then, playing his role to the hilt, he began beating his breast once he had the pearl in hand.

"It is agony!" he wailed. "I have been duped! This insignificant pearl seemed much larger from a distance. This is so unfair! I am cursed to forever be a fool. . . . What can I do, what can I do?"

Some of the watchers cursed the fat man for insulting their intelligence, and others laughed at his antics. All knew that he had struck a bargain that made him one of the richest men in Hlupallu. The men aimed jeers and lewd suggestions at both buyer and seller.

Meanwhile, the Pearl of Perfection had continued to gyrate, seemingly unaware of the transaction and the near-tumult that followed it. As her dancing display reached its frenzied climax, she performed a thrilling series of whirling undulations and shakings during the course of the bargain and the uproar that followed. As the gross proprietor whimpered his last mournful pleadings, the girl slowed her dance and moved toward a young man sitting alone at a

low table at the edge of the dancing floor. The room
fell silent as she gracefully folded herself into a prostrate and submissive form in front of the man. Then
she looked up at him, and with her silver-gray eyes
riveted on his return gaze, she smiled and said
loudly, "May you hold this Pearl forever in your
heart, as I shall hold you, Noble Master."

The audience gasped at this boldness. Omar gave
out a shriek and waddled toward the dancer with a
furious expression, shaking his fist over his head. Ignoring this outburst, the girl removed her single remaining scarf and wrapped it around the young
man's neck. She was supine before the lone man, a
tall and handsome warrior of the Tusmite people
judging from his looks and dress.

The young tribesman smiled. The Pearl of Perfection was covered now only by a gauzy strip of silken
cloth at her loins. She was perfection indeed, and
her honoring him in this way was singular. The
young man reached down, with one swift and powerful motion drew her up so they were both standing,
and kissed her. The audience cheered at this and
voiced lewd comments — except for the Shah
Kufteer, who was livid and scowling, and Omar, who
had pushed his way through the crowd to a position
next to the pair. The gross Kettite swung his sweating hand toward the girl, but the blow never landed, for the tribesman's hand moved more quickly,
stopping the thrust and holding the fat man's wrist
in a viselike grip. The young man swung his other
hand around, fist balled, and caught Omar flush in
his copious gut. The Kettite's knees buckled as he
clutched his stomach, and by the time he hit the
floor he was nothing more than a mountain of quiv-
ering blubber.

Now it was time for Shah Kufteer to take matters
into his own hands — or, more properly, put the
task into someone else's. "Kill that dog!" shouted
the enraged Jakifi. "He dares to defile my chosen
concubine, and he must pay with his life!" A dark,

evil-looking man at his side leaped up, snarling.

The men between the shah's bodyguard and his target stepped aside, none of them wanting to get in the man's way — all except for a small easterner who not only stood his ground but actually took one step toward the bodyguard, as if to make his intentions unmistakable. The short, tan-skinned fellow was clad entirely in black leather, attire that made his cold, gray eyes stand out as he gazed upon the man who stood less than ten feet in front of him.

Shah Kufteer's lieutenant didn't know, or care, if the shorter man was Velunese or some other sort of foreigner. The glowering killer had only one thing on his mind — skewering the young man who, after recovering the girl's shoulders with her thin scarf, was embracing her with one arm while his other hand moved toward the dagger he kept at his belt. What the young man had done was tantamount to signing his own death warrant, and the scowling servant of the shah was determined to carry out that sentence. Apparently, though, he would have to take a few seconds to deal with the interloper who stood in his path. With a snakelike movement the Jakifi drew a long, wickedly curved dagger, threatening the black-clad man. The easterner held his ground, simply staring at the angry Jakifi.

"So, foreign dog, you try to impede the progress of Zameer Dey, do you?" the paid assassin snarled, meaning to distract the easterner with sound and motion. As he cried aloud those words, the Jakifi also waved his curved dagger menacingly. However, the assassin had also brought forth a short, perfectly balanced throwing knife in his left hand. This was his real threat, for its blade was coated with deadly venom. As the black-clad foreigner stood still and presented a perfect target for the blade, Zameer Dey raised the knife above his head and loosed it in a downward line toward the man's throat, sneering as he did so. "Then *die*, insolent whelp!"

His intended victim was not what he seemed.

The instant the poisoned blade left the assassin's fingertips, the easterner became a blur of motion. Where bare throat had been inviting keen-edged death but a split-second before, empty air was now. The blade whistled through the space where its target had been, clattered against the tiled floor a few feet farther away, and skidded harmlessly to a stop. In the instant after the knife was thrown, the lean easterner had thrown himself sideways, knocking a few onlookers off their feet. By the time the blade slid to a stop on the floor, the young man had rolled over to a position flanking the Jakifi killer. When the black-clad man sprang to his feet in the next instant, his right hand was holding a long, needle-pointed dagger and his body was poised for combat.

The easterner had already demonstrated, by action and by his current posture, that he could move with catlike agility and quickness. His face also had a feline aspect — mouth set and expressionless, eyes wide open, flat, and unreadable. The Jakifi assassin, staring back into that face, could not suppress a shudder of fear. Zameer Dey was a murderer, but this man was a model of unfeeling death. The patrons, meanwhile, alerted that the black-clad man was no easy victim for slaughter, backed away to clear a circular space around the antagonists.

The young man with the girl stayed by her side in the background, weapon in hand, still prepared to confront the assassin himself in case this benefactor turned out to be less than he seemed. He did not consider trying to escape the place with the girl, both for the sake of upholding his honor and because he was as interested as the other spectators in seeing how this duel would be resolved. This sort of entertainment spectacle was not one the crowd wished to miss. Mercenary, warrior, and jaded noble alike appreciated such a test of manhood far more than dancing, and these two promised to provide a show of the finest sort — the mysterious, unfeeling easterner with a deadly-looking dagger against the fiercest of Jakifi assassins armed with the curved and razor-edged blade of the west.

"You are fast, pig of the pale-skinned east," the snakelike killer hissed as he readied to face his opponent. "Fear of your imminent death must lend you such quickness, but it only puts off your end for a bit!" Those from Ket, Tusmit, Ekbir, and other parts of the west generally cried their encouragement to the Jakifi at this. Bisselites and Perrenlanders growled and spat in answer, while a group of Velunese mercenaries voiced catcalls at the fighting prowess of westerners and their weapons.

The dark-skinned assassin held his weapon blade upward, the curve running along his forearm, as he spun inward to engage the foreigner. This style of fighting was unusual but deadly. Those opposing it were usually sliced to ribbons before they understood that even as the curved dagger parried and caught blows, its wielder was cutting arm and body as he whirled and twisted in tight infighting. The peoples from the westernmost portions of the Caliphate favored this fighting style, but it was seldom seen in the middle western regions such as Ket.

The leather-garbed man made no reply to the taunt and threat. He watched his opponent with hard, unwinking eyes. As the Jakifi spun to close, the easterner moved away, his straight dagger always between him and the assassin. He watched and assessed the movements and style of the Jakifi, but made no attack himself. The man named Zameer Dey wore a brightly striped, short kaftan of the typical Jakifi sort. A broad, cloth-of-gold sash held the tuniclike kaftan tightly around the waistband of the assassin's baggy pants of bright blue satin, the bottoms of which were thrust into the slightly curled, long-toed boots favored by the folk of the Caliphate of Jakif. Over the kaftan, Zameer Dey wore a short, padded and embroidered garment similar to a gambeson but cut away in front.

The smooth line of the chest area of the kaftan suggested that some protective cuirass was beneath it, possibly a leather shirt. The assassin looked impatient and seemed a bit more confident than before.

"Come, Ourmi cur!" he said with a false grin etched on his sneering visage. "Do you seek to dance with me? Or are you brave enough to use that silly blade you poke in front of you so warily?"

Zameer Dey crouched forward as he spoke, dagger still held with blade upward, his black, beady eyes watching for the slightest mistake on his opponent's part. The Jakifi was ready to block, cut, slash, or stab as opportunity presented. His movements were difficult to follow, and would be as hard to counter once his weapon went into motion.

There was laughter in the crowd when Zameer Dey spoke his insults, but the black-garbed man seemed totally unaffected. When the assassin began to slowly shuffle in an arc to his left, the young man's only reaction was to edge left so as to keep the Jakifi's eyes and weapon in full view. Although his skin was as dark as that of some of the Kettites who jeered him, and his hair too resembled that of folk with Baklunish heritage, there was no doubt that he was from the east and had Oeridian blood. If the Jakifi thought that referring to him as an Ourmi, the derogatory term for all easterners, would upset him, then Zameer Dey was disappointed. The young foreigner showed the deadly calm and steely caution of an experienced knife-fighter. He had a short, straight-bladed sword at his side, but the stranger made no move for his other weapon. Instead, he held the foot-long blade of his dagger swordlike before him — also a very unusual fighting style.

Tiring of this standoff, or perhaps worried that his master would grow impatient, the dark Jakifi darted in, feigning a sweeping cut. The long dagger met the curved blade, sending the latter slightly downward, but then the straight steel was pulled away before the long dagger could be trapped and the arm holding it sliced by the curved weapon. The Jakifi assassin was fast, and he started to come out of his semi-crouch immediately with an upward stab. The stranger darted back, but only a step, and his long poniard began to thrust out and down.

This first motion was the feint, designed to draw the assassin's dagger farther to the side. The next part of the move did the "damage"; the young man in black simply flicked his wrists and changed the direction of his blade in mid-stroke. He aimed high as Zameer Dey was straightening up, drawing the slender tip of his blade diagonally across the front of the Jakifi's silk turban. The slash, aided by the upward movement of the assassin's body, sliced through several layers of the thin cloth. The easterner sprang backward just as the turban-cut ran its course, apparently content to let matters develop instead of trying to continue the infighting.

The remnants of the turban promptly began to cascade down around Zameer Dey's face, revealing in the process that he wore a spiked tarboosh underneath. That was of no import, but if he did not break off his countermove and get rid of the cloth, the distraction would make him vulnerable to attack. The Jakifi leaped backward, yanking the tattered cloth up and away with his left hand as he did so. His metal cap, no longer fixed firmly by the turban, fell off the side of his head and landed on the floor in front of him. The clattering noise of its fall was drowned out by Zameer Dey's voice.

"Filthy, diseased son of a dozen unnatural fathers!" the assassin cursed, his swarthy features distorted and even more darkened by rage.

"Know me as Gord of Greyhawk, you slinking murderer," the young man replied with neither expression nor force as he lowered into a crouch. "The last man you will ever attempt to slay by treachery and poison."

The Jakifi began his next move before his opponent had finished speaking. With his first step, his left foot struck the fallen helmet and sent it spinning on a low arc toward the young man. He continued the lunge, following the helmet's path and moving in to finish the fight. But the young man who had just named himself Gord of Greyhawk was not there to receive either the spiked helmet or the curved blade. Instead he shot his body upward and out, somersaulting over the attacker's head. Turning and twisting in mid-air, Gord landed facing the assassin's back. By the time his feet hit the ground, Gord's dagger was already penetrating the space between Zameer Dey's shoulder blades. Almost faster than the eye could follow, Gord withdrew the dagger and once more drove it in to the hilt. The man coughed once, weakly, then sprawled face down, dead. His blood began to run over the bright tiles and smooth marble of the floor.

Dead silence enveloped the wine house. Not even the mercenary fighting men from the east had expected this startling finish to the duel. The Kettites and other westerners were in shock, for they had anticipated an easy victory for the Jakifi killer. Then the stillness was broken.

"*Kill him!*" The shout came from the Kufteer, Shah of Wadlaoo, Vizier to the Caliph of Jakif.

This time the command was obeyed not by a single assassin but by the half-dozen men who formed the Shah's personal guard. They had slowly started to move from their position along the back wall of the establishment during the contest between Zameer Dey and the foreigner. Now, as the crowd frantically parted to let them through, they sprang to do their lord's bidding, confident that their superior numbers would tell.

The foremost of the onrushing guards was a giant sporting a bulbous turban and diaphanous pantaloons. He wore a byrnie of chainmail adorned with thick breast chains and swung a monstrous tulwar one-handed as if it were a willow wand. The remainder of the Vizier's guardsmen trotted several paces behind, ready to follow up their leader's rush even though the giant warrior alone seemed more than sufficient to handle the slight Ourmi dog who had dared to slay the servant of a noble Jakifi.

"A...a...l R...u...u..h...k!" The huge man bellowed his name, drawing it out in the form of a battle cry, as he rushed upon the smaller opponent, his tulwar held high for a cleaving stroke. Such a blow, if carried through, would surely split the black-garbed foreigner in twain. Instead of seeking escape to one side or the other, Gord drew his short sword with his left hand, bent his knees slightly, and stood still — ready to take the blow head-on!

If the towering Jakifi thought that his furious rush and bellowing shout had frozen or disconcerted his opponent, he soon found out otherwise. As the giant closed and started his downward stroke, Gord brought both of his blades up and crossed them. He caught the descending tulwar in the X formed by his weapons and pivoted his body to the left at the same time, turning the tulwar away from its original path. Then he abruptly bent at the waist and leaned his upper body back to his right. The guardsman's momentum turned against him; his long, heavy blade sliced downward and to Gord's left, hitting nothing but air until it struck the floor, shattering the tilework where it hit. Off balance and confused, the huge Jakifi sought to recover, but Gord would not give this one a second chance as he did for the assassin. A backhand slash with the left, and the short-bladed sword fell across the giant's exposed neck. A lightning-quick thrust with the right, and the dagger penetrated the thick steel mesh of the guardsman's mail byrnie, right over his heart, as though the armor was not there.

"So goes the elephant," the stranger said aloud, tugging the dagger from the corpse. The huge guardsman was dead before he hit the floor.

Murmurs of astonishment swept through the

crowd as Gord withdrew his dagger — even on the way out, the blade severed chainmail links as if they were strands of cotton! Never had any of them seen Keshrun chainmail severed thus by the mere edge of a dagger. The five remaining bodyguards had stopped their rush as Al Ruhk fell dead before them, but were now being urged on by catcalls and advice from the spectators. However, the eastern mercenaries were lending vocal support to Gord again, and this time even a few Kettites joined them. Here was a swordsman, and a weapon, the likes of which they had never seen!

The Jakifi guardsmen formed an arc and came forward slowly and with deliberation. They had encountered hard-bitten opponents before. Their plan was apparent; they would surround this foe and as two or three engaged him, the others would strike his unprotected flanks or from behind. Certainly, five of Kufteer's Own would make short work of this Ourmi cur. All were large, although none as big as the dead Al Ruhk. The tallest of the group, in the center of the bowed line, was also broad, with layers of fat overlaying his muscular body. This one sought to engage Gord first, to keep him busy while the others got into position. He came ahead, even before he got into striking range with his tulwar; as the senior member of the remaining group, he would get his chance to dispose of the foreigner alone — but the others would surround him, too . . . just in case. The big Jakifi rushed in and started to flail at his opponent with a series of furious cuts, shouting curses and insults all the while.

"You fight well, for a greasy pile of pigshit," Gord said, getting off the remark while he was in constant motion parrying and sidestepping the first few blows. The four other swordsmen had almost finished fanning out to cover Gord's sides and back when the foe in front of him took time for a long backswing.

Gord leaped toward the man suddenly, thrusting

his sword out and upward. Caught off guard, the fat Jakifi swordsman tried to back away. He barely avoided the thrust, but was far too slow to prevent the followup strokes. Gord wounded him first with a dagger strike to the torso, then a painful backhand sword cut across the man's unarmored upper right leg. The big guardsman fell over backward, clutching at his leg, and lost consciousness when he hit the floor. Gord somersaulted over the man even as he fell and landed facing the four remaining attackers, who found themselves about to swing at empty space.

"Sheathe your swords now," Gord said flatly to them, "and I will forget this incident. If you continue to attack me, I will give you no quarter."

"*Kill!*" urged the Shah Kufteer.

Somewhat uncertain now, the four warriors came against their opponent once again, obligated to obey their master's command but loath to face this small and terrible foeman.

"To your deaths, then," Gord said without threat or emotion.

The guardsmen of the Shah of Wadlaoo did not take the easterner's words lightly, but they really had no choice. Not to attack him meant death to them as surely as if they did come on and the small man's warning came true. Kufteer would boil them alive for failure, while at the worst this Ourmi offered them a clean and quick end. The four warriors launched themselves nearly simultaneously at the lone foreigner, not bothering to organize a plan of attack. Furious blows, lunging thrusts, and a flurry of slashes poured upon the black-garbed man from front and sides. It was frustrating to these attackers, for the small foreigner never seemed to be where he had been but a split-second before when a tulwar was sent swishing toward him.

In the course of this confused series of exchanges, the four men seemed to get in each other's way, while the stranger's own weapons inflicted many wounds of small sort upon the sweating guardsmen. The crowd was silent, awed by the feats of this single man. First he had dispatched a deadly assassin, then a giant swordsman, both without emotion or seeming strain. A third man was helpless on the floor, as good as dead if not already gone. Now he contested to the death with four expert warriors all at once. He stood still unwounded, holding four large tulwars in play, while those who dared wield them against this black-clad man were dripping blood from wounds he had given them.

Events were becoming too much for the westerners in the audience to bear. The insult inherent in all this was unacceptable. Onlookers from Jakif, Tusmit, and Ekbir grew angry and loosened their own scimitars and curved-bladed daggers. The various nomad tribesmen in the crowd watched the show without apparent allegiance, commenting to one another on style and form as they viewed the display before them. Most of the Kettites, along with all of the eastern mercenaries, however, were rooting openly for the small man called Gord of Greyhawk. They cheered his successes and laughed at the clumsy attempts of the Jakifi to strike him.

It was becoming obvious to all that the melee could end only one way, and that ending must come soon. All of the Jakifi guardsmen were wounded and panting with fatigue from raising and swinging their large blades repeatedly. In no more than a minute or two, one of them would fall, then another. Soon, all of those who had come against the small man would litter the floor as three already did.

When yet one more corpse crashed to the tiled floor, the shah had seen enough — and Kufteer himself entered the fray. Although the noble's dagger had a jewel-encrusted hilt, its silvery crescent below these gems was sharp steel, highly functional, and glittering with a dark enchantment. Kufteer came in a silent rush from a point slightly behind Gord, heading toward the young man's left side, with his curved dagger held across his body, set to deliver a disemboweling stroke as the black-garbed easterner concentrated on the three guardsmen still standing before him.

Gord gave no indication that he knew Kufteer was coming, but at the last instant he sprang aside suddenly, allowing the startled Shah of Wadlaoo to pass on a slant in front of him. The wickedly gleaming blade of Kufteer's dagger cut empty air; then, with a cross-body thrust of his dagger into Kufteer's side and a shove of his left foot against the nobleman's hip, Gord pushed the shah off course right toward the exposed blades of his own guards. The nearest of the swordsmen tried to pull his weapon up and away, but succeeded only in running the edge along Kufteer's neck as he did so. The mouth tried to scream, but no sound came out as the nobleman crumpled in his tracks.

The guardsman whose weapon struck the blow stood frozen for an instant, horrified at what he had just done. Gord's weapons flashed again, and the Jakifi warrior no longer had to concern himself with having slain his master, for he too was a corpse. As the guardsman's body collapsed on top of Kufteer's, the two survivors dropped their tulwars and ran. They would rather risk being captured some time later, given a thousand cuts, and then rolled in salt until dead than continue to face this terrible, black-garbed man any longer.

Silence reigned in the wine house for the space of a heartbeat. The flesh of the blubbery proprietor shook as he peered angrily about his establishment and realized his plight. It was bad enough that this upstart had won — now the bargain could not be sealed, and Omar would lose the thousand gold dokshees and the fabulous pearl. Worse yet, the death of so great a personage as the Shah of Wadlaoo in his establishment would probably bring the wrath of the shah's own ruler, the Marcher Lord of Ket, down upon his body. Trembling and growing more furious by the second, Omar realized that the young foreigner must be killed at any cost. He vented his wrath in a shrill scream, pointed at Gord, and shrieked an order to "Attack!"

Several of Omar's armed servants reluctantly approached the circle where Gord still stood amid the fallen forms of his adversaries. At the same time, an uproar of sound and activity spread through the audience; these men had had enough of watching.

"*Hoddo Ekbir!*"

"*Veluna and Struthburt!*"

"*Tusmani Akbur!*"

In seconds, a cacophony of battle-cries and challenges erupted and the place truly became a battleground of east versus west. Kettites fought on both sides, each according to his feelings at the moment, brawling and using blades. The eastern mercenaries and outlaws generally contended with the dark-skinned and turbaned westerners, while Gord stood alone, an island in the turmoil because no one dared deal with him. Off to his right he saw the Pearl of Perfection making her way toward him across an uncongested area; the young man she had been with was nowhere in sight. One of the fat owner's servants lunged at the girl as she got near Gord, but with a lunge of his own and a flash of steel, the young man handled the threat easily. Then the crowd lost all semblance of cohesion, and the surge of the melee engulfed the open space that had surrounded Gord just a moment before. The girl moved closer to Gord and grabbed his arm.

"Quickly — follow me!" the gorgeous girl shouted in his ear. Then her shapely arm released his, and she began running and dodging through the crowd of fighting men, heading for a curtained archway at the rear of the large court.

Gord ran after the nearly naked girl. The brawling seemed to ebb in an area she passed through; seemingly, no one wanted to be responsible for injuring this beautiful and coveted prize. Nobody directly attacked Gord either, for they all had seen what he could do, but the young easterner had to be constantly on the alert to avoid being stabbed or slashed by an inadvertent stroke as he darted along the same course the dancer had taken. Charging behind the girl through the still-swinging cloth that screened the portal, Gord found himself in a broad but ill-lighted hallway. He caught a glimpse of the Pearl's pale hair disappearing around a corner ahead. The smell of stale, spicy food was strong in here. He guessed that the girl was heading for the kitchen and some back exit, so the young swordsman dashed down the short passage and around the corner into a large room.

"Hurry!" she urged as Gord came into the deserted place. This was the cooking room, all right, but the cooks and scullions must have either joined the melee or fled earlier. "We must get away quickly," the Pearl said as she led Gord across the room, out another doorway, and through a small, walled garden. A tall man, his body covered by a voluminous burnous and his face veiled in the fashion of many Tusmit tribesmen, stood holding open a heavy back gate. At his feet was a guard; in the hand not holding his dagger was the dead man's robe.

"Who is—" the man started to ask, but the girl cut him off.

"Can't you see?" the Pearl scolded as she and Gord came up to the portal. "It is the Ourmi who stood between you and death!"

The veiled warrior made no reply. With a swirl he draped the unclad dancer with the burnous he held, guiding her through the gate as he did so. Gord leaped through the portal on her heels, and then the tall Bakluni pushed the heavy door shut and jammed an iron bar into place.

The man and woman had to stop for a moment to get their bearings, because the alley in which they stood was almost pitch dark. But Gord had a special night-sight that served him automatically, and he could see as clearly as if the sun illuminated the sky, not merely a sprinkling of stars and the tiny, pale-blue half-sphere of Celene, the lesser of Oerth's twin moons. "Thanks, Pearl of Perfection, for showing me the way out of that place," he said sincerely. "My sword arm was growing weary."

"Why did you fight on my behalf?" the tall man asked, pulling back the hood of his burnous.

Gord suddenly recognized him as the tribesman who had been the object of the Pearl's affections inside. There was no doubt that Gord had saved his life, but the young easterner also understood that the man's pride had been injured. He answered without irritation. "To be honest, this whole night was like a bad dream. I once knew a beautiful dancer of Ket myself, and she too was to be sold. No matter. I did as I chose, and I trust you are satisfied with my work," Gord said.

The girl squeezed Gord's leather-clad arm. "Thank you, stranger, for you have helped give me life and hope! I can never tell you how much what you did means to me."

"Yes, many thanks, warrior of the East," the tall Kirkir said with a ring of grudging admiration in his tone. Then, more enthusiastically, he continued, "Come with me. I carry the Pearl home to the Pennors, where the Al-babur tribe of the Kirkir people roam free. There will be welcome there for a man such as you."

"Oh, yes, Zulmon, do have this Gord of Greyhawk come too!" the dancer agreed. Then she added urgently, "But we must hurry, for all Hlupallu will soon be in hue and cry over what has happened. We must get out, and then we can talk on the way."

Gord didn't mind leaving the issue unresolved for the time being. The three went quickly down the alley and into a narrower side passage that turned several times before giving into a small, open square. Four horses were tied here, two of them saddled. Zulmon went to one of the horses' packs and produced a robe similar to his own, but drab instead of colorful. He tossed it to Gord, and the young man quickly put it on over his leather garb.

"Can you ride bareback?" Zulmon asked as he helped the girl into one of the saddles.

"Yes," Gord replied.

"The two there are spare steeds," the warrior called back softly as he mounted. "Take whichever pleases you and bring the other behind."

The three left the little bazaar by the narrow road opposite the passage they had entered it from. To Gord's sensitive ears, the iron-shod hooves of their horses made enough noise sufficient to awaken all of Hlupallu as they rapidly walked the mounts along the building fronts that walled the lane. He peered nervously about, but nobody was watching, no windows above were opened.

Thinking that he much preferred his own silent mode of movement through sleeping cities, Gord hunched low atop his mount and followed the fleeing pair ahead. It was better, he decided, to stay with the warrior and the woman for now; they did seem to have a plan for getting out of the city, and Gord certainly had to do that. Everything he wasn't carrying would have to be left behind, but that was no matter. Only some clothing and small coins remained in the caravansary where Gord had been lodged.

"Get off your horse and lead both of them," Zulmon called back softly. "We come to the gate, and you must be my slave for the moment."

Gord complied without comment. Trotting briskly to keep up, the young man followed the riders on foot for the next hundred yards or so up to the gate. There were four guards flanking the closed doors, well armed with recurved bows and long spears in addition to their swords. These men refused to open the portal and called their corporal out from inside the guardhouse. This man started to complain and threaten, but when Zulmon put some copper and bronze coins in a small purse and tossed the bag to him, the corporal quieted down and made only a cursory inspection of horses and riders, not even bothering to look at Gord. Then the gates opened, and they were free of the city. In seconds the night had swallowed them.

Chapter 3

BY MORNING THE GROUP WAS miles away from
the city, but they had been moving in a direction
that made no sense to Gord. When he questioned
the other man, Zulmon explained his deception.
"We ride southeast into the middle regions of Ket —
but the garments we wore at the city gate last night
were of Tusmiti sort. I think that pursuit will sweep
the northwest and west, expecting us to head for
Tusmit," the big nomad said. Then he gave out a
barking laugh and added, "Who in their right mind
would seek safety from the agents of the Marcher
Lord by riding deeper into his very realm?"

"That is a novel approach to escape," Gord commented dryly. "It also places me in a most unde-
sirable situation, for I desire to travel southwest."

"Why that way, Gord of Greyhawk?" The Pearl
asked in her sweet voice. "Why not just come with
us and dwell with Zulmon's tribe?"

Before the young thief could answer, Zulmon
spoke to the point. "We will turn due southward
soon enough, Gord. The Toosmik River flows to our
left hand, and as it bends southward so too will our
path." The tall hillman looked inquiringly at Gord,
and the black-garbed thief nodded for the Kirkir to
speak on. "The land between the great forest you
easterners call Briartangle and the river is a wild
and lawless region. Bandits might try to molest us,
but none of Ket's soldiery will be in our way. We will
ford the Toosmik and be in the hills by tomorrow
evening."

True to Zulmon's prediction, the three riders came to the first slopes of the Pennor Hills before the sun set the next day. The locals avoided them, and a handful of motley-dressed outlaws posed the only threat they encountered. The Kirkir's huge bow, so large the nomad had to dismount to nock an arrow and draw it, easily discouraged the ragged men from coming close enough to ply their weapons against the three.

The Pearl was silent for several hours as they rode, her expression impassive. Finally, when the sun had all but disappeared below the horizon and Zulmon decided they would stop for the night, the girl dismounted with a huff. As if getting off the horse was a signal for her to begin talking again, she told her troubles to no one in particular. "I hate horseback riding!" she shouted. "I *hate* it!" This was the first time Gord had ever heard her voice sound so harsh, and the dancing girl looked bedraggled and cross, too. "I will never be able to dance again if I must sit on a horse for so long, and I want a soft bed and a place to bathe!"

"I am sorry, my golden dove," Zulmon told her softly, "but we can rest only a few hours here. In but one more day of riding we will be in the lands of my people. Then all will be made right."

The Pearl grumbled and still looked miserable and unhappy, but she sighed with resignation and tried to get comfortable on the hard ground. "Ow! Rocks stab me all over," she cried, "and the smell of horse sweat makes me sick!"

Zulmon offered to take the first watch, so Gord found his own piece of flat ground, lay down on his side, and tried to get to sleep. Meanwhile, Zulmon helped his intended bride get more comfortable, assured her over and over that soon all would be fine, and urged her to rest while he stood guard over her. Things were not going to be all mare's milk and honey for this couple, Gord reflected. He knew a little of nomadic life, and these hills would not provide the every comfort The Pearl seemed to desire. Nonetheless, he thought to himself, eventually she would get used to it. A better man than Zulmon would be unlikely for her. The adjustment, however, would be difficult for both, he mused. Then Gord fell asleep. When Zulmon woke him later for his turn at the watch, The Pearl was sleeping fitfully — but at least she was sleeping, and she dozed that way until dawn.

The Al-babur tribe welcomed the three of them joyfully when they rode up to the camp late the next afternoon. Gord was surprised and mildly impressed to find that Zulmon was the first son of the tribe's hetman — a fact that Zulmon, to his credit, had not seen fit to reveal. The young man's return with four splendid horses and the gorgeous girl who was to be his wife was more than sufficient cause for the whole group to celebrate wildly. Gord was accepted as a member of their people by the hetman, named Mulha, after Zulmon described the fight in the Dar Peshdwar and the young adventurer's victory over so many swordsmen.

Like all the Kirkirs, this tribe was not truly nomadic. The Al-babur built stone villages and their women tended crops. Periodically the tribe would move from one village site to another, each place matching one of the four seasons. The men of the tribe hunted and fought. Occasionally there would be disagreements or even feuds between the tribes, but usually the Al-babur and the other Kirkir tribesmen made war upon the wandering Bayomens and the roving Yollites. Their celebration on this evening of Zulmon's return was a dual one, for it was also time to move from the village they occupied in high summer to the fortress in which the tribe dwelled during the coming autumn months.

Just as promised, the latter part of his journey with Zulmon had taken Gord back in the direction he wished to go. And with the move of the Al-babur tribe, if he remained with the group, he would be taken farther along his intended path, ending up in the hills between the southern grasslands claimed by the Yollites and the broad steppes where the Bayomen tribesmen roamed in bands with their herds of grazing animals.

"Stay with us this season, Gord of Greyhawk," The Pearl pleaded when the three of them found themselves alone inside Zulmon's tent during a lull in the revelry. "I am bored here, and it will be nice to have someone who knows more of civilized life to converse with."

A scowl crossed Zulmon's countenance momentarily when he heard that statement, but he did not allow it to remain and even managed a slight smile to go with his next words. "As my bride wishes, Gord my brother, let it be. I too ask you to remain with us. A warrior such as you will be a great honor to the Al-babur, and you will soon become wealthy and respected. Already my father tells me there are two men who wish to have their daughters married to you!"

Gord had to laugh at that last remark. "I am honored," he said quickly, so as to show no offense to his host, "but imagine a man such as I trying to settle down — and with *two* women, not just one! I would be crazed or fleeing within a month. I am much honored, Zulmon my brother, but my feet can never be still — and I have duty to consider also. On the morrow I must bid you farewell."

"You are too young for such wandering," The Pearl said petulantly.

Zulmon started to retort angrily on Gord's behalf, but Gord managed to interject his own reply. "Not so, dear sister. I look but a youngster of twenty summers, but I am older. The years have been kind to me. . . ."

"Hah! At sixteen, warriors of the Al-babur tribe ride alone to steal horses from our enemies," the tall hillman told his wife-to-be. "You shame Gord by suggesting he is not equal to his manhood!"

Offering vague excuses, Gord managed to slip away from the two and go outside. He was greeted heartily by several warriors, and soon they all were drinking wine and talking of horses. The gathering lasted well into the night, with Zulmon's father repeatedly singing the praises of the young easterner who had so much to do with his son's safe return. When Gord departed the next morning, he was mounted on a small, swift stallion named Windeater, given to him by the leader of the Al-babur as a gift of thanks. The animal was far stronger than it looked, Mulha said, assuring Gord that it could run for hours without tiring. The young adventurer sat in a silver-studded saddle, and behind him were silver-embellished saddlebags filled with his old clothing and ample provisions. Gord now wore the garments of the Kirkir people over his mail shirt.

Before he left, Gord got himself alone for a moment with Zulmon and The Pearl, intending to say a quick good-bye. The girl spoke first. "I am sorry, Gord of Greyhawk, that I had to involve you in the unpleasantness at Dar Peshdwar," she said. "You understand, I know, that I did not wish to end my days as a harem slave." She was back in form, sounding seductive even while making an apology.

"It was my privilege to be of service, lady," Gord said, anxious to end the conversation and be on his way. But the girl insisted on explaining further.

"Omar, that pile of pig fat, planned to use me as an instrument to further his influence at the court of the Marcher Lord," The Pearl told him. "I tried everything to escape his toils, and Zulmon spoke on my behalf, but to no avail. When I salaamed before Zulmon in the traditional offering of my body, I was taking an enormous chance. I expected that Zulmon would be able to contend with fat Omar, as he did indeed. But I knew that both of us would need help to overcome or escape all of the force that Omar and the Shah Kufteer would use. I had a good idea that you, Gord of Greyhawk, would somehow interfere — but I could never have guessed how formidable you actually were."

"She speaks the truth," Zulmon interjected. "Each time I sought to come near The Pearl, Omar prevented it. Neither would he listen to any of my offers to purchase her. I am sure he was scheming with agents of Ket to place her within the seraglio at Jakif as a spy. Promises of freedom would have been made, of course, if she had provided all the information the Kettite agents demanded. Perhaps their promises might have been kept eventually — although poison after her usefulness had ended would have been more likely."

"Why did you think I might help?" Gord asked, finding himself drawn into the conversation despite his sense of urgency about leaving.

"Something in your eyes," The Pearl said. "You had no expression on your face, Gord, but your eyes were like a window to your heart. Those gray eyes looked at my dance, but they saw some other one performing. I could tell you were too much of a man not to hate the likes of Omar and the Shah Kufteer, but I could only hope that you would somehow help us to escape from the Dar Peshdwar by using those straight blades of yours."

"I could have died," Gord said, a bit of irritation creeping into his voice as he realized that he had been taken advantage of.

"As I could have — and The Pearl too," Zulmon said. "But why look as if you have just learned that your best stallion has become sterile?" the tall nomad added, his dark eyes crinkled with mirth. "You helped and added much glory to yourself in doing so. Now we are happy, and you are an honored blood brother of the Al-babur tribe! I will not beg you to stay with us, Gord, but I pledge you my brotherhood and the welcome of the Kirkir always."

Forsaking offers of horses, flocks of goats, and many wives, the young man rode west without looking back into the steep hills behind. There were many leagues to go and much to consider before he entered Yolakand. One hundred leagues, in fact — more than three hundred miles of travel across the open, rolling plains that stretched westward from the Pennors farther than anyone knew. Just why he was bound for the great city of the Yollites, Gord still wasn't certain, but go there he would.

As he cantered along on Windeater, Gord recalled The Pearl's comment about his being too young, and he chuckled to himself. How old *was* he? It was a fine question, and he wasn't really sure of the answer.

Since the time when he grew up as a child of Greyhawk's Old City slums, Gord had had no accurate idea of his age. His foster mother, such as she had been, never told him — if she knew, which Gord doubted. Old Leena cared only for herself, never for Gord, except as a means of providing things that Leena could not otherwise get. His adolescent years as a beggar and thief, the time he spent studying at the city's great university, and his periods of traveling in the wide world he could reckon. Counting in the time between travels, when he had roamed throughout Greyhawk as Blackcat, the most successful thief and burglar the city had ever known, and as Gord the free-wheeling gambler and rake, and adding that total to the other years, Gord arrived at a good reckoning of his age. He also took into account the time he had spent in the strange realm of the Catlord, but he had the distinct impression that somehow he had not aged, or had aged only very slowly, during that time. All things considered, Gord's best estimate of his age was between twenty-eight and thirty. In light of this, he was always amazed nowadays to hear others remark on his youthful appearance — and when he viewed his reflection in a mirror, he was as puzzled as anyone else. Judging by looks, he was barely past twenty. Perhaps, Gord mused, this was a side effect from the time he had lingered in the Catlord's domain. Having nothing better to do while Wind-eater carried him west, Gord allowed his memory to drift back through the strange series of events that had brought him to this place and time. . . .

He wrote an end to his adventures in the city of Greyhawk when Gord agreed to accompany his half-elven friend, Curley Greenleaf, on a quest for what the druid-ranger referred to as the Middle Key. It was a portion of an evil artifact meant to awaken a being who was the embodiment of all wickedness, should the three parts of the malign thing ever be joined. One evil group, known as the Scarlet Broth-erhood, held the Initial Key. Gord and his comrades sought to gain the middle portion so as to keep the artifact from the grasp of those who promoted vile darkness. Although he and his group failed, the Middle Key fell into the hands of the half-demon Iuz — an outcome that was not all bad. That evil cam-bion had no more desire to see the whole artifact united than did the other forces of Oerth, either those on the side of good or those who sought balance between good and evil.

In the process of returning from this perilous mission, Gord encountered and fought a terrible creature — a devil in the form of a monstrous boar. In the process, the beast tore him to shreds and actually killed him! Gord was still amazed whenever he thought about this. The fiend was likewise slain in the awful contest, but it had no magical protec-tion from death as did Gord.

The young thief stroked his ring idly as he re-called these events. On one other occasion, before confronting the devil-boar, he had been killed and then awoke to find himself in the otherworldly realm of one known as Rexfelis the Catlord — only Gord hadn't realized immediately that he had been dead and then restored to life. The Catlord told him that the green cat's-eye chrysoberyl he wore set in his ring was special. This ring, which Gord had somehow become attuned to, had been made by Rexfelis himself, along with eight others of similar sort, for some purpose that the lord did not reveal to the tan-skinned young adventurer. Even after his first rescue, Gord hadn't believed the Catlord's assertion that the ring had the power to restore him from death nine times, the proverbial number of lives a cat was said to have. The second time he found himself recovering in the realm of the Cat-lord, however, there was no doubt left in his mind.

As he recuperated, Gord experienced nothing but comfort and pleasure, and he was tempted not to leave. After all that had befallen him, it was no wonder that he wished to linger in the strange but peaceful domain of Rexfelis and his cats. There were felines of all sorts there — subjects of the Cat-lord? Perhaps. But if subjects these animals and others were, they served willingly and from respect. Gord himself was a werepanther of sorts, for the ring he wore also empowered him to take the form of a black leopard whenever he chose. For all of the ring's benefits, Rexfelis never demanded anything of Gord. Homage was freely given and majestically received by the Catlord. In addition to the attraction of the fascinating nature and beauty of this realm, Gord was tempted to stay for another reason . . . and her name was Tirrip.

She was a human, yet she was a tiger. She explained to Gord that on her own world the dominant species was of the latter sort, and that only here, with Rexfelis, could her folk take both human or feline form at will. Gord didn't care that she wasn't really a human. He loved this strange female, and he and Tirrip had spent uncounted days and nights together. They roamed the place in cat bodies or in human ones, as they felt at the moment. He hoped that their idyll would never end . . . but it did, of course. One day Tirrip told him sadly that she had to return to her own world, for a reason she would not reveal. There was discussion — argument on his part, actually — but that could not alter things. She left a few days later, and afterward Gord felt more alone than ever before, even more than when he had been sentenced to the workhouse in the Old City of Greyhawk for theft when he was still a very small boy.

After seeing Gord mope around for too long a time, Rexfelis summoned the young man to join him in his private area of the seemingly endless villa that served as court and home for the Catlord and who knew how many cats of all sorts. Stroking a sleek, black tomcat, the Master of Cats said, "I am journeying to Oerth soon, Gord, to the town of Bardillingham. Will you come?"

Gord was perplexed. "Bardillingham? That name is unfamiliar. In what land does the town lie?"

"Have you been here so long that you forget your own world, Gord?" Rexfelis laughingly asked the dark-haired young man.

Gord wasn't quite certain how to take that remark. It seemed like a jest, but then again he had to admit to himself that perhaps he had tarried in the Catlord's lair too long. "No, Catmaster," he said carefully in reply. "I fear that my real knowledge of the Flanaess is confined to that bit I have traveled in and what I read about other parts in books when I was a youngster at college."

"Little portion of the Flanaess? Come, come, my boy. From all I have heard, you have covered a good bit of eastern Oerik. It is not surprising that you know nothing of Bardillingham, though," Rexfelis went on. "It isn't much of a town and lies in a place most folk are ignorant of. The community boasts scarcely three thousand inhabitants, and it lies deep within the land governed by the Demiurge Basiliv. You might know the place as the Vale of the Archimage."

The Flanaess was named for the old race originally dwelling in the heart of the continent of Oerik, one of the four great land masses of Oerth.

The Flan nation was ages gone, although Flan peoples still inhabited the continent, some still relatively unmixed with the other races that had eventually settled the Flanaess and carved their kingdoms and states thereon. Having wandered the east as a gypsylike entertainer and later as an adventurer, Gord had seen some of this territory, and then more of it when he had sought the Middle Key. The Vale of the Archimage, however, was a near-fabulous place, or so he had thought, supposedly lying somewhere in the mountains that separated the Baklunish states of the west from the Oeridian and Suel nations of the east. For all of his travels, Gord had been no farther west than Veluna, and Rexfelis's definite words about the Vale of the Archimage were music to his ears.

"You mean there *is* such a place?"

"Yes, my friend, there certainly is . . . and a Bardillingham town, too. The headwaters of the Chaban River rise in the Barring Mountains range, form a series of deep, cold lakes, and have carved a great, lush valley in the eons since this watercourse began flowing. This is the Vale of the Archimage — at least, so it is named on those maps that show anything there at all. The so-called Archimage is actually a Demiurge, and his name is Basiliv. I have business with him."

"Bardillingham?"

"That is the only real community in the whole of the valley. There are some scattered villages and hamlets, but little else. The town is rather dreary."

"I have read a few things about the Vale of the Archimage," said Gord. "Whether the tales are fanciful or not, it is said that strangers are . . . most unwelcome there."

"You'll be welcome enough if you should care to come along," Rexfelis purred reassuringly. "I, of course, am no stranger at all, and whomever I bring with me is accorded acceptance and respect. Besides, Basiliv has asked to meet you."

This last statement made Gord very uneasy. The reputation of this secluded land and its ruler was anything but amiable. And why would the Catlord be discussing him with Demiurge Basiliv in the first place? Gord didn't think he wanted to know, so he suggested to Rexfelis another course. "Hmmm," he murmured, pretending to consider the matter carefully. "Perhaps another time, Master Cat, for I have things to attend to in Greyhawk soon now. Perhaps thereafter I can travel westward and pay my respects to the Demiurge. Meanwhile, could you not simply transport me back to my home city?"

Rexfelis laughed softly. "Diplomatic, very diplomatic! I would indeed fulfill your request if I could, Gord," the Catlord said with a sincere smile, "but many powers weave and interlock over the Flanaess now, as they have done for some time past. All is not well there, you know — but I suppose you do not need to concern yourself with such matters any more. To give you a short answer, though, I am able to send you back to Oerth via the terminus that Basiliv's force keeps open and operative. You must go there if you wish to return to your world. But you can feel at home here, too, Gord. You may spend all of your life here if you wish, for you are now certainly of my own ilk," the Master Cat added warmly.

His heart sinking, Gord asked, "Cannot one of your power go where he wills?"

"I? Yes indeed. I can go where I desire. You would not survive the rigors of such a work, however. Would you use another of those precious lives — only to end up back here where you started?"

"Pray, Catlord, tell me what is going on," Gord asked him earnestly.

"Time here is different," Rexfelis explained. "Sometimes a day here is a month long, by Oerth reckoning, while the obverse might prove true before or later. The months and months you have lingered here have been moving less rapidly on Oerth. Evil still strives to gain that tool which you have sought a part of. Many of the demons of the Abyss have united, melding their powers. They contend with the Hells and all others of evil, and in such warfare we all profit. Who can object if demon slaughters devil? Those great ones from the higher planes take a hand also, and strange twists and fluxes abound in the multiverse. It is quite impossible to use planar travel without expending great power, and even then there is risk. Established gates are now watched, traps are set, misdirection abounds. Basiliv is strong enough to maintain an unwarped gate. In this matter I assist him, naturally. Even the Demiurge is not strong enough by himself to hold against the ones now bestirring themselves."

Gord had no reason to doubt the truth of these words — or any others the Catlord spoke, for that matter. Still, he could not be entirely convinced that the course laid before him was the best one for him to follow. But after some more discussion and still with reluctance in his heart, Gord agreed to go with Rexfelis to the Vale of the Archimage.

Bardillingham was a plain and unattractive town. At least, that's the way Gord perceived it in comparison to places such as Greyhawk, Dyvers, Rel Mord, and even Wintershiven. Contrary to what he had read and heard about the Vale of the Archimage, these people seemed neither hostile nor secretive, and their town was anything but glamorous and lavish. The officials of Bardillingham received them with ceremony. The earl who resided in the nearby castle did them honor, and Gord was surprised to be included not just as the Catlord's guest but as some minor personage in his own right. Despite all the pomp and circumstance, he found the whole place uninteresting. After almost three days spent walking the corridors of the castle and the streets of Bardillingham, Gord was bored and impatient.

"When will I find out why I am here?" he asked Rexfelis in as polite a tone as he could muster.

"That will come soon enough," said the Catlord. "In another day or so, Basiliv will be seeing us."

The next day, as Gord and Rexfelis were strolling through the town, the Catlord brought them both to the front steps of an unimposing stone building in the center of town, a site they had not yet visited. Gord had a feeling that their audience was about to take place — but could this be where the Demiurge held court? The place was barely large enough to contain a town bureau, let alone the sovereign of the land! When Gord made a remark to this effect, Rexfelis merely laughed and reassured his young charge that wonders were abundant in the strange realm ruled by Basiliv.

Once they were inside the building, Gord realized the truth of those words. Somehow, the interior of the place was as large as the largest palace Gord had ever heard of. He presumed that some mighty dweomer allowed a vast space to be contained within the small shell of the building. This was such a contrast to the drab and ordinary appearance of the rest of the town that Gord could not contain his wonderment. Rexfelis, of course, was considerably less impressed.

"Be not amazed. Others can manage this little trick, too," the Catlord told him. "Did you know, Gord, that when Basiliv is elsewhere, all this is too? Had we come yesterday, we would have found only a small and empty structure." Gord, feeling a bit embarrassed by his awestruck reaction, kept silent as he and the Catlord crossed under the archway that led to Basiliv's audience chamber.

Basiliv, wearing an impassive, businesslike expression, nodded in Gord's direction as if to acknowledge the young man's presence. After exchanging pleasantries with Rexfelis, the Demiurge addressed himself directly to the young adventurer.

"You no longer serve those of the Hierophants and the Cabal."

It was a statement of fact, not a question, and for

a few seconds Gord wasn't sure how to reply. The affair of the Middle Key had left him feeling worn and disheartened, believing that he and his comrades had been little more than meaningless pawns in a struggle far beyond their comprehension. When that portion of the Artifact of Ultimate Evil was reported by Rexfelis to be in the possession of Iuz and his horrid associates, Gord had felt less than useless. The young man detested evil, that he was certain of. But he disliked being used, too. During the short silence that hung over the chamber, Gord decided that he would continue to strive against the ascendancy of malign powers as well as he could, but he intended to do so in his own way and as he chose to. He would have knowledge before he entered any new quest, and never again would he contest blindly if he had his way.

"Yes, Great Demiurge, I am my own man," Gord said quietly to the waiting Basiliv.

A secret, knowing smile passed between the Demiurge and the Catlord. Neither sought to conceal the exchange. "None of us are actually quite that, young Gord of Greyhawk," Basiliv replied, smiling benignly. "Yet the desire to be one's own is admirable . . . if actions match ideals!"

Now Gord was truly puzzled. What could this great magic-user be talking about? And why was Rexfelis nodding in agreement? "I am at a loss, My Lord Demiurge, to know how to reply."

"No need. Your life is known to me, Gord. You have come far and accomplished much for one of so tender an age. Thank your progenitors for supplying you with such splendid genes! But let's get down to business, shall we?"

What on Oerth this bizarre spell-worker was speaking of, Gord had no idea. Genes? Perhaps they were some form of guardian genies — he didn't know. And what manner of business Gord and the Demiurge could possibly have between them was totally beyond him. Despite the awesomeness of the two figures he was with, the young man actually began to become annoyed. "It seems that you have the advantage of me, as does the Master of Cats," he said. "I am at a loss, as I already stated. I must know what is going on if I am to do anything at all!"

This brought laughter from both Demiurge and Catlord, and their laughter was both real and friendly. "Seldom does anyone manage to get the advantage of you these days, Master Gord," Basiliv said after composing himself. "Let us depart this too-formal audience hall for my private chambers," and so saying he got up without ceremony.

His guests followed him, and soon all three were seated in a crowded but comfortable study of some sort. Gord didn't recognize much of what lay around him, but there were books, maps, and charts in profusion along with the paraphernalia of dweomer-craefting. There were also strange, large seats of padded and most comfortable sort for each of them. Refreshments floated in the air, trays of beverages and tidbits of tasty food that served each of them in turn — Catlord, Gord, and then Basiliv.

"Now, that's better," the Demiurge said contentedly as he leaned back in his chair and sipped the fruity concoction he had selected. "Rexfelis," he went on while looking at Gord, "you told me this one was unusual, but I hadn't appreciated until now just how unusual he might be."

"As always, dear Basiliv, I have a tendency to understate. Let us suppose it is simply a case of blood telling. . . ."

With a shake of his large, black-maned head, Basiliv turned to stare at Rexfelis a moment, shook his head again, and returned his gaze to Gord. "So it is information you must have, is it? I shall now do my best to supply you with just that."

Then the Demiurge related to Gord how he had kept track of events in the past, events surrounding the three portions of the evil device that would awaken the slumbering Tharizdun, Lord of All Evil, the one who would weld demon and devil together and bend the Abyss and the Hells to his vile will. Basiliv said that he knew of the Scarlet Brotherhood's discovery and use of the Initial Key, and that he had done what he could to confuse them so that the middle portion of the artifact would not also fall into their hands.

"Contending factions work against the forces of Good and Those-Who-Seek-Balance as well as Evil," the Demiurge noted. "Too many desire to use the malign powers of the artifact for their own ends. Nothing beneficial ever comes of Evil, Master Gord — remember that! Even I, in my young and foolish past, have misused my powers and wrought badness, seeking nothing but seclusion. Now folk fear and hate me, I know. Though their feelings are misplaced at this time, the past gives them cause. But I digress." Basiliv paused and quaffed his concoction again, then continued.

"My friend and associate, Rexfelis, has always believed as I do now. That is why he and I are united now to achieve a certain goal. He suggested that you, Gord, might be the one to bring our desires to fruition. I believe his perception is correct." After another short pause, the Demiurge explained himself further.

"The contending factions which would have the Final Key are so busy fighting with one another that most have effectively taken themselves out of the contest, as it were. That is as it should be. But can the Lords of the Upper Planes use, or even hold, the Key? Not likely. Its base vileness would soon bring it into the hands of those who want to awaken . . . that dark being who sleeps. Do the Cabalists have better skills? The Hierophants? Never! And I am no more fit to employ such an object than is Mordenkainen or any of the others who would have it. Despite intentions, they would find themselves growing as evil as the one whose essence is the artifact. Do you understand?"

"I hear what you say, Lord Demiurge," Gord replied slowly. "I think I perceive the point you are driving at. I do not understand, however, why you are telling me that you have no desire to yourself possess the Final Key."

"Quite so! You do not yet understand because you are unaware of what has recently transpired. Let us have another round of potables, and then Rexfelis and I, my boy, will provide you with all there is to know on this matter."

Several hours later Gord saw the whole matter in a new and very different light. He had taken no oath, nor sworn any vow, but he knew within himself what he must now do. After shaking hands with Basiliv and bowing in farewell to the Catlord, Gord simply walked out of the Demiurge's strange palace and into Bardillingham. In less than an hour he met up with a party of the Demiurge's soldiers (who apparently had been awaiting him), packed his possessions (which had been brought from his room in the castle), and was on his way out of town.

He rode northward in company with a mixed group of close-mouthed men and taciturn elves. The latter were called Grughma by their own kind, and "valley elves" — a term of derisive sort — by men and other sorts of elves who dwelled outside the realm of Basiliv. It was not a particularly pleasant trip. The soldiers of the Demiurge showed great respect and deference to Gord, but kept themselves isolated from him. The landscape was interesting, at least, which made the journey somewhat more bearable. They traveled from valley to foothills to mountains — the first peaks Gord had ever seen.

On the second day after leaving the town, once the group was well into the Barring Range, the elves and men turned back, taking with them the horse that Gord had ridden. They would not go farther than the boundaries of their lord's domain. New escorts took over, though, so Gord did not have to worry about being abandoned in the vastness of rock that jutted and towered so majestically.

The fifty soldiers of the Demiurge's troop were replaced by four times that number of dour dwarves dressed in iron and steel armor. The long-bearded mountain dwarves dealt summarily with any predatory creatures foolish enough to approach them. Gord and this small army of dwarves trudged upward into the mountains, going ever higher. Soon, Gord recalled, the very air seemed so cold and thin that he felt like he was being strangled. The broad-chested dwarves appeared not to mind the rare atmosphere, but they deferred to the young human, taking a path through the mountains that was not the shortest but which enabled the group to avoid climbing to even higher elevations. Gord was glad when their path led downward, and some of the deep breaths he took were genuine sighs of relief.

He was surprised that the dwarven company remained with him when they all finally left the mountains, four days after beginning their descent toward less rugged ground. They had come to the rough foothills on the north side of the Barring Mountains, an area called the Pen-Wilds, where few folk lived and game abounded. Gord hunted with success and greatly enjoyed the wild lonesomeness of the place. Noticing this, the dwarves warmed to him a little.

"Do you, Gord of Greyhawk, roam thus in your own lands?" the captain of the band asked him one night as they camped. Gord replied in the negative, but then told the broad dwarf of his adventures in other places, his hunts, his combats with monsters.

I see why you are a Chosen One," the fellow rumbled when Gord had finished. "Our gift to you is this," he said, and held forth a broad armlet of vari-colored gold. It was a work of odd design, its material being gold of hues like palest sunlight, deepest sunset-orange, gold-green, and violet-gold intermixed with the usual yellow gleam of the ore.

"I cannot accept such a treasure!" Gord said.

"No, man, you cannot refuse it," the dour demi-human rebutted. "We all depend on you, and this is our offering of success."

Gord took the band, clamped it around his bicep, and nothing more was said on the subject.

The next day they came to a place where the hills became more gentle and trees dotted valleys and hilltops alike. In the distance the mass of a forest could be seen, blanketing the last, low ridges and mounds of the Pen-Wilds. Here the company of dwarves told Gord that they would go no farther.

"You are now at the edge of Briartangle Woodland, Gord," the gnarled captain of the demi-human band said to him. "That little brook there is the headwater of the river the Baklunish humans call the Toosmik. If you keep it on your left hand, it will guide you through the forest to Hlupallu."

Such a speech was quite a bit for a dwarf to say, and this impressed Gord. "Many thanks, Good Captain. May I ask a question?" When the dour fellow nodded assent, the young adventurer went on with, "Why do you name me as a Chosen One?"

"Our folk know Basiliv the Demiurge, and the Master of All Cats, too," answered the captain. "We neither serve them nor care overly much about their whims. But some greater force is at work now — we know this. They send you, but their purpose is not of them. It is of the greater power." And then the broad-shouldered, curly-bearded dwarf clamped his mouth shut and folded his arms. He had said all he would say in response to Gord's question.

"I see," Gord replied, not fully understanding but accepting this mysticism as something the dwarf chose to believe. "Fare you well, captain and company all!" As he turned away and began to stride northward, the stout demi-human rumbled after him, "The armlet you wear, Gord of Greyhawk, was forged long and long ago by the smiths of Grotheim. It bestows the strength of our folk upon you in certain ways."

At this, Gord turned back toward the dwarves and bowed slightly in a gesture of thanks and respect. He had never suspected that the armband was anything but a valuable piece of jewelry; now he had been told that it was special for a greater reason than the gold it was made of. The dwarven captain nodded to Gord, and behind him his fellow warriors raised their weapons in a silent salute. The whole incident moved Gord deeply.

"Venoms and dweomers, man — dwarves are very strong against them!" the captain shouted out. Then he and his men turned and trudged on corded legs back toward the rugged hills of the Pen-Wilds.

Whether or not the dwarves had any idea of Gord's abilities, their directing him through the forest proved to be exceptionally useful for the young adventurer. Once alone and concealed within the thick growth of the Briartangle's southern verge, Gord transformed himself from man to panther. He was relieved to find that the armlet changed with him, as did his other possessions.

There were dangerous beasts in the forest, monsters too, and occasional outlaw bands. Those that Gord was unable to avoid either avoided him or discovered after a brief encounter that it was better not to attack such a creature. A black leopard the size of a jaguar was an unusual creature, to say the least — too much of a match for lion, carnivorous ape, or green forest ogre.

When he eventually came to the open, cultivated lands beyond the Briartangle, Gord changed to his true form again. The herdsmen and farmers of Ket were a mixed race, although Baklunish blood predominated. Although Gord was dark in complexion as they were, his dress and speech gave him away as a foreigner. The natives shunned a lone wanderer of this sort. Nevertheless, his passage was swift enough, inns and caravansaries providing for his needs.

When he finally arrived in Hlupallu, Gord sought

and found service in the army of the Marcher Lord.
When he demonstrated that he could ride well,
Gord was assigned to a troop of mercenary lancers.
Tests of his weapon skills showed that the new
Ourmi recruit had no ability whatsoever with the recurved bow but could at least point a lance correctly. He was appointed a private in the company
of lancers commanded by Malik Ibn Urchi. Wearing
the brown cloak with the white and orange emblem
of the Kettite kingdom, Gord rode over the lands
around the capital for hundreds of miles, chasing
Bayomen tribesmen, raiders from the tribes of hill-
folk, or local bandits. He learned a smattering of
Kettite Baklunish speech, and his comrades told
him that his accent no longer sounded eastern.
Then abruptly one night he deserted the troop,
leaving without farewell or regret, and went alone
into the teeming streets of Hlupallu.

The city was a mixture of cultures, but it was
more of West than East. Hlupallu was divided into a
fortress compound of great size, the *casbah;* a
crowded market district, the *souk;* a residential
quarter, the *medina;* a sector for foreigners known
as the *ourmistan;* and a place of warehouses and the
like. Each portion of the city was walled off from
the others. This was purposeful, not a case of hap-
penstance as it was in some eastern towns and
cities. He took up residence in the foreign quarter,
traveling here and there in Hlupallu dressed in native garb — looking, listening, and learning so that
he could pose as a Kettite. He managed to do well
enough in the few weeks he had to further study
the manners and speech of Hlupallu.

As he had been told by both Demiurge and Catlord, some event would occur that would take him
from the capital of Ket. What the event was, neither
could say for certain, but Basiliv had said that
Gord's journey would be west and southward, and
Rexfelis assured him that once it was underway he
would recognize the enemy and know instinctively

what he must do. More than that, neither could tell
him.

Gord stayed in Hlupallu and waited for fate to
move him. He continued to practice his skills —
thievery, gymnastics, weapon play — as much as he
could; but he did not actually ply any of these arts
beyond mere rehearsal. In fact, at times he felt frustrated, for it seemed to him that he was becoming
more and more a swordsman and less and less a
thief and burglar. This boded ill for his purse, for
the pay of a mercenary, no matter his ability and
prowess, was laughable when compared to the return from a single successful mission such as the
ones he had undertaken as Blackcat the burglar.

Then came the night when he was seated in the
Dar Peshdwar, watching one incredibly lovely dancer perform but recalling another dancer, another
time, and another place, long past, much distant.
Was the combat there and his flight with Zulmon
and The Pearl to the Pennors the sign he was supposed to wait for? Perhaps, perhaps not. It didn't
matter now, for there was nothing he could do
about those events. What had occurred had occurred, and Gord was now committed to action. Although he had seen no enemy as he had been told
he would, it seemed to be time for him to move
westward. Once he had left Hlupallu, the young adventurer felt strongly that he must follow a new
strand spun by fate. Those who sought the last portion of the malign artifact would have to travel this
way, Gord reflected. It stood to reason, then, that
he must ride forth to meet them in some other locale than the city.

Whether it came from native intelligence or by
the hand of some greater power, this belief was to
prove correct.

Chapter 4

OBMI STOOD FIDGETING before the fearsome trio. Zuggtmoy, Demon Queen of Fungi, was in human form, looking ravishingly lovely even to the jaundiced eye of the dwarf. Beside her lounged Iggwilv, likewise seeming to be nothing more than a young and incredibly beautiful female. Between exchanges of "girl talk," these two would chatter with Iuz. The cambion was irate at this behavior, but he dared not speak to either female about his anger. In fact, Obmi gloated mentally, when the towering cambion had started to take out his frustration by snarling at Obmi, Zuggtmoy and Iggwilv had intervened.

"Stop that!" the great witch had commanded.

"Yes, Iuz, you know that the dwarf is no longer yours," Zuggtmoy had added. "Obmi is mine now, and I will not tolerate meddling from another when it comes to my servants!"

Finally, unable to stand it any longer, Iuz interrupted the two females with a loud demand. "If you are going to waste your time, that is up to you, but I have better things to do. If you ever get down to important matters, you may inform Me. Perhaps I will attend and give you the benefit of My wisdom!"

"Stay, Iuz," Iggwilv said. The tone was conversational, but her look and meaning were unmistakable. She would have no such conduct from her son.

Zuggtmoy smiled at the glowering cambion. "Very well, dear Iuz. We have had enough of gossip, I think. It is just a matter of letting those who must obey you know exactly where they stand," the demoness said, giving Obmi a casual glance.

Iuz ground his hundred little fangs in fury at the manner in which his mother treated him. He said nothing, but he held in his heart a growing hatred for the most ancient and powerful of witches. One day soon, Iggwilv would regret her treatment of him. First, however, he would use her to attain rule of all Oerth. "I consent to your wishes, Greatest of Ladies," Iuz said, smiling and nodding. "It is merely that I believe My dear father, rot his scabrous skin, will be acting with more expeditiousness. . . ."

"Your apology is accepted, Iuz," Iggwilv said, knowing full well that statement would annoy him. She meant to teach this sprat some manners soon, but not until his usefulness was ended. The witch waved a hand toward the sweating dwarf. "Are you ready for his instruction, Zuggtmoy?"

"Did you enjoy being My toad?" the demoness inquired, smiling at the dwarf as she did so.

"Well, great queen, I must say that it was an experience which I had never had the privilege of prior to your kindness," Obmi replied.

"No matter!" Zuggtmoy interrupted before the clever dwarf could speak on. "You will not have the opportunity to experience the . . . pleasure . . . of that form again — *if* you obey Us and succeed. You *will* gain the Final Key for Us, won't you?"

"Yes, great Queen of the Abyss. You may always rely upon—"

"I rely upon no one!" The statement thundered in startling fashion from Zuggtmoy's slender, full-bosomed form. "If you fail, dwarf, you will either be dead or wish for death."

"Iuz trained you well, did he not, Obmi?" Iggwilv inquired, redirecting the conversation. She wished Zuggtmoy to get to the point now.

"Yes, greatest of witches," Obmi said with a bow toward Iggwilv.

"He is very strong, Zuggtmoy," Iggwilv said to the demoness. "See those knots and bands of muscles? That one is as near to extraordinary strength as is possible for mortals, be they men or dwarves."

"No, dear," Zuggtmoy contradicted. "He is not as strong as a dwarf can be through supernatural means. That favor I shall bestow upon him soon, to assure he does not fail."

"An excellent idea, Zuggtmoy!" Iuz said, so as not to be left out of the matter. After receiving sour looks from both females, Iuz scowled and did not go further. Iggwilv, however, had something meaningful to add.

"Obmi, I too shall give you a special gift in order that you may serve Queen Zuggtmoy better." With that, the witch took out a small square of folded cloth, odd material bearing glyphs that writhed and changed before one's eyes. She unfolded the stuff carefully, and as she did so the cloth seemed to stretch and alter. It became larger unfolded than the small packet ever could have been, if it had been normal cloth. Soon the material actually blanketed Iggwilv's lap and spread to the floor around her pretty little feet. Lying across her lap, somehow revealed from within the package by the unfolding of the cloth, was a strange-looking object. "There, Champion of Zuggtmoy, is your second weapon!"

The dwarf stepped forward and took the gift as Iggwilv held it out to him. It was a short-handled, hammer-backed military pick known as a martel. Its color was odd, and inlays of silver ran through beak and butt. "I am eternally grateful, munificent lady of witches," Obmi said ceremoniously, but his nervousness was obvious from his expression. He sensed that Zuggtmoy was annoyed about the exchange that had just taken place. Indeed, the demon queen wanted to be the one to extol the virtues of the weapon, but she had not been given a chance to examine it before Iggwilv handed it to Obmi, and without a careful study of the weapon she was quite unable to inform the dwarf of its values.

A beatific smile spread across Iggwilv's gorgeous

features. It was obvious that she appreciated and enjoyed Queen Zuggtmoy's discomfiture. She allowed the moment to stretch on . . . a bit too long.

"The martel, Obmi-My-Former-Slave, is obviously magically forged of latten, inset with silver against the dogs of the Hells, and magicked to a degree of much power," Iuz said smugly.

Iggwilv, her thunder stolen, gave her son a stare that would have withered any lesser creature, but the cambion simply bowed slightly, as if she had paid him a compliment, and smiled so as to show his rows of pointed teeth. "Iuz is correct, dwarf, as far as he could go," she said acidly. "The pick is of such enchantment as to be powerful enough to wound the greatest of Hell's dukes. Its metal of copper and tin is finest latten, as Iuz mentioned, but its dweomer is such that it is as strong as adamantite. Better still, no magnetism nor iron-eater will affect it. Should you not choose to use your little hammer, Obmi, this weapon will serve you most ably . . . and I give it in honor of your mistress, Queen Zuggtmoy," the witch concluded, with a sweet smile toward that person.

"I thank you on behalf of My servant," Zuggtmoy said with a regal tone. "Of course, you are wise, dear witch, to recognize that My cause — and it *will* succeed — is best furthered by aiding My champion and thus assuring your own ends will be met. We must now get to the serious matter of this contest."

There followed a period of express instruction. Zuggtmoy told Obmi that he was to depart the grim city of Molag the next day. All of his magical gear, armor, hammer, and boots would be restored to him. In addition, the dwarf would don a dweomered hat, a magical head covering that would enable him to appear far different from his true form. When he ventured forth on the morrow, Obmi would seem to be an aged female elf, one making a pilgrimage to Celene and the Great Temple of Ehlonna before she died. Of course, no such destination would ever be reached. Once in the Kron Hills, the dwarf would use the magical hat to appear as a gnome, crossing westward to gain Yolakand over the Larkill Mountains, the Longridge Hills, and the Pennors.

"It is a slight deviation, Obmi, but you must turn north and go to Hlupallu in Ket. There you will find your assistants and guards. Understood?" Zuggtmoy queried.

"Yes, Queen of the Abyss."

The demoness seemed pleased. "When you leave the hills to go to Hlupallu, eliminate any of those still with you in the party — this poison and your own weapons should serve for that," Zuggtmoy told him as she handed him a tiny vial. "It is certain that one or more of those who accompany you will be spies, agents of Graz'zt or some other meddler. Enter Hlupallu as a half-elf with a spade beard and yellow eyes. Go to the place called Dar Peshdwar, and there your assistants and guards will await."

"Whom should I seek?" Obmi asked meekly.

"No!" admonished Zuggtmoy. "That you will learn when you arrive in Hlupallu — those you seek will find you, not you them. I want no slip of the lip occurring in the meantime. Those who will serve you will bear my further instructions."

"Leave us now, dwarf," Iggwilv commanded coldly. Obmi hesitated but a moment, glancing up to see if the demoness would countermand the order. Zuggtmoy's face was absolutely expressionless, as beautiful and unreadable as a portrait by a master limner. Falling to his hands and knees, Obmi crawled backward from the metal-walled little chamber, thanking all with flowery profusion as he departed. His underlying thoughts were carefully screened by mental images of gratitude and desire to serve — a trick that he had become quite good at since falling in with witches and demons.

When he was gone, Iggwilv brought the others to attention by saying, "That one is a snake and a jackal!"

"A fitting servant, true," Iuz commented.

"And a nonesuch among dwarves. He is a warrior more able than most, if not all, living humans," the Queen of Fungi boasted of her new servant. "He is the best tool We have to defeat Graz'zt!"

Iuz sneered. "Bah! He would have failed Me earlier, had not you two rescued the situation in the Vesve and captured the Middle Key."

"He has learned much since then, I think," the demoness said.

"With those We support him with, Obmi will succeed," Iggwilv said with an iron ring in her voice. "But let Us now converse on a still greater topic — Graz'zt and his filthy slaves!"

Zuggtmoy sat up at that, and Iuz stared hard at his mother. The witch smiled warmly at both of them. Seeing that she had their rapt attention, Iggwilv explained, "It would never, never in a thousand years, be to Our benefit for Graz'zt and his lackeys to possess any of the Theorparts."

Iuz started to interrupt. "But you—"

"I said otherwise? Of course! We need his cooperation in gaining the Final Key. Once dear Queen Zuggtmoy has it safely, she can turn on him and the vile Kostchtchie and the rest. They will be powerless against her then, and their foes will rend the braggarts' petty kingdom plane from plane."

"You are a dear!" the demoness said, leaping up and hugging Iggwilv.

The cambion had to smile broadly himself, thinking of how his hated progenitor would fare in such a situation. "I am proud to be your son, Mother!"

"Just so," Iggwilv said dryly, smirking slightly in Iuz's general direction. "Moving ahead, though, We must lay out exactly what course We will follow once Zuggtmoy gains the Final Key." The other two assented eagerly, so the ancient witch went on. "Graz'zt will be hard-pressed by his growing number of enemies. Worse still, for him, the boastful swine will be confined to his own personal domain.

These circumstances, Zuggtmoy, will enable you to send aid to Us. Then you, Iuz, with your demons — and you will command many hordes with the Theorpart — and My skills and powers, will overthrow the Brotherhood. You will destroy those scum, and then the Initial Key will be in Our hands as well."

"I will be Emperor of Oerth!" Iuz crowed, barely able to suppress the urge to beat his massive chest in delight as he did so. Zuggtmoy started to frown slightly as she witnessed this outburst, and Iggwilv acted quickly to soothe her.

"Be not alarmed, sister!" the witch said, taking and holding Zuggtmoy's shapely little hand. "Iuz, in his excitement, wrongly assumed that he would retain possession of the Initial Key once the Brotherhood is obliterated. But in truth, he will not need it to maintain his power. And what could be more fitting than a bestowal of that object upon she who assured Our success here? What more proper, adored Zuggtmoy, than you using the Initial Key to become Queen and Ruler of all the Abyss?" Iuz bristled a bit when he heard this, but was wise enough to hold his tongue.

Still suspicious, the demoness looked sharply at Iggwilv and asked, "Why would you hand so great a thing over to me so willingly?"

"Without mention of the undying love that Iuz and I hold in Our hearts for you, great queen, I need only point out two simple facts. First, with the whole world Ours, what need do either of Us have for more than the single key We now possess? Second, who better to hold two, and thus assure rule of the entire Abyss, than Our staunchest friend and ally?"

"You speak with wisdom beyond mortals and the powers beyond them," the Queen of Fungi said solemnly. "I had resolved to speak of the problems which the unruly Graz'zt might cause should he somehow blunder into possession of the Final Key, or even the initial one. I am happy that you, dearest Iggwilv, have anticipated My needs thus. Your once-husband will never forgive the humiliation he once received at your hands. Graz'zt will cause much trouble for both of you, should he ever manage to gain a Theorpart. Your understanding of this fact and your pledge of loyalty to Me indicate that My past judgment has been correct. You, Iggwilv, and you too, Iuz, shall be the most favored when I rule the Abyss. You have the word of Queen Zuggtmoy!"

Thanking her profusely, Iggwilv and Iuz both embraced the demoness. "Shall we now refrain from this tiresome business and enjoy ourselves?" the witch said with urging in her voice.

Iuz implored Zuggtmoy to let that be the case, but the demoness demurred. "There are matters on My own plane which need My attention now. After all, I must alert Szhublox and the others and make preparations." Promising to come back as soon as possible, the Queen of Fungi took her leave.

As soon as she was gone, Iuz turned angrily to his mother. "Are you growing senile? How dare you suggest that she possess two keys, let alone *pledge* them to her?!"

"Mind your tongue, lest I have reason to severely punish you, Iuz. Never forget that I am your mother and guide!" Then, softening her tone and smiling, Iggwilv hugged the scowling cambion. "You are My own, dear son! I would never betray Mine own flesh and blood thus. Never suppose I would actually give anyone but you the Theorpart. You will rule Oerth with the strength of two keys, and none will ever be able to remove your yoke then. Let the Abyss squabble and contend as its princes will — so much the better for Us! Not even Zuggtmoy will dare challenge Us when We hold two thirds of the artifact."

"What if Graz'zt should somehow manage to win the contest and gain the Final Key?"

"Leave that to Me. It is an outcome I have considered, and one which I will deal with soon. You run along and enjoy yourself as you please, Iuz. I will personally descend to see your father in the Abyss and handle the contingency you speak of. I will act, and you need have no further concern. Soon all Oerth will bow to you, My son, as Emperor Iuz, Lord of All!"

Humming a deep dirge, the cambion went off to do as Iggwilv had suggested. Desporting himself always cleared his mind of cobwebs, and Iuz knew that he must work out careful plans for ridding himself of that woman's oppressive and interfering presence as soon as he held two parts of the artifact. Meanwhile, it was only fitting that he did enjoy himself a bit.

Chapter 5

THE DEEP DARKNESS of Graz'zt's own layer of the Abyss pleased Eclavdra. The blackness reminded her of her own homeland deep beneath the surface of Oerth. The mockery of a tropical paradise where demon-inflicted pain and suffering befell helpless and unsuspecting creatures satisfied and pleased her senses. The worst of the drow city of Urlisindatu, a sink of debauchery and base cruelty, could not compare for a moment to this wonderful place ruled by the demon king.

Best of all, the beautiful dark elf female enjoyed her status on this weird Abyssal plane. Because of her own prowess and Graz'zt's evident favor, Eclavdra was rightly accorded a station very near that of the great lord of the place. Of course, the hyena-headed Yeenoghu and the scum Kostchtchie and certain other demons as well took precedence over her. That matter would be set right in the fullness of time, that she knew. As champion of Graz'zt in the contest for possession of the Final Key, she would certainly prevail. Then would Graz'zt bestow even greater favor upon her, and Eclavdra would be a Princess of Demonkind, a fitting ruler, too, for all drow to bow before!

Before Eclavdra sprawled the polished, jet-pillared structure that was the grand palace of King Graz'zt. Its black marble and obsidian gleamed with mirror brightness, reflecting more darkly still the ebon foliage and fire-opalescent sky of the demon lord's realm. Soon now she would stand before the assembled court of King Graz'zt and receive his charge. The prospect was exciting, and she relished the opportunity. Was she not named as his handmaiden, after all? Now only further honors and greater power could come to her, Eclavdra of the Clan of Eilserv, soon to be known as the greatest ever of that house.

The dark elf squared her perfect shoulders, shaking her head so that her shoulder-length tresses fell like a silver frame around her lovely face, each delicate feature presented to perfection. Eclavdra's violet-hued eyes looked out from beneath long, curling lashes of bright silvery color, and her sensuous mouth looked ripe and inviting as she chose, or hard and unyielding if need be. All drow females had near-perfect skin of shining black, but none among the dark elves could boast of a complexion such as she had, and well she knew this. Shoulders back, perfect breasts pointing the way beneath her filmy gown of violet to match her eyes, a single large amethyst at her throat, Eclavdra entered the palace and strode toward the great valves that gave onto the demon king's throne room.

"Eclavdra, High Priestess of King Graz'zt!" the huge pair of nabassu boomed in unison to announce her arrival. Eclavdra noticed the leers on both of these demons' hideous visages as she passed under the tall archway. They would need correction when she returned in triumph, she thought as she strutted past them without apparent notice of their disrespectful behavior. She made her way down the center aisle between two large groups of onlookers, approached the throne at the rear of the chamber, dropped to her knees, and bent forward at the waist in a gesture of supplication.

"Arise, high priestess," Graz'zt said.

Eclavdra drew herself erect before the demon lord's opaline throne. Graz'zt had had it carved out of a single great stone, and was proud of the fact that it complemented his own coloration perfectly.

Graz'zt's hair was blue-black, but the demon king's complexion was the same color as Eclavdra's, and the drow agreed very much with his choice of thrones. Perhaps one day she would have a similar one, slightly smaller (for that would suit her physical stature) and of even more perfectly polished black opal than that of Graz'zt's throne. Being careful to display her body to best advantage as she stood, Eclavdra bowed her beautiful head and replied, "Thank you, King of Demons, Lord of the Abyss. I, Eclavdra, am before you as commanded."

"I have summoned you here before Me, high priestess, so that My peers and vassals may see you and hear your oath."

"Yes, mighty Graz'zt."

"Speak then, Eclavdra!"

"My life and obedience are in your hand, sovereign lord. I humbly accept your charge and will serve as your champion in the coming contest. I have only one desire — to succeed and please My king in doing so. My life is nothing without your favor, and before accepting failure, I will die!"

"So be it," Graz'zt said with no expression. "You said well, high priestess," he added. Then, turning to look at the crowd of demons present, the demon king boomed, "We are now done with this audience. You are dismissed — all save Our steward Vuron and Eclavdra herself. We have small matters to discuss."

The demon princes and lords departed readily, followed by those greater demons high enough in Graz'zt's favor to be numbered as special vassals.

Eclavdra's high hopes had sunk a bit at the mention of Vuron. The Lord Steward was an androgynous albino, as white as Graz'zt was black. Of all the demons who associated or allied with the six-fingered demon lord, Vuron was possibly the most evil and intelligent. Surprisingly, the dark elf had found him — it? — unswervingly loyal and devoted to Graz'zt. This made her both uneasy and very suspicious of the competition. Eclavdra had aspired to a private conference with her master. Vuron's participation was a cold and unwelcome douche to her anticipated opportunity.

After taking his guests to a secluded chamber that was magically proof against all forms of spying, Graz'zt sprawled on a divan. He motioned Eclavdra and Vuron to similar furniture. Vuron spoke first.

"You know I like not this proposed contest, My king. Why do you call Me to counsel you on it?"

"Because you advocate against it, Lord Vuron!"

This took the white-skinned demon aback. "If you plan to go ahead with Iggwilv's scheme, of what use is My opposition?"

Eclavdra couldn't believe her ears. Vuron had just put himself in an exposed position, and she would certainly take the opportunity to see that he regretted his foolishness. After all, was she not far better qualified to be Graz'zt's chief advisor? Of course! Just as the dark elven high priestess marshaled her thoughts and readied her comment, however, the demon king spoke.

"He who trusts a devil must have a dozen lawyers to advise him on the terms that will surely be written by those of the Hells. He who trusts a demon must be so powerful that no treachery can affect him. He who trusts the witch Iggwilv is no more than a sorry fool!"

"My lord?"

"Vuron, you are My right hand in such matters as this, for you are the least like a demon of any of the Abyss that I have ever known."

Vuron bowed, replying with great sincerity, "But for yourself, great king."

"Bah! I have the same weaknesses as the rest of our kind, My lord steward. If I exhibit any other behavior, it is because I learned the trait from you."

"My liege is most wise in his choice of servants," Eclavdra managed to insert ingratiatingly.

"You honor Me too much," Vuron said with humility that seemed actual — a unique thing among demons. "How may I serve you, lord? I have said all I can on this matter."

"Perhaps, but I think not. Attend Me now, both of you, and I will give you My rede," Graz'zt told them. "There is no question that all concerned desire the continued separation of the three keys — or at least two from the remaining one. Zuggtmoy certainly plots to gain two, just as Iggwilv and that whelp Iuz likewise must even now scheme to hold a pair of the Theorparts. I would have two Myself. Treacherous dealings on all fronts are no surprise under such circumstances."

Eclavdra spoke as soon as the demon king paused and glanced at her. "As your champion, King Graz'zt, I will not fail in securing the Final Key for you alone! With its power, you will surely be able to wrest the other you desire from either Iuz or the Scarlet ones."

"Do not seek to gain two of the keys, My liege!" Vuron said as forcefully as he dared. "There is a deep foreboding within me which demands I give you such warning. I believe that to hold two will surely attract the third. All know what disaster that would yield. . . ."

"You counsel weakness!" the beautiful drow shot at Vuron. "If Zuggtmoy should gain even a single one, what would be My lord king's fate then? If that mushroom-lover possessed two keys, all would be lost! Iggwilv is as bad, if not worse," Eclavdra continued. "She would see that her associate Zuggtmoy held the third, for she is surely the enemy of King Graz'zt. You preach downfall to My lord king!"

"Not so, little elf," the pale demon shot back. "I urge Graz'zt to take the Theorpart held by Iuz from him. Then let Iggwilv howl and lament with her spawn, let Zuggtmoy grow wroth and full of hate, let all of them contest with one another for the Final Key, for My king will have that which he needs! Best of all, he will hold it safe within the vastness of the Abyss, and the whole will then never be joined."

"With the key, Iuz and Iggwilv are too strong for our lord to do as you suggest, for the human bitch has defiled King Graz'zt and her tricks confined him unnaturally for yet decades more."

The black demon king raised a finger. Vuron closed a mouth just opened to retort, and Eclavdra bowed her beautiful head in a submissive manner.

"My champion speaks well, Vuron. Her words are true. I must have the Final Key, and so I must agree to the contest Iggwilv has decided upon. I do not forgive her, nor do I forget the slightest injury. I bide My time. Opportunity will come. . . . What you must do now, Vuron, is to assist in assuring My victory in the coming struggle. Thereafter, We will consider what course to take, and then you may again counsel as you choose. Now, give Me your mind as I direct!"

Vuron calmly bowed, accepting the order with no show of emotion. "Yes, lord. I think thus. Witch and cambion will use all of their power to see that the weaker of the contestants gains the prize. Obmi will thus be favored. Then, once the dwarf has gained the Final Key, those two will have traps and snares ready to take him and relieve the fool of the Theorpart, if possible. If they fail in that, they will allow Zuggtmoy to have it — nay, *help* her as if faithful to a bargain they have surely struck with her. If that occurs, and Zuggtmoy is deceived, she will assist in warfare against the Scarlet Brotherhood and their diabolical helpers. At such point, I can not ascertain which faction will prevail — Zuggtmoy, or Iggwilv and Iuz — in actually gaining the Initial Key. There will be dissension between witch and cambion, between Zuggtmoy and Szhublox — that I know. Unless they fall to bickering immediately, My liege, they cannot fail to take the Initial Key, for they will wield the powers of two parts against a single one."

"You are agitated, Vuron," Graz'zt said as he observed the albino demon closely.

"I am, My king. If two parts are played against

one, I think that the powers will enmesh and draw the three into a whole!"

The statement just spoken made Eclavdra shudder, but the dark elf concealed this and said, "Yet if My lord king has *two* of the keys, he need not fight for the third! Let the Scarlet slaves of the Hells piddle with it — all the more discomfiture for Iggwilv and the wretched cambion she bore!"

"How do you propose that King Graz'zt gain *two* keys?" Vuron's question was the challenge Eclavdra had been waiting for.

"Quite simply, Lord Vuron," the drow female replied, making the honorific seem somehow insulting through her inflection. "I will gain the Final Key for My liege. Then Iggwilv and Iuz will need to beg his aid in getting the one held by the Brotherhood — ostensibly for the horrid Zuggtmoy, but of course actually for themselves. Possession of the Final Key will *free* My lord king from the confines of this plane! To dupe or take by force from the two that which they hold will be a slight matter for one so powerful as King Graz'zt."

"Excellent!" Graz'zt cackled. He placed his massive, six-fingered hand on Eclavdra's silver-haired head and said, "I commend you, champion. Succeed, and I shall elevate you to My nobility and accord you status as First Concubine as well!"

"My liege is too generous. . . ."

Vuron, seeing that his words would no longer fall upon hearing ears, turned to practical matters. "How may I assist in assuring the victory falls to your champion, lord?"

Graz'zt didn't seem to notice how Vuron avoided giving any honor to Eclavdra, but the dark elven high priestess did. Another cause, she thought, for which I shall exact full payment from this pale worm when My time comes. Instead of showing her anger at the slight, however, Eclavdra smiled most charmingly at Vuron, making sure that Graz'zt saw her display. Then she said, "Yes, wise lord steward, please give the benefit of your thinking. All that assists me in succeeding as champion only helps us all to better serve our king."

Again Graz'zt beamed. The albino demon barely raised a snow-white eyebrow at the spectacle, though. "I will meditate and study the whole matter constantly, My liege, so as to be prepared to intelligence your champion when she departs. . . . Will that be soon?"

Without waiting for a reply, Vuron added, "I also have at hand certain things which she will find helpful when venturing forth on Oerth. From My own store I offer cusps — shields to protect her eyes from the burning radiation of the sun." As he said this, Vuron closed both his eyes tight for a second, as if he felt the very brightness he spoke of.

"What else, lord steward?" Graz'zt asked with a tone that conveyed his dissatisfaction with so paltry a provision. Eclavdra was quite pleased at that, although she too thought more must be given, for the contest was no easy matter, and her victory was by no means assured despite her boasts. Let this Vuron provide more means for her to displace him!

"There is more, of course, King Graz'zt," the albino steward said with a ring of hurt in his voice.

"Oh, please tell me what, noble Vuron!" Eclavdra said with pleading in her tone, casting a look of anxious need toward the albino demon.

Vuron saw Graz'zt's expression as well as that of the high priestess. "Amongst the many ideas I have are protections, weapons, and more. I beg My liege lord's pardon for not detailing each at this time. You have charged me with My best efforts, and I crave a bit more time to deliver to your ultimate satisfaction."

"Be certain you do deliver!" Graz'zt admonished in his deep, commanding voice. "You have Our permission to leave Us now, steward. Report to Us daily on your progress. It will not do to delay the departure of Eclavdra much longer."

The snow-skinned demon left the private chamber with dignity, as Graz'zt turned his attention to the dark elf. She had launched into an explanation of her plans to emerge victorious in the coming contest, and the demon king was listening to her speech with pleasure.

The king's daily checks with Vuron produced no results, and the monarch grew more and more agitated. Many days later, Graz'zt angrily summoned Vuron to another audience in the shielded little place. "This delay is unconscionable, steward!" the black demon thundered. "Explain yourself to Us, or there will be punishment meted out!"

"May it please your Abyssal majesty," the Lord Steward intoned formally to Graz'zt as he bowed from the waist. The demon king nodded but made no suggestion that Vuron be seated. Eclavdra observed the exchange from her own divan next to the royal one. After a short pause, Vuron stood straight and spoke.

"After great thought and most careful planning, My liege, I have just this day finished devising a plan which will meet your majesty's needs. It is very simple, yet very complex. In all, My lord king, it will give you the advantage over the others."

"Advantage? What of surety?"

"Surety, King Graz'zt, must be bestowed by one far more powerful than I. The advantage of surprise, that of precaution, and those of special equipment I can offer . . . but no more."

Instead of flying into a rage as he seemed about to do, Graz'zt glared at the albino demon for a moment. Then he relaxed and smiled. "Your words, Vuron, bring sense into mind as usual. We take your meaning and appreciate it. Relate your plan."

"Eclavdra, well cloaked and protected, will depart from the free city of Dyvers. There is a temple of yours, lord king, in that city, and it will be possible to transport your high priestess to the catacombs beneath that place without arousing undue suspicion. Even the risk to her is slight, for those who opposed you are not concerned — pardon, lord — with your leaving your plane."

Graz'zt scowled at this, and Eclavdra openly sneered. "That will put me many days behind that toad, Obmi!" she snapped. "Spies report that he rode from Molag a week ago!"

Ignoring her outburst, Vuron went on calmly. "With her will be an escort of half-drow able to tolerate the sunlight they will be exposed to for so long a period of time as the journey will take. Her lieutenants will be two able cavaliers with high skill in the art of dweomercraefting. The six additional guards will be half-drow also — an assassin of dire prowess, a thief with fighting skill, and four with only warrior training, but doughty nonetheless."

"The rules Iggwilv laid down allowed a full dozen to escort me!"

"Yes, priestess, and others will later join the group. After the party reaches Ket, six of the strongest barbarian horsemen of the Yollites will enlist. These horsemen will meet you in Hlupallu, at a secret rendezvous there. They will serve to further protect the expedition, and guide it, through Yoll and the Barren Plains to the Ashen Desert."

"Nonsense!" Graz'zt said, standing in fury and pointing menacingly at his steward. "You counsel a sure loss. The group will be seen, watched, dogged, delayed, and thwarted! At best it will arrive well after Zuggtmoy's jackal has gained the City Out of Mind and departed!"

"I know that, King Graz'zt," the albino demon replied without emotion. There was a moment of shocked silence; then the towering Graz'zt began to advance toward Vuron with a terrible look in his eyes. The pale demon seemed paler, but he did not flinch. "But Eclavdra will *not* be in the group, My liege. That is the beauty of the whole plan."

The demon king drew erect, rocked back on his heels, and stared at Vuron. Then he boomed forth a deep laugh. "I should have never doubted your cunning and duplicity, good Vuron! Say on."

"The Great Cavern of the Drow, lord, is open to Eclavdra's entrance by magical means. There we will send her. From there she shall go up into the world. There is an entrance to the underworld near Ghastoor, is there not?" The query was directed at the dark elf, and when Graz'zt's quizzical gaze followed that of the albino demon, Eclavdra nodded her head to confirm that there was such a place. "There, My king, her true escort will be waiting. Tough, obedient camel-riding warriors of the Barren Plains, along with two rogues who have robbed the dead in the Ashen Desert beyond. One is a spell-worker, the other a thief of highly resourceful sort. While our enemies watch the false Eclavdra and feel content to be well ahead of her, the real one will be delving into the City Out of Mind to gain the Final Key as your prize, My king."

"How can there be two of me?" Eclavdra asked with a carefully neutral tone. "Surely a simulacrum will be detected."

"There you are correct, High Priestess of Graz'zt. When you are well away, safely within your homeworld's deep Cavern, we will bring forth a clone."

"But . . . a clone will—"

"Be done away with before difficulty befalls you, drow priestess. When the enemy fails, I will see to it that your duplicate does not remain to dispute with you which has the right to exist."

"The plan is accepted, lord steward," said the ebon demon prince. "We are pleased!"

Vuron smiled a small, careful smile. "Thank you, majesty. There is just a bit more. To make certain none recognize her, your servant and champion Eclavdra will be given an oil of special dweomer. It will lighten her skin so as to make it no darker than that of the nomads of the steppes. The splendid armor and weapons of her people betray no aura, but in the radiation of the open sky, and without the rays of the Cavern, the metal becomes less. Another solution I have alchemically prepared will serve to stop the decaying process for weeks, if not months. She will make her journey armed with undetectable protections. The elixir will even protect cloth, so she may utilize drow clothing as well."

"Now I am truly delighted with you, Lord Vuron, My faithful advisor."

Again a small smile played across the white features of the demon's narrow visage, a small expression of satisfaction that Eclavdra alone saw as he bowed humbly to Graz'zt at the compliment. "Also, my lord, there are a few trantles which I have gathered for the use of your champion. A decanter which spills forth water when needed, a magical mask to allow your high priestess to breathe and move freely as if dust or water were air to the lungs, and an assortment of other items which might prove useful to her in fulfilling your command."

"What perils and hazards do you envision, Vuron?" the demon king asked, pulling his steward down to sit beside him on his royal couch. Vuron answered at length, with interjections coming frequently from Graz'zt. After some time, the black-skinned demon glanced up and noted Eclavdra sitting petulantly, barely concealing her annoyance.

"You will depart tomorrow, Eclavdra. You will return to your chambers now and rest. I will see you on the morrow. There is much I would yet discuss this night with Vuron, and there is nothing you can contribute to this discourse."

Eclavdra was clever to hide her shame and fury. Bowing, she quickly obeyed King Graz'zt's command and departed. Her triumph would come, and then Vuron would be cursing.

Chapter 6

"SALAAM, STRANGER. May I have permission to enter your camp?"

Gord had been aware of the nomad's approach for some time. He was but one of three riders who had walked their horses to a bowshot's distance, dropped the reins, and split into three. There was a warrior on either flank even now, just beyond the range of the firelight. The third was just inside the circle of illumination from the small blaze the young adventurer had kindled to cook the grouse he had brought down with his sling at twilight. Gord called back casually, "Of course you may come closer, and so can the two who lurk to either hand."

The nomad laughed at that, for the Ourmi, as he surely was from his accent, had not even bothered to look up from the fowl he was eating. "You must have the eyes and ears of a cat, stranger! Come, my brothers," he called to those beyond the light. "We have the hospitality of this one's fire!"

"I do not like those who creep up on lone wayfarers," Gord said as the fellow approached.

"One must be cautious on the plains," the man replied with no hint of apology in his voice.

"That is true, Okmani," the young thief said as he eyed the swarthy-featured man in the firelight. His striped robe of green and gray, the leatherwork of girdle and boots, and the big sword across his back identified the man as from the Okman tribes, which held the area north of the Yolspur Tors.

The nomad seemed surprised that Gord knew

his people. "Does the fame of the Okmani stretch all the way to the Ourmi kingdoms, then?"

"Robbers and muggers are recognized throughout the whole of Oerth," Gord noted dryly. "And tell your . . . brothers . . . to stop skulking out there and come openly into my camp, or I'll have no choice but to kill you all here and now."

"You are either a great warrior, gray-eyes, or a stupid braggart," the Okmani said. He looked Gord over, noting the sword and dagger he wore, and the lance that lay nearby. The small man's movements were smooth and precise. He used economy in all he did, and his bearing was that of one who had no fear at all. "Come now, as I told you," he said to his comrades. "Our host is a paragon of warriors, and we will be safe camping here tonight."

Gord stared at the nomad. The fellow seemed to admire Gord's casual demeanor and self-assurance in the face of three potential foemen. "I am called Gord," he said to the Okmani.

"Hail, Gord-the-Ourmi. I am Eflam. These are my fellow warriors, Hukkasin and Ushtwer," he added as two similarly garbed and armed men came hesitantly into the circle of soft firelight.

"Be not shy, boys," Gord said without smiling. "Sit, all of you. There is but half the bird I roasted left, but you may have it if you hunger. With it, you will eat of this bread and flavor it with my salt."

The other two hesitated to accept the offering, but Eflam grinned and took a piece of the flat loaf Gord had produced. The Okmani smiled, sprinkled a pinch of salt atop it and swallowed the piece in a gulp. "You too!" he managed to say through a mouth crammed with bread. As Hukkasin and Ushtwer did the same, gobbling the stuff hungrily, the Okmani warrior swallowed, then grinned again and said admiringly to Gord, "So you know that my people honor the customs of those who dwell in the dry lands. You are indeed a most unusual man, even if you are an outlander. I like not calling you Gord, though. It has too foreign a sound for one so well versed in the ways of true folk. I will call you Pharzool, our name for the gray-striped cats who hunt the hills of Okmanistan."

Gord shrugged indifferently. The two other nomads clapped their hands and cried agreement, however. "He sees and hears like a pharzool!" said Ushtwer. "That one is as fierce as such hunters — Eflam, you name him well!"

Then the four men settled down to conversation and a bit of bragging. When Gord mentioned the Al-babur, all the Okmani scowled. These were hereditary enemies of their tribe. Then Eflam, the brightest of the three and their natural leader, laughed. "We Okmani are very perceptive, too," he said. "You are adopted by the Al-babur — the Tribes of the Tiger, do you see?" Gord shook his head.

"We have named you as a cat!" Eflam exclaimed. "The tiger-folk have no merit in their adoption. I now make you a brother warrior of the Okmani, Pharzool!" All three then jumped up and pounded the young adventurer on the back. Gord, although he did not wish to belittle the privilege just bestowed upon him, could not help wondering why these tribes were so free with their pronouncements of brotherhood — first the Al-babur, and now these Okmani. He was just about to say something to this effect, when he found out what "brotherhood" meant in the Okmani sense of the word.

"You have nothing much to give us as presents for this honor," Ushtwer said as he eyed Gord's fine stallion. The horse laid back its ears at the approach of the nomad, and then it snorted and bared its teeth. Ushtwer took a cautious step backward.

"Don't worry, brother," Hukkasin said to Ushtwer. "Tomorrow we will find a caravan to plunder or wild horses to capture. Then will our new brother, Pharzool the Generous, bestow his gifts of appreciation upon us."

"I have a much better idea," Gord said loudly to

be sure that he had the full attention of all three Okmani warriors. "In gratitude for your generosity in making me a fellow warrior of your worthy tribe, I will give you all a lesson in the weapon play of my people." With that the young man was on his feet, and his hands displayed long dagger and short sword. Not having seen him draw either blade, the nomads made signs against magic.

"There is no need for any gifts, brother," Eflam assured the small, gray-eyed man who stood poised before him. "We have sufficient honor in sharing your food and camp and in counting you amongst the ranks of the Men of Okman!" Both Hukkasin and Ushtwer seemed to agree very much with that statement. They stopped sweating when Gord put his weapons away and sat down again. Then they began sharing stories, and kept that up until they settled down to spend the night around Gord's fire.

Morning brought with it a heavy, patchy fog. Gord could make out large features of the landscape, but details were not visible from more than a few hundred yards away. He realized that his special sight did not give him any advantage in this sort of condition, and this worried him, but only briefly. After the group had readied for the day's travel, Eflam suddenly pointed into the distance and began to shout a high, yipping call. The other two Okmani warriors took up this cry, and Gord demanded to know what was the matter. "Nothing is the matter, Pharzool," said Eflam in a vaguely condescending tone. "That line of riders there, see? That is the rest of our group. Soon the other warriors of our tribe will greet you, and we can all ride to ravage the lands of the Yollite dogs!"

The nomads mounted and kicked their mounts into a gallop, not bothering to see if their new brother was following, intent on going to meet their fellow Okmani raiders. Hukkasin, the smallest of the three and the one riding the swiftest horse, took the lead, opening a gap of a few dozen yards be-

tween himself and the other two. Gord followed
their lead but kept Windeater to a canter, allowing
the nomad warriors to stay ahead. A minute later he
still could not figure out how many men were approaching through the fog, because they seemed to
be riding in close quarters. Then Hukkasin's yipping cries turned to another sort of sound, a bray-
ing shout, and he reined in his steed.

"Hurry, Pharzool!" Eflam called over his shoulder. "Those are the curs of Yoll before us!" As he
spoke, he and his comrade slowed their movement
to a trot. Hukkasin had wheeled his horse and was
almost back with the rest.

"What made you so sure that these would be your
men?" Gord said as he came up near the nomads.

"See the two low ridges on the horizon?" Eflam
said, pointing with his head as he fumbled free a
small bow from its case on his steed's flank. "The
space between them marks a place of rendezvous
for the Okmani warriors. The disease-ridden Yollites must have accidentally come through there."

"What now?" the young adventurer asked. The
question was voiced in an offhand tone, but as he
spoke it Gord pulled his sling from his belt and
reached into his pouch for a stone.

Eflam looked resigned as he nocked a broad-
headed arrow. "We stand and shoot until they are
upon us. Then we fight," and so saying he released
the shaft at the charging Yollites.

Gord saw that the other two Okmani had done
likewise, so he spun his sling and sent a stone flying forth. A pair of the foemen fell from arrows, and
a second later Gord's stone hit a horse. The steed
stumbled and sent its rider tumbling, to be trampled beneath the hooves of the other animals.

"Good shot, Pharzool!" Eflam cried. "Give those
dogs another such kiss!"

There was no time for that, Gord knew. The Okmani were drawing back their next arrows, but it
would take him too long to reload his sling. Gord

tucked away that weapon and drew his light lance from its leather sleeve just as another Yollite went down with an Okmani arrow in his chest. Crouched low, his lance aimed, Gord coaxed Windeater into a trot, heading toward the Yollites. The trot changed to a canter and was just opening into a full gallop when he was all but closed with the enemy.

From this close distance, Gord could see what he and the Okmani were up against. The Yoli warriors were armed with scimitars, and many also carried lances similar to the one that Gord plied. They had bow cases too, and as he approached the charging line of enemy warriors Gord supposed they either disdained using missiles against so numerically inferior a foe or else didn't wish to risk wasting arrows. Shooting from a galloping horse was difficult, and few could perform such a feat with accuracy even in clear air. In this fog, it would have been all but impossible to hit a solitary target. There were about a score of the Yoli nomads still — five to one against them, Gord estimated. And now they had fanned out, apparently trying to surround the four of them. Gord was glad to see that they held their positions in this spread-out formation, because that meant he would only have to contend with two or three of the enemy at one time.

"*Yoll-Yoll-Yoll!*" That sound washed over Gord as he maneuvered to keep the Yollites from getting at his back. He chose a target at the same time the target chose him, and a warrior voicing this strange chant at the top of his lungs lowered his lance and thundered toward Gord. As they closed, Gord swayed quickly in his high saddle to avoid the wavy-bladed lance that threatened to pierce his chest. The point of his own lance took the Yollite in the shoulder — a poor hit. He had been aiming at the heart, but his movement to avoid the foe's weapon had spoiled his own attack. Nevertheless, Gord's hit was sufficient to dismount the Yoli warrior, and then Gord was past the enemy and pivoting Windeater to charge again. Just before he turned back toward the fray, Gord thought he detected another group of riders approaching in the mist, and he instantly feared the worst. If the Yollites they were now engaged with only comprised an advance group, then he and his compatriots were surely doomed. Gord silently resolved to make one more pass through the enemy ranks and do what he could, but then he would turn from the battle and drive Windeater as hard as he could away from this futile cause.

Gord lowered his lance again and charged toward a warrior who was trying to cut down Hukkasin from the flank, hitting the orange and red-garbed nomad full in the side. The blow broke the shaft of Gord's lance, but the young adventurer used the splintered piece of wood to confuse another attacker, hurling it into the fellow's face. Gord drew his short-bladed sword and prepared to take on one more warrior who stood between him and his escape. Just as he began his charge, he heard from behind the sound of pounding hooves and more loud shouts. The second group of men was closing on them — but this time, the war cry was different.

"*Yii-yii-yii, Okman!*" Into the suddenly confused ranks of the Yoli rode the two dozen and more warriors of the band that Eflam and his men had been expecting. Green-and-gray-striped cloaks intermixed with the flame-colored and reddish-pink checks that adorned the Yoli warriors' clothing.

Although surprised at the arrival of these additional enemies, the Yollites were neither discouraged nor intimidated. They stopped their casual approach to the combat and fought more fiercely now that the odds had suddenly shifted against them — roughly two to one in favor of the Okmani, Gord figured. He exchanged cuts with one rider, then the press separated them, and the young adventurer was engaged with a new opponent. After each man countered several blows, Gord managed to slip un-

der the horsed Yoli's small shield, and his short
sword pierced the swarthy nomad's heart.

All of the Okmani were not faring as well as Gord,
however. The Yollites had regrouped and were cutting and stabbing furiously. The young adventurer
had a moment to wonder what would happen if the
fray continued, but then the tide seemed to turn
against the Yoli warriors, and a half-dozen of them
reeled and fell in as many seconds. As this occurred
Gord heard yet more battle cries in the distance,
followed by screams that came from the opposite
end of the battleground, the area closest to this
new group of attackers. He turned to look in that
direction and saw that the screams were coming
from Okmani warriors being felled by streaking
darts of glowing light. Knowing magical missiles
when he saw them, Gord instantly flattened himself
along Windeater's back. Kneeing the stallion into a
trot, he headed away from the approaching knot of
newcomers.

A fast glance backward told him that the new
group contained a handful of Yollites and a larger
number of men dressed in unidentifiable, but non-
Yoli, garb. Gord thought he saw a dwarf with these
new attackers, but he wasn't certain, and there was
no time now to study the onrushing band. Again the
young adventurer urged Windeater, this time with
both booted heels. The small stallion broke into a
run. In moments the swift courser had carried him
away from the melee, heading west. Gord peered
over his shoulder. He saw a few striped cloaks
fluttering behind fleeing riders; these would be the
surviving Okmani, spreading out from their enemies in all directions.

Windeater topped a low rise and pounded down
the reverse slope. The young adventurer turned his
mount's head slowly toward the left, so that they
were now galloping southwest. Gord knew that for a
time at least, possible pursuers would be unable to
see him, and he meant to stay totally out of sight if

he could. In the direction he was riding, the ground fell away to form a long depression between swales of land to either side. Once in the depression, Gord knew that the enemy riders would be unable to see him. Whether the weapon was bow or spell, he had no wish to be a target. Windeater ran on without faltering. They covered fully two leagues, and had long since outrun the fog, before Gord called soothing words to the gallant animal and pulled gently on the reins. The horse fell into an easy canter, and Gord allowed him to remain at that pace.

When it seemed likely that he had thrown off any who might have been following, Gord brought Windeater to a halt, dismounted, and quickly unsaddled the horse. Before he could begin wiping the steed's flanks of the coat of sweat, Windeater whinnied with pleasure and began rolling in the long grass. "Well, my friend," Gord said to the stallion, "I appreciate you doing that job for yourself, but don't take too long at it." As if he had understood the young man's words, Windeater stopped and got to his feet with a lunging motion. The stallion began to crop grass, tearing mouthfuls of the stuff as quickly as he could.

Gord left Windeater busy thus and scrambled up the bank to his right. It was high enough to allow the young adventurer to see what lay ahead of him to the west, and back from where he had come, too. There was nothing of interest ahead, but far to the east Gord saw a line of mounted men moving toward him at a trot, moving along the route he had been taking. "Shit," he murmured disgustedly under his breath. The Yoli seemed determined to dog him; even though he was a few miles ahead of them, they were apparently following Windeater's tracks, and as long as they chose to do that there was no way Gord could avoid them. Wondering why they would bother to pursue a single fugitive from a chance encounter, Gord slid back down the slope and put the blanket and saddle back on the stallion.

"Hoy, Windeater! Let's move on! You don't want to belong to some Yoli master, do you?" The horse snorted and shook his head. Gord laughed and sent the stallion toward the west, going at a slow trot to match the speed of those who followed.

For two days and one night his pursuers kept on his trail. Gord was able to stop at night to allow Windeater to rest, and he even got a little sleep himself when it became apparent that the party behind him had also stopped for the night.

On the second night, Gord decided to take matters into his own hands, so to speak. He left Windeater grazing contentedly, loosely tethered to a sturdy bit of scrub brush. After getting well away from the horse, Gord shifted from human to panther, using that form to travel back along his route. About three miles to the east he came upon the camp of the group that was pursuing him. Three guards stood on duty while about ten other men slept. From where he crouched, Gord-the-panther thought that at least one of the sentries was a demi-human with night vision, for his eyes reflected the firelight when he peered back toward the camp. Gord was careful to stay as far away from that guard as possible as he slunk around the perimeter of the encampment in the form of a great cat. He managed to get close enough to inspect the equipment of some of the sleepers. Not all of those whom he viewed thus had armor and weapons laid carefully nearby. This meant that there were probably at least a pair of spell-workers in the pursuing party. That was all he could learn, so he departed as silently as he had come.

The young adventurer was disappointed. At best he had hoped to be able to get among the horses and chase them off, leaving the enemy afoot. That would have meant the end of their pursuit, for finding their mounts would have taken them at least a full day, if indeed they ever found all of the horses. Unfortunately, the night-seeing sentry happened to be posted at the place where the horses were tethered, so this spoiled his plan. At worst, Gord had decided, he would attack the group and try to reduce it in number, but he was deterred from this plan by his discovery that the group contained magic-users or clerical spell-casters or both.

Gord was frustrated but undaunted. If he could not use easy means to rid himself of this unwanted group of followers, then he would have to rely upon Windeater's ability and simply outdistance them. Solving the problem in this way would be harder and take longer, but Gord was confident that the pursuit would eventually cease. Even the best trackers would lose his trail when distance was sufficient to enable him to use terrain, weather, and movements of herd animals to cover his tracks.

As if the elements favored him, the morning sky dawned gloomy, and intermittent light rain showers began shortly after sunrise. While Gord dozed in the saddle, Windeater trotted along, seeming to enjoy the dark and foul weather as much as he liked sunny days. Suddenly, a clap of thunder brought the young rider to wakefulness. The grass around him was tossing like wind-whipped water. Huge, flat-topped clouds loomed in front of him, black and ominous, their interiors illuminated by great flashes of lightning. Windeater did not mind the gentle rain, but thunder and lightning were another matter. The horse's eyes grew huge and wild, showing white, and his nostrils became dilated. Gord patted his neck and spoke soothingly to the stallion, but the streaking lightning and booming thunder undid his work as quickly as the young thief did it. Then the wind increased, rain sheeted down, and the crack and bang of the great storm hammered so at the senses that Windeater became unmanageable. Gord swung the animal's head toward the south, the only direction where the fury of the weather seemed less, and gave the courser his head. Windeater ran, and Gord held on for all he was worth.

After a time, the ground beneath Windeater's hooves became harder and more slippery. This rocky landscape made traveling difficult, but Gord let the horse pick his way through the terrain instead of trying to search for a safer route. He knew that somewhere in this area would likely be a cave or projection where man and horse could find a dry and safe haven. And they did indeed find a large overhang, which provided the two with a relatively dry and comfortable place to wait out the storm. After unsaddling Windeater, Gord hobbled the exhausted stallion and fed him a handful of grain. Then the young adventurer stretched out on the hard stone and instantly fell asleep.

When Gord awoke it was dawn, and he was stiff, sore, and miserably damp — but at the same time heartened by the fact that it would be impossible for his pursuers to continue to track him through the rain and over the rock. Windeater seemed to have recovered from his harrowing experience. Sometime during the night, when the rain had let up, the animal had moved out of the sheltered spot; he was now a hundred feet distant, working on eating the bits of vegetation that cropped up here and there among the stony ground and precipitous walls of rock around them. The storm still lingered, for Gord could see occasional lightning far to the north. Southward, the sky was clouded but undisturbed. To his left, Gord saw a dark line of the sort that could only indicate mountains, while to the west deep clouds bumped the plain and showed that the storm traveled southwest.

"Windeater, we must ride south, between the storm and the mountains," he said to the stallion as he placed blanket and saddle upon the horse's strong back. "At least we will no longer be troubled by any hounds of Yoll dogging us!"

Chapter 7

EVERYWHERE THE LAND was parched. It wasn't
all sandy desert, or even a combination of sand and
rock. There were patches of such ground aplenty,
but more frequently the land was cracked earth dotted with skeletal plants. There were cacti and stunt-
ed trees too, growing in depressions and along
steep-sided gullies.

"I guess it does rain here . . . sometimes," Gord
said, patting his horse's neck as he peered around
at the waste. "I am glad you are a hearty one, Windeater, or else we would be in desperate straits."
The stallion moved on, ears twitching to indicate
he heard his master's words, but he had interest
only in where his hooves were placed. They had
been traveling across the barrens for two days. Windeater had been able to find sufficient forage, but
didn't like the cracked ground. Sand and rock
troubled the stallion not at all — in fact, the courser
moved with ease through the loose grains of such
stuff, and trotted easily on hard sheets of bare rock.
However, broken and powdery dirt, prickly succu-
lents, and potholes made the courser uneasy, and as
he paced through such terrain he paid attention
mainly to his footing.

The ground became very rough. Gord
dismounted and walked his mount then, not
wanting to risk a fall or a broken leg. Clambering
down a steep bank, they found themselves in a
boulder-strewn wash that apparently served as the
bed of a swift watercourse at times. The relatively

smooth and level terrain here offered a fairly sure and easy means of travel, so Gord and the stallion shifted their path from south to southwest, following its course. At mid-morning they rounded a sharp bend, and Gord's eyes lit up in the same instant that Windeater's nostrils flared.

"Look, Windeater!" Gord boomed. "Water at last!" In a moment both man and horse were drinking from a deep pool off to one side of the dry wash — a place where the flood that came periodically sweeping along the wash had deposited some of its content. It was a well-used waterhole, judging from the signs of hoof and paw imprinted around it. As thirsty as the two travelers were, neither man nor horse cared. After checking quickly to see if any predatory animals lurked nearby, Gord dismounted, dropped to his knees, and began splashing and drinking. Windeater lowered his head and sucked up great gulps of the precious liquid even as his master did likewise.

"If you move, Bayomen dog, you are dead!"

Gord froze. Lifting his head imperceptibly, the young adventurer could just see shadows that indicated men behind him, advancing as they came down the slope of the wash. The horse jerked his head up and snorted wildly at the sound of the unfamiliar voice. Then came a clatter as rocks were dislodged by approaching feet, and at that Windeater snorted again and bolted, trotting away on down the dry wash.

"Kodan! Vahkta!" cried out the same voice that had threatened Gord. "Stop that horse! He is worth more than this one in the Great Bazaar!" A short distance ahead, Gord saw a couple of men riding camels appear over the edge of the wash and head down into the depression, trying to intercept the runaway horse.

In the bit of confusion this incident caused, Gord decided to take a chance. With one smooth move he rolled to his right, gained his feet, and started to dart away along the same route Windeater had taken. But before he could take more than a couple of steps, a lasso circled his upper arms and drew them tight to his sides, stopping him in his tracks. A second later, another lariat tightened around his neck. The point of a weapon touched the small of his back at the same time. Gord stood stock still. He was captured, and there was no use attempting anything now to compound the peril. The weapon at his back was taken away. Then two of his attackers, mounted on camels, came around to his front, and he glared at them as they examined him.

"This is no Al-baburi, even though he is dressed like one. See his eyes?"

"Had he different hair, he might be of our own people."

Gord looked from one speaker to the other. Both men were swathed in buff-colored garments, turbaned and veiled too. All he could see of them were patches of dark skin where their hands held weapons, and gray eyes through the slits in their veils.

"Who are you?" one of the voices demanded. The rope that circled his neck was pulled tighter by one of the men still behind him, and the young man had to shake his head a little to enable his constricted throat to get words out.

"I am a peaceful traveler from the north."

"Liar!" boomed the questioner. At the same time, the other man confronting Gord brought the tip of a lance to within inches of his stomach. "Only bandits and rogues come from the north! Where is the rest of your party?"

"I am alone," Gord said.

"Liar still!" the one holding the lance against his belly said as he pushed the point forward a little to make his statement show how he felt about falsehoods. "You are a scout for that band of Yoli dogs who ride but a little distance behind."

That statement made Gord's blood run cold. Could his old pursuers still be on his trail? If so, and if they were really that close, then all of them, camel-riders and Gord alike, would soon be dead. "Those Yoli are enemies who seek my death!" the young man said as forcefully as he dared.

"When we take them, snake-tongue, we will make all of you speak truth."

"Have a care, warrior," Gord shot back. "There are workers of spells among those after me."

"Let's be done with this one now, Yahoud. I think he is a renegade who leads our enemies to our waterholes and oases."

The lance-bearer demurred. "Perhaps, Haradoon, but I am not so sure. See that he is bound and guarded." Then this man, apparently the leader of the group, looked past Gord and gave another order. "Bohkir, take your men and spy out the Yoli."

"Aye, Yahoud," Bohkir replied from behind Gord. "What should I do when I come to the enemy?"

"Use your eyes, think, then act. You are my right hand," said the one called Yahoud. Bohkir turned his mount around, gestured to a small group of nomads, and all of them headed back in the direction from which Gord had come.

Gord was half-led, half-dragged to a sheltered spot a hundred yards away, a place where the curve of the gully and an outcropping of rock hid him and his captors from view. The nomads remaining with him, four in number, stripped him of all his weapons and gear, leaving him with nothing but his simple clothing, and trussed him with coils of rope so that he could barely move. Two took up positions as sentries nearby while the other pair stayed next to Gord, their long, straight swords ready to cut him down if he tried to get free. Shortly after Gord was bound, he heard the sound of approaching riders, followed by telltale snorts that could only mean one thing: Windeater had been captured.

"The beast is fast, and ornery too," said one man to the others, "but we finally got a noose around him. Quite a prize, is he not?" Gord was saddened that Windeater had not escaped — in fact, he felt worse about that than he did about his own plight.

The shade disappeared as the sun rose to its zenith. Gord sweated and wondered what was going to happen. Right now, he was as good as dead any time the men who held him chose to kill him. He considered, then dismissed, trying to change to panther form; that would take time, and he doubted that he would be invulnerable to their weapons during the transition, even if none of these warriors bore magical blades. The young adventurer waited and watched for an opportunity as patiently as he could, but his guards never took their eyes from him. After nearly two hours more he heard the soft sounds of camels coming down the streambed, and then conversation that took place right outside where he was being held.

"What did you learn, Bohkir?"

"This one spoke truth, Yahoud. The Yoli were after him, and with them were workers of spells."

"So?"

"I parlayed with the fools. When I told them we had captured a stranger garbed in Al-baburi dress, they asked for his surrender. They offered me silver for him, threatening to slay us and take him by force otherwise."

"Well, you are not dead. Where are the Yoli?"

Bohkir laughed derisively. "They are as stupid as all the rest of the Bakluni, my shaik. When I signaled for my warriors to allow themselves to be seen, the Yoli dogs seemed impressed. The warriors made themselves seem a hundred, and their crossbows were in evidence. At such range, and with so much cover, the outland spell-casters with the Yoli would be of little use once fighting began."

"What did the dogs offer then?" Yahoud asked, heavy contempt for the Yoli evident in his question.

"The leader of the group was one of the foreign spell-workers. He and the chief warrior of the Yoli conferred for a time, and then the dung-eating Yoli actually told me that through the kindness of his mighty captain's heart, *they* would spare *us* — if we promised to slay the prisoner we held."

"So?"

"I laughed at the statement, asking why the interlopers thought we would spare them. 'The Arroden can kill whomever we wish, as we wish!' I said. Then the Yoli babbled to their pale-skinned leader, and we began to bargain."

"From your tone, Bohkir, I would guess that the Yoli were as easy as always," Yahoud said mirthfully.

"In the end, shaik, they gave over a hundred silver pieces, these two good horses, and a necklace of gold. In exchange we allowed them to ride back the way they had come, unmolested. The silver is to assure that our 'guest' dies," he finished.

"You gave your word?" Yahoud asked the man incredulously.

"That he would surely die? Yes, shaik, that I did. But *when* he would die . . . that I did not say at all! He will fetch our tribe yet more silver in the slave market at Karnoosh. Slaves sold there die quickly anyway — at least, those who go to the mines of Zondabad do. One such as this one, small but well muscled, will surely be bought by the Kizam's agents for just such work."

"Well done, Bohkir! Make sure the Yoli are carefully watched, for I trust them not. Join us as soon as you can. We will ride south to Karnoosh."

After his captors freed him enough so that he could ride, Gord was unceremoniously placed atop a camel. Bohkir and a small band of warriors headed north and the remaining nomads, with Gord, went in the opposite direction under the leadership of the one called Yahoud. After they had ridden about two miles, they met up with the main body of the nomad force, so that the group traveling south now numbered about a hundred camel-riders. Besides the camels the men rode, there were quite a few other humped beasts bearing equipment and supplies. With these pack camels were his own horse, the two gained from the Yoli, and a half-dozen less desirable animals — probably either wild horses taken by the nomads or else prizes from some raid. Gord saw no other prisoners, so he supposed that the small horses were wild ones.

His guards still numbered four, even though Gord was virtually helpless — precariously perched atop a camel that was being led by one guard, flanked by two others, and covered from the rear by yet another of the nomads. These Arroden, as they called themselves, were both thorough and cautious. Even though they had confiscated everything from Gord, they were still taking no chance that he would escape, or that they might be forced to kill him if he made such an attempt.

Apparently, Gord thought, he had enough value to the Arroden that they strongly desired to keep him alive and in their possession until they reached the slave market. But they did not know just what resources he still had at his command, both natural and not so natural. He felt sure that he could get out of his bonds in moments, if he ever got the chance. In addition, he had the power to see at night — an ability first bestowed upon him by his cat's-eye ring, but something that his long contact with the ring now enabled him to call upon even when he was not wearing it. He might be helpless at the moment, but he was certainly not beyond hope.

Although he was treated roughly by his captors, and riding a camel proved to be sheer torture for him at first, Gord was given food and water whenever the Arroden ate and drank. After a couple of days the young adventurer became fairly accustomed to his strange mount, and the pain of his sore muscles lessened enough so that Gord was able to actually pay attention to his surroundings as he rode. The land they passed over was similar to that which he and Windeater had encountered before.

The guard on Gord's right flank, Brodri by name,

had shown himself to be a bit more sociable than the others — in other words, Gord could occasionally speak to him and get an answer other than a growl and a painful blow. When the young captive saw that they were no longer heading south, he risked punishment and asked Brodri about it.

"We now go more eastward than south," Gord said without expression.

"There are caravans near Ghastoor."

"You trade?"

"Don't be stupid. Arroden warriors take what they need from the Yoli," the veiled warrior said, turning his head to speak directly at the captive.

"Such men as you Arroden can surely do that," Gord said with a note of humiliation in his voice, "but surely the swarms of Yollite horsemen resist that. Are so few real warriors as this able to overcome the many who must protect such caravans?"

"Sometimes there are only a few guards. Sometimes others of our people join us—"

"Stop chattering like a woman!" This command came from one of the lieutenants of the warrior band. Brodri shot an angry glance at Gord when he was rebuked, and with this he turned to face forward and spoke no more. What the nomad had told him, however, gave Gord some slight hope. A fight, or even the confusion of new warriors joining the group who held him captive, might allow him the chance he needed.

The Arroden warriors rode in a broad arc. Their path curved to the southeast, and their pace was now slow. A dozen scouts trotted to the left and an equal number rode ahead, all of them beyond sight of the main body of camel-riders. It was evident that the leader, Yahoud, was looking for a passing caravan, just as Brodri had said. Nothing occurred that day, though, and the next morning they turned due east, for the rising sun was directly in his eyes as Gord was hoisted up to begin his day's ride with his feet, as usual, lashed under his camel's belly.

Near the end of the day, Gord detected a line of undulating darkness on the faraway southern horizon — a stretch of hills, he suspected. The nomads stopped and went through the usual camping routines. Gord watched for an opening as usual, but the Arroden guards were as alert as they had always been. The young adventurer forgot about thoughts of escape for the time being and slept as comfortably as his bonds permitted; tomorrow was another day. The veiled nomads swung southward the next morning, riding perhaps two leagues in that direction. Now Gord noticed mountains to his left hand — perhaps the Barring Ridge, but he wasn't sure. Then the Arroden abruptly turned and headed their camels west, sweeping back toward the area they had come from. Gord was perplexed by this, and decided to probe Brodri for information.

"Do we now ride for Karnoosh?" he asked.

The nomad stared hard at Gord for a moment. Then his visage softened slightly and he said, "It is only because you might have our blood, the blood of the Arroden, that I speak to you. . . . I would not wish to die in slavery either, outlander. Karnoosh lies to the south, several days' ride. We will make for the city, but as we do we will travel eastward and westward as well. Our shaik seeks prey, so we sweep the land for Yoli or others who are so bold as to ride through the land of the Arroden."

"There are others who are your foes here, then, too?"

"Of course. Many come and go to and from Lake Karnoosh and the rich markets of the bazaar there. Bayomens, Yoli, and the dark Jahindi all travel to and from that place. Even the folk of Sa'han and Behow are seen at Karnoosh. We abide most of these visitors, requiring only that they pay us in goods and livestock when we run across them. But when the dogs of Yoll dare to pass over our lands, they are subject to our special tariff."

"Tariff?"

"Plundering and death," Brodri said with a thin, grim smile.

The very next day just such an encounter occurred. Running camels, their curious side-to-side gait still seeming strange to Gord despite the time he himself had been riding one, brought a handful of the veiled Arroden scouts back to the main body. They shouted that Yoli were coming toward them from the north.

"There are many animals laden with goods, shaik!" one warrior called, and then added, "Many slaves — women slaves! But the dogs have many guards with them, too."

Yahoud immediately called in his lieutenants and held a council. When this broke up, Gord overheard the plan that was passed down to his guards by their leader. "We will wait for darkness, for those cowardly mongrels do not like to fight when they can't see to use their bows. When we halt at dusk, keep that one wrapped well," the veiled warrior said, nodding toward Gord. "All but one of you four must come with us when we attack."

"No one wants to lose honor and spoils," one of the guards remarked. "Which of us must stay?"

"The other groups of sentries are drawing lots," said the lieutenant as he turned to ride away. "You can do the same, or settle it any other way you wish, so long as no one is injured."

The guards decided to leave the question to chance, and the other three insisted that Brodri draw last since he was the youngest. To no one's great surprise, Brodri lost. He was furious and insisted he had been cheated, but of course the others would not admit to such a thing. Gord did not say a word during the rest of that day's ride, knowing full well that Brodri was in no mood for talking.

That night, Gord stayed awake but silent until several minutes after the Arroden horde had ridden out to take on the Yoli. He knew that Brodri was still furious, but tried to approach him with a question anyway — and got a kick in the ribs for his trouble. "Keep that wagging tongue still, or by Lightning and Wind I'll tear it out of your head!" the young guard screamed. So, Gord thought, it wasn't going to be possible for him to draw Brodri into talk and then persuade the guard to loosen his bonds a bit. He would have to play a waiting game instead — and, as it turned out, the wait was not a long one.

Gord kept his peace for another few minutes while Brodri sat nearby, facing his prisoner and brooding. Then the guard's expression changed to one of resignation. He stood up, looked around, went a few paces over to his gear, and pulled out a small pot. Gord could smell the heady odor of date wine as Brodri sat down in front of him again and swigged occasionally from the container. The container was drained in less than half an hour. Brodri stood, belched, heaved the empty wine-pot disgustedly to one side, then stumbled heavily off to Gord's left, looking for a place to relieve himself.

Possibly Brodri believed that the many loops of cord and complex knots were sufficient to secure the prisoner. Possibly the potent wine had made him incautious. Whatever caused him to be careless in the first place, Brodri made an even greater mistake when he heard the sounds of fighting coming faintly over the still night air of the arid land. When his ears picked up the distant yells and din of battle wafting in from the north, the warrior ran several dozen yards farther away from Gord, in the direction of the sounds, in hopes of hearing more clearly.

Gord had already managed to loosen his bonds somewhat during the two minutes when Brodri had been busy relieving himself — literally the only occasion on which the young thief had been left unsupervised since he was captured. In the time it took Brodri to cover the additional distance and then stand for a moment with his ear cocked toward the faraway sound, Gord finished the job of getting free, then quickly and noiselessly crept up behind the careless guard, one of the ropes that had tethered him held fast in his hand.

A barely audible choking noise was the last sound Brodri made, just before the rope Gord had drawn around his throat cut off the noise and his breath all at once. Gord felt a slight pang of regret as Brodri's body slumped to the ground, for this Arroden was the closest he had had to a friend during his captivity. But even at that, thought the young thief, it was certainly not the sort of friendship that was bound to last. Strengthening his resolve to its fullest once again, he bent over the corpse and claimed the nomad's long sword and heavy-bladed dagger. Now Gord felt a lot better. He owed these Arroden much, and tonight he would repay them for their kind hospitality.

He wanted to get back his belongings, and using his special night-sight and his keen ears he did not see or hear any guards around the warriors' tents — including the one belonging to Shaik Yahoud, where he supposed his gear would be stored. But Gord didn't go there immediately. He assumed that there would be sentries stationed with the pack animals and horses to keep them from hurting themselves or straying away, and he wanted no men in the camp left alive when he searched the shaik's cloth shelter for his precious gear.

His reasoning was correct. After creeping along the perimeter of the camp, using tents and shrubs to conceal his movements, he detected two guards in the area where the remaining camels and the horses were tied on a long line. The first he struck from behind, using the unfamiliar but deadly sword. The nomad never knew what happened, and he was dead before his body fell to the sandy ground he had been walking on a moment prior. The sound of his collapse alerted his comrade, however, and the other Arroden warrior called out.

"What is wrong, Lafdan?"

"Hsssst . . ." Gord replied, allowing the indistinct

sound to trail off.

The nomad crouched and came cautiously toward the noise that had risen out of the darkness. He moved with all the stealth of any of his kind, and his sword was held ready before him as he advanced. That maneuver did him no good, for Gord had already flanked him and came to the attack from his left. The Arroden, sensing the young thief's silent rush, tried to bring his blade around at the last second, but both sword and dagger struck before he could defend himself. Choking on his own blood, the veiled warrior followed his comrade to wherever dead warriors of the Arroden go.

"There, slaver, is your pay for the work you have done," Gord muttered bitterly. Not bothering with either dead sentry further, Gord went swiftly to the rows of tents and sought out the largest one, which was Yahoud's. In his haste, he pulled aside the flap covering the entrance — and almost ran directly into the sword of the warrior on guard inside.

The man's sword slashed through the air as he lunged forward, and Gord had to throw himself sideways to avoid a mortal wound. As it was, he suffered a long, shallow cut. The nomad followed up his advantage, slashing and stabbing so furiously that it was all the young adventurer could do to avoid another wound while he retreated back out of the cramped confines of the tent's entryway. Once the battle was carried to the outside, Gord's opponent got his blade caught for a moment in one of the ropes that held a nearby tent, and as he freed it, Gord managed to spring back and take a proper position. Then the two engaged in a fencing match.

The contest was silent except for the ring of steel on steel. The Arroden must have known that either the noise of fighting alone would be sufficient to summon his fellows, or that no amount of noise would help, so he saved his breath and fought without outcry. Within seconds, both combatants realized that no other men remained in camp — no live ones, at any rate. The nomad was a little taller than Gord and very skilled. Whether or not a contest in daylight with equal weapons would eventually have gained the warrior a victory, Gord wasn't sure — but the young adventurer was in no mood for gallantry and honorable tests of arms at this point. The Arroden had taken him, stolen all of his precious possessions, and thought to sell him into a short life of slavery and death for a few bits of silver. Revenge and recovery of what was his were the only thoughts in Gord's mind as he acted.

With a lightninglike flick of his wrist, Gord brought the heavy dagger down. His arm shot outward as he did so, and the weapon flew from his hand, point first. The sharp point of the blade hit where he had aimed, imbedding itself in the bicep of the veiled man's sword arm just as he was bringing forward his weapon for a sweeping cut targeted at Gord's neck.

"Aargh . . ." the nomad cried, a half-stifled sound of pain as the dagger pierced his flesh. The stroke could not be held, and neither could the warrior's grip on his sword hilt. Gord ducked, but need not have done so. The long blade went flying on an incline into the darkness, sailing well over and past the young adventurer's head with a whirring sound. The Arroden tried to continue the fight, standing his ground and reaching for his dagger with his sound left arm, but with two sword slashes and a final dagger thrust, Gord cut him down.

It took only a little time for Gord to locate the Arroden shaik's hidden wealth. It was buried, of course, and kept safe in a locked chest. Gord had it out from under the carpet and the dirt quickly. He used the long sword to hack the container open, for he feared that poisoned needles protected its lock and he had no time or desire to try to use his skill as a thief to defeat any protections that might have been built into the nomad chief's strongbox. Inside were all of his treasures except for his shirt of magical elfin mail.

"So, Yahoud, you like my armor, do you?" he said aloud as he buckled on his shortsword and tucked his enchanted dagger back into its sheath. "Let us see how much good it does when my long-fanged poniard here kisses your lousy body!" His ring, his armband, his sling, and all of his other possessions were here as well, and he savored each thing as he reclaimed and donned it. Adding a largish leather pouch full of coins to what he had recovered of his own, Gord ran out of the tent and headed back for where the animals were kept. He was curious about what was happening in the battle to the north, and besides that he was not yet done with revenge. With luck, it might be possible to find Yahoud in a position where he had only a few of his warriors around him. If that happened, Gord vowed he would risk the odds to even the score with the Arroden shaik.

Windeater recognized him as soon as he came near the stallion. It was a simple matter to untether him, then find and put on his saddle. Just before Gord broke camp, so to speak, he cut the rope that held the camels and other horses together. Then he galloped Windeater along their length, hooting and waving his arms as he went. Frightened dromedaries and equines ran off in all directions, and horse and rider pounded off toward the sounds that still came faintly from the north.

After about twenty minutes of hard riding, Gord brought Windeater to a halt atop a low rise. A few hundred yards in the distance he could see the Yoli encampment. Spread out in an arc along the flat ground were clusters of Arroden; from this vantage point, Gord could see that the camp was about two-thirds surrounded. Inside the camp, several unwinking lights glowed brightly. They looked like magical globes of illumination, evidently cast by the Yoli sometime during the combat. There had probably been more, but Gord supposed that the Arroden had priests and shamans of their own to counter such light with magically wrought darkness. A few burning tents added a flickering glow to the steady brightness of the enspelled light spheres. Even though his night-sight did not operate at such long distances, Gord could discern what was going on in the camp, and some of what had transpired, thanks to this strange combination of illumination.

It appeared that at one point the attacking force must have been right among the defenders. There were bodies dressed in the pale ochre robes of the Arroden strewn throughout the camp. Many Yollites had died there, too. Because of what he was now witnessing, the young adventurer assumed that the defenders had managed to push back the first onslaught of the veiled warriors. He saw no combat activity within the camp, but with every passing minute the Arroden were expanding the ends of their arc and clearly intended to encircle the Yollite encampment. The beleaguered Yollites were lying low, for the attackers were sending buzzing bolts from their crossbows toward the camp. Any figure that showed itself in or against a light source was a target. Before, the Yollites had needed the light to use their bows, just as the Arroden had suspected they would prefer to do, but now the illumination was a liability, and the lit areas were being generally shunned. Gord could make out burned and smoking patches of ground here and there around the camp. If any spell-workers still lived among the defenders, no sign of this was evident. Either their magic was exhausted, or these men had died after casting their spells. Gord wondered how many Yoli warriors remained. It was hard to tell from this distance.

Gord tied Windeater to a scrubby bit of brush a hundred paces away, in a place where an upthrust fold of ground would conceal the stallion's presence unless someone came within ten or so yards. Moving quietly down the slope and then working to his left, the young thief began moving toward the veiled warriors who were besieging the camp. The Arroden strategy was a logical and unsurprising one; by encircling their enemy, they could contain them and also gain maximum sniping advantage, just so long as the attackers were careful not to hit the'r allies on the other side of the circle with their crossbow fire. The Arroden camels were ground-reined in small groups along the outside edge of the circle, but the animals' senses had already been assaulted by so much commotion that they paid no heed to another man in their vicinity. And, as Gord soon found out, the attackers themselves did not even consider that someone might be coming up behind them. . . .

It was so easy as to be almost laughable. Each of the Arroden warriors was stationed roughly one hundred fifty feet from the fringe of the Yoli encampment, and more importantly each one was at least seventy-five feet, sometimes as much as a hundred, away from his nearest neighbor — not enough space for the Yoli to attempt an escape as a group, but plenty of room for Gord to work undisturbed.

He picked a spot in the loosely spaced circle to begin, and then moved relentlessly along the Arroden rank. He killed as silently as the whisper of an owl's wings, as swiftly as that nocturnal predator does when its great talons strike an unsuspecting rat. From one of the first men he felled, Gord appropriated an attractive-looking necklace. Then, as he went on, he amused and revenged himself by stripping many of his victims of the silver bracelets they wore, stringing them on the necklace as he went along. Old habits die hard, Gord thought to himself as he did this — but the Arroden were certainly dying a lot more easily.

One of the men he did in was Yahoud himself, and he was careful to take this man with a dagger thrust in the neck so that he could reclaim his mail shirt in whole and unharmed condition. Gord's only regret was that he had had to strike the shaik from behind to kill him quickly, and thus the Arroden leader never knew by whose hand he died. He lost exact count after a time, but Gord thought that he had managed to slay no fewer than a score of the veiled men, and had worked his way around about a quarter of the circle. Then his presence was noticed — but not by those whom he was killing.

It was his own success that proved his undoing. The lack of missile fire from the segment where Gord had been wreaking his revenge must have become apparent to the besieged Yoli. A brief, tentative movement in that direction by a group of Yollites failed to bring any reaction from the attackers, and, unbeknownst to those along the circle, some intelligent leader among the defenders' ranks managed to spread the word of this development.

As for the attackers, they were so widely spaced, and one side of the circle was so far from its opposite section, that they remained oblivious to the fact that their ranks had been thinned. The closest Gord came to discovery was when an occasional warrior remarked to himself that the comrade on his right must have used up his crossbow bolts — just before that man himself fell to Gord's blades.

There was a sudden burst of activity in the center of the beleaguered encampment, but much of what went on was shielded from the view of outsiders by tents and large canvas shields. Some of the Arroden continued to fire indiscriminately into the mass, but most of them held their fire and did what they could to prepare for what was sure to be a last, desperate rush. Then the rush began — but it went in two directions at once. While expendable animals were driven out toward the side opposite Gord, a rush of men and animals headed toward the unguarded portion of the circle. The ploy was detected by the veiled nomads within a couple of minutes, when those on the still-intact side of the circle realized what they were being "attacked" by. Shouts and cries traveled along the arc, and an Arroden shaman stationed close to the gap in the circle

125

brought forth a globe of light to show his brethren what was happening.

The brilliant sphere sprang into being not far from where Gord was crouching. An Arroden warrior who would have been Gord's next victim got to his feet nearby, shifting his attention from the onrushing Yoli to the strange sight the globe revealed. "It is the prisoner!" the veiled nomad shouted, pointing his small crossbow at Gord and jerking the trigger to release a hasty shot at the young adventurer. "He has escaped the camp and slain Thotir!"

The shaft plucked at the baggy robe that covered Gord, but did him no harm. Gord shouted a curse at the fellow, ran forward, and attacked without thinking. By this time he was mad with fighting lust and blood madness. The Arroden dropped his crossbow and defended himself with his sword, and before he died the man managed to keep Gord occupied long enough to enable another and then another of his tribesmen to join in the melee.

Even as this occurred, the escaping Yoli saw that not only were their enemies caught totally unaware, but that the Arroden were not nearly as many in number as they had made themselves seem to be. This knowledge offered the Bakluni fighters an opportunity to revenge themselves upon their hated foes. Spread out as they were, the Arroden would find it hard to regroup to counter the nucleus of warriors who had just broken through the encirclement and were now ready to fight ferociously again. While the noncombatants among their number rode pell-mell to escape, the warriors of Yoll began to fan out along each side of the broken circle, riding down upon their dismounted enemies and trampling and stabbing as they went.

As the sound of hooves came toward him, Gord disengaged from the two Arroden who fought him and darted away from the scene. A half-dozen mounted Yoli descended upon the place where he had been but a moment before. The two veiled warriors managed to unseat one of the Yollites, but they lived only long enough to see him trampled beneath the hooves of his cohorts' mounts.

All of the Arroden now knew what was happening, and many of them had regained their own mounts and begun to form into groups. The fight was far from over, and it was anyone's guess as to what the final outcome would be, but Gord had no interest now. It was time for him to forget about thoughts of revenge, to get clear of the confused battle and ride away. He had no trouble getting back to the spot where he had left Windeater. Gord mounted the steed and rode off, heading along a route that angled away from the direct line of escape that most of the fleeing Yoli noncombatants had taken. He could not avoid the flight of these dozens of people entirely, for they had fanned out once they were away from the Arroden circle and were heading in many different directions at once.

Gord hadn't gone far when he saw the shape of a fallen horse outlined against the lighter-colored ground ahead of him. Farther in the distance he heard the sound of several other horses, camels, and shouting riders heading away from where the fallen animal lay. The sound of steel on steel rang out intermittently from this cluster, and Gord assumed that some of the Arroden had broken off from the main battle to chase down the Yollites who were riding away. He slowed Windeater's pace; he saw no sense in coming too close to the fighting at this point. The frenzy of killing had left him now, and Gord felt disgusted, nauseated, and exhausted. He was drained of emotion and strength, and what he wanted most now was a place where he could rest and regain his energy.

As he came within about twenty yards of the fallen horse, a high-pitched but tentative cry rang out: "Help!" Gord reined Windeater to a halt and peered intently toward the horse, able to see it at this distance as if the dark night were brightened by both of Oerth's moons in full splendor. He spied a heavily robed, slender figure lying on the ground beside the horse. Or was it partially beneath the animal? His vision of the form was somewhat obscured from this vantage point. He edged Windeater closer, circling to get a better view, and cautiously drew his dagger just before he identified exactly what was before his eyes. The animal was indeed dead, seemingly from a wound suffered in combat, and the figure was a woman with one of her legs pinned beneath its body. Evidently, she had been unable to free her foot from the stirrup in time when the steed collapsed and died.

"You are not going to hurt me," the woman said groggily, phrasing the question more like a statement. Then, in a more panicky tone, she continued, "How did I get like this? Who are you?" It was obvious to Gord that the woman was not seriously injured, but she was disoriented and puzzled.

"I am neither friend nor foe, just one who is glad to be done with fighting," said Gord in response, trying to put reassurance into his voice.

"Will you please help? My leg is trapped!" she said, a tinge of panic creeping into the statement. "Aid me, and I will see that you are rewarded!"

"No need for a reward, lady," Gord replied, dismounting and walking to her. "I will free you, and then we will both be gone from this charnel place."

Chapter 8

LONG, LONG AGO two great empires fought a war of mutual annihilation. One empire, the Baklunish, was fractured and made backwards, and the land of this race was turned arid and poor. To this day, the Bakluni are not a nation any more, but a collection of tribes that contest with each other for the dubious privilege of controlling the harsh, featureless lands of the western part of the Flanaess.

The people of the second empire, however, suffered even more when the Bakluni retaliatory strike came. Their fair land was scathed by a magically created storm of fire — colorless flames that consumed all life. When all was done, virtually all of the once-mighty second empire, known as the Suloise, was covered in a layer of dust and fine ashes. Gray and lifeless, wind-driven and parched, this covering of ruin blanketed the land for a thousand and more miles in every direction from its center. Indeed, it stretched like water across the landscape, and the area became known around the continent of Oerik as the Ashen Desert. When the Invisible Firestorm finally ended, all who viewed this seemingly endless vista of dust and ash, a gray-black desert born of destruction, assumed that nothing could live in such a place. Of course, they were quite mistaken.

The dweomercraefters of the decimated Suloise empire were so accomplished in the magical arts that they were able to shield their capital city from the fiery storm before it fell. For a time, at least, life continued in this metropolis, buried beneath a hundred and more feet of dust. A few of the other major cities of Suel managed to prevent the ravages of the colorless fire from fully affecting them, and there were isolated strongholds of powerful magi and priests that persevered despite the devastation. The ash and dust covered so much of the landscape, though, that the blanketing might as well have been complete. To make matters worse, volcanoes born out of the upheaval erupted, adding even more flakes and grains to that which was already there, and great storms drove and shaped the whole mass. One after another the Suloise outposts of survival were smothered and buried as years became decades, decades centuries.

But life is persistent, especially on those worlds where the mutable laws of magic take precedence over the immutable laws of science. As humans died, other forms of life discovered the Ashen Desert and found it desirable. At the same time, certain living things that had somehow managed to survive the destruction that had fallen upon their land adapted and mutated to survive in the new environment. Monstrous, single-celled amoeboid creatures flowed under the dust and ashes, feeding on the residue of the fire and leaving traces of matter and moisture for other, tiny organisms to thrive upon. Giant, multicelled clusters, colony animals, fed on silicates and carboniferous materials, returning the favor by depositing as waste other sorts of minerals that smaller life forms found beneficial.

After these lower creatures prepared the way, monstrous things grew up in the domain that the amoeboids and colony growths had dominated. Various types of slugs, all of them small at first, found that they had no enemies beneath the layers and layers of dust and ash, and they thrived on the growth that had sprung up there. These slugs got much larger, but the biggest of them was still no larger than an average man. Then they burrowed even farther down and found the springs and bubbling wells that still flowed deep, deep under the dust. By feeding in such places, engorging themselves with water, the slugs became more and more gigantic, and they made still other life possible.

Because of their size, and as was their nature, the slugs moved with the aid of trails of mucous, which they secreted from all around the exterior of their bodies. This slime, once exuded, hardened quickly. The less massive slugs left small tunnels through the ash and dust, and the big ones left comparably large passages. A network of twisting, turning, pipe-like burrows grew beneath the Ashen Desert. These passages generally led from one water source to another. Eventually, old tunnels collapsed. Some were destroyed by the passage of larger slugs, others by the still-surviving amoeboids and colony monsters — puddings, as their relatives elsewhere were referred to — and many fell due to pressure caused by the growth of vegetation beneath and through the dust. While all this was going on, new passages were being made continually anyway, so the change was hardly noticed — and certainly was not perceived as such by the nonintelligent creatures that spent all their lives in this strange and forbidding domain.

Plants are hardy, and some survived the destruction to grow anew. Seeds sent roots deep beneath the surface, seeking the moisture that still lay there, and thrust stems and tendrils up through ash and dust, seeking sunlight. Where tens or hundreds of feet of the stuff covered it, the vegetation failed. But in a few places, only a relatively thin layer of dust lay between the plants and the light above. Still, most of the growths that made the journey upward successfully didn't survive. The searing heat and the tearing wind that buffeted the plants with fine, abrasive particles saw to that. Many sorts of vegetation that managed to survive the elements still fell prey to insects and hardy mammals still dwelling on the surface, who fed on their leaves, seeds, and stems. As all forms of life will do, the plants adapted. In their changing, they grew defenses of many sorts. Eventually, over the centuries, a dozen species with a dozen varieties each managed to survive, if not always flourish, in the sealike desert of ash and powdered dirt.

Insects burrowed beneath the stuff; some few of them lived in a symbiotic relationship with plants, and others survived by eating the vegetation. A few birds, too, dwelled among the plants or adapted to making their homes in burrows below the dusty surface. Some fed on vegetation, others on insects. And not all insects ate vegetation; some sought other insects, avians, or even small mammals to feed upon. A complex ecosystem developed. Cacti of new sorts grew. Wirelike trees stretched up, showing only their branch tips unless a storm shifted the terrain and exposed more. Flat vegetation relied on photosynthesis or else trapped protein-rich creatures to survive, and scores of other sorts of flora awaited the infrequent rain to germinate and then grow in a frenzy while the moisture was available.

Rats, mice, and other rodents moved into the waste. Some took to the mazes underneath, while others found conditions on or near the dusty surface favorable. Shrews and moles burrowed there. Badgers came to dwell in the subterranean portion; foxes and wild dogs roamed the hot, black and gray desert above, and with them were snakes and lizards who likewise hunted their own prey.

A few hundred years after the Invisible Firestorm, the Ashen Desert was known throughout the continent as a place of death and desolation, a location whose deadly nature was sung of in eastern Oerik, related in the Baklunish poems chanted in Jakif, and told in legends elsewhere throughout the Flanaess. If there were men alive to contradict this reputation, none of them stepped forward. The few explorers and travelers who related their own experiences simply said that the Ashen Desert was a void, a place where nothing but the toughest and craggiest of plants could survive. Considering the few areas where animal life could have been seen, and the camouflage and protective coloration that was prevalent among the fauna — green that was either so dark as to appear black or so faint as to be gray to the eye, dun-colored skin and hide, black feathers, sooty fur, dusky hair — no casual observer could in truth state otherwise. But of course life did exist in many forms in this strange desert, and if it did not exactly thrive, it was fierce and tenacious enough to make up for the difficulties it had to overcome daily in order to continue.

Certain tight-lipped or otherwise uncommunicative sources did know of the true nature of the Ashen Desert. Among them were the nomads who roamed the northern boundary of the place; horsemen and camel-borne men of the Barren Plains and the savage folk of the Grandsuel Peaks that walled the steppes from the dust and ash beyond occasionally ventured into the fringes of the place. Explorers from the Seakings' Lands managed to cross the Inferno Peaks to seek wealth in the eastern portions of the Ashen Desert, as did certain expeditions sent by the head of the free state known as the Yeomanry.

Possibly, folk from the other borders of this waste likewise penetrated at least a little way into the Ashen Desert; the legendary peoples of such fabled states as Changol, Jahind, and Mulwar to the south, and the folk of Sa'han, Behow, and Chomur to the west, were the sort who would dare such activity. That the waste was a dead and deadly place, however, most would agree. Even those who had entered the Ashen Desert would not disagree that the expanse of powder and ash was hostile, had no possibility of supporting human life, and could never be explored at length beyond its edges.

Sages and savants of the arcane, if they were asked, would relate that the very place had supported life, at least for a time, when the very worst of conditions prevailed. These same scholars would also inform the interested listener that the centuries had certainly moderated the severity of the initial conditions. These ones knew that some life forms had adapted to survive in the Ashen Desert. But would they themselves venture into the heart of this sooty wasteland? Not likely! Could they suggest ways and means of survival to any — foolish or deranged — who sought to do so? Well, yes, they could *suggest*, but they offered no guarantees.

As a matter of fact, there were now at least three parties who were intent on venturing into the Ashen Desert — individuals ready and willing to risk its perils, intending to overcome them and seek out the lost metropolis that had been the center of the destroyed empire of the Suel people.

Obmi the dwarf was out to find the City Out of Mind.

Eclavdra, dark elven high priestess of Graz'zt, was bent on doing the same.

Gord, citizen of Greyhawk, once a beggar, thief, and cat burglar, now a free-willed agent of Rexfelis, Lord of All Cats, and the Demiurge Basiliv, likewise was on a mission to somehow trek across the uncharted waste of ash-strewn dust and sand to discover the hiding place of the Final Key, the last portion of the Artifact of Evil — which, if joined with its other two parts, would awaken Tharizdun, the greatest force of malign power ever known. That one would bind all evil to his wicked will, destroy light, and bring a reign of such terrible woe to the very multiverse that all good might be stamped out forever. Somewhere, buried beneath the Ashen Desert, was the object sought by these three — and perhaps others as well. Between all of them and the object lay the vast stretches of this arid waste . . . and everything that dwelled within it.

Chapter 9

"SUCH A THING is impossible!"

The spell-binder bowed in acceptance of the assertion. After all, he was but a lowly warlock, a functionary serving a far greater mistress. "It would seem so, Lord Obmi," he said. "Yet, I can only relate the information passed to me from one who stated it was the word of Iggwilv herself."

"I no longer am subject to that witch, knave! I am the champion of Queen Zuggtmoy!" the dwarf told him in a heated tone.

"Yes, lord, but is not the greatest of witches herself an ally of the exalted demoness? It was Kalfeen, the Mistress of Black Covens, who told me of what great Iggwilv would have you know. She also said that the same intelligence was Zuggtmoy's."

Obmi grimaced through his thick brush of beard. "Then let my mistress tell me of it," he growled. Before continuing, he looked around to make sure that none of the other patrons in the tavern were eavesdropping. "Bah! This is some ploy of Iggwilv's making or Iuz's twisted thinking to slow me in my passage to victory. No clone can be made so quickly, and none existing can continue whole and sound, while the true Eclavdra herself still lives. Even I, a magic-disdaining dwarf, know at least this much of dweomercraefting."

Daring the wrath of this fearsome fighter, the warlock persisted. "Duplicates *can* be grown and kept unactivated, Lord Obmi, by those of superior powers. Perhaps still greater spell-workers can remove the fell link and compulsion for sole existence which ties self to clone."

"Deceptions and lies! I myself arranged for the slaying of the scum guarding the drow filth, and her along with them. Eclavdra, the would-be champion of Graz'zt, is dead. Only I remain to complete the contest. You may inform your mistress of that, and she may tell whomever she pleases — Iggwilv, or Iuz, or all Oerth!" The dwarf was flushed with rage now, and the nameless warlock took a step backward, fearing that Obmi would fly into a murderous fit. As the underling began to retreat, the livid dwarf calmed himself somewhat.

"Don't hasten away quite yet, man," said the dwarf in a more even tone. "Tell your superiors that I, Obmi, have abided by every single rule and constraint of the whole affair, and I have done this so scrupulously that even Iggwilv herself could not find fault with my conduct. Although the dark elf was waylaid, I did not harm her myself. Others saw her and her entourage as an easy target, once I simply made them aware of her existence and location, and it was they who laid the black-skinned one low. I was nowhere in the vicinity when they put her to the sword. I was far away when all that occurred, and none can gainsay that. Now, begone!"

The warlock bowed his cowled head, perhaps a little deeper than he normally would have for a dwarf, even though this demi-human was the sworn champion of the terrible Zuggtmoy, Demon Queen of Fungi. The important fact to the warlock was that this one was mad, and the magic-user had no desire to become a victim of such a creature. Those whom he served would be the arbiters of all this; he was merely a conduit of sorts. "May you prosper, lord," he said in departing. But having already dismissed the man in his mind, Obmi was paying no attention.

In fact, despite his braggadoccio, the dwarf was not at all sure that he would succeed. Just two days earlier, he had completed a significant part of his journey, the trek from Hlupallu to Ghastoor. But he knew the most difficult tests still lay ahead, even now that he considered himself to be without competition. The contest was not just one of individuals; it was a trial of survival against the elements as well, and all that Obmi knew of the Ashen Desert boded ill. Then there was the problem of locating the City Out of Mind and finding the Theorpart somewhere within the buried ruins of the ancient metropolis.

Even as he thought about all of this, Obmi reassured himself that he would discover the way to manage everything, but right now he needed information and time to plan further, time enough to prepare for leaving Ghastoor and traveling to Karnoosh. Meanwhile he would have a little relaxation and diversion, enjoy the hospitality of the city of Ghastoor, and gather the facts and aid he needed for venturing onward. At the caravan town on the shore of Lake Karnoosh there would be need for final preparations, but by then he would have the wherewithal he needed. Now he was quickly regaining his confidence: He would not fail, and Zuggtmoy would appreciate his accomplishments. Along with his renewed faith in himself, the dwarf regained his cruel demeanor as he realized that the attendants of this tavern had left his cup empty for too long.

"You there! Bring me more wine!" bellowed the surly dwarf to a nearby serving maid.

She hastened to obey, spilling a bit of the stuff on the dwarf's sleeve in her nervous anxiety to please. That was all the excuse Obmi needed. He grabbed the girl's arm and twisted it. Pain was written on her face as she meekly begged his forgiveness. Obmi simply smiled and bent her arm farther. When it broke, she fainted, giving the dwarf only the satisfaction of a brief scream and a few whimpers before unconsciousness relieved her of the torture. The dwarf kicked her, but the servant girl remained unaware, so he got no pleasure from that. After calling for others to remove her, Obmi hurled a handful of silver pieces after them to avoid any recriminations from the local authorities. Then he sat back, savored his wine, and reflected on how masterfully his plan had worked so far. . . .

It had been a simple matter to have the two "lieutenants" among his original group of guards agree to slay the rest of the escort that had accompanied Obmi to the outskirts of the city of Hlupallu. "One of their number is a spy," he had told the duo. That had been sufficient to persuade the dull-witted half-orc to use Obmi's poison on the others. But then it had taken a bit more effort to convince the priest of the pair that his half-orcish companion was an enemy also.

Eventually, by exceptionally imaginative lies and dint of persuasion, including the promise of gold, the dwarf had brought the cleric around to his viewpoint. With the aid of a paralysis spell, the priest managed to incapacitate the half-orc, and then had the fine idea to offer the helpless part-humanoid as a sacrifice to the demoness all three of them served. Obmi congratulated the cleric on this bit of thinking, and accompanied the man on a trip to a secluded canyon outside the city. The trusting cleric had done away with the paralyzed half-orc and was on his knees, engrossed in finishing the ritual of the sacrifice ceremony, when Obmi caught him from behind with his enchanted martel. The dwarf rammed the weapon's sharp pick into the man's body repeatedly, so as to baptize it in the life blood of the unsuspecting fool. "This too is in sacrifice to our queen!" Obmi chortled, but the cleric was already unconscious and on the brink of death. Then Obmi finished the doltish priest with a solid smash to the skull, thus properly tempering the hammer head of his new weapon as well. Now he had disposed of all the members of his first retinue, as ordered, and he entered the Dar Peshdwar in disguise to await word from his new group of servitors.

Hlupallu was a diversion in more ways than one. Obmi had tarried there longer than he should have, principally because he was enjoying himself too much. But, the dwarf thought pridefully in retrospect, it must have been his own innate sense that caused him to linger, for the delay had been most profitable. A few days after he met his new agents, they informed him that Eclavdra was traveling toward Hlupallu, slowly, days behind. "You should hasten on, lord," one of them urged. "You can be a hundred miles or more in the lead if you hurry."

Instead of following this advice, Obmi had bided his time and used his clever wit. With a word here and a bribe there, he acquired and developed some contacts with bandits, and his scheme began to function. Of course Obmi was too smart to violate the conditions of the contest. He would not harm any of Graz'zt's minions . . . personally. In fact, he had been most careful not to purchase any harmful services either, for the twisted mind of Iggwilv might somehow cause the demons to construe that as a direct assault upon Eclavdra. No, the device he had come up with was even better. . . .

Four days later, Obmi received word that Eclavdra and her entourage had entered Hlupallu, and that she would be making the rounds of various places of entertainment that night. He went to the Dar Peshdwar, encountered one of the bandit leaders with whom he was acquainted, and invited the man to share his table. Less than an hour later a regal-looking elven woman arrived in the company of two burly bodyguards.

"That one — the strange elven female. Do you see her?" Obmi asked casually. The nomad seated next to the disguised dwarf nodded. "She travels with a fortune in precious gems, valuable magical items, and stores of coin!" the dwarf whispered.

The raider shook his head. "This city is too well policed to risk causing trouble here," he said. "Taking her and her guards is a major operation."

"If I give you the route she will take south from the city, plus details on her guards, and the name of a sorcerer who would be helpful in assuring your victory, would your warriors be interested?"

"*I* would be interested — but what share do you get of the loot?" the ugly bandit chieftain asked.

"None at all," said the half-elf that was Obmi, with a sly tug at his magical cowl. "That one is a sworn foe of my own clan." This the nomad could understand, and he nodded as Obmi spoke. "All I require for the aid I give is that the female elf be slain. Do you agree to that?"

"She is as good as dead even now, effendi," the bandit said with a crooked smile. "Now tell me all!"

Pondering the matter, Obmi too had to smile. How useful it was to have a spy acting on his behalf in Eclavdra's party! At first he had doubted the truth of the intelligence given to him, but those early assertions had proven true, and Obmi excitedly accepted the fact that traveling with the drow high priestess was one figure bent on her destruction. Using the information gained by the unknown spy and transmitted to him, he had been able to place the whole party in the hands of the bandits — and his subterfuge would not be traced back to him, for soon the spy would be dead too. "Very well," said the dwarf. "Now, listen closely. . . ."

Two nights later, the still-disguised Obmi was again seated in the wine house when he was approached by one of the members of his new group of servitors, a sorcerer known as Bolt.

"I bring news of a tragedy," said Bolt with a wry smile on his face. These were not the words Obmi had expected to hear. The sorcerer's sarcasm was lost on him for a moment, and he reflexively raised a hand to strike the man. So, the spell-worker wasted no more time in getting to the point. "Word has it that a contingent of easterners, a party containing a beautiful female elf, was ambushed and slaughtered by bandits last night, just a few miles outside of this fair city. A rare occurrence indeed, and one we should hope will not be repeated," he finished. Bolt, of course, was the sorcerer Obmi had referred to in his conversation with the bandit leader, so the spell-worker was not in fact a bringer of second-hand news but actually had been a participant in the assault.

The dwarf merely grunted in acknowledgment of the information. Angry at Bolt for beginning with a misleading remark, and embarrassed that he had not understood it for what it was, Obmi was not about to condone such flippant behavior by congratulating the sorcerer or even displaying any pleasure at the news. Bolt, sensing the tension in the air, took his leave a couple of moments later — and it was only then, in the privacy of his own thoughts, that Obmi allowed his face to display an evil grin.

Obmi and his group left Hlupallu the next day, then spent the next twelve days on a somewhat leisurely journey southwest from Hlupallu to Ghastoor, generally following the edge of the grasslands where they bordered the Pennors and the Barring Mountains. The travelers were not molested or even appreciably delayed along the way, for three main reasons. First, the group was small and unimposing enough so that no troop of nomads or bandits would expect to get any real spoils from a raid. Second, as Bolt had alluded to in his recounting of the earlier events near Hlupallu, it was rare that a band of western tribesmen would assault a small group of foreigners; although all the nomad tribes shared disdain for easterners, their real quarrels were with and against each other. And third, on the three occasions when a smattering of scavenging tribesmen did threaten to approach Obmi and the half-dozen who accompanied him, all it took was a show of force from Bolt to kill or maim one or two of the raiders from a long distance and send the survivors away, cursing and scurrying back the way they had come. The nomads of the west were not ignorant of magic, but few of them had any experience with dweomers of the sort that Bolt could call up. . . .

Out of the corner of his eye, Obmi noticed Bolt take a seat at his table, and he vaguely heard what the man said to him, but the main thrust of his thoughts was elsewhere. His reminiscing had come full circle, back to the conversation he had had earlier this day with the warlock messenger. "No," he muttered to himself. "There is no second Eclavdra, no clone. Someone seeks to give me false information to slow and confuse me. Perhaps a clone might be growing, but it will be weeks too late!"

"You spoke, lord?"

Obmi turned and glanced at Bolt. The dwarf was angry at being overheard; he had not meant to speak aloud. "No, I merely allowed my tongue to move in conjunction with my thoughts. If you heard anything, forget it!"

"There is nothing to forget, lord. I only heard the sound, not the sense, of what you uttered."

"That had better be so, or I will separate your ears from your head. So, why are you here?"

Bolt bowed his head only slightly, trying not to be intimidated. After all, he told himself, this despicable creature needs me far more than I need him. "Preparations are nearing completion," he said politely, repeating his earlier statement. "I have obtained our supplies, plus the documents and plans needed for the . . . vehicle . . . and now I have come to ask you when you will be ready to depart."

"Good," grunted Obmi. "Now find a secure train, a caravan of size and protection sufficient to deter attack from the swarming bandits who litter the way between here and Karnoosh. We will be heavily laden for this part of the journey, so there is no sense in trying to go alone. The leisurely pace of such a caravan will gull our enemies. They will never suppose we would travel thus."

"I have taken the liberty to investigate departures, lord, and a caravan such as you desire is assembling even now. It is scheduled to depart in two days," Bolt told the dwarf.

"How many will there be?"

"Three squadrons of guards, ninety warriors all told. They will cover the front, flanks, and rear of a train of two hundred camels, half as many horses, some of those odd carts favored by the locals, and several hundred handlers, drivers, and bearers," the sorcerer said as he ticked off the composition of the caravan on his fingers. "This is the main group journeying to the slave fair held annually in Karnoosh. My agents relate that small bodies of slavers with their merchandise will be allowed to travel with the caravan, and known merchants who have hired fighting men to bolster the strength of the mercenaries there to protect the main body will likewise be permitted to accompany the train. All told, a thousand or more will be going south."

Obmi could not help being startled at the size of this pilgrimage, but concealed his surprise beneath a screen of gruffness. "How many guards will there be all told?" he asked.

"Probably near to a hundred and a half, lord."

"Good!" said the dwarf. "As large as it seems, that is still a paltry number when the size of raiding nomad bands is considered. Even the most loutish of these Baklunish tradesmen must realize that. Our group of a dozen of the toughest horsemen — better, certainly, than twice their number of ordinary guardsmen — will be assured passage, for we have such strength as these louts cannot decline."

"Most aptly put, my lord," Bolt said unctuously. "Even the twenty camels we have will be useful, for these pigs always count on losing some of their number to raiders. But, we should expect that they will surely place us at the tail of the caravan, hoping that any attackers will fall upon us first."

The dwarf scowled. "That is unacceptable!"

"Of course, lord, under most circumstances the position would be most perilous. But with our men bearing Muzier banners on their lances, and the wagon drivers we have hired all displaying heavy crossbows as well, most who see this show of strength will decide to strike elsewhere in the train, if at all. Besides, my own spells will blast any who are foolish enough to attack."

"This whole country is not fit for a civilized dwarf to be in, let alone have to travel through," Obmi growled. "I want no fighting of any sort. It might delay my progress or make the journey even more unpleasant than it will be. Use more of the funds at our disposal to have your agents bribe the steppe nomads not to raid this caravan."

"That is sound thinking, lord," Bolt agreed, even though he doubted that any sum of money would actually prevent the wild tribesmen from taking what they could if the pickings looked easy or rich. "Yet your words make me think of another alternative, noble dwarf. Could you not employ the gold to enable the smaller slavers to hire their own mercenaries? Another hundred warriors would be sufficient to discourage raiders from molesting us."

Obmi thought about that for a minute. "It is pleasing to me, sorcerer, that you are learning from my wisdom," he said then. "You may use the coins as I now tell you. Select the most likely prospects amongst the local slave dealers, and make certain that they use the money to hire guards. We will show our unswerving exactitude in adhering to the rules of the contest, because the guards are not for us, you see. . . . Still, sorcerer, make sure that the ones in our debt know who their benefactor is. A few extra men between us and an attacker might mean the difference between life and death."

The caravan departed from Ghastoor three mornings later. It was even larger than Bolt had originally described, thanks to the late addition of several dozen guards attached to various slave merchants. The whole operation of getting under way was confused and slow, of course, because of the last-minute changes and the overall size of the train. It was not until just before noon that the last of its elements rode out of the city and down the long slopes leading to the Barren Plains. The main body was encamped and finished with the evening meal by the time Obmi and the rest of the tail end arrived at the campsite, just ten miles from their starting point. The next morning's routine went more quickly, for all components of the caravan now knew their places and had a greater sense of urgency. Some news had reached the caravan in its first encampment, and that information caused things to tighten up immediately. Bolt, while walking through the campsite with his ears open, heard the information and rushed to tell the dwarf what he had learned.

"Lord Obmi, may I enter?" he called from outside the dwarf's silken tent.

"Come in, come in! This had better be important, though, to interrupt me thus."

Bolt parted the flap and ducked inside the low pavilion. Obmi had few amenities in his tent, despite a demeanor that implied he was accustomed to such things. The dwarf was hard as iron and tough as boiled leather. The sorcerer bowed and said, "Survivors of a Yollite caravan which preceded us have just come into the camp. They were attacked a week ago by Arroden warriors — a group of more than five hundred, they say."

"Have you learned any other details?"

"I am not certain of the truth of the rest, great dwarf, but from what I understand, the Yoli had spell-workers who inflicted great loss upon the raiders before they died. These survivors claim that they actually defeated the Arroden — although the

145

Yoli fear and hate those camel-riders, so they always report victories and sometimes lie. They do have several heads and trophies, as well as some loot, but such stuff can be snatched even in defeat if a rear guard manages to disengage and flee."

"Incomplete information is useless, sorcerer! Go back and find out more. Whatever you learn, you keep to yourself. Report to me in the morning, after we are under way."

Bolt stood. "I obey, lord. May you rest well." Then, muttering under his breath, the dweomer-craefter withdrew and set about his assignment. Although he would prefer to rest, he didn't trust anyone else in their group to gather the facts he knew Obmi would demand. Besides, if he delegated the responsibility to another, the one he selected might — no, *would* — take advantage of his knowledge to supplant Bolt in some way. So far, the sorcerer had managed to be the chief lieutenant of the group, and he meant to remain in that position. If anything untoward should happen to the dwarf, then Bolt would become champion in his place. The sorcerer smiled at that thought, and went about his work.

Bolt rode at Obmi's side when they broke camp the next morning, but did not volunteer any information. He was determined that the dwarf make the first overture, and after several minutes that was what happened. "Well, what more did you learn?" Obmi growled.

Satisfied to have won the battle of wills, the sorcerer withheld none of what he knew. "The Yollite train was smallish, my lord," he said. "It carried goods and slaves to Karnoosh, the merchants hoping to be amongst the first there and thus gain highest prices for their wares. Knowing that they stood greater risk of attack because of their small number, the merchants were well guarded by warriors and a pair of fairly strong spell-binders — one a dweomercraefter, the other a priest of some sort. There is but a single merchant amongst the returning party. His goods are lost."

"The Yoli did not defeat the Arroden, then," Obmi said flatly.

"Pardon, my lord, but I suggest that perhaps the survivors speak truth for once — as unlike the Bakluni as that is."

Frowning, the dwarf demanded to know why Bolt thought the way he did.

"Because, great dwarf, the merchant made sense even as he beat himself and tore at his beard over the loss of his goods. To travel ahead, or back, slowly, laden with such stuff, and with only a handful of men, would be to invite every predatory nomad to fall upon oneself. The Yoli, even though they slaughtered great numbers of the attacking Arroden and drove them away, dared not recover their property and try to travel with it. They came back northward with their most precious possessions — their lives."

"Well done, sorcerer!" said Obmi, his spirits abruptly and unusually high. "Your news is splendid and your assessment sound, I think. That is an excellent omen for us. The Arroden will be licking their wounds for a time. Oh, yes, they'll gather their warriors again, and that band will be larger and more bloodthirsty than any seen for a long time by the Sons of Yoll. We will be long past, however, safe in Karnoosh . . . or beyond. Tribes less fierce than the Arroden — and that is most — will hesitate to come against any caravan of any size for a while, anyway. The story of the Arroden defeat will spread quickly through this wasteland, and will dishearten other raiders. Our trek will be a quiet passage through a peaceful land, I'll wager."

Obmi's pronouncement proved to be true — but it was fortunate, in a way, that his optimism was not shared by most of the other travelers. The big caravan made a little more than twenty miles each day — a good pace for so large a train of men and animals. Drivers, merchants, and guards alike were spurred on by the thought of vengeful veiled warriors, the terrible, camel-borne Arroden, coming down upon them by the thousands.

Their route was along the more westerly of the two wide trails that ran from Ghastoor to the city on the shore of Lake Karnoosh — slightly longer in distance than the easterly track, but a path that was generally parallel to a dry riverbed that ran southward from the Yolspur Tors to Lake Karnoosh. Every two or three days they came to a wadi where water could be found, either lying in pools remaining along the watercourse or waiting just a foot or two beneath the surface of the ground. Two times during the journey through the dry steppeland the caravan came upon a permanent source of water — once a true oasis, another time a well.

At the well site, the oasis, and some of the other places there were fortified villages. Although the tribesmen dwelling in such spots were neither strong nor numerous, the caravan master always paid over a tribute in coins or gifts for water and whatever other supplies the train needed that the villagers could spare. The local folk started out demanding exorbitant prices for dates, eggs, chickens, and all the other produce they had. But a few rounds of hard bargaining brought prices down into the realm of the believable.

This dickering was obviously the chief amusement of these tribesmen, for there was little else for them to do to enjoy themselves. The leaders of caravans through these parts quickly learned how they were expected to conduct themselves, or else they paid a high price for their obstinance. Purposely poisoned water and tainted food were only two of the more obvious means the locals had of revenging themselves upon any who sought to take water, provisions, or lives without proper payment. Anything the village could do without could be had, but money or goods in return must exchange hands. Such was the way of these places, and no wise person expected it to be otherwise.

The route to Karnoosh was fairly direct, for the steppe was relatively level and few obstacles stood in the way. The six-hundred-mile journey was accomplished in just more than thirty days. Every veteran caravaneer was astounded at such speed, especially for so large a train. Occasional encounters with savage carnivores were handled with ease, for Bolt and other spell-binders in the group were well prepared for such contingencies. The small bands of steppe nomads who came near the caravan were impressed by its size and capability. They approached without threatening, talked, traded, and rode peacefully away thereafter. One experienced guardsman informed Obmi that these petty warriors roaming the steppe were a sure sign that the Arroden had suffered a severe defeat, for normally these nomads they were encountering dared not come so far north for fear of the terrible veiled warriors.

About halfway along their route, the nature of the land changed. The steppes were seldom favored by precipitation, but in areas well away from the intervening mountains, the clouds did drop rain upon the land regularly. As the caravan proceeded southward, a little more than halfway to its destination, dry plains gave way to a well-watered grassland. Camels were no longer essential in this place; although they certainly could survive, they were no longer the most appropriate means of conveyance. Horses were favored by this terrain, and thus the camel-riding Arroden did not venture into the prairie to raid. The threat of the veiled warriors, small as it may have been, was safely past.

Large tribes and clans of horsemen roamed the grasslands around Lake Karnoosh, but many were paid tribute by the city of the same name to refrain from molesting trade. These warriors, then, tended to prey upon those groups that did attack caravans. The continual warfare that resulted kept the nomadic warriors in check while distributing some of the caravan loot — that which actually reached the city

— to even those who protected the merchants' trains. Of course, the least slight or pretended offense could send some formerly nonhostile tribe into a frenzy of raiding. When this occurred, other clans would happily take bribes and tributes to reverse their roles. Then these nomads would ride out to seek the now-hostile group, being paid to do so and relishing the prospect of taking loot from those who had recently gained it by pillaging some caravan or other. Obmi greatly admired this system, remarking pleasantly to Bolt on its practical and logical workings, and the sorcerer had to agree.

Turrets and domes dominated the brick city of Karnoosh. The walled portion of the place — the actual city — was relatively small; no more than seven or eight thousand souls were enclosed by the high barriers. All around the city, except on the side that abutted the shore of the big lake, were ancillary villages and towns that quadrupled or quintupled the total population of the area. Most of these smaller places were liberally dotted with caravansaries and wine shops where traders and laborers could find housing and amusement during their brief stay.

Continual streams of merchants came to the city, for Karnoosh was a hub where purveyors from north, south, east, and west could exchange commodities. An open bazaar was always busy. Slaves, spices, animals, ivory, and a multitude of other goods were sold and traded there. The brick casbah housed sufficient troops to encourage everyone to do business peacefully, but just in case auxiliary fortresses also stood on either flank of the city. The Shah of Karnoosh was very rich and very powerful. There were no strong states around his little realm, so for a century there had been no warfare troubling the place. Such peace and prosperity brought even more merchants to Karnoosh, and it was a thriving cosmopolis by all measures of the whole of Oerik.

Obmi's attitude about the place was in conflict with all the obvious facts. "This is no real city," he observed petulantly. It was obvious that the dwarf belittled Karnoosh for one simple reason. Men, not demi-humans — and in particular, not dwarves — dominated it. In the whole of the city, there were not more than a half-dozen of his own kind. In fact, there were so few of any nonhuman sort here that even Bolt was amazed. An easterner like Obmi, he had long been accustomed to encountering at least a fair number of nonhumans in any city or large town. Even in the western cities of Hlupallu and Ghastoor, they had seen enough dwarves and elves so that neither Obmi nor Bolt felt terribly out of place. But out here on the steppes, such was not the case.

Here there were males and females with deep brown, dusky, swarthy, tan, yellow, or reddish hues to their skin. There were short men and women, tall ones, stocky folk and lean. Some had small noses, others beaks. They looked different from one another, but with few exceptions they were all humans. These folk lived and worked together in harmony of a sort, at least bound to each other by their common racial heritage, but they did not consider elves, dwarves, or the like as their equals.

So, instead of desiring to linger in this exotic city as he had wanted to do in both Hlupallu and Ghastoor, Obmi demanded to leave Karnoosh as quickly as possible. This edict placed a terrific strain on Bolt, for the sorcerer had to gather more equipment and supplies, see that all was properly packed and loaded, and all the while make certain that no spy discovered what was taking place. It required four days for Bolt to handle all the details, but then the dwarf's group was away from Karnoosh, going along the southeast track that followed the lake's edge for more than seventy miles before splintering into three smaller trails heading in different directions of the compass. They led their carts and wagons, horses and mules along the smallest of the three paths, the center one that led south toward the town of Tashbul and then east and south into the Grandsuel Peaks.

"Tashbul will provide all the rest of what we need," Obmi told Bolt smugly, even though he himself did not know the whole truth of the matter, for he was aware that the sorcerer had no knowledge of this part of the west, and Obmi had picked up some intelligence on the subject back in Karnoosh. Although even most sages and savants of the Flanaess could boast no great store of knowledge on the subject at hand, the sorcerer's ignorance was a tool the dwarf enjoyed using against Bolt.

"You are most learned, lord," Bolt replied with a touch of sourness evident in his tone.

Obmi basked in the glow of this grudgingly given praise. "This verge of the old Baklunish Empire, my dear Bolt, still retains some small vestiges of the once-great culture lost in the Invoked Devastation. They are a decadent people, but interesting nonetheless, and they will understand our needs."

"I bow to your wisdom, lord," the sorcerer murmured, vowing to do his best to return the favor at the first opportunity.

Between five and six days later they arrived in Tashbul, found suitable lodgings, and set about the final preparations before entering the Ashen Desert. This city was as devoid of nonhumans as Karnoosh had been, but here Obmi and his ilk were looked upon more as a novelty to be enjoyed than a lesser to be shunned. The dwarf actually had a good time, in his sense of the term, during a week of debauchery in the ancient town. But then it was time to be on his way. Bolt had spent his stay in the town acting under more of Obmi's orders, seeking out some personnel and materials they still needed, enlarging and reorganizing the train, and generally doing his utmost to see that all would go as planned. He was tired, frazzled, and near his wits' end when the day arrived for departure, but he had accomplished everything he was responsible for.

The journey from Tashbul to the mountain pass that would lead them through the Grandsuels to the desolation of the old Suel lands was relatively quiet. But then, after covering a little more than ninety miles in six days across grassland and then again over dry ground, they came to the place where the guides Bolt had hired in Tashbul would take over, leading them through the mountains. The pass was winding, steep, and treacherous. To traverse a distance of twenty-five leagues as the crow might fly, they had to go twice that far overland, following the rocky path that was the only sure route between the crags. The journey was even more difficult because of the carts that were necessary to haul the equipment Obmi needed, but after more than two weeks of climbing, carrying, and stumbling through the rocks, the party made its way to the place where barren rock gave way to the vast stretch of dust and ash that rolled away to the south, east, and west as far as the keenest eye could see.

Most of the party turned back now. The mountain guides, of course, were not needed any longer. Likewise, the caretakers of the carts did not have to go farther, because the carts themselves had served their purpose. Before the majority of the group left to head back north, artisans assembled the stuff that the carts had brought through the mountains. They worked day and night while Obmi brooded and paced, occasionally overseeing the work but more often simply waiting out the delay inside his tent. At sunrise of the second day since the group had camped, Bolt came to Obmi at the end of his master's morning meal and gently led him outside.

"There she is, Lord Obmi — faithfully recreated from the drawings I obtained in Ghastoor," said the sorcerer, making no attempt to conceal his pride.

The object that the sorcerer pointed to was a shiplike device that rested on four great tubes. These cylindrical wheels were made of the skins of grubs, immature giant beetles that were native to

the lush, semitropical valleys that lay west of Tashbul. These, along with the pieces of the dismantled
craft, had been carted from that city to the edge of
the Ashen Desert to form a unique mode of transport across the waste. The skins were cut to the
proper shapes, then laboriously sewn together, and
the seams were sealed by heat before the cylinders
were inflated with bellows. The body of the vehicle,
its shape resembling that of a seagoing vessel, was
filled with stores of provisions and equipment. Even
though the group that would travel across the desert included a cleric who would be able to supply
magical provisionings, it was wise to carry real food
and water in case something should befall the man.
The vehicle had a single large sail, as yet not raised.
The whole thing was a sight that was at once in-
congruous yet quite logical, considering the "sea"
over which it would be traveling.

During the group's sojourn in Ghastoor, Bolt had
managed to find some very helpful information — a
treatise on an expedition into the Ashen Desert carried out more than a century ago by an adventurous
savant. This brave fellow recorded his travels in the
desolation and gave detailed drawings of the vessel
he used to accomplish his long journey from the
western side of the Inferno Peaks along the edge of
the Grandsuels. This bold savant had found ruined
cities along his route, managed to discover the
mountain kingdom of Zufon, and eventually make
his way back to his own home again.

From the drawings and information he discovered, Bolt worked hard to not only duplicate the savant's feat but also to learn all he could about what
the journey held in store. Survival was foremost,
knowledge second. Even if he did not eventually become the leader due to some mistake made by the
dwarf — and there would be plenty of opportunity
for that in the vast and hostile basin of ash — then
at worst the sorcerer could claim the accolades for
providing the vehicle that brought success to the

champion of the demoness. Obmi, of course, would derogate any contribution of his, but Bolt knew he was clever enough to be given credit when the time was ripe. He was not, after all, shy.

"You are certain, sorcerer, that the winds will propel this device?"

"The hot breezes always come from the east, great dwarf. I have sighted on the stars, and we are at the same degree of longitude as the place we seek — directly north of the buried ruins. The wind will try to drive us away to the west, but by steering carefully, we will travel southward, on course, just as a ship would navigate the ocean. In two weeks, three at the outside, we will see the broken spires of the City Out of Mind thrusting upward from their shroud of ash."

"So you say. We will set forth, then, and we will see how accurate your pronouncement is." Obmi signaled, and his dozen men clambered aboard the vessel. Some of their number were familiar with how watercraft worked, and they would teach the others how to rig, set, and furl the great sail. Unlike a waterborne ship, this craft was steered from its prow, and the dwarf went there to seat himself beside the pilot. When he was comfortably at ease, Obmi gave a signal, and the lateen-rigged sail was hoisted. Even though the wind was not brisk this day, the canvas bellied out, and the rigging creaked and hummed. In moments they began to roll across the powdery stuff of the Ashen Desert, the man beside Obmi straining to keep the steering roller canted so that the wind-powered vessel stayed on a southerly heading. "Good," the dwarf murmured to himself when he was convinced that the vessel would in fact move. "Failure is unacceptable — and had Bolt been mistaken, his failure would have been mine." While thinking about how he would have to carefully keep watching the clever and ambitious sorcerer, Obmi leaned back to enjoy the ride.

Chapter 10

"I AM SURE I can use this," the slender half-elf said as she finished stringing the short, recurved bow. "Name a target, and I will hit it!"

Gord was impressed by how easily the girl had readied the weapon for use, for the rather short Yoli bow was a compound of horn, sinew, and wood that was hard to bend. He turned his gaze to the terrain ahead of them, and after a moment said, "There are three gazelles grazing in that thicket — see? Slightly to your left, about one hundred yards away, Leda."

As the girl nocked an arrow and drew the shaft back smoothly so that the fletching just touched her cheek, her arm trembled for just an instant, but then the steel point held steady. Leda released the arrow, and it shot out in an arc that was almost impossible to follow. One of the animals sprang into the air a couple of seconds later, and then all three began bounding away. "There!" she cried happily. "You and I shall have dinner now."

"I fear not, Leda. Don't you see them running?"

"Of course, Gord, but the one I hit won't go far. Come on!" The half-elven girl leaped into the saddle of her horse and galloped away in the direction the gazelles had taken. Gord was atop Windeater a moment later, and before long was beside the girl. "Have a care! This ground is too rough to ride across at such a pace!" he called to her.

Leda only snickered and urged her mount to

greater speed. The steppe-bred horse that bore her was swift, but it was not a match for Gord's courser, and she knew it. It was exciting to gallop along like this, however, and laughing with the thrill of the race, Leda did her best to win the contest by choosing the worst course so that sheer speed would not prevail. Even though she was not highly skilled at riding, the half-elven girl was daring and athletic, so what she lacked in ability she made up for in aggressiveness. "Catch me if you can, slowpoke!" she shouted back over her shoulder.

Gord had checked his stallion so he could observe Leda as she rode. This was dangerous work, and the young adventurer was fearful that she would come to grief. Still, he knew by now that trying to call off the race was useless, so his only recourse was to slow Windeater so that Leda's own horse would not compete with the stallion, and stay close behind, just in case. They covered about four hundred yards thus, and then Gord spotted the dead gazelle at the same instant that she pointed to it. "You win!" he shouted to her. "I see the kill!"

Leda slowed her horse, jumped off when it stopped several yards away from the quarry, and ran to where the gazelle lay. "I shot it, Gord, so you must skin and dress it for supper," she told him gleefully as he stumped up beside her.

Grumbling in mock displeasure, the young man complied. Soon he had the task completed, and the two made a little camp. It was already late afternoon, and this was a good place to spend the night.

"What troubles you, girl?" Gord asked after he and Leda had finished a fine meal of game and wild berries. She had stopped speaking a while ago and was now staring moodily into the little flames of the dying bonfire.

"Have you ever heard of a tribe called Al Crevad?" she asked in reply to his query.

"No, but I am no expert on the west, Leda. Why do you ask?"

"I am troubled by the whole situation, Gord — wouldn't you be? When you rescued me a week ago, I thought my loss of memory was only a temporary thing, a fault of the fall and no more. Leda is a nice name, and I like it, but it doesn't seem quite right."

Gord smiled reassuringly at her. "Come on, girl! A week is not sufficient time to fully recover from such a nasty fall as that, you know. In a few more days your memory will come back."

"Gord, I hope you are right, but I am uneasy about the matter. Who am I? Why was I riding with a group of Yoli to Karnoosh? Where are my people? You and I both know that this is not a land where elves roam, yet I am surely half-elven. It all seems wrong, very wrong!"

Gord had to agree in his heart, but he wasn't about to reveal his doubts to the girl. "Leda, I think the answer lies in Ghastoor. The caravan was coming from there when the Arroden struck. I still think you should have let me take you back there."

"And delay your mission? How could I? If it is as important as you have told me — and I know you are speaking whole truth, Gord — it would be unthinkable for me to put myself above your duty." The young man started to speak, but the half-elven girl hushed him, adding in a gently scolding tone, "Besides, as I have told you before, I have some deep conviction that I too must go southward; that is probably why I was with the Yoli caravan to begin with. There is a vague sense somewhere within my mind, a feeling that I am needed for some purpose that lies to the south — just as you are."

"There are strange and unknown forces at work in this matter, Leda," Gord said seriously, "and it is possible that you are an agent of one, just as I am. I was doubtful about you at first, I admit. When I saw how well you managed a sword and dagger, I was only slightly less so. Now that we have spent a week traveling across these arid plains, Leda, I am becoming convinced of your ability to survive, and your need to press on with me." The young man paused for a minute, thinking. "I do agree with you," he continued. "You — we — must do all we can to bring your memory back. If you are a part of this business, there must be knowledge hidden in your mind that will aid us in winning through."

Leda replied as earnestly. "Yes, Gord, I know. That's why I asked about the Al Crevad — the name just came to me, unbidden. Perhaps the tribal name is El Cravad . . . well, no matter. I think I am . . . from a secret tribe of folk who keep their presence hidden from the savage nomads around them. I . . . we . . . are a careful folk who must always be alert, for there are enemies out on the plains around us. Yes!" she said excitedly. "I am sure of that. Perhaps I am from the mountains to the south, the very place we are going! I know those peaks are the Grandsuels, and the thought of mountains seems sort of comforting to me, like home."

"Good. This could mean that you are slowly recovering. And a solid night of sleep will help you, I'm sure. You turn in now, Leda, and I'll stand watch. When it's dawn, I'll rouse you to break camp and make some breakfast. I'll grab an hour's sleep then, and then doze in the saddle as we travel. I've become used to living that way," he said matter-of-factly. "Besides, I can catnap and feel refreshed," he finished, smiling at his own joke.

After a half-hearted protest against such coddling treatment, Leda rolled herself in her burnous and seemed to fall asleep instantly. Gord went off a bit from the fire and began his silent patrol around the outcropping they were camped by. They had covered a lot of ground since the night he had pulled the girl free from beneath her dead horse.

Windeater had found no difficulty in carrying the two of them away from the area of the battle, but it was a good thing the steed did not have to be taxed this way for long. At dawn the next morning they had come across a saddled horse grazing peacefully beside its dead rider. The animal accepted the half-elven girl readily, and the arms of the dead Yoli provided her with the wherewithal to protect herself. The dead warrior was a smallish man, and Leda put on his armor as naturally as if she had been a veteran fighter herself. She had likewise picked up the fallen man's weapons and tested them with a show of such experience at handling scimitar and dagger that Gord was convinced the girl was no soft courtesan or noble lady.

"Just who and what are you?" he asked her then.

The question stunned the girl, and she nearly collapsed from distress when she realized that she was unable to answer. "I . . . I . . . don't know!" she cried. "What's wrong with me? Trying to think of my name, who I am, where I come from — it makes my head hurt and my stomach twist." She reeled as she said that, and Gord had to rush and grab her to keep the girl from toppling over in a faint.

"Never mind that now," he told her reassuringly as he helped her to sit down. "Enough for now that you are alive. Memory will come soon enough."

That day he had suggested names as they rode along. When he began on names that started with the letter L, she had seemed more interested than before, so when Gord came to Leda, a name he personally liked, she had agreed that it sounded right — at least until she could recall her real name.

In the intervening days, Gord had kept trying to help her remember about herself, but the process was strange and slow. Leda seemed to be able to draw upon ingrained abilities to do what she had to do — handle weapons, ride a horse, shoot a bow. It was unsettling, though, that her memory of each skill made her uneasy even as it pleased her to recall information. The name "Leda" pleased her and bothered her at the same time — she said the word like it was an echo of her real name. At first, using the dead warrior's arms seemed to provoke stirrings that gave her a headache, as if the familiarity was trying to evoke another memory. Even riding made the half-elf uneasy at times.

"You are the strongest part-elf I have ever seen, Leda," he had remarked once. She got angry at the remark, seeming to take special exception to the phrase "part-elf," although she admitted later she didn't know why this happened. "Your pardon, girl, but I have met many elves and half-elven folk in my travels," Gord went on. "Even the dark-haired sort have fair skins. The elves of the west must indeed be of unique sort, with such a deeply tanned complexion and pale hair as you have."

"As a child of two races, Gord," she had said crossly, "could it not be that I inherited my dark skin from the Bakluni?"

"You have neither the olive cast nor the bold nose of the Baklunish folk . . . but I suppose it could be. You do look more elven than human at that!" Then they had spoken of other things, and no more was said about the subject.

Now, as he mulled over recent words and events, it seemed likely to Gord that Leda was right about her heritage, for she did ply the Bakluni weapons with skill, as her bowshot the previous afternoon had demonstrated. In any case, Gord was happy to have her company. Not only was she very lovely, but Leda was able and lent strength to this mission. Until this night she had been taking her turn on sentry duty as staunchly as any man, and her elven eyesight was most useful in the dark.

The usual nocturnal carnivores prowled the land as Gord stood guard, but no animal was so fierce that the little fire, a bit of noise, or a well-aimed stone from his sling didn't discourage it.

As the eastern sky became faintly light, Gord went to where the half-elven girl slept. She awoke at his slight touch, and in minutes she was on guard and Gord fast asleep. Leda let him doze longer than he had wanted to, for she felt they could easily spare another hour or so. Then she knelt beside him and gently poked him in the ribs.

"Come on, sleepy man!" she said boisterously. "The sun is up two hours now, and you are still abed! Food is ready, and the horses saddled. Refresh yourself, eat, and then we can be on our way."

Gord rolled over and was just starting to get to his feet when his eyes spotted several specks on the northern horizon. At the same time he was drawing Leda's attention to the sight, Gord was up and arming himself, all of his fatigue dissolved in a flood of adrenaline. Both of them mounted their horses and stood in the stirrups to gain a better perspective. Four — no, five — riders were coming toward their encampment at a trot. They were in a good place to defend themselves, for the rocky outcropping and brush provided both cover and concealment. Leda set out the eight arrows she had remaining in her quiver, and Gord selected from his belt pouch a dozen good stones for his sling.

"I'll hail them at a distance, and see if we can parlay," he told the girl. "If they are hostile, or prove treacherous, send your shafts at the one with whom I speak, for he will be the leader."

Leda nodded and returned to checking her bowstring, bow, and arrows. The best of the shafts were set for first use, for the shots would be the longest. This would change if a battle occurred, so the arrows with poor feathers or a slightly warped shaft would serve for close work. "Good luck, Gord," she called as he climbed up onto the outcropping to make himself seen to the approaching warriors.

The burnoused men immediately slowed their mounts from a trot to a walk when Gord stood up on the spur of rock and raised one hand. He remained motionless like that for a minute as they continued to advance abreast. At about three hundred yards distance, the five horsemen stopped their advance and gathered momentarily for a conference. Then one of their number broke away from the cluster and came forward, keeping his horse to a slow walk and holding the point of his lance sky-ward. Hoping to impress the visitors, Gord jumped down from the jutting stone, a distance of about twelve or so feet to the dry grass below. He landed, rolled once, regained his feet, and began jogging toward the lone warrior, all in a single fluid motion.

The nomad stood in his stirrups as the young adventurer came toward him, staring at him because of the unusual activity he had just demonstrated. As Gord approached to within twenty yards, the nomad dipped his lance toward the young man, indicating that he had better come no closer. "I am Achulka aka Saufghi of the Al Illa-Thuffi," the stranger shouted. "Who are you, outlander?"

"Those who name me comrade have called me Pharzool," Gord replied.

"Do any Arroden name you?"

"Perhaps from the Hells," the young adventurer retorted, and spat as he did so.

The nomad stared hard at Gord's necklace — the Arroden trinket with the silver bracelets adorning it that he had acquired during his solitary attack upon the veiled warriors. "You took those silver bands from the veiled men?" asked the nomad.

Gord plucked absently at the necklace and dangling bracelets, never taking his eyes from the horseman before him. "Well, I had many more than this under my blade," he said with a straight face, "but I took only these few things as souvenirs."

Achulka raised the long lance he held upright, so that its yellow-tufted tip was far above Gord's head. Then, with a slow and careful motion, he turned the weapon to a point-down position and sunk the steel head into the earth beside his leg. At the sight of this, his four fellows began to ride slowly ahead. "We now speak as not-enemies, Farzeel the Outlander. You may tell your comrades this, for we would not wish fighting by mistake."

"I will have my woman join me, but one other will remain behind until we see if you speak truth, warrior of the Al Illa-Thuffi. And my name is Phar-zool," he added. Then he turned his head slightly and called, "Leda, bring your bow and join me!"

The swarthy Achulka laughed a real laugh, showing white teeth and an honest smile as he did so. "Yes, Gray-Lion-of-the-Mountains . . . Farzeel is certainly a good name for you. Why mispronounce it as those from the north do? And why pretend you have three in the camp when you are only two?"

Then it was Gord's turn to laugh. "Fair enough, man of the Al Illa-Thuffi. I greet you as a not-enemy and ask what purpose you have in conferring with my woman and me."

The four other tribesmen joined their leader just as Leda trotted up beside Gord, her bow and arrow still raised and her eyes narrowed. Achulka raised his eyebrows at his first good view of her and whistled like a hawk, his way of extolling the girl's strange but stunning beauty. Leda was both annoyed and pleased at his display, but more the latter than the former. She lowered her bow and held it and the arrow loosely in her left hand thereafter.

Achulka dismounted, and his fellow nomads followed suit, forming a loose line spread out behind him. The leader kept his eyes on the girl while addressing Gord. "I see now why you are so fierce. Had I a woman like that, I too would be a lion! Is that not Yoli garb she wears? I recognize it as such, and the weapons too. Which of you took them from those dogs?"

Leda answered without the slightest hesitation. "I did, with my own hands. The one who wore this mail and bore these arms now feeds the vultures."

At that, Gord nodded solemnly, keeping his face a mask. The girl looked so intense as she spoke that it was all he could manage to not laugh. She said nothing but the absolute facts, of course.

"It is time for a council between us," Achulka said, gesturing back toward his fellows to indicate whom he meant. "Perhaps I have something to propose, but my brother warriors must agree first."

Gord would not be put in the position of waiting for these nomads to decide what to do. "We are riding south," he said curtly. "If you wish to speak further, you will surely find us in that direction. Leda, bring our horses forth. Farewell to you, men of the Al Illa-Thuffi." As the woman turned and began walking back toward the camp, Gord continued to face the nomads and maintained an alert but unthreatening posture, legs slightly apart and hands on hips near his weapons.

The horsemen behind Achulka looked surprised at Gord's statement, and several black looks shot back and forth as hands touched sword hilts. Their leader hissed over his shoulder at them once, softly but sharply, and the other four regained their composure. "Very well, Farzeel," he said after a few seconds, his jaw set. "If we care to speak with you and your warrior-woman further, we will seek you to the south. In fact, we are headed that way ourselves, but not until after we parley."

Gord looked at each of the tribesmen in turn, not smiling but not challenging. He simply gazed so as to be able to recall their faces later, if he needed to. Each warrior looked away from the young adventurer's eyes after but a moment — except for Achulka, the last one Gord stared at, who returned his stare calmly but firmly. Gord broke the silence by saying, "Come in peace if you come at all." Then he turned on his heel and followed Leda back to where their horses were tethered. He did not expect the men to try to attack him from behind; indeed, when he reached the outcropping he turned back to see the five of them sitting in a circle on the ground, obviously engaged in conversation.

Gord and Leda rode for most of the day. He acted especially alert, casting furtive glances over his shoulder when he thought she was not looking. After they had trotted their horses due south for a time, Gord angled their path slightly to the east and picked up their speed to a canter. Leda knew without being told that he was doing this to widen the distance between themselves and the five nomads.

Speed and distance were important to them, but not at the expense of their steeds. Periodically, both Gord and Leda dismounted and walked for a short time to allow their mounts to rest. The horses snatched mouthfuls of tough grass as they walked, and Gord and Leda also ate on the move. This way they managed to keep covering ground with no pause. However, fatigue began to tell on Gord by mid-afternoon, for he had not been able to doze in the saddle as he had said he would do.

"How much longer can you manage, Gord?" asked Leda as they walked, with a look of genuine concern for him.

Gord smiled at her. "For the rest of this day and tonight too, if necessary, girl. We won't have to keep up this pace much longer, though. I'm beginning to think that those nomads aren't likely to bother us — I'm just being extra cautious."

At that the half-elven girl seemed momentarily relieved, but then she thought of something else. "It's because of me that you are being so careful, isn't it?" she said. "Achulka was very interested in me, and you think that he and his fellows will try to steal me."

Gord had thought of that, but there was more to his desire for putting distance between themselves and the five horsemen than that. Gord was certain the nomads wanted something from them, and he saw no sense in tempting fate. "I mean no offense, Leda, but even as beautiful and exotic as you are, we also have valuable horses, weapons, and other possessions most of these nomads would kill for. Before you came close enough for him to see, the man seemed very interested in these silver rings," Gord said, gesturing to the bracelets on his chest. "For many reasons, I wanted us to press on as quickly as we could. Better to have distance between us and possible friends than to be in proximity to foes."

"If that's the way of it, then we should get to riding," Leda said with a wry face as she turned and mounted her horse. "But tell me, Gord. Which is more precious to you — me, or your stallion?"

Without waiting for an answer, she rode off at a canter that quickly became a gallop. The young adventurer was after her in seconds, and Windeater promptly closed the lead she had. "I think it is a standoff!" Gord shouted as he drew abreast of her. "You're better looking, but this horse is more manageable and even-tempered!" She smiled warmly at him, and they settled their mounts down to a walk, spending the next two hours in comfortable silence. Gord's sense of urgency was much lessened now, and he was able to snatch a few moments of sleep as Windeater followed the other horse's lead.

In late afternoon, Gord and Leda both glanced backward at the same time as they topped a low rise, and both saw the same forms moving toward them at a rapid pace, scarcely a mile away. "It seems they are coming after us, Gord," said Leda. "What should we do?"

"Let's get this over with," Gord said as he dismounted and she followed suit. "I hate being chased, or even trailed. We will stand here, but be ready to drop behind this slope if they display their bows. Meanwhile, get arrows out for that bow of yours, and try to knock a couple out of their saddles before the others close. When they get to us, I can handle two of them easily enough, if you can manage the other."

"Oh, what a man," Leda said with mock reproof as she nocked an arrow. "Perhaps *you* will manage one while I deal with the rest. The proof will be upon us soon — shall we wager?"

Just then the racing horsemen slowed their galloping steeds to a walk, seeing that those they pursued had stopped. When they were all still out of range of Leda's bow, one figure detached from the group and came on at a slow trot. It was, of course, Achulka. Leda raised her bow and sighted on the man, ready to fire at him if he or the others made any aggressive move. He closed to within a hundred yards, then halted and called out. "Hold your arrows, warrior woman! We come in peace to offer our swords to you and Farzeel!"

"Why would they chase us so far to do that?" asked Leda skeptically.

"Hmmm . . . I'm dubious myself, girl," Gord replied. Then, to the approaching nomad, the young thief shouted his conditions. "If you speak truth, have your men join you. Then leave your horses and come to us on foot, without arms."

Achulka dismounted immediately, then waved to his fellows to come up to where he stood. Soon four of the Al Illa-Thuffi were approaching them on foot while the fifth warrior held back, staying with their horses. Much of their gear had been left behind, but Gord could see that they were not unarmed. He was on the verge of telling Leda to begin shooting, but when they got within forty yards, Achulka halted the group and spoke again.

"You are cautious, but this we can appreciate," the hawk-faced leader said. "We have left bow and lance behind, but I and my brothers still have our swords." Achulka drew his tulwar and held it up across both hands as an offering. "If you will but promise two things, we will be your men."

Gord simply waited, and Achulka took his silence as consent to continue. "First, we ask that we get our fair share of any spoils when we meet enemies," the nomad offered.

Gord nodded and allowed himself a small smile, which Achulka could not have seen. It was beginning to seem as though these nomads were serious, because that was certainly a reasonable request. "Fair enough," he responded noncommittally.

"Second, at the end of our time of service, we ask that you give us the bracelets of the Arroden you wear as trophies."

This made Gord grin even wider, this time in mild derision. "You will then pass them off as something you won from the Arroden?" he ventured.

"Never!" Achulka said in a pained tone. As he continued talking, he slowly approached Gord, his sword still held peacefully before him. "I am hurt, Farzeel, that you think so little of warriors of the Al Illa-Thuffi. But I forgive you, since you are an outlander. You do not realize the power of the armlets you wear as mere decoration. Do you not know," the nomad said with great earnestness, "that each is worked with great charms to protect the life and aid the arm of the wearer?" The nomad leader paused in his advance, waiting for a response.

Rather than pointing out that the dead Arroden to whom the bits of metal had formerly belonged hadn't received much benefit from the silver hoops, Gord folded his arms — a reciprocal gesture of non-aggressiveness — and remained silent for a moment. Then he told the burnoused nomad, "We ride for the Grandsuel Peaks."

"There is naught beyond but the Ashen Desert," Achulka informed him.

"That is where we plan to go," Gord countered.

The nomad shrugged and then said to Gord, "May the rain fall upon us, then, as we trek there."

"You would risk your lives there for these baubles I hold?"

"Not only for those. We have been amidst the powder and ash once or twice, Farzeel. We know there are many other things to be found there," Achulka finished with a knowing grin.

Leda placed her small hand upon Gord's shoulder. "There is no use trying to stay ahead of these clever warriors," she said softly to him. "We should accept their service, instead of having them behind us all the way to our destination."

Gord mulled everything over for only a moment; actually, he had made up his mind even before Leda spoke. "Your terms are acceptable," he shouted to Achulka. "Join us."

Soon all seven were riding together over the dry, flat land toward the long line of peaks that scribed a jagged line on the southern horizon. Two days later they were heading eastward through the foothills of the Grandsuels, paralleling the peaks while Achulka continually scouted the terrain to their right. The nomad leader claimed to know a route through the mountains, and Gord had no reason to doubt him, so he went along with him in more ways than one.

Finally, Achulka gave out with a whoop and stiffened in his saddle. "There, see the big rock like a fist with its thumb upright?" he asked, pointing to the southeast at the landmark he had just noticed.

When both Gord and Leda nodded, the nomad grinned with pride. "Why do we care about a strange-looking rock?" Leda said caustically.

"That is the entrance to a pass which only we Thuffi know about. All others think there is but a single way across the Grandsuels to the desert beyond. We know better!" the warrior boasted.

Sure enough, they found the pass and began traversing it. As they started the gentle part of their ascent, Gord expressed surprise at seeing little towers in the foothills. Achulka explained that these were built for protection and were used by his people in high summer, when the worst drought was upon the steppes but a little rain and frequent ground fog covered the foothills of the Grandsuels. Herds were pastured in this area, and some few crops were also raised. At such times, however, the Hokrodden, a southern branch of the fierce Arroden camel-riders, made forays into Thuffi territory. Sometimes, Achulka told Gord and Leda, the guard towers actually meant the difference between life and death to his people. Now these mud-brick fortifications were unpopulated, however, for the full heat of summer was not yet come. The little band simply rode past these places and upward along the defile called the Pass of the Clenched Fist.

It took two days to reach a spot that the nomads told them was about halfway through the mountains. There was a small, green valley at this location, and high up on the mountainsides could be seen stone walls and buildings. "Who lives here?" Leda asked.

"The Chepnoi. They are mountain people — a strange folk," Achulka told her in reply. "Can you believe that they are our cousins? Why any Al Illa-Thuffi would give up horse and steppe for such a cramped and unchanging existence is a marvel under the sky! We exchange visits in high summer — they travel to us in the month of the boar, we come here in the time of the squirrel. The trade is good for both peoples. In four moons' time, this valley will be filled with the mountain folk and my own tribesmen, trading and contesting. I'll give the Chepnoi credit for some things," the nomad said earnestly. "They make good wine in their little valleys, and they know the land of dust too!"

"What mean you by that, Achulka?" Gord asked. "And I am not speaking about wine, mind you!"

"These mountain folk are used to walking, so they don't mind doing so even in the Ashen Desert. The Chepnoi taught us the value of such work, for they first brought stuff from the desert to the gatherings with our people."

"Now do the Thuffi people go into the ash often?" the half-elven girl asked.

"Well, not frequently," Achulka admitted, "but my uncle has been there and returned with a big gold coin and shield of bronze to prove it!"

On that note, they dismounted and made camp in a shaded sward just off the path leading up to the nearest village on the ledges above. In a few days' time, they would be in the waste to the south, and much more than gold coins and bronze shields was at stake.

Chapter 11

NO CHEPNOI WOULD JOIN the expedition into the desert — not after Gord told the mountain warriors that it would take them out of sight of the Grand-suels. "That is death, Gray-Lion," said the Chepnoi hetman solemnly. "Even if one stays close to the safety of the mountains, a storm can bury you alive in minutes. To trek out of sight of the peaks is to invite death in many ways, but surely from being smothered by ash — never a week passes without the wind blowing that powder into a scouring fury."

Achulka took the lead at this point and tried to shame his mountain-dwelling kinsmen. "You have stout silken covers and hollow poles for that. What is a little dust storm when one is safely burrowed beneath the very stuff you fear? We will find enough water, surely, and much treasure too! Old women and young boys might fear the dangers of the Ashen Desert, but are you not Chepnoi warriors?!"

"We will live to fight, thank you," the hetman replied laconically, not even taking the nomad's response as insulting. "All but crazed ones shun the interior of the Ashen Desert."

"Then we *men* of the Thuffi, plus Farzeel and his woman, are crazy," Achulka said with a sneer.

"Yes, you are," was all the Chepnoi chieftain said in reply. That was the end of the discussion.

The mountain folk would not go with them, but they did cooperate in other ways. For a price, they provided the travelers with provisions, gear that would help them negotiate the ash and dust, and they allowed Gord to make a copy of their sketchy map of the Ashen Desert, which vaguely marked out some of the land's major features and indicated the location of the City Out of Mind. Whether or not this latter aspect of the map — or any part of it — was accurate, Gord had no way of knowing. But he supposed the information was better than none at all.

Gord and Leda remained confident and determined despite the Chepnoi leader's negative words. However, the Thuffi nomads grew glum after hearing what the hetman had to say. Even though the prospect of wealth was a strong motivator, the warnings about deadly storms and lurking death from their mountain-dwelling kinsmen had severely dampened the enthusiasm of the five warriors. When Gord paid in silver for what they had obtained from the Chepnoi, the young adventurer took the opportunity to hand each of the Al Illa-Thuffi several nobles, too — all he had remaining, in fact, with Achulka getting the odd extra silver piece. That brought cheerfulness from the steppe horsemen only for a brief period.

"Why not just loot the ruins off to the east?" Achulka suggested, indicating a spot marked on the map. "We know there is much wealth remaining in that place, there is only slight peril in the journey we must make to get there, and we can keep the mountains easily in sight for the whole distance."

"Those ruins must have been visited by many over the years — but the treasure is untouched where the two of us intend to go," Gord said in counter to that plan. He didn't know that for a fact, but he was quite willing to stretch the truth to keep Achulka and his men in the group, for now that the Chepnoi had given him a clear idea of what had to be faced, it seemed unlikely that he and Leda could succeed without the help of the nomads.

Achulka was in no mood to argue the issue. He shook his head, then sat tight-lipped with his arms folded across his chest. Gord tried taunting the Thuffi leader, just as Achulka had done earlier with the Chepnoi hetman. "If you five no longer desire such riches, and if you have decided that the Arroden charms I would give you no longer have power, then perhaps you should stay safe at home with . . . those who are not daring."

Achulka lowered his gaze, remained silent, and was getting more sullen with every passing second. Clearly, the man would not be influenced by a tactic that had failed to work when he had tried it. Things looked bleak . . . and then Leda spoke up.

"In my mind," she said bitterly, "there is one kind of man lower than a coward, and that is a hypocrite. I listened to you cajole and insult the leader of these mountain people, which was fine. But now, by your inaction, you are proving yourself to be an empty shell — one from which words flow, but which contains nothing of substance. It is easy to *talk* about being courageous, isn't it, Achulka?"

That was all it took. Leda's scathing words, coupled with Achulka's attraction and admiration for her, turned his thinking around. The nomad leader lifted his head to meet her steely gaze, then turned for a brief, hushed conference with his cohorts. When he looked at her again, it was with a combination of respect and anger in his eyes. "I am glad I have never met any of your people, warrior-woman," Achulka said in a dry tone. "If your men fight as well as I suspect you do, and if their tongues are as pointed, then they are surely more fearsome than a band of Arroden warriors in the charge. We will come, and may the fates be kind to us all."

Gord was a bit taken aback by the whole affair. Using words the likes of which he had never before heard her utter, this beautiful and mysterious woman had accomplished something he could not do. Just what *was* this warrior-woman, anyway?

After several more days of traveling through mountain passes and then along the craggy fringe that bordered the Ashen Desert, the seven treasure-seekers bade farewell to the Chepnoi men who had accompanied them this far. As part of the bargain Gord had struck with his silver, the mountain tribesmen would care for their horses and gear for three months. By then, if they had not come back for their property, the whole would belong to the Chepnoi. It was a fair enough arrangement, under the circumstances. Gord hated to part with Windeater, but the powdery wastes were no place for horses, even the finest of stallions.

The travelers wore white tunics and robes, so that the heat of the desert would be reflected away from their bodies. They each carried their own provisions and other needed materials in large backpacks. They walked on strange, flat shoes made of woven-leather strips held fast in circular frames of tough wood. Each held a long, hollow pole with a little shoe at one end and a plug in the other. With the shoe end down, the pole could be used for support and balance while walking. By reversing it, the pole could be used to test the depth of the dust.

The shoes were large and strong and distributed the wearer's weight over a good-sized area. But the Chepnoi had warned the group about places where the powder was so fine that even their dust-walkers, as the wood and leather shoes were called, would prove insufficient to keep a man above the surface. To sink was to be smothered and dead within a minute or two, as the tiny abrasive particles would fill ears, mouth, and lungs immediately. By temporarily removing the shoe and the plug, each pole could be used as a breathing tube if someone found himself being covered. This tactic would only succeed if the user also had time to bind small pieces of finely woven silk over both ends of the pole to serve as filters. Even this would not assure survival, but any chance was better than none.

Each of them carried a cocoonlike tent — bulky, but light, and absolutely essential. The only way to

survive in a serious storm on the Ashen Desert was
to get below the surface, out of the wind. Otherwise
the flying particles would tear cloth from body and
flesh from bone, in as little as a few minutes. The
proper procedure was to take off the dust-walkers,
get oneself and one's equipment into the sack, and
then hop up and down in the powdery stuff. This
would cause one to sink, and as this occurred, the
cloth was pulled higher and higher about the body.
Once a person had worked himself down to below
the surface, the pole-tube came into play — along
with prayers that the storm would not pile up a
dune of dust and ash that was higher than the tip of
the breathing device.

The heat was terrific, and although he did not
like the look of them at first, Gord was soon glad
for the white garments that swathed him. The Chepnoi had directed Gord to take his group along a
route that was not the shortest path to the City Out
of Mind, but was in all likelihood the safest. Because
of the rolling terrain of what was once the Suloise
Empire, there were places where the dust was
fairly thin on top of the old landscape — and others
where it was so deep as to be immeasurable or even
impassable. So Gord took their advice, which was to
go east for a short time to begin with, keeping the
mountains on their left shoulder until they became
accustomed to moving on the dust and otherwise
coping with the environment.

Gord saw evidence of life in the wasteland almost
as soon as their trek had begun. Of conditions farther out, he was not sure. The evidence of strange
plants and small life here at the edge of the desert,
however, made him suspect that tales of the area's
absolute desolation were not wholly accurate. Then,
when they came upon an actual pool of water, his
suspicion became a known fact.

Dark-leafed plants grew low around the place
where the blackish water spilled forth and ran into
the powdery ground to the south. Here and there,

wherever some crack or fissure permitted, trees and other normal-looking sorts of vegetation thrust upward. "It is said that the leather-leaf palms have tasty fruit," one of the nomads remarked as he gathered up several handfuls of hard, wooden pods. "Soak these for an hour, and see what happens."

They all followed suit, and then set about getting a supply of water to replenish their stores. The pool was filled with tiny particles of dark ash suspended in the water. A cloth quickly filtered the stuff out, however, leaving clear, drinkable liquid. Even the unfiltered water was not harmful, but removing the particles gave them more room for liquid in their containers. Everyone was glad for a chance to pause in relative comfort and unstrap their dust-walkers, even if only for a short time. As they relaxed, Achulka gave Gord and Leda a summary of his tribe's lore concerning the flora of this place.

"The low trees which grow near the place where the brook disappears are called deathvision trees," he began. "One leaf chewed will give strange and portentous dreams and visions. Two leaves can kill, and three are deadly always. The deep green plants which grow around the edges of this oasis we call fatleaves. Singe them, and they provide food, although it is waxy-tasting and will make you sick in the belly if you eat too many. There are hairs on the leaves which make the skin itch and burn, but flame removes them quickly — just be careful not to char the whole leaf."

There were various sorts of cacti, brushy growths, and varieties of other plants here as well. Living around and among the plants were several kinds of insects, little birds, lizards, and jumping mice. All were colored in tones to match the area, ranging from pale gray to sooty black. "There is plenty of life here, Achulka," Gord said, looking around. "What is the great danger in going on into the middle of this waste? Anyone wise to the ways of such arid places can survive easily."

"Not so, Farzeel. Directly to the south, beyond this rocky area, the dust deepens, and there are no waterholes such as this one. Storms and thirst can easily kill all who venture out there."

"Nonetheless, *you* are going," Gord said, voicing this partly as praise and partly as a point of fact.

The nomad shrugged. "You and the warrior-woman seem capable and determined, and you might be lucky as well. The welfare of me and my men is now a matter of kismet—"

A shriek broke up the conversation. One of the Al Illa-Thuffi warriors had walked over to examine a striped-leafed bed of little plants that had silvery fruit dangling beneath their leaves. As he approached these shrubs, the ash beneath him had suddenly shifted, and he sunk as if in quicksand. His cry brought the others, but without their special shoes they had to step gingerly to avoid suffering the same fate, and by the time they got to the site, the nomad had disappeared into the stuff.

"Poor Hammadan! He should have been more careful," another of the nomads cried, sorrow written plainly on his swarthy features. "I have never before seen such a terrible thing. Let us not go on!"

This tragedy brought on another round of doubts from the nomads, countered by arguments from Gord and Leda. Eventually the four remaining men agreed to continue accompanying the pair, but it took more promises of gold and gems and much convincing besides. And, instead of turning south at this point, the nomads demanded that they continue eastward along the mountains' edge to a southern arm of crags and hills where, according to Gord's map, another pool could be found. When they ran up against this finger of rock that thrust into the Ashen Desert, then they would turn and head in that direction — but they would not go south until they had to.

Although the easterly route would take them away from the supposed location of the City Out of

Mind, Gord rationalized that it made sense to follow the high ground for as long as possible. First and foremost, of course, the nomads would have it no other way. But also, they all would gain more experience in desert travel during the diversion, and before they headed away from the mountains they would be able to replenish their water supply. Perhaps most importantly, the terrain around the spur of rock seemed likely to provide a means of relatively easy access to the heart of the desert. From the information the Chepnoi had given him, the young adventurer thought that there would be hills running southward from this area. Recalling the advice of the mountain people, Gord had noted for himself that the dust and ash was indeed much like water. The powdery stuff flowed and ran, filling low regions and lying thinly on high ground. So, the six survivors trekked east.

"If I could, Gord, I would turn back now," Leda said quietly one night. "Even now that I am fairly used to it, walking on these platters is murder."

Gord put his arm around her shoulders. "You handle the dust-walkers better than I do, Leda," he said, "and you're as tough as the leather they're made of. Whatever reason you have to be here, you'll make it. Why, girl, even your skin has darkened and become like part of the dusky world we travel in."

Leda snuggled closer to him. "I know, Gord. Even with my body covered in this cloth, I am getting darker and darker. My dreams are getting more vivid each night, too. I think that soon I'll recall everything — and that frightens me more than anything." Then she put her arms around his neck and kissed him. "Will you be here with me when I need you?"

"Of course I will," Gord told the half-elven girl. He kissed her back, tenderly at first, and then with a hint of growing passion. He pulled his face slightly away from hers and met her eyes with his own as he continued, "For whatever reasons fate has decreed, you and I are following the same path. We'll be side by side when we enter the City Out of Mind," he assured her with all sincerity. "You and I are comrades, and friends too."

"Then let's become lovers as well," Leda said, using her little hands to stroke the sides of his face and his shoulders as she brought her lips to his again in a lingering kiss. Soon passion ruled both of them, and they made love to each other for a long and wonderful time.

As they lay together afterward, Gord felt Leda's body shudder. Then the girl began to cry. "What's wrong, dearest love?" he said with deep concern. "If I have somehow—"

"Don't be foolish, Gord," Leda said. Then, forcing herself to stop sobbing, she tried to explain. "It is because of *me* that I weep! What am I to do? Each day something grows within me. I have terrible *evil* inside me — I feel it! I fight against it, but as little memories come back unbidden, the malign thing inside my head becomes more powerful too. You are all that is keeping me from becoming lost in the darkness of what lurks inside, Gord. Help me!"

The young man didn't know exactly what to say, but he tried to console her. "I see you every day, Leda, and you are no more wicked than any other person — human, elf, or whatever — would normally be. In fact, you are more generous and kind and brave than most I have known."

"But that is because I fight and fight to be that way. You see what is happening to me, Gord. You yourself commented on how my skin grows dark. I am a drow — or at least part dark elf, anyway. Who and what I am is still hidden, but there is badness inside — the evil of the worst of elvenkind and who knows what else besides."

Leda started to sob again, and Gord held her close. "You and I will fight it together," he said. "I have seen that you are good, so if there is other than that within, we will drive it away together so that the better can rule. I too have my malign side,

Leda, and it often tries to come to the fore. Sometimes the evil part of me succeeds, and then I must work especially hard thereafter to push it down and bind it. If this is happening within you, then it is something that can be dealt with. Love will help, too! It must be a part of your memory returning, the bad resurfacing before the good does."

"Yes, Gord," the half-elven girl said weakly. "Perhaps that is it. Please love me still, though, no matter what."

"You may count on me, love. My word on that." Leda calmed down at this point, and the two soon fell asleep in each other's arms.

The following days were filled with heat and danger, the nights with passion and reassurance. The party reached an area of low hills, some actually showing stony clay, with deep drifts of ash and dust between. They swung south, for the Grandsuel Peaks thrust down into the barren wastes ahead. The hills and powder-filled valleys between continued. By staying on hill and ridgetop, they made good time. Then they turned slightly to the east again, and in a half-day of hard trekking came to the second oasis. It was very much like the first one they had encountered, and it became apparent that the life forms that managed to exist along the edge of the desert were all pretty much the same.

That was one pattern, and Gord could see that the nomads were exhibiting another. Whenever they reached a waterhole, it seemed, their resolve to travel farther grew weaker. Gord observed a couple of the men pointing surreptitiously toward the east and witnessed a hushed conversation involving all four of them during the early part of their stay at the oasis. Later, Achulka approached Gord and Leda where they sat, trying to seem casual but failing to keep his self-consciousness from showing. "Shall we go on eastward now, Farzeel?" he asked in an artificially friendly tone. "The ruined city is but a few days' travel that way. Let us go there and return soon — sound, and rich men!"

Because of what he had seen and sensed, this sort of talk did not take Gord by surprise at all, and he was prepared for it — determined to exert his own influence fully this time and not let Leda carry the burden for him. "Achulka, you amaze me," he replied with obvious contempt. "I thought you were a warrior whose word was a bond. Instead, I hear the mutterings of an old man, lazy and afraid. One fit only to tend children and campfires should certainly turn away from man's undertakings. Go!"

This time, Gord's insults worked — ultimately. After a brief exchange of breast-beating, argument, and threats, all four of the Thuffi warriors agreed that they would continue on with Gord and Leda as planned, but as recompense Gord had to start giving over the Arroden bangles. If Gord did not believe that their apprehension was real, he would have accused the Thuffi of taking advantage of him. Achulka wore the first bracelet proudly. One more was to be handed over every other day, until each of the nomads had one. Gord would retain the necklace and the remaining pair of bracelets for the duration of their quest, the tribesmen receiving those items when the party returned to the Grandsuels.

With the matter resolved — at least for the moment, Gord said to himself pessimistically — the group headed south instead of east. On the second day afterward they ran into a terrible dust storm, and only their being in the rocky terrain of the worn hills saved them from its full fury. In fact, they didn't even have to resort to using the tent-bags and breathing poles, for there was sufficient shelter to be found behind the stony ridges they traveled across. The hills disappeared four days later, and the band was reduced to shuffling across the dusty terrain on their webbed shoes once again.

At this juncture, Gord turned the group southwest. They traveled in a line abreast, each member of the party about a hundred yards away from the next. This way it was hoped they would be able to spot any sign of water. They had at least another week of water still, if it was carefully rationed, but very soon the risk of thirst would become serious.

Leda discovered the ruins. She was on the far right of the line and thought at first that she had come across a natural stone outcropping that could mean water a short distance beneath the surface. She called out and waved, and one by one all of them lumbered over to see what she had discovered. They carefully dug away the ash and dust from around the upthrusting stone, and it soon became apparent that the stone was not a natural formation. What they found were broken towers and the remains of walls.

The nomads were excited. "Dig deeper!" one of them said. "We must search here for treasure!" exclaimed another.

Leda agreed that they should search the area, but for a different reason. "Gord, there could have been no city here unless there was a supply of water to support its citizens. Let us see if we can get into this building below us and try to locate a spring or an old cistern," she suggested.

Gord consented to this, and the six of them renewed their efforts to dig away the dusty covering. In a certain spot, just three feet beneath the ash and powder, was a solid surface that turned out to be an intact roof. When they had cleared away a fair portion of this area, Gord noticed a rectangle of wood that was separate from the rest of the roof. He pried at the seam with his dagger and discovered it to be the edge of a hatch. Two of the nomads laid hands on the side opposite the hinge and lifted. A moment later, the hatch came open with a creak, causing a bit of ash and dust to cascade down into a three-foot-square hole that opened the way to the darkness below.

It was not hard for Gord to hang on the edge of the hole and drop to the floor below. He was a little

nervous about the wooden planks being rotten and
giving way when he struck the surface about twenty
feet beneath the roof, but he managed the incursion
with no problem. The rest could have used a rope
to climb down, but Gord found a ladder nearby, its
wood perfectly preserved in the arid place. Soon
Leda, Achulka, and the other three nomad warriors
were standing beside him. They left the hatch about
halfway open, resting on the end of the ladder, so
that shifting dust wouldn't bury the exitway and
trap them inside. They all took off their backpacks
and set aside other nonessential equipment such as
their poles and dust-walkers. Gord and the nomads
kept their weapons, but Leda left her sword and
bow with the rest of her gear.

"There is a flight of steps descending over
there," Gord said, pointing to a corner. "Shall we
begin exploring?"

"How will we see in the dark?" Achulka asked.

Leda's elven vision and Gord's enchanted sight
made the issue no problem for them, but the nomads had no such advantages. Once they were out
of the slight illumination provided from above by
the open hatch, they would not be able to function.

Gord glanced around the room and saw nothing
suitable. "Wait here," he told Achulka. "There must
be some means of illumination within this place."
Then he went below and returned a few minutes later with a pewter pricket and a rushlight. "This
thing is so old that the grease has become hard as
wood," he told the four steppemen, "but it will
shed enough light for you to see — at least until we
can find some torch or lamp that will serve better."

They went down through five stories before getting to the ground floor. The charts and wall hang-
ings he saw along the way led Gord to assume that
the square tower had been used for stargazing and
astrological calculations. All of the equipment and
maps, books and scrolls, were stored in the floors
beneath the upper level, dusty but otherwise intact.

"The priests of this place must have left without commotion," Leda said as they walked through the great, echoing temple they found below. "It is good that they did, for otherwise the windows would have been unshuttered, and the weight of all the dust and ash from above would have filled this chamber with powder long before now."

Little ramps of dust had sifted in over the centuries through the seams around the windows, so that an inch of the stuff lay on the floor in most places. The sediment puffed up around their feet as they walked, but was undisturbed elsewhere. "Enough of the desert has entered," Gord observed, "to tell us none has been here for long years before us."

"This is perfect!" Achulka exclaimed. "Priests always extort money from the faithful, and those who were so careful to secure their place of worship before leaving it must have been exacting in their demands for wealth. Let's find the coffers of those clerics, for none can claim their gold but us now!"

"The treasury is certainly hidden below," Gord said. They all began searching for a means of going into the cellars, and a stairway was quickly located. Gord was thinking about water more than gems, but he didn't mention that to the nomads. Let them hunt for loot while he sought more precious stuff. "Come on, let's see what the ancients who ruled this place hid below," he said. "Leda and I will form one team, and you four split into two others. Call out as soon as you locate anything worthwhile."

After they began descending, Gord took Leda's arm and spoke to her sternly. "I did not want to bring this up in front of the others," he said, "but I noticed a short time ago that you are not armed, and I am dismayed that you saw fit to leave your weapons in the chamber above. What will you do if we run into a problem down here?"

"I am sure we will encounter no problem that you cannot solve," she said with a tender smile, trying to make light of the matter. When she saw

185

that this response did not satisfy him, she frowned slightly and spoke further. "I can give no real reason, except that I simply wished to be free of the weapons for a while, because they cramp my movement and make me feel heavy. Also, something in my head tells me that I have weapons other than those that are held in the hand. I am not worried right now, dear, and I beg you not to worry either."

Gord didn't know exactly what to make of her cryptic remarks, but decided to let the issue pass. In truth, he did not feel that their lives would be endangered while they searched this abandoned place, so perhaps the whole thing was not worth thinking about. "As you say, my love," he told her. "Now, let us see what we can see."

Minutes later, Leda discovered a low tunnel that led to a downward-spiraling stair hewn from solid rock. "Look over here," she called. "This building is like a fortress, and such places always have their own source of water in case of siege. I think I've found it, for there is a damp smell rising."

Not bothering to call the others, Gord and the girl went down the narrow, slippery steps. They twisted and wound into the ground about thirty or forty feet, then opened into a place whose ceiling indicated that at least a portion of it was a natural cave. Marks on the walls showed that at one time water had filled it about halfway, a depth of seven or eight feet. But now the water was gone, and the floor was covered with nothing but dried mud.

"Damn it, the conditions above must have dried out the source of supply," Gord muttered.

"No, Gord, look yonder. There seems to be a dark patch over there, as if there is wet mud on the floor, and there is an opening in the wall just at the place where the floor meets it. Let's look more closely." They walked across the chamber to the place she had indicated.

"Wet is right, you sharp-eyed vixen!" Gord said, giving the silvery-haired girl a pat on her round lit-

tle bottom as he said it. Crouched on his hands and
knees, the young adventurer peered down the narrow passage that had allowed the water to escape.
"Not only mud, lass, but a big pool of fresh water
beyond! I can smell it and hear drops hitting the
sur— *Ouch!*" Gord whirled around and raised himself to a kneeling position to find out what had
struck him so sharply.

"Take that, you molesting swine!" Leda had taken
the choice opportunity offered to revenge herself
for his earlier attack on her posterior.

"You drow *are* creatures of great evil," he
laughed, trying to grab and kiss her. Leda backed
away with an expression of anger on her face.

"One day you might learn the truth of that, you
pale pig! Until then, don't joke about dark elves."

Gord got to his feet and grabbed her by the shoulders. "And you, Leda, remember that I am no one to
trifle with, either!" he said, giving her a shake that
rattled her teeth. "You will fight off the darkness
which is trying to overwhelm you, or else I'll know
the reason why. The woman I love is *not* about to
transform to a demon before my eyes!"

Leda grabbed him and held on. "Thank you, dear.
I don't know what happened. But I feel fine now, so
let's get the others and show them this pool."

"Hells, no! Let's you and I have a bath and enjoy
ourselves first. Those barbarians will be busy for
quite a time searching for loot, and we'd be crazy
not to make use of the time that gives us."

Leda agreed readily, so it was much later when
the two of them clambered back up the spiral steps
to search for the four Al Illa-Thuffi nomads.

Finding them wasn't very difficult. The tracks in
the everpresent thin layer of powder went here and
there but eventually joined up in one passageway.
Gord and Leda came to a partially open door with
light leaking out from the other side of it. Indeed,
the four warriors were in the room beyond. The one
called Nizamee was lying on the ground in the cen-

ter of the chamber, stroking a dark red, swollen hand and groaning weakly. The others were farther from the door, facing their comrade but standing motionless — seemingly entranced — before several huge stone chests.

"What is going on here?" said Gord, confused and angry at the same time.

"I . . . I can help this one," Leda told him haltingly. "Go see what is wrong with the rest of them."

While Leda bent over Nizamee, Gord rushed to where the other three nomads stood like statues. One glance at what was in front of them told him what the problem was — overwhelming greed. They had managed to open the heavy lids of four of the stone boxes that stood in the center of the room. The young thief saw that each container held a fortune in precious stuff — coins, jewelry, uncut gems, ingots of metal. The tribesmen were obviously too taken with this find to pay attention to other things. His entrance with Leda had gone as unnoticed as the stricken condition of their brother Nizamee.

Gord stepped over to Achulka, grabbed him firmly by the shoulder, and shook him. "Your comrade is dying, and you stand gazing at treasure!" sneered Gord. "What sort of men are you?" He slapped the other man sharply across the face, and this seemed to bring Achulka out of his dazed condition.

"This is so much . . ." Achulka said, slowly shaking his head as if to clear it of cobwebs. Then his eyes seemed to clear, and his voice became agitated as he noticed Leda and Nizamee in front of him. "I remember . . . Nizamee! He was careless, and a sharp needle stuck his palm. But that is the last thing I remember before— "

"No worry now," Leda said. She was kneeling by the white-clad nomad, passing her fingers slowly over the injured hand and arm. The dark swelling had vanished, and the nomad seemed to be asleep. She looked up at the two men facing her, both wide-eyed in amazement, and explained. "As I realized he had been poisoned, something seemed to snap inside me, and a flood washed over my brain. I recalled that I could use spells, so I knelt down, thought hard, and remembered the one which alters toxins to harmless waste within the bloodstream or body. As you brought Achulka from his fascinated daze, Gord, I worked my spell upon Nizamee — just in time. He sleeps now, for a bit, and he will feel bad when he wakes, but he will live."

"You see what your stupid greed has almost done?" Gord scolded the nomad.

Leda interceded for Achulka. "Don't blame him entirely, Gord. The stupor he was in — which his two fellows are still under, if you'll bother to look — is induced by a dweomer placed here as a part of the guards and wards of the treasure room. Think you that such a place as this would not be most well protected?" she asked the young adventurer with a hint of acid in her tone.

"Yes, you're right, Leda dear. Sorry, Achulka. Bring your comrades out of their transfixed state, and let's see what is to be done about all this. Excuse me, but I need to speak privately with Leda for a moment."

Taking her by the arm, Gord steered the dark elven girl from the treasury into the corridor outside. "What sort of spell ability have you?" he asked in a hushed tone.

"Clerical, Gord. I have spells of the sort common to drow women — females, more properly. I guess I am becoming a typical dark elven female."

"No, not typical! You are Leda. You are special, and you are my love! If you are a priestess of some sort, what deity do you call upon?"

At that she shrugged. "I have no recollection of that, and nothing to give me any clue — not even a symbol of any sort. The spell-working I just performed came to mind as naturally as any thought, so there is no hint there either."

"As I recall, Leda, clerics are able to bring water

forth from the air, so to speak. Am I right?"

"Hmmm, let me concentrate a moment." There was a pause, and then the beautiful dark elf maiden smiled at him and said, "I can, Gord, and that I know for certain! Now we have no more problems in our quest!"

The two stepped back inside the chamber. Without even really thinking about it, Gord pushed the heavy wooden door until it was only open an inch or two — a habit picked up during his days of thievery. He and Leda stood casually a few feet away from the doorway. The nomads were now lively and alert, except for the comatose Nizamee. The three who were able were busily sorting through the vast array of treasure, selecting and storing away in their packs the choicest items. Gord and Leda both laughed at the sight of the scene, and the warriors stopped their looting and turned sheepish faces toward the two.

"No need to stop that on our account," Gord said with a chuckle. "No matter how much the three of you stuff away, there's more here than ten times our number could manage. Help yourselves!" Leda walked over to where she could get a better look at the haul, and Gord enjoyed seeing her eyes widen as she viewed the contents of the coffers.

There were big, golden coins, thick wheels of yellow metal that bore the head of a haughty-faced man on one side and a sun on the other. Only a few of the coins were silver, dark with tarnish from the years they had lain undisturbed in the long-lost treasury of this unknown temple. With all of this were faceted gems, uncut stones, pearls, amber, ivory, and coral. There were strings of gems, wrought jewelry, and more. All of these riches held Leda's attention for a few moments. Then she picked up an ivory scroll case, casually pulled out its contents, and spent the next several minutes apparently studying what was written on the parchment. Gord wondered what she was doing, but didn't bother to ask. The nomads paid her no heed whatsoever, preoccupied as they were with picking out the choicest of the valuable items.

"When you have all you can reasonably carry — and remember that we have a long way to go yet — I'll show you where we can replenish our water," Gord said to the nomads. "We'll rest here until tomorrow, and then we head out again for the City Out of Mind."

Achulka listened to whispered words from the two warriors who demanded his attention. Then he turned to Gord. "My brothers say there is no need to go farther, Farzeel. They say that here is all anyone could ever want — and I agree," he said. "We will head back for the mountains tomorrow. Come with us, and you will be made the chief of our tribe! Not one of the Thuffi would deny you such honor."

"You pledged your service," Gord said slowly, without apparent anger.

"Yes, but we have agreed to give back the Arroden charms, and we do so now." With these words, he and his fellows stripped off the bracelets and laid them on top of the treasure piles they had been sorting through. "You may take Nizamee's too, of course, and now we are even."

Leda gave a sarcastic little laugh at the easy manner in which the nomads disregarded their sworn bargain, and began to berate the men. Gord turned disgustedly away from Achulka and took a couple of paces toward the doorway. He intended to assume a barricading position and then tell the nomads that if they didn't live up to their word, they would have to fight him here and now. Suddenly, he heard a faint shuffling sound coming from the corridor. He whirled, made a short hissing noise to quiet everyone else, and then gestured to indicate that he thought someone or something was outside. As he drew his dagger and shortsword, the nomads took out their swords, and the three of them moved to a position where they could shield their fallen comrade from further harm.

Gord motioned for Leda to take Nizamee's sword for her protection, but she shook her head and said in a near-whisper, "He will need it, should he awaken. I have . . . other ways of defending myself." Gord was not about to waste precious time arguing about it. Wordlessly he directed her to move toward a far corner, and as she complied he took up a position beside the doorway. The shuffling got louder and closer for a few seconds, until it was apparent that the noise was coming from right outside the door. Then the sound ceased altogether for the space of two heartbeats — and all of a sudden the heavy portal flew inward with a resounding crash.

Chapter 12

A LIVING WALL of albino apes was coming through the doorway. Their faces twisted in snarling expressions, showing their yellow canines but making no sound, the mute, baboonlike things began to plow through the opening. The front wave had impacted the partially open door and pushed it inward. Because they had paused outside the door and thereby lost their momentum, and because the portal was heavy and not easily moved, the beasts' initial entry was slow. The apes behind the first wave had an opportunity to build up some speed in the corridor, and they ran over the ones in front of them. The result was that a few of the apes were stunned or injured by their allies, and the haphazard nature of the charge gave the adventurers inside the room a few valuable seconds to prepare for the onslaught.

From his position beside the door, Gord was able to strike and defend himself at the same time. As the initial wave surged into the room, he thrust one through the neck with his sword as he gutted the one nearest him with his long dagger. The apes did not come for Gord right away, since he stood out of their line of movement. This gave him a couple of moments to assess the situation as the albino beasts fanned out and began to advance upon the others.

There were still four or five dozen of the little apes on their feet, Gord figured. Most of them were not rushing forward recklessly now, but were circling and shuffling, looking for ways to put their teeth and claws to use without being hurt themselves. The three healthy Thuffi nomads had formed themselves into a rough circle around Nizamee. They slashed and thrusted with their blades, keeping most of the apes at bay and doing in a couple of the beasts that got too close.

Meanwhile, Leda had found her secluded corner and escaped the immediate attention of the apethings because of her isolation. As Gord cast his gaze toward her, the dark elven girl was reaching up to where the natural ceiling of the chamber curved down to meet the wall. She broke off a handful of tiny stalactites and held them aloft for a few seconds. Gord was bewildered by this: Was she intending to use these tiny things as weapons? If so, they would not last long or do much damage. Figuring that the Thuffi warriors could fend for themselves for the time being, Gord began using both of his blades to hack and slash a path across the room to the corner where Leda was located.

"Keep them off me, Gord!" Leda called to him as he approached.

"I'll do my best!" Gord replied. As he got closer, he saw that stalagmitelike spikes had sprouted up from the stone floor of the chamber all around Leda. These protrusions were from a quarter of a foot to a foot long, serried about a foot apart, and sharply tapered. The little monsters that were trying to get at Leda were having a hard time of it. Apparently, the hedge of spikes had sprung up just as they were about to strike. A half-dozen of the ape-creatures lay dead, impaled on the field of stone spires.

In one place, three of the corpses formed a line that led through the spiky area. If the beasts behind these dead ones had thought about it and used the bodies of their packmates as a bridge, they could have been upon the girl before Gord got to the scene. However, the ones still alive seemed to get more excited at the sight and smell of so much blood. In their lust, they were so eager to get to

Leda that some more of them fell on the spikes, and others fought and tore at one another for the privilege of using the pathway of bodies — with the result that none of them actually got that far. Had these terrible little apes been other than mute, the room would have been a bedlam of snarling and howling, but the things attacked without sound and died in silent agony.

Tensing his muscles, Gord slashed around him to clear away the little apes that were pressing round to attack, took one step backward, and then sprang forward with a bound. He cleared the hedge of spikes and landed beside the girl. "Don't worry any more, Leda," he said to her over his shoulder.

Without turning toward him, the dark elf called her thanks, then added, "If you can manage to keep me safe for another minute, Gord, I'll give these little bastards something to be sorry about."

"You've got it," the young man said just as he got very busy. So many of the apes had died on the spikes that now there were pathways in many places, and he had all he could do to stem the tide. He thrust and cut in a blur of motion, seeming to be everywhere at once. Although he bled from a bitten thigh and arm, and the monsters' nails had clawed cheek and leg, Gord was not seriously hurt. He had lost count of how many of the yellow-haired white apeoids he had killed. Out of the corner of his eye, Gord saw Leda crouching down next to one of the dead apes. He wanted to ask her what she was doing, but then he heard the girl start chanting and knew that she was working some spell, so he dared not interrupt.

An apeling leaped through the air, mouth agape, fangs bared to bite off his face. Gord caught the thing with dagger and sword, the shorter blade taking the apeoid through its upper jaw, the longer one piercing its abdomen. He held the creature above his head for a moment, its blood dripping down upon him in a gory shower. Then, using all of his might, Gord hurled the corpse full into a trio of its charging fellows. Two of them were knocked down and stunned, and one was driven backward to die writhing upon the stone spikes.

"That does it, Gord. I'll be fine now — see if the others need help," Leda shouted to him. Then, in a different, deeper voice, the dark elf said, "To me, apelings! Kill any of your fellows that come near!"

Gord turned quickly to look at her. Leda was gesturing to the forms of dead baboons nearby, and the corpses were responding. Before his eyes, about a dozen of the dead apes rose up, blood-smeared, entrails spilling, to form a crescent around the girl, their backs toward her, facing their own, living kind with ready fangs. Indeed, Leda seemed able to care for herself, with some strange and grisly assistance, so Gord took advantage of the moment to go to the aid of the hard-pressed nomad warriors.

"Two can play your game!" Gord shouted to the mute creatures that had momentarily recoiled from the stone spikes and the fury of the young adventurer's blood-drenched blades. He sprang upon the bridge of dead monsters, stabbing and thrusting as he advanced, and fought to the side of the spiky area farthest from Leda. The apelings there sought to recoil from the savagery of their foe, but those behind the ones in front were not quick enough. A severed head flew; another baboon, its arm lopped off, fell writhing on the hard, blood-covered floor of the chamber. Using each weapon-stroke with murderous efficiency, whirling and darting continually, Gord chopped his way through the pack. Now the survivors were moving backward, toward the chamber door, and Gord was able to get clear and join the beleaguered nomads. Another of the men had fallen beside Nizamee, but Achulka and the one called Jahmut were still holding their own.

"Die! Die!" he shouted over and over as the young adventurer fell upon the group of things that were between him and the steppemen. Two of the yellow-maned baboons fell instantly, caught from behind as Gord assaulted them like a whirlwind.

Heartened by this, the two tribesmen still able to fight redoubled their own efforts, calling "Illa-Thuffi! Illa-Thuffi!" as they struck about them with their swords.

Gord cleared a path through the dozen or so apeoids who were clustered to attack the tribesmen. Counting those already killed by the nomads, not half of the creatures were left alive. The remainder turned suddenly in panic or fear, bounding and capering to escape from this red-smeared room and the terrible humans who were cutting them down in droves. Gord thought that some spell of Leda's might be at work, helping the panic to wash over these near-mindless little killers, but he didn't spend any time dwelling on the matter. "Cut them down!" he called to the two nomads, and then the young thief leaped after the routing troop of albino monsters, leaving red tracks wherever his blades touched their blond-maned heads or dead-white backs as the things sought to flee.

Both Al Illa-Thuffi warriors joined Gord in the work of slaying the apes as they scrambled to get clear of the chamber and back to the safety of wherever they had come from. Then, from outside the chamber, in the passage where the remainder of the pack was routing through, human voices cursed and shouted.

"Stop! and "Back! Back!" echoed in the arched corridor beyond the doorway. "Kill!" and "Obey!" could be heard as deep-voiced commands directed to the retreating monsters.

The two Thuffi warriors were busy finishing off some wounded apeoids that were thrashing about or attempting to crawl to escape. As the voices shouted their orders to the things beyond, Gord acted to delay a second inrush of the terrible little monsters. Kicking aside a carcass and cleaving one of the braver apes as it tried to re-enter the chamber, the young man grabbed the thick door with his left hand and began to swing it back toward the closed position.

A flying spear grazed his shoulder, for the light coming from inside the room made Gord a distinct target. In the next instant, the swinging door stopped and bounced back slightly, as if it had struck something. As the door rebounded, there was a thud and an audible groan from the empty air — and, amazingly, a crossbow bolt that had been heading directly for Gord abruptly stopped in mid-air. Scarcely a second later, a heavy billet of wood with protruding spikes came flying through the doorway and struck Gord's chest.

The spear wound was only a trifle, and the hurled aklys, as the spiked club was called, did little more than bruise Gord, for the mesh of elfin armor beneath his robe warded off the piercing iron hooks and points. But the metal projections of the aklys caught on the heavy cloth of Gord's burnous, and the one outside the chamber who had thrown the weapon hauled hard on the leather thong attached to the club's handle. Gord was jerked from his feet and toppled headlong toward the stone floor. Before he struck the rough granite, however, something only scarcely softer broke his fall.

Fortunately, Gord's comrades were right behind him as all this occurred. Achulka grabbed Gord's feet and hauled him out of the doorway and back into the room, just as Leda got behind the half-closed portal and shoved with all her strength against its thick planks. The door banged closed, and an instant later Leda dropped its bar down. In the interim, several more spears and a half-dozen quarrels had been discharged into the room, but none had scored a hit. More missiles could be heard thudding into the planks of the great door even as the dark elf shut it fast.

The invisible mass that had held Gord away from contact with the floor had been dragged into the chamber along with the thief. Grateful for this invisible cushion but unnerved by the whole affair at the same time, Gord hurriedly hoisted himself to his feet. The young adventurer bent down and prodded the seemingly empty air with his sword point. The weapon encountered a solid . . . something. Leda knelt beside the area and felt around, her hands moving swiftly over the unseeable thing they touched. A moment later she held a strange ring in her fingers and a very visible dead body was lying face down at her feet.

"Invisibility ring," she said to Gord and the nomads as she put the loop of dull metal into her sash. "He is a strange-looking sort," she added, gazing down at the form.

The corpse was that of a thin, pygmylike albino, a human who closely resembled the yellow-maned baboons that had attacked them. "He was slain by that little bolt," Gord observed, noticing the object that was protruding from the corpse's upper back. "The flesh is black around the shaft . . . poison?"

"Yes," Leda answered. "Are either of you wounded?" she then asked, turning to the nomads.

"Not heavily, and not from such missiles," Achulka replied, "although I fear that the apes have done for our brothers. Perhaps we were too hasty in removing the Arroden charms. . . ."

Leda interrupted. "Gord, see what you can do about blocking the door," she said. "Those beyond are sure to try to force it, magically or physically. Meanwhile, I'll see what I can do for our friends."

As Leda turned to her spell-work, Gord did what he could. First, he took the spear that had been cast into the room and jammed the point into the door so that it kept the bar held down in a locking position. Then the young adventurer began to toss the bodies of the dead baboons into a mound that further blocked the portal. By the time he had made a pile as high as his chest and was dragging the last of the lifeless creatures over to finish the task, Leda had completed her ministrations and come to his side.

"Nizamee is finished," she whispered to the young man. "Those filthy apelings did for him. The other three will be fine in a few days, even though I hadn't sufficient power to heal them fully. I knew that you'd also need some of my magic, Gord, for you are a mess of wounds. Now hold still, and I'll do what I can to cure the worst of them."

After a few seconds spent murmuring and gesturing, the dark elven girl began to touch Gord here and there, each probe on a painful area, each making him want to wince and draw away. His pride kept him motionless and silent. Then her touch seemed to grow lighter and cooler, and was no longer painful. "You're doing it, girl," he said.

"I've done it man!" she said with a tired swipe at her blood-smeared forehead.

The three nomads were on their feet and cleaning their swords. As Leda sat down on the floor next to Gord to rest, fatigue showing plainly on her lovely face, Achulka walked over to where the two were. "We will be ready to fight again in a little while, Farzeel. We owe you and your warrior-woman our lives. We will fight with you to the death for that, but . . ."

"But?" Gord said with puzzlement.

"But if we manage to live and get clear of this place," the nomad said solemnly, "we will go no farther into the Ashen Desert. Two of our brothers have fought their last because of this place, desert and ruin. We will take our chances and go back alone if need be — or with you two, if you are wise. It is not the way to repay a debt of life, Farzeel, but neither is dying uselessly a measure of manhood."

Before Gord could speak, Leda answered the warrior's pronouncement. "We are held fast within this place, Thuffi. Let us deal with the matter at hand before worrying about going north or south above. Such talk is so much wind until our enemies outside the door are dead."

Achulka smiled grimly at that, hefting his tulwar. "We will do that, dark warrior-lady. Never fear."

"We can remain bottled up in this chamber for a long time, Leda," Gord said to bring things back to the reality of the situation, "and we can die quietly in doing so. I also think that talk is foolish, and so is this hiding. Our foes can regroup and gather reinforcements if given enough time. That enables them to come at us when *they* are ready. Instead, let's prepare to attack them now, and fight the battle on our terms."

Everyone was quiet for a moment, and in the interval the clank of weapon on stone and the shuffling of feet could be heard outside the barricaded doorway. "You make good sense, Gord," Leda said. "I will do what I can, although I have little left in the way of spells. Once I am done with the priestess-craft, I will take up poor Nizamee's sword and do the best I can to fight by your sides."

The nomad warriors struck their breasts at Leda's words, a signal honor. Gord too was bolstered by what the little elven girl had said. "Be ready then, my dearest lady, to lay on with spell and weapon," he told her. "We four will clear the door and attack when you give the word."

In a couple of minutes, the four men had quietly unstacked the mound of corpses that Gord had piled up. Then all five of the comrades gathered at a spot away from the door, so they could not be overheard, and Leda explained her strategy.

"Jahmut and Gord will open the door," she said. "Do not look out right away when he pulls open the portal, for I will cast a spell there to disorient the enemy. When I shout, then you will be able to look, and the passage will be lighted. You other two, loose arrows as quickly as you can, and then all charge to the foe with your blades." Gord had no bow, but he could use the spear that had been thrown into the chamber, and he would throw that as he rushed to close quarters with the apelings and their masters who awaited outside.

Jahmut stepped to the door and put his hands on the heavy iron ring that hung stapled to the planks. Gord lifted the bar, softly, placing it firmly in its upright position and securing it with another little bar that kept it from falling and accidentally locking the portal — a precaution made by the ancient keepers of this stronghold centuries ago. The other two Thuffi warriors were crouched a few feet away behind a wall of baboon bodies, their bows ready. Gord looked at Jahmut and nodded. As the nomad pulled on the door ring, Gord jumped back to be shielded by the door jamb. Leda was prepared, too; as the heavy construction of planks came open, she uttered an incantation and cast her spell.

A chorus of shrieks and cries sounded as the light created by Leda's casting blossomed forth and made the passageway bright. There were perhaps a dozen of the white pygmies and twice as many of the yellow-maned, albino apes there, caught unprepared by the sudden assault. Leda gave a shout, and Gord stayed out of the opening as the nomad warriors sent a pair of shafts into the turmoil beyond. As soon as he heard the clatter of their discarded bows, though, he jumped into the doorway, aimed rapidly, and hurled the small spear with all his strength. Jahmut was there beside him, tulwar in hand, and the two rushed into the enemy. The pygmies and apes were still in disarray, milling about as they tried in vain to keep from being hindered by the globe of bright light that floated near the ceiling of the corridor. Their eyes, accustomed to darkness, bulged and ached as they were exposed to more illumination than they could stand.

Gord was quickly separated from Jahmut by the press of enemy bodies, but he didn't mind. He was too busy laying about with sword and dagger to notice anything but his targets. For fully two minutes he fought alone; then Leda was beside him, holding the tulwar that had belonged to Nizamee. "Beware,

Gord!" she shouted to him, pointing ahead of where they stood. "That one there is a spell-caster!"

Her warning came just in time. Gord saw that one of the pygmies was making passes in the air. As the little man called out the last of his incantation and thrust out his hands toward the young adventurer, Gord leaped up and ahead in a vaulting jump. For an instant while he was in the air, he felt as if all the muscles in his body were stiffening. But then the feeling passed as quickly as it had come, and he landed in front of the startled little dweomercraefter and wounded him before the pale midget knew what happened.

Now it was Gord's turn to be surprised. A small fighter nearby stabbed at the young thief, forcing him to dodge and parry instead of quickly finishing off the spell-worker. Simultaneously another, lesser spell-crafter finished a work of his own, and Leda's magical illumination suddenly vanished. In the confusion and darkness, the chief dweomercraefter of the pygmy warband expected to slip away from his attacker, not reckoning with Gord's exceptional visual capacity.

With his long dagger, Gord fended off the curved-bladed pole arm the fighter had thrust at him, knocking the weapon's hooked portion aside so that it struck one of the baboons that was moving to assist in the fight. As the warrior tried to clear his weapon, and the dark suddenly engulfed the combatants, Gord kept his eye on the wounded spell-binder. The little fellow turned away and ran down the corridor and around a corner to be clear of the melee. When he got a fair distance down this escape passage he turned, bent on summoning some new mischief. The pale pygmy's eyes, already huge, nearly started from his head as he saw the supposedly night-blind human figure bounding after him, dodging from side to side as he advanced with sword and dagger at the ready. Behind Gord came a small crowd of apes and pygmies, not chasing him so much as they were escaping from the swords of his companions.

"You cursed oaf!" the gray-clad midget shouted, gesturing and muttering furiously. A fat, crackling streak of violet-blue electricity issued from the little man's hands and came close to striking Gord full in the chest. The young thief threw himself to the side as the sizzling bolt was released, and the full force of it missed him, but the stroke was still close enough and strong enough to burn him and knock him flat. The lightning continued down the corridor and played among the caster's own fellows, dropping several of them in their tracks. Then it hit the wall where the passageway turned, and it came sizzling straight back along the corridor it had just traversed.

From where he lay, dazed and nauseated from the shock of the bolt's passage, Gord saw the bolt blazing back in the direction from which it had come. An instant later he heard a loud sizzling sound, immediately drowned out by a shrill scream, and the pygmy keeled over, dead from his own electrical attack. Gord managed to climb to his feet and stumble back through the passageway, stepping over the dead bodies, getting back to where Leda was swinging away furiously with a sword that was really too large for her to handle. The nomads had been blind since the moment Leda's globe of light was extinguished. She had shouted for them to stay behind her and was singlehandedly keeping off five or six of the pale little fighters and their yellow-maned baboons. When Gord began hewing them from behind, they fell like wheat before a scythe. At this point, the survivors scrambled and got away as fast as they could. The battle was over.

While the men of Thuffi regained their rushcandle from within the treasure chamber and sought for stragglers to dispose of, Gord and Leda followed the signs left by the fleeing band of underground dwellers. Only a handful had managed to escape, but they left a trail that was easy to follow, for several bore wounds that still bled. It led the two down the spiral steps to the old well room and disappeared through the hole that led to the pool beyond.

"I feared it," Leda said to Gord. "They must use this place, but from some other access point. When we bathed and made love here earlier, we were seen or heard. Those baboons probably have noses keen enough to follow scent."

"Yes and no, love," Gord replied. "You are right about our being detected, I think, but not about the apelings. They don't have noses that good — don't forget I handled a lot of dead ones, and I got a good look at them. They followed us by looking at the signs in the dust. I think those so-called baboons are nothing more than the same species as the pygmy men, degenerated perhaps, or bred to serve as hounds."

Leda didn't believe him until she too had examined several corpses after they returned to the treasure room. "Devildirt, Gord! These things *are* men!" she exclaimed with revulsion in her voice.

"Not men, actually," Gord said. "Pygmy spawn, albinoid descendants of once-humans who have probably dwelled underground for a hundred generations. It isn't surprising, though. Slavery is just a step away from deliberate breeding for desired characteristics, degenerate or otherwise. I have seen the losels that the vile Iuz breeds, too — a disgusting thing to do to human, humanoid, or ape!"

At the mention of the cambion's name, Leda's face became a mask of hatred. "I hate that gross pig!" she said. "Somewhere, somehow, one named Iuz has harmed me or someone close to me. I would kill him very slowly if I had that lump of dog dung in my hand!"

"Perhaps you would . . . if you could," Gord said laconically. "Still, I am interested to note that his name evokes such a response in you, girl. What other memories now return?"

Leda looked at him blankly. "None, other than disgust and hatred for that despicable dog. Let us speak of something else."

"Yes," interjected Achulka. "It is time for us to talk of returning to the mountains. My brothers and I have gathered all the wealth we can hope to carry, and when we are rested we will set forth. Come north with us, Farzeel and Leda-Warrior-Woman!"

"We have been over this before, Achulka," Gord said. "Leda and I have a . . . a . . . vow which must be kept. But if you wish to begin acting like old—"

"Enough, Gord!" Leda interrupted. The dark elf — and she fully looked the part of a drow now as they stood in the subterranean chamber — held Gord's arm and pressed it to gain his full attention. "These warriors of the steppes have served well in this unnatural desert. They helped us to gain this place. They helped us survive against our foes. We should show them the water we have found, and then Achulka and his brothers are entitled to take their spoils and return."

Gord gazed incredulously at the girl. "What are you saying?"

"Excuse us for a moment, friends," Leda said to the nomads, who were as stupefied as Gord was by her support of their desire to go back. She stepped outside the chamber, bringing Gord along by the arm, and spoke softly to him. "Gord, I think we can travel the rest of the way to the City Out of Mind underground! I know you see as well as I do in the lightless world, but those warriors are unable to. They are a handicap to us, so let them hazard a return alone. We two will forge on by passage beneath the dust."

"Have you lost your reason?" he asked caustically. "There is no means of traveling beneath the Ashen Desert — unless we change to ashworms, moles, or those sharklike things the Thuffi call dustdevils. Why not birds, to wind our way above the ash?"

"This is no time to jape, man!" Leda stared hard

at him, impressing her seriousness upon the stubborn human. "I have not lied to you, nor have I misled you, have I, Gord?" The query was obviously a rhetorical one, for the dark elf went on immediately, "And I do not do so now. I found a scroll amidst the treasure coffers, a piece of writing concerning tunnels which run under the dust. There it will be cool, safe from wind storms, and easy to find water. Think, Gord — instead of ten miles of plodding on dust-walkers, we can go two or three times that far each day without fear of dust mires, venomous plants or reptiles, or being cooked by the sun."

"This sounds . . . wrong," Gord rebutted. "How do we know which direction we are going — assuming that there *are* passages that lead outward from this place — and what makes you think that even if there are tunnels, they will go to the City Out of Mind?"

Leda had to admit to herself that the man had a point. "You might be right, dear one," she said. "The little information I have read mentions only that there are miles of tunnels of some sort which go from this place in many directions. Perhaps one will not serve to take us all the way to our goal. Still, going just part way below the dust is better than nothing. We can then make or find some new equipment and travel aboveground again, that much nearer our destination. As for knowing direction underground, don't you know that we drow have an innate sense of things like that?"

"I know little of your folk, Leda," Gord admitted. Then, hugging her, he said, "But if all are like you, then I wish to know much, much more!"

"Don't joke about that. I am not like the others — of that you may be certain. This little dark elf is all you need to know about drow," Leda said firmly. "Your education begins and ends with me. Now, let's be serious. I was getting very uncomfortable traveling across the ash and dust, to put it charitably. The sunlight seems to be a problem for me. Aside from all other considerations, I feel that I can not abide much more of the environment above, Gord. Whatever I was before, part-elven or who knows what, this change you have seen me going through is affecting me greatly. I think I will die before reaching the City Out of Mind if we continue on above the ground. But if you insist, I will go with you, my love, across the ashy plains and dunes of dust. Perhaps my fear is unfounded, and we will find our goal together. . . ."

"Or?"

"Or I will die, and you will find it alone. At any rate, the nomad warriors will never go on, shamed or not. If you keep on about their pledge, all you will accomplish is to make them your enemies. Let them go. We can travel by ourselves, whether in the inferno above or in the lightless realms below."

She paused for the response that both of them knew would settle the matter, one way or the other. Gord looked into her eyes, as if trying to see into the depths of her soul and beyond the present into the future. After a minute, he made the decision he knew he had to make. "We will go on . . . below," was all he said. Leda embraced him, and they held each other for a few seconds before going back inside the chamber.

All of the nomads were injured from the most recent combat, but they had cleaned and bound their wounds with skill born of long practice. Each of them had drunk as much of the contents of his waterskin as he could hold. "Show us to the water now, Farzeel, so we can fill our skins and set off!" Achulka said heartily.

"Come with me," Gord told the warriors. "I'll lead you to the pool." While they went off, Leda busied herself by rummaging through the coffers, picking up some odd items that she thought might be useful later.

By the time Gord and the nomads returned, the young thief was totally resigned to what was about to happen, and he decided to make the best of matters by being friendly and thoughtful. "Shall we lay Nizamee in one of the stone chests?" he suggested to Achulka. "I think he would appreciate resting on more wealth than most men see in a lifetime."

"Agreed, Farzeel. A hero's tomb for a brave warrior of the Thuffi!" the nomad leader said. Then, after seeing to this task, Achulka grinned and pointed to the door. "Let us all now get above to see the sun and feel the air of the real world — even that of this stinking desert!"

Leda was surprised to hear talk of this sort; apparently Gord had not yet informed the nomads of their final decision. "You go alone, warriors," she told them. "Gord and I will rest here a little time, and then set forth again for the City Out of Mind."

"You cannot mean that, warrior-woman! Is this true, Farzeel . . . ?"

"She speaks the truth, Achulka." With no further words, all five retraced their path and ascended back to the room through which they had entered the building.

"Here," said Gord as the nomads were organizing and packing their equipment and treasure. "Take our waterskins with you. Our rations, too. We will not need them, for we know places to gain both as necessary."

"I could not trust such a statement," said Achulka, "if it came from anyone but you, Farzeel. You are not bent on dying — I know this, for otherwise, you would now be lying on the floor in the cellars below us. So, you must believe the truth of what you say, and if you believe it, then I do too." He accepted the provisions, and the three nomads bowed deeply to Gord and Leda in a sign of great respect. The two of them helped transport dust-walkers, poles, and other gear up the ladder, and then they said their final farewells to Achulka and his comrades.

Gord and Leda took what little of their equipment they would need and returned, at her suggestion, to the treasure chamber below. He wanted to move out immediately, to be free of this forbidding place, but she actually seemed relaxed in the same environment. "Let me rest a bit first," she told him, "and then I will be able to heal your burns and the wounds you still have before we set out."

"You can do that so easily? Why, then, did you not tend to Achulka and his fellows?"

Her expression turned abruptly cold. "They deserted us," she said disdainfully. "Let time care for them." Gord was a bit bewildered by this sudden change in her attitude, but attributed it to the fact that she really did need to rest.

"Now, let me sleep and regain my powers," she said tersely. "I'll have to use them to see to our food and drink too, probably, so stand guard while I rest and recover."

"As you wish," the young thief replied in an equally curt manner, but if Leda noticed his tone, she chose not to react to it. By the time he had put the bar in place across the door, she was prone and well on her way to sleep. He soon forgot about her cool demeanor and had a fine time for the next few hours browsing through the great piles of treasure that remained in the stone coffers. He knew he could not take any of it with him, but for the time being, at least, it was all his. What more, he thought to himself wryly, could a thief ask?

Chapter 13

THEY HAD BEEN FOLLOWING an old passage leading away from the pool for only a few hundred yards when a pile of broken rock loomed before them — a cave-in that, at first glance, seemed to keep them from going farther. Then Leda saw a small opening in the ceiling just in front of the heap of stones and rubble. "Look, Gord," she said, pointing to the hole. "That is how the apes and pygmies come and go."

Gord scrambled swiftly up the pile of rock and hoisted himself up into the vertical passageway. It was a very snug fit, but that actually enabled him to climb better because he could exert constant pressure on the sides of the tunnel. He disappeared from Leda's sight for a couple of minutes, then came down feet first and dropped lithely back into the chamber where she stood. "There is a maze of passages above," he reported. "The hole in the ceiling seems to be an escape tunnel, Leda. Above it are what were sewers, subcellars, and who knows what else. Some of the work is newer than the rest, so the pygmies must have made them. Those places are only about four feet high, and narrow too."

"Do any of the routes go in the direction we want?" the dark elf asked.

"Yes, but only one of the little ones, and it heads upward, too."

"Then let's see if we can clear away the debris here and move onward in this tunnel."

"What makes you think we can do that, girl?

Those white midgets would have done so long ago if it was possible."

"Why would they bother if they had their own egress from the area? Just be still, and watch while I use a little trick to discover if there is a way," Leda told him.

She knelt and, using a sharp stone, scratched a strange symbol on the tunnel floor. It was composed of three swords, two pointing downward at angles and one perpendicular, point upward, to form a starlike symbol. The girl began to chant under her breath, and then from within her robe she produced a tiny bead of quicksilver. As she intoned her chant, she worked the stuff into a bit of clay she had picked up from the temple's cistern. Then she smoothed the mixture out onto a large piece of the fallen rock, sang out a strange series of syllables, and stepped back. Gord was about to ask her what she thought to accomplish with her actions of the last several minutes when Leda spoke — but she did not address him.

"Tell me, stone, what lies beyond you?"

A hollow, toneless voice, barely audible, replied, "More of the passage you stand in."

"Between it and you — how much more stone?"

"Ten times the length of your arm."

"Everywhere?"

"No."

"Where is there less?"

"Above."

"Where above?"

This question-and-answer routine went on. The very rocks would speak, it seemed, to those clerics able to employ the correct power to enable or compel them to do so. Finally the weird voice related that in the far corner near the roof of the passage, only an arm's length of fallen rock was between them and the continuing tunnel.

"But is there more loose stone above that place, which might come down if we clear away what lies there?"

A long pause. "Yes," the slab of rock finally admitted.

"What of the corner on the opposite side?"

"But little more, and above there the roof is solid," the hollow voice told her. Gord sensed a grudging tone in the sound. At this, Leda turned away; the communication was apparently ended.

"How can a stone speak?" he asked as she motioned him toward the place where they could clear a way.

"The stuff is of the plane of earth. The spell awakens an elemental who can read impressions within the rock as you or I would read a book," the dark elf explained impatiently. "Let's get on with clearing the stones away now."

Leda stood well away as Gord accomplished the work. It wasn't too difficult once he freed the first couple of chunks. The remainder were loose, and then it was only a matter of working them free and tumbling them down, first on this side, then shoving them away to fall into the passage beyond the pile. "Whew!" Gord said after about ten minutes of work as he contemplated the small space he had made. "That was heavy going, but there's a hole big enough for us to use now. Shall I give you a hand?"

"No," Leda said. "I can manage myself." She suited action to word by climbing nimbly up the heap of rocks to a place just behind him. "Go through, and I'll pass you our gear. As soon as you have it all, go on down the other side, and I'll follow."

The corridor continued for another hundred or so paces beyond the cave-in, then it divided in a rough T-shape. One branch seemed to head almost due west, so they took that one in preference to the route that veered to the east. This tunnel slanted upward, and in a short time they had moved aside a concealed stone and were gazing down on a circular pipe cut through the sandstone that prevailed here.

"It is an underground aqueduct, Gord. See there.

213

A trickle of water still flows along it."

"That seems to be what we've found, all right," he agreed. "The flow goes back toward the temple and whatever urban complex was around it. Even though this conduit leads southward, Leda, I think we should take it. Going back and heading east is certainly no better."

"Agreed. If this brought water to the town and temple, it will take us a long way. We'll have water, too, as we go."

"How in the Nine Hells could the Ancient Suloise have managed something like this? This tunnel is almost twenty feet across and, if we are correct, it must run for miles!"

Leda laughed at Gord's wonderment. "Any kingdom so powerful as to make a fertile plain into a place of arid devastation, and to get in retaliation a burying coat of dust upon them, could do something like this as easily as you and I walk along it now. Think of the powers they possessed! Had I but a trifling of those old ones' strength, I would be queen of . . . . Oh, no matter."

"Right, love. We had better save our breath for what comes, for by any calculation there are a hundred leagues and more between us and the City Out of Mind."

The next day they encountered their first slug. It was by no means a giant among its kind, only about six feet thick, and it wasn't the variety that expectorated its poisonous saliva, either. The thing was basking in the streamlet that flowed along the pipe. It had sensed their coming, however, probably by picking up vibrations borne by the water. As they came close it surged suddenly, sliding forward on its slimy track, feelers waving and a sharp-tipped tube outthrust.

Gord, in the lead at the moment, was nearly taken by the unexpected lunge made by the seemingly slow and senseless monster. Instinctively, he jumped back and batted with his left hand, the one holding his dagger, for the barbed tube was coming at that side of his body. Even though the slug's hide was tough, the keen-edged blade sliced the stabbing member cleanly off, and a jet of vile-smelling stuff shot forth as the severed tip fell away. The liquid hit Gord's leg, and the pain was so intense that he screamed reflexively. Then his nerves shut off, and he remembered no more, until . . .

"How are you now, love?"

Leda's dark and lovely face swam into view before his eyes. Then Gord recalled what had happened. "My leg is still a little tender," he answered after a little thought and a flexing of his limbs, "but otherwise that stuff it squirted on me seems to be pretty harmless — other than the searing pain it causes."

"Searing is right," Leda said with a shake of her platinum tresses. "That thing's poison seared you almost to death, and that's the truth. I had to use a spell to detoxify you, then heal you after. You've been unconscious for half a day!"

As soon as he felt strong enough, Gord pulled the dark elf to him. Despite the conditions, they found kissing and making love was as healing and restoring as any magic. "Now, my dear drow queen," he said to her, "we are even. I have saved your life, and you mine. Whatever occurs from now on is on a clean slate, as the scholars are wont to say."

When they went on, both were more alert for danger. It was a good thing, too. The farther they proceeded along the conduit line, the more dangerous were the things they encountered. A tannish agglomeration was seen, a pudding of awful sort that scavenged and hunted as well. There were several sorts of amoeboid creatures, slimy bundles or ribbons that lurked in the water or on the curved ceiling. There were more slugs of various sorts, too. Only some of these latter monsters were unavoidable, since they lurked directly in Gord's and Leda's path and, as Gord had found out the hard way, they were capable of quick, rapid movements over a short distance. They took care of all the small slugs they could not go around — but then, as they rounded a bend in the tunnel, they came upon a monstrous one that nearly filled the entire tunnel with its bulk, and it was crawling toward them.

"What do we do now?" Gord asked as they retreated from the advancing horror. "That mindless blob will probably pursue us all the way back to where we entered this tube."

Gord might be helpless in this situation, but Leda was not. "Hit it with your sling stones if you can," she said. "Try to make it stop, or at least come on more slowly. I'll go back and bring up something that even this thing will not like."

Gord waited for a few minutes while the thing moved inexorably forward. Then, when he thought the slug might be in range of his weapon, he tried his best. Unfortunately, because of the height of the tunnel, he had to send the stone on a flat trajectory, and it did not travel as far as he had wanted. It hit the creature on the bounce and did not hurt it, but evoked a glob of spittle from the slug. The shot of liquid fell short, just as his stone had, but Gord got the message. If he was able to send stones to strike the creature with any effect, the slug would be in range to retaliate with its juices, and one dose of that stuff could kill him. He loaded and spun his sling a second time, loosed one more heavy stone just for the sake of doing so, and then ran back to where Leda was standing just as she finished making a series of passes in the air.

"I love your legs in that modishly short robe you're wearing, Gord!"

"Not very funny, Leda," he snapped. His burnous had been eaten away by the first stinging slug's poison, so she had cut it off to make a tuniclike garment. "That son of a bitch is coming, you know."

"Not for long he isn't. I managed to work up what is needed. Let's watch."

The gigantic slug moved along toward them for

another minute or so. Then suddenly it stopped, its feelers waving wildly, and its bloated, grayish form began to heave and writhe. A strange piping sound came from the monster, a sound Gord had never heard from any of the slugs they had avoided or killed prior to this encounter.

"Look at that bag of slime now, dearest one. See how the visitors I have called get its attention?"

"What is happening?"

"I have summoned insects to attack that thing. Even down here there are many to answer the calling I sent forth, and arachnids will obey too, sometimes. It will take a time — we had better get back from here now. Eventually the little ones will do their work, and the bites and stings will finish the slug. The beetles and bugs will feast on that slime-coated flesh, and we will go on thereafter."

Gord shuddered at the thought. Even a ghastly thing like that deserved a cleaner death. Still, when it came down to it, it was a matter of their death or the slug's. Leda was more practical than he, no two ways about it. "You have saved us, girl," he said with calm admiration. "Nice work . . . but couldn't you have managed it some other way?"

Leda shrugged. "I don't think so, but what's the difference? The swarm of insects came to me, and the summoning has worked. We will go on, and the matter is closed. Do you really concern yourself with that slug?"

"Stupid of me, isn't it?" he replied with a tone of self-disgust. "That bastard would suck me up for lunch without thought, but it is a nasty way to die, that," he said, turning away from the thrashing thing and walking back a short distance with Leda to wait for the insects to finish their work.

After a time they proceeded forward again, stepping gingerly around the area where the bugs were still feasting on the slug's remains. "One thing is apparent now," Gord mused as they walked. "The number of life forms we have encountered lately spells it out clearly for us."

"What's that?"

"Somewhere pretty close ahead is a place where this tunnel gives way to the desert above. All these monsters and other things don't come from inside this aqueduct."

A few minutes later, Leda spoke. "You were right, Gord. There it is ahead, see?" She pointed to a wall of rock and soil about a hundred or so feet farther on up the tunnel, in front of which was a sliver of light that leaked down from the surface above. "Another barrier," she added with disgust as they approached the site.

"It would have been handy to take this tube all the way to our target, and it did seem to be heading southwest, too. Maybe there's a way past this blockage like there was before," said Gord hopefully.

A minor earthquake must have caused the collapse of the tunnel. The fall had totally blocked passage along the aqueduct, although a trickle of water issued from the broken stones and fell to the floor of the corridor. However, Gord and Leda found that they were not without alternatives. There were several dark openings in the sides and floor of the aqueduct at this point. All they needed to do was choose one of the several tunnels they could fit into.

"Now we venture into more interesting places," Leda said to the young adventurer. "This kind of thing makes me feel right at home."

"Do you remember your home, Leda?"

"No. . . . I have no personal memory of that. Still, we drow live in such conditions, I hear — don't you? What more natural, then, than to go traipsing off under an Ashen Desert?"

Gord made a wry face but began checking out the options available. Eventually he narrowed their alternatives to two. "We can try the big hole here," he said to the girl, pointing to the place a slug must have made as a means of entering the aqueduct, "or we can follow the smaller one on the side there. It goes in our general direction, but the large one seems to turn that way also. Your choice."

"Big passage, big monster. Let's give the small one a go."

It turned out to be a good decision. They had to stoop, but the hard-walled passage went almost straight southwest, if slightly upward as well. Pretty soon it intersected with the floor of a bigger hole, the trail of a much larger slug that had come this way a long time previously, judging from the decaying condition of the tunnel it had left. Neither liked the looks of the place, but they had to follow it anyway. The smaller creature had done so, evidently, for there was no sign of its continuing passage anywhere nearby.

The new passageway took them more south than west, a bit off course, but still they were making good time. There were odd growths here, some sorts of fungoid material that needed little moisture, creeping things, and occasional chitterings — bats, rats, and probably even little mice. Leda didn't turn a hair at any of it.

"Now what?" Gord asked as they arrived at another decision point. There was nothing but dust and soil directly ahead, and only three possibilities for them. A hole slanted down, and another slug burrow intersected their tunnel at a right angle.

"Down," said Leda without hesitation. "That's where water would be. We must be close to the surface by now, and it's high time we delved downward again. With luck, we'll find a maze of new passageways there."

"What if the creators of the tunnels are there, too?"

"Have your weapons ready," Leda answered dryly.

Gord sent a large, flat stone down the slope of the passage first, listening to the sound of its slide. After several seconds he heard a faint clatter; then there was silence. "Hmmm . . . . Be prepared to slow yourself after a couple of seconds, Leda. I think there's a drop at the bottom of this hole. Give me a short time, then set out behind me," he told her. Then Gord got out his dagger with his left hand and lowered himself gingerly into the opening.

Negotiating this passage wasn't as easy as he had hoped it would be. Gord found that by some perverse instinct, the slug that had formed this tunnel had decided to alter course to a more steeply slanting, nearly vertical, one after about thirty feet. It took all of his strength, pushing with forearms and knees against the sides, to slow his drop into the tube. The tunnel turned slightly toward the horizontal again for a few yards. Then, without warning, there was nothing beneath his feet.

"Hellish hoppin' toads!" The expostulation came unbidden. Fortunately, so did his frantic reaction to keep from falling. As Gord felt the solid ground disappear from beneath him, he instinctively tried to halt himself. His right hand slammed hard against the side of the tube, while his left shot out to do the same. The sharp point of his dagger pierced the hardened slime that formed the passage. It held there, nearly dislocating his arm as the solid hold it gave him jerked him to a stop.

"Whew, that was a close one," Gord muttered to himself as he rested on his elbows at the edge of the hole, feeling his lower body swinging free in space. A wind blew, ruffling his truncated robe. "I must be hanging out over the edge of a chasm!" Then he heard a shuffling, grating sound from above that terrified him. Leda was sliding down the passage after him, just as he had told her — no doubt holding her sword out, ready to run him through!

Chapter 14

SOMEWHERE ABOVE, WHERE the wind sent great clouds of dust and ash flying across the rolling wastes that had once been the Grand Empire of Suel, the struggle for life continued as it had for centuries. Wire-tentacle trees snared incautious animals, as did stinging whips, the low bushes that never grew near the predatory trees' wire-tentacles. Eight-barbs and snakeweeds fought for smaller morsels, while hungry rodents and insects feasted on the seeds and sprouts of these plants. Jumping cacti and touch-me-nots caught unwary birds and other flying things, as sliver sticks shot sprays of stuff at any warm object that passed near, so that the bits of wood would lodge in flesh, grow, and flourish. Basin plants offered the mirage of water; shower shrubs gave occasional sprinkles of the precious fluid — and deadly poison thereafter as well.

The ashworms just below the surface ingested minerals and deposited wastes upon which other things fed and grew, and of course the multitude of these worms fed insects, birds, shrews, moles, and many other creatures as well. Dust archers exchanged shots with needle-birds; spotted pit vipers and deadly ash arrows slithered through the powdery land after their own prey. Dust striders and wolf spiders of large size lurked or ran, chasing or being chased by paddle-foot lizards and long, black centipedes. When darkness fell, packs of dogs, wolves, jackals, and big-footed, long-legged foxes ran over the dust. Sometimes the lurking dustfish took one of these canines, other times their packs dined on the flesh of the high-finned denizens of this place. In many forms and at many levels of activity, life went on.

To the north, three nomads struggled across the drifts and dunes. They were still a good distance from the mountains, but soon enough they would come to the oasis they sought. Their water was running low, for a bed-of-nails plant and an incautious moment had cost them two full skins. Also, because all were still recovering from wounds, they traveled more slowly than they had on the way south. With luck, though, the three would make it.

More than a hundred leagues to their east, and totally unaware of the existence of the struggling tribesmen, a dozen souls rode across the Ashen Desert on a strange, wind-powered vehicle. Already half of the bladderlike tubes it rode upon had been destroyed by sharp rocks or strange plants. Worse still, it had encountered a dust mire, and the morass of fine powder was so vast and deadly that the craft had been forced to detour a hundred and twenty miles to go around the obstacle.

The delay, the extra days of hardship, and the very fact that such a thing could happen infuriated the captain of the dust cruiser. Obmi gave the wizard called Bolt a tongue-lashing on account of the matter, and then he ordered the chief pilot flogged for good measure. The dwarf took over from the man doing the lashing, for he wasn't hitting the offender hard enough. Obmi was a bit too zealous, though, and the victim died before the sun rose the next morning. The dwarf didn't mind, for it meant one less person to eat the scanty food and consume the dwindling water. Besides, there were two others aboard who were almost as knowledgeable as the dead pilot.

The wind-powered cruiser that bore the dwarf and his party across the powdery terrain wasn't the only strange craft plying the Ashen Desert. Another, smaller and odder still, was skimming along at a speed much higher than that of the sailed vessel. This vessel was fishlike. In fact, it not only resembled a grouper but was painted like one and had dark eyes — crystals of smoky sort that allowed anyone inside to see out, but not vice versa. The craft was fully enclosed against dust and wind storms. Perhaps three or four could fit inside it without discomfort. There was no way of knowing how many the vehicle contained as it moved over the dust.

Viewed from a distance, the fishlike thing appeared to float just about a foot above the ash and powder. Actually, about midway along the sides of this piscean vessel were revolving blades. These turning blades were made of stiff, thick leather. As the leather strips turned, their edges came into contact with the surface of the ground over which the craft floated. Puffs of dust and ash were spewed toward the tail as the vehicle's paddles revolved, one blade after the other brushing against the powdered ground. The craft moved along very quickly in this manner.

From a dead stop, the thing was slow to get under way. A walking man starting out at the same time would be a bowshot ahead of the craft two or three minutes later, for each sluggish turn of the vehicle's double wheels moved it only a few feet ahead. As the paddles turned, however, the thing gathered momentum, and after a few more minutes it moved faster than the strongest man could walk. Once under way for a fairly short time, the strange device could shoot along at the pace of a galloping horse, but such a rate of speed was dangerous. Too dangerous, in fact, for long distances across the barren, ash-coated land it sailed above. Upthrusting stone, sudden dropoffs, and other dangers were too numerous to allow it to move as fast as its occupants desired. Even though its belly was scaled with metal plates, the first few difficulties of high velocity told them that care was needed. Some of the dents and scars that the vessel bore spoke eloquently on the dangers of haste.

Still, the fish-thing moved swiftly, slowing up-slope, speeding down, traversing an average of ten miles each hour, not counting stops for rest and maintenance. It had come seven hundred miles in but four days' time, and the particularly smooth and level stretch of land it now negotiated enabled its riders to increase its velocity without undue risk. The craft was virtually flying along, and its helms-man reckoned its speed at thirty miles an hour. He was humming as he steered.

"What is that dark line on the horizon?" the co-driver queried.

"Ashstorm, perhaps," he replied.

"I think not, but we could be closing with winds ahead," the co-driver said thoughtfully.

The one steering kept his eyes on the looming color ahead. "It is unmoving, I think," he ventured. "Are there mountains shown on the ancient chart?"

"Any mountains were destroyed in the Invisible Firestorm, dolt," the driver shot back.

"There is only one way to determine what is there, then," the fellow said grimly. He jerked on a line next to his right side, and the rotation of the leather-paddled wheels increased in speed. There was a wheezing and puffing from the rear of the vessel, but both driver and co-driver ignored the sound. They didn't worry; the craft would manage the speed. Minutes later, the thing was doing forty miles per hour and still gaining velocity.

"We'll be close enough soon to see what it is. Should I slow us now?"

"Keep traveling! We must get there quickly," the co-driver snapped.

It wasn't long before the line resolved itself. The dark etching across the western horizon was a black bluff of stone. It stretched north and south as far as the eye could see. It seemed at least fifty feet high in its lowest places, higher elsewhere.

"Slow us, and turn south," the co-driver instructed, cursing all the while.

The fish-shaped vehicle eventually curved its course to follow the cliffs, bearing south and now going only as fast as a horse trotted. Nonetheless, it still ate up the ground with relentless regularity.

Chapter 15

LEDA HURTLED DOWN the shaft made by the long-dead slug. The tube resembled a J, the upper portion tilted about thirty degrees from the vertical and the hook truncated so as to have about half missing. Although she hardly cared about it as she descended, the portion that was gone might have been sheared off by the same cataclysm that created the great chasm into which the J-shaped passage led. As she reached the spot where the tube curved back toward the horizontal, Leda's precipitous descent was slowed slightly, and for this she was glad. The dark elf had no idea that in the next second or two she would be catapulted from the tube into empty space, with the next solid ground to be encountered lying hundreds of feet below.

Gord feared that Leda was sliding toward certain death. He also feared that unless he did something fast, Leda would carry him with her, and both would plunge to become gory smears somewhere far below the place he precariously held onto.

As the sound of Leda's too-rapid slide down the tube came nearer to him, Gord reacted with speed and daring. With a heave, he jerked himself back up into the end of the tunnel, pulling his dagger free from the wall as he did so. In the same action, with the momentum of his surge to propel him, Gord shoved himself upward so that his back was pressed against the curving roof of the pipelike passage. By looking down and backward between his legs, he would be able to get a glimpse of Leda's form an instant before she slid past him. Just as a dark blur of motion came shooting beneath him, he acted.

In the same motion, Gord plunged his dagger into the tunnel wall above his head and dropped his lower body down from the ceiling, his legs closing from the full diameter of the tunnel to a clamping position similar to that which would be used to stay on the back of a wild horse. The magically keen point of the dagger was imbedded in the tunnel, and both of Gord's hands were wrapped around the hilt in a death-grip. His legs struck something soft as they scissored together. There was a muffled scream, a terrible pull that made his straining muscles shriek, and then he felt a pair of arms clamped around his locked legs. Gord was again hanging part way out of the passage; he could feel the sharp edge at the lip of the tube cutting into his shins.

"Don't let go," Leda's quavering voice called faintly. Fortunately, she had not been holding her sword when she came sliding down, or Gord's legs would have been severely sliced.

"I'm not," he replied through clenched teeth, "but you'd better pull yourself up here in a hurry!"

"I . . . I . . . can't. I don't dare let go of your legs. There's nothing below me!"

"Great," he groaned. "Just hold on, then. I'll try to pull us both up." The young thief was strong enough to manage that, but as he started to draw himself upward toward the imbedded blade, Leda screamed and Gord felt the dagger move slightly.

"Stop, Gord! When you do that, my lower back pushes against the wall and it forces my grip loose."

"Forget it, girl," Gord told her. "I won't try it again, because the dagger that's holding up both of us is loosened when I try that."

"Then what will we do? I can't hold on like this forever!"

His feet were touching, but not securely locked together, behind Leda's upper back. She held onto

227

his legs awkwardly as she attempted to secure herself by grasping as high as she could. "Move your hands to just behind my knees, Leda. Lock them there." He felt her shift and then comply. After the girl had done this, Gord pulled himself toward the dagger, then slid back and repeated the process twice more.

"What are you doing?" The query from below was both frightened and angry.

"Hold tight!" Gord growled through a grimace. He hauled himself ahead once more, pushed his elbows against the tunnel wall as firmly as he could, and levered the buried blade up with wrists and forearms. It jerked free suddenly, and Gord was immediately pulled toward the sheer drop below.

"E...e...e...k!" The cry of horror came in a long, shrill scream as Leda felt them both beginning to slide and head for certain destruction.

But Gord had a plan, and his catlike reflexes made it work. At the point where his waist passed the rim of the tube, he raised the dagger and drove it downward again. It struck home as before, this time on the very edge of the opening. Gord hung at arm's length now, with Leda dangling below and moaning in abject terror. There was true method to his seeming madness, however.

"Stop that!" Gord said. "Fear saps strength. You have nothing to worry about now. I'll have us out of this mess in a second." He flexed his leg muscles, both to make certain that they gripped the dark elf securely and to reassure her that she was in good hands, so to speak. Holding firmly to the dagger with his left hand, Gord released his right from its iron grip and felt around the lip of the passage. His exploring fingers found what they sought — a crack deep enough to use as a hold. He pulled himself up a few inches, using the right hand to do so, then he released his left from the dagger hilt and held it down toward Leda..

"Grab my wrist!" he ordered her as he felt her

upstretched fingers groping against the back of his left hand. She complied readily, and her right hand grabbed his left wrist with a viselike grasp born of fear. "Now hold tight. I'm going to release my legs, but I'm holding your wrist, just as you have mine." he explained slowly and carefully to her. "I'll find a toehold once my legs are free, and then I'll draw you up. . . . Now!"

The sudden tug of Leda's full weight on his arm nearly made him lose his handhold, but the fingers of his right hand retained their position. He braced his right foot against the wall to keep his body from swaying while moving his left foot here and there, seeking any hold he could find. For a few seconds it seemed to him that the clifflike wall must be as smooth as glass, but then his toes found a little ledge. After carefully raising his foot and setting the sole of his boot on the outcropping, Gord placed weight upon that foot. This helped relieve the tension on his right arm a bit, allowing the muscles to relax just a little so that blood would flow more freely and lend strength to that member.

"Up now!" he cried to Leda, digging his fingers into the crack again and pushing down on his left leg for leverage as he hauled upward with his left arm.

As the girl's slim body was pulled upward, the strain shifted from Gord's arms to the foothold. If the little ledge of limestone crumbled, or his boot slipped, they would both be lost. Gord prayed silently. Then Leda managed to grab his belt, and using this new grip the girl pulled herself up to a position beside Gord. The young man's left hand guided Leda's own left to the handle of the imbedded dagger. "Let go of my wrist now, girl, and grab the pommel of the dagger — it's buried fast in the stone and will hold your weight easily."

Leda did as he said. "I have it!" she exclaimed in joy. Then she freed her right hand, and using both arms pulled herself up and over the lip, back into the tube above.

In a second Gord had hold of the dagger again, pulled himself up, and then he and the elf were wedged into the tube side by side, the cramped conditions actually giving both a sense of safety and security for the moment.

"How do we get back up the tunnel?"

Gord paused to think before answering Leda's question. "I am not sure we do," he said.

"Have you a flying carpet now?" She sounded exhausted and cross.

"No, but there might be some means of getting down that both of us can manage. That monstrous cavern, or whatever it is, seems to head off toward the southwest — just the direction for us."

"You go ahead if you like. I'm going to climb back up the way we came," Leda said acidly. The dark elf turned and began to wiggle away.

Gord remained where he was, waiting to see if she really meant what she said. But before she had gone twenty feet back along the passage, Leda froze in her tracks, and Gord heard the same sound that stopped her — a sort of slurping, snuffling noise. He had no idea what made such a sound, but decided he didn't care to find out just now anyway. As Leda began making her way carefully back toward Gord, the young thief eased himself over to the place where the tube opened onto the chasm and peered down and around. Five or so feet to his right and about ten feet down, a ledge ran along the face of the rock for as far as he could see. That looked like a usable route, and Gord could use his acrobatic skill to gain the place with no difficulty. But Leda would find it impossible to get to the ledge without his help.

"Don't lose your dweomer now," he muttered to his dagger as he began chipping away at the limestone just beneath the edge of the hole. By doing this, he turned a small toehold into a sort of step — at least in his climber-experienced eyes. Then, farther down and to the side of the passage he leaned out of, the magical blade went to work again, cutting the soft stone to provide another holding place.

By now Leda was back, and she was terrified again. "What are we going to do?" she moaned.

Instead of answering her, the young man redoubled his efforts. Then he moved away from Leda, swinging out to the step he had carved beyond the opening and working with one outstretched hand to hew another hold farther toward the ledge.

"Don't climb away without me," Leda pleaded.

"I'm not, and don't worry. Come to the mouth of the tube and climb out quick, or that thing coming behind you will have you for dinner." As Leda cautiously looked out, Gord showed her where the places for her hands and feet were. She was reluctant at first, but then a squishy, plopping sound from close behind her propelled Leda down and out onto the first step in a flash. "Just follow me, keep three holds at all times, and don't move too quickly," Gord said, making it all sound much easier than it was for her.

A rubbery appendage came snaking out of the hole Leda had just vacated. It paused, quivered for a moment, then quested in her direction uncertainly. With no hesitation, she moved to the next position, her head now about five feet below the mouth of the tube. Gord was working on gouging out another pair of holds. The protruding member lengthened, and was only a foot from Leda's body now.

"Gord, do something! It's going to grab me in a second!"

Gord moved to his right and let himself drop to the ledge below. By using the stone, he slowed his fall easily, and what shock there was to the drop he absorbed with flexed legs. As he turned to face the girl, Leda saw that she could move sideways a couple of feet to where he had been but a moment before and did so. The tentacle lengthened too, nearly reaching her with its searching tip. Then it did touch her, and with an involuntary cry, Leda jerked away from it, lost her hold, and fell — about two feet down into Gord's waiting arms.

"Let's move along," he suggested to her as he put her down on the two-foot-wide shelf of limestone. "Who knows what that thing can do?" With that, Gord began walking casually along the ledge. Leda followed, facing inward and doing a rapid side shuffle to keep up. After about two hundred feet there was a gap of six or seven feet before the shelf resumed on the other side, a bit lower than the elevation they presently occupied. Some fall from above had apparently carried part of the ledge away.

"That thing is still after us," Leda hissed.

"No time to waste," Gord observed. An amorphous glob with several waving stalks that pointed in their direction was oozing its way methodically along the ledge about fifty feet behind them. A little work, and Gord had a single handhold about two feet out along the sheer surface. Grabbing that with his left hand, the young adventurer swung his body like a pendulum, arcing over to the far portion of the ledge and landing nimbly on his feet.

"Leda, go back a couple of steps, run, and jump. I'll be here to catch you." The monster was now only about ten feet away from her, so the dark elf nodded and immediately did just that.

"Now move on past me," Gord continued. "Let's see if that lump of dung can follow us across that space." Leda went forward a few steps and then turned to watch what he was doing. Gord stayed at the edge of their new pathway, watching the blob. One of its tentacle-pseudopods waved out toward him, as the mass of the monster hesitated where the ledge ended. Gord moved away from it a bit. The member snaked around, then down. It contacted the new ledge and appeared to fasten itself there. Then it began to thicken, and the blob on the far side seemed to dwindle at the same time. "I'll be damned!" Gord said in wonder and disgust.

"Do something!"

Even as Leda urged him on, Gord was drawing his short sword. "That I am, girl!" he muttered. With an oath, Gord struck downward, hitting the black band of stuff just in front of the arriving swell. The blade sliced keenly, and a rush of vile, dark stuff washed over the steel. There was a keening sound, and in the next instant the mess fell from sight. Then Gord heard a faint sizzling sound coming from his weapon, and as he looked down he could barely believe his eyes — the ichor of the monster was dissolving the metal of his sword!

"Now I'm screwed!"

"There are other swords, love," Leda said and squeezed his arm. "We are safe now, and alive. That, not your sword, is what matters."

"Until it comes time to fight again," Gord retorted. There was nothing to do about it, though. He finally dropped the hilt and scabbard down after the dead horror, shrugged, and resumed his position in the lead along the narrow walkway of stone. "At least I retain my trusty dag," he finally said.

"Of course, Gord, and I still have my sword. Let us be bold!"

He didn't feel very bold just now, but at least the dark elf was now recovered from her fright at the near plunge into the abyssal subterranean rift they'd chanced upon. Let her handle the next problem with her spells and her weapon. Right now, Gord simply wanted to get out of this underworld and see the sun again — even if it meant plodding through the Ashen Desert once more.

The ledge slanted downward and grew broken, much as if the natural forces that created the place desired long, sloping steps, and it also broadened. So, it was actually very easy to travel along, as long as they didn't encounter a wide stretch where it was missing altogether. Eventually the ledge came to within ten feet of the floor of the rift, and they were able to jump down. They moved into the middle of the cavern to investigate it. The ceiling was higher than they could see, and the place had to be nearly three hundred yards from side to side.

"There is no dust or ash in this place," Gord said wonderingly.

"Some great magic still lingers over this rift, Gord. I thought so when we first encountered the place, for so strange a gap underground does not exist without powerful spells protecting it."

They went back to where they had descended from the ledge and began to follow it again, now heading gradually upward. The place they were traveling in narrowed in all dimensions, until finally the ledge became an actual floor and the cavern had tapered down to the size of a large tunnel. "We have gone for miles now, sloping up all the while," Gord observed some time later. "We should be amidst the powdery waste of the desert by now, Leda, and still we are underground. This wide ledge seems almost as if it were a roadway, too. What do you think?"

"That we should rest a moment," she said. As they both reclined on the ledge, Leda started to speak a legitimate answer to his question. "I am familiar with subterranean living. It is apparent to me that this area was fashioned by someone's hand — probably those who commanded the lost Suel empire. Perhaps that vast place we visited earlier was meant to shelter them until they managed to recover from the Invisible Firestorm and restore their lands." She paused and was lost in thought for several minutes. "I *feel* somehow that there is a city back there. Empty, deserted. A place never really used as its builders conceived it would be."

"What makes you think that?"

"Just a sensing of things, I guess. Consider those albino pygmies, too, Gord. I think that those are the descendants of the masters of the Great Empire of Suel, their degenerate aristocracy. And the apes are the less fortunate survivors of that unhappy race."

Gord had propped himself up on one elbow and

stared hard at Leda as she spoke. She was a drow, but regardless of that, had he ever seen a more beautiful girl — no, woman? Even though he used only half of his mind to ponder the thought, Gord knew the answer quickly. Leda was certainly the most lovely female he could think of. . . .

"Gord, are you listening?"

"Oh, yes. You seem to be thinking and remembering a lot, Leda. Do you recall who you are now?"

Now it was her turn to stare at Gord. He was looking at her with an open, assessing gaze, and when Leda smiled a little smile, he returned it with interest. Leda answered as truthfully as she could. "I know who I am *not*, Gord. I know what I am, when I came to be, and what I must do."

"That is confusing as hell, woman."

Ignoring his use of the human appellation, Leda sat up and said urgently, "I do not want to confuse you. I need to tell you and have you accept me. Will you, Gord? Can I count on you?"

Making a wry face, the young man sat up too. "All of this deep, dark mystery — tut! *I* don't know who I am, really, you know, Leda, for I was orphaned . . . no matter. Go ahead and say your say. You and I are closer than any, so how can you doubt me?"

"We shall see. I was born only months ago. That's right, *months!* I am a clone — a special one, somehow nurtured to develop fully in a very short time, and one given something a clone is not supposed to have. . . . Gord, I am the duplicate of the most evil and degenerate drow ever — the one who calls herself Eclavdra Eilserv."

"Never heard of her," Gord told Leda with a grin. "And somehow you don't fit the description of your twin — or should I say parent? — either. Aren't ones grown from the flesh of another supposed to be exact replicas? But you are by no means evil and degenerate, as you put it."

Leda breathed a sigh of relief. Despite his seeming to argue over this last point, she could tell that he believed her. She moved over and gave him a hug. "Thank you, dearest! I was afraid you'd think me a liar, demented, or hate me!"

"Only if there is reason to," Gord replied. Then he hugged her in return, saying, "Go on. I can tell you have more to say."

"You see, I have two sets of memories. There are mine, and they really begin with the night you rescued me, love. Then there are *her* memories. That is a cesspool! Eclavdra's experiences are so vile and full of evil that I keep them locked away. If I could only burn them from my mind! Well, never can that be done, I suppose, so I will tell you a little. You know about me, for what I am we have shared. Now I will tell you about *her*.

"Eclavdra is the handmaiden of the great lord of demons — the one as jet-black as I, and bearing six digits on hand and foot. His name I will not speak; do you know the one I refer to?"

Gord nodded slowly. "I have had some cause to study demonology in my time, Leda. I have fought and slain one or two of the lesser sort, and I know a little of those great ones who lord it over the Abyss. The one you speak of has a name known to me."

"She is his high priestess, and I too must open a channel to his place to draw power for certain of my spells, Gord. But Eclavdra is his *willing* slave, and I am no part of that! It is only that I am attuned to her. We have the same vibrations in many ways — but I, Leda, repudiate the link!

"For two centuries she dwelled in the Vault, that home of the drow deep under the ground. Eclavdra sought power, desiring to rule the Great Cavern of the Drow and all who dwelled therein. When her plans were thwarted, Eclavdra deserted her clan and sought power elsewhere. The demon lord I referred to — he accepted Eclavdra. Then did she come home with fury, bringing a horde of that demon's own retainers to ruin her enemies. There was a civil war, Eclavdra's side triumphed, and now the Eilserv clan and its supporters rule all drow.

"Once exposed to what was beyond the deep world, however, Eclavdra was dissatisfied with being queen. At least, that's how I read the memories which fester in my mind when I can bring myself to examine them. Perhaps it was more a matter of having to serve him, that great demon, elsewhere. It is not a matter of concern. She now desires to rule far more than a few thousand dark elves who live in the subterranean realm. Thus, she deals with all manner of demon lords and evil ones. . . ."

At this pause, Gord had to ask, "And where is this Eclavdra now?"

Leda shrugged. "I am supposed to be her, a duplicate who knows the whereabouts of my 'parent' and hates that original. I should desire that one's death, so that I can become the only Eclavdra. But I do not know her mind fully, and I do not wish to become Eclavdra. I *will* slay her, for kill her I must, but only to rid Oerth of one so vile!"

"What are you saying, Leda? Please don't allow your emotions to muddle your thinking," he said earnestly. "I need to know clearly what is going on if I am to help you."

"You're right. Let me calm myself a moment," and so saying, Leda visibly relaxed and gathered her composure. "Because I have been given, or somehow developed, a separate and unique identity, a persona my own and apart from Eclavdra, I do not know her exact whereabouts. Perhaps she is near here. I somehow sense she is, but that could be nothing more than a desire that she be, so I can confront and exterminate her. Eclavdra allowed my creation so that I would be a target, a decoy to be slain while she went unhindered to her goal."

Gord prompted her again. "What goal?"

"What you seek, she is also after. There is a contest, Gord. Two demonic factions struggle for possession of the . . . Final Key. I name it, for you are knowledgeable. The gross turd Iuz, the one who

rules from Dorakaa, and now Molag too, and his unnatural mother as well, meddle in the game. They
would be kingmakers, perhaps. I suspect that the
two would possess the key themselves. I know that
I am here to stop them all from succeeding!"

"My mission too, Leda, and one which I accepted
freely. But why must you do this?"

"Eclavdra would consign the multiverse to thrall-
dom to further her own ambitions. If she lives, let
alone gains the Final Key, there will be terrible con-
sequences. That is why I am so glad I found you,
dear one, and you are with me. If there is no other
choice, Gord, I must exchange my life for that of
Eclavdra. I will die to see that she is expunged. If
that must occur, then you will be there to take the
last portion of the artifact to wherever you must."

"So two great demons contest for the Final Key,
do they?" Gord said, reflecting on the words Leda
had spoken. "Eclavdra on behalf of the one, but who
for the other?"

"The dwarf," Leda said with hatred plain on her
beautiful face. "Obmi."

"Aaah, *him* I am familiar with. There is a score to
settle between us," he said, patting the place where
his sword used to hang. "Blast! That filthy dungheap
to fight, and me with no sword!"

Leda was practical. "If we find none to replace
your loss before you must confront the dwarf, I shall
give you my scimitar — a poor substitute for your
own blade, I know, but better than nothing. We both
have handicaps, Gord, but we also have a great
advantage."

"Namely?"

"Eclavdra and Obmi came bent on taking the
Final Key each for themselves. Both are demon-
serving filth, but they will oppose and hinder each
other while we work as a team, you and I. Eclavdra
fights against three, and so does Obmi, but we have
but two foes, do you see?"

"Oh, yes, I understand that well enough, Leda.

You are apt in your reasoning, but you overlook a major factor. Who else will accompany those two?"

The dark elf frowned. "Let me think . . . . So, you are right," she said after a bit. "Eclavdra's memories contain a plan which includes many retainers, a half-dozen at least, able and well-equipped so as to counter whatever force Obmi brings in support of his effort."

"Will these factions slay each other?"

"The contest allows for such, but they would fight us first, I fear. I guess I was too quick to think us victors, too overconfident," she said ruefully, looking at Gord with a downcast air.

The young thief cocked his head, considering the matter. "Yes and no. With that intelligence, Leda, we are better prepared for the enemies we must face, so we have an advantage — surprise. They have no such information. True, the drow might have an inkling of your presence, girl, but not so with Obmi. Neither foe will know of me — unless I choose to reveal that fact. Now, let us plan, for to be prepared is to hold a host of weapons . . . and speaking of which, we must also attempt to find me some suitable blade. That dwarf is a doughty fighter, and his hammer is to be respected."

They conferred for a time, and then Leda used magic to bring them food and drink. Rested and refreshed, the two continued on, discussing their plans as they went. After a time Leda suggested that they were ascending a passage that must make its way up some high plateau in the heart of the Ashen Desert, for she concurred with Gord's earlier assessment. Were they not so doing, they would certainly be amid the wastes by now, for their pathway still climbed gradually upward. All mountains, even the high hills, of the ruined empire had been eaten away and brought down by the devastation that was brought upon Suel. Nubs and mounds only remained. Yet a great plateau might have, must have, withstood the colorless fire that devoured the rest.

"That's it, Leda!" Gord exclaimed suddenly. "Think of a river which began on a plateau, flowed there and grew, then plunged down to the land below, cutting a deep bed and feeding some great lake. That is what the rift, and this way, bring to mind."

The dark elf thought a moment. "You might be right, for with great magic and many workers, the thing could be done by such ones as once ruled these lands. Would not their chief city, their grand capital, be situated on such a river as you envision?"

"If they had any inkling of what might befall them, Leda, they would utilize the natural advantages to make their secret hideaway too. The destruction would end the flow of water, but a remainder would continue deep underground — a supply for the survivors to use for generations, if not forever."

"Then this passage — actually an old riverbed, it seems — should eventually bring us to the City Out of Mind itself, Gord."

There was doubt on the young man's face as he replied, "We will travel another hundred and more miles, all of it underground? This seems too far-fetched."

At that Leda laughed. "You are a surface-dweller, dear Gord, and not steeped in the darkness which exists beneath the world where sun and moons shed their rays. A hundred miles? That is no distance at all! There are tens of hundreds of miles of passageways in the subterranean realms, my dearest one. Be assured, this is certainly the route for safety and survival that the lords of the lost empire laid down for themselves an eon ago."

Leda's words were indeed prophetic.

Chapter 16

A SOUND BEHIND THEM made them start. After a minute it was clear that a large body of things, whatever they were, was approaching from down the tunnel, and there was no place for Gord or Leda to go. They were in semi-secluded positions about a hundred feet in front of a guarded entranceway, a crude wall and two square towers of stone manned by a group of albino pygmies. They had spent a few minutes standing here, pondering what to do next. Now their choices were much more limited, since they could not retreat.

"I can climb and conceal myself, I think, Leda. First we must think of some way for you to hide."

"Help me up there," she replied, indicating a ledge about nine or ten feet above their heads. "And don't worry — see?" As she said that, Leda disappeared for an instant, then flashed back into Gord's view again.

"The ring you took!"

"Yes, from that spell-caster you flattened with the door. It fits on my little finger perfectly. Now, boost me up."

Gord made a stirrup with his interlocked fingers, and the dark elf stepped into the proffered palms. The young adventurer then lifted her to where she could grab a jutting bit of stone, placed her feet on his shoulders, and with that Leda was able to get up to the ledge. Gord saw her step into a recess there, and then she was gone from sight.

It was no challenge for him to scale the wall of the passage. The sandstone had so many projections and indentations in it that climbing it was almost as easy for him as walking up a flight of steps. Gord clambered up as far as he could without being upside down, then moved sideways until he found a place where he could squeeze between two slabs of rock. Shielded from even infravisual sight, he could still peek and see what happened, who passed, and what passed when they arrived at the blocking position ahead.

He had hidden himself just in time. A score of the mute, blond-maned baboon-things came loping along the passageway, traveling on all fours most of the time. Now and then one or two would stand upright and peer around, then resume their shambling progress. Behind them came as many of the white, midgetlike men, a half-dozen in front, ten flanking, and four at the rear, behind a double file of humans who were bent and groaning under incredible burdens. These bearers were blind in the darkness and moved with a shuffling gait to avoid stumbling. All were men, and some looked fit and hale still — but only a few. Most looked very bad off in Gord's estimation, and the way they staggered and groaned reinforced his opinion. He figured that more than half of them would never again serve as beasts of burden after this ordeal. Gord wondered if their pygmy masters would simply allow them to die or kill them out of hand. Cannibalism was likely, he suspected, with fiends such as those albino creatures were.

With sharp prodding and cruel titters, the line of pygmies and their enslaved bearers went past, never realizing that they were observed by the dark elf and Gord. When they came near the wall and its pair of towers, the pale little creatures there made hand signals, to which the leader of the train replied in kind.

Then two of the pygmies actually spoke to each

other, but even Gord's acute hearing was unable to pick up their conversation. As they spoke, the rest of the albinos kicked and prodded the slaves into motion, and the procession filed through the gap between the blocky towers that guarded whatever lay beyond.

He was almost fifty feet away from where he assumed Leda to be, but it took only a brief time for Gord to slip out of his hiding place and sidestep over and down to the spot where Leda waited. As Gord descended onto the ledge, the dark elf appeared, in the act of coming forth from the niche in which she stood. "Could you see what transpired?" Gord asked her.

"No, the slaves blocked my line of sight. What happened?"

"The chief of the group made some sort of sign-talk with the captain of the guards, and then they spoke together. I don't know what was said, but the whole band marched in while they talked. What are we to do now?"

"Can you scale the wall beside the guard towers and remain unseen?" Leda asked.

"That, dear girl, is a good question. The wall is nothing, but I am not sure about how alert those little white bastards are. If they are on their guard, I doubt they could fail but to notice my activity."

"But if there was a distraction?"

"Then it should be no problem. I can be up and on the other side the moment that the sentries are occupied elsewhere."

Leda smiled at him. "That's what I hoped you'd say. I can move very quietly myself, Gord, and with the ring I can remain unseen, too. I will sneak up to the guards. When I am near or inside the gateway, I'll find something to do to cause a commotion, and that will be your cue. Watch the guards, and when they look elsewhere, or go away, make your move. Get away from the wall quickly, and I'll wait a bow-shot along the path for you."

Gord helped Leda down to the floor of the tunnel, whereupon she became invisible again and went off to do her work. He crept up along the side of the tunnel until reaching the juncture where wall met cavern side. The matter was almost laughable, for the stones that were piled up to ward the passage were so badly fitted that a child could have scaled the twenty feet to the top without danger of falling. There was an ample number of sentries in the area, though, and most of them bore small arbalests of odd design. Recalling what happened to the former owner of the invisibility ring when he was struck by one of the envenomed bolts these crossbows shot, the young man was especially glad that the attention of the guards would be elsewhere when he topped their barrier.

Without making his presence known, Gord kept careful watch on the sentries. Several minutes went by, and still the guards seemed undistracted. Then the one nearest Gord, some thirty feet away on top of the wall, started to gesture violently, evidently replying to some fellow of his located closer to the towers. The first albino then let his weapon drop to his side and jogged toward the towers himself.

Now that there was no one within at least forty or fifty feet, Gord took the opportunity to climb up and over the barrier, which he accomplished in a matter of a few heartbeats. Once atop the parapet, the young thief simply crept across to the far edge, hung from the dropoff by his fingertips, and lightly dropped the fifteen feet to the rock floor beyond, collapsing into a ball and rolling away from the wall as he landed.

The passage on this side of the wall was much the same as on the other side. Why then, Gord wondered, the outpost and guards? But then he noticed the slant of the corridor. It climbed fairly steeply, rising about one foot for every forty or fifty of its length. He assumed that the higher they got, the greater their chances of encountering some sort of actual civilization. From that reasoning, something certainly lay close ahead.

"Pssst! Gord!"

Leda blinked into view at his side as she said that, and despite himself Gord jumped. He had a vague feeling that she was nearby even before she took off the ring, but her sudden materialization disconcerted the young man still. "Don't *do* that!" he said reflexively.

"Do what?" she responded coyly.

"Never mind. . . . How did you manage to distract the guards?"

"Simple, really. I stole up close to the opening between the towers and started tossing small rocks up in the air so that they would hit on top of the structures. No one could see where they were coming from, of course, so the guards all assumed that a small landslide or cave-in was taking place. As the word went down the line, they all ran for safety inside the towers. They probably cower there still, waiting for a rain of rocks that will not come. As for me, I simply strolled through the opening while they were all babbling at each other, and here I am," she finished with a smug smile.

Gord was silently amused at the mental picture she had given him, but still piqued at the way she had startled him, so he maintained a businesslike air. "Did the guards say anything useful? Do you have any idea where we are?" he asked.

"No," Leda replied. "But from the appearance of things, we must be near the City Out of Mind — or whatever these little runts call it nowadays. That, and the fact that we have to be really careful now, is about the sum of my knowledge."

Gord grunted noncommittally. He pointed up the passage. "Let's get going and see what we can see. I do take heed of your cautionary words, though, girl. Be prepared to act swiftly."

"I have the ring, love, but what will you do?"

"Whatever the situation demands. I can be rather

resourceful myself, you know," he replied with a grin as they set forth at a brisk pace.

No more than a quarter of a mile farther on, they discovered the reason for the guard post. They reached a place where the already large riverbed-tunnel they were in abruptly widened and gave onto an enormous chamber. They looked up and out at a sight that was truly amazing. If this was not the City Out of Mind, thought Gord, then there must be a second place beneath the dust that was even more deeply hidden — because this certainly was a city.

The broad way on the lowest level directly ahead of them was spotted with foot traffic — albino pygmies in small groups, some of them herding even smaller groups of human slaves. On either side of the roadway, stairs and ramps led off and headed up to another level containing an even busier thorough-fare fifty feet above their heads. On the topmost level, Gord could see low buildings of strange, ancient design, their upper storeys serving to support a solid roof of stone that spanned the whole complex as far as he could see.

The whole place was practically devoid of the sort of illumination that Gord considered natural. A sprinkling of oval globes gave off a dim, unwavering, luminescent red light. These bulbous shapes were spaced at great distances, each held several feet above floor level by a stone receptacle. Their glow did not affect Gord's night-vision; despite the illumination they provided, he could use his special eyesight to see a considerable distance into the near-darkness that pervaded virtually every corner within this odd, subterranean city.

"I believe that the roof overhead is domed," Leda said as she took in the sight of the place. "That would be the way we drow would handle things, were we setting about preserving a city from something raining down from above."

Gord observed the space above where they stood at the moment. The ceiling of stone slabs was at least a hundred feet above their heads. "Do you think they created a dome of rock over the whole city?" he asked her.

Leda shook her head. "No, not over the whole place. My guess is that there is a hemisphere which encompasses the heart of the place only, and that we have arrived by a seldom-used side passage at a place near the perimeter of that dome."

A distinct problem faced the two. They had to get around, but the City Out of Mind was a place where only the albino pygmies could come and go freely. Humans were there, but they were slaves and were overseen by their pale little masters at all times. Activity seemed to be slowing, however, and the number of folk on the streets was thinning.

Gord made a suggestion, and Leda was quick to agree. The thief slipped into the deepest shadows at the place where the riverbed splayed out into the chamber; then he moved ahead with Leda following him invisibly.

Gord crept along slowly, allowing time for the cessation of activity on the level above them to match that which had taken place in the lower thoroughfare. Selecting a narrow stair, Gord ascended deliberately, his boots making no sound. The dark elf followed just as noiselessly.

There were a few of the little men still abroad when Gord and Leda reached the next higher level, but they were moving purposefully toward various places. Within another couple of minutes, they had all entered one building or another, and none of the pygmies were coming out. Then Leda became visible and whispered, "I hear a faint, high-pitched note. I think it calls those small ones in."

"I can hear naught," Gord replied, "but whatever the cause, we must take advantage of the situation while it lasts." He looked around hastily, noted what appeared to be a disused structure, and then pointed toward the arched roof overhead. "Let us go into that place and climb to its upper storey. See

247

those flying bridges?"

"I had thought them supports for the roof, Gord. Perhaps they are, but I now see that there are piercings in the stone too — windows! They must be upper walkways."

The young adventurer nodded. "This place was once thronged with people, I'd say, especially if all the citizens of the City Out of Mind dwelled here at first."

"They and more," Leda suggested as they entered the building Gord had selected.

It had no door, and the entrance was sized for humans. Whatever it had been before, the place was now a warehouse — perhaps abandoned even, for the crates and bales piled inside appeared very old and as though they had been untouched for years. They briefly scanned the contents of the room, but took nothing away except for a couple of lengths of rope that Gord thought might come in handy. After a search, they found a hatch in the ceiling leading to the next floor, and from there another one to the floor above. Because the building had high ceilings, the third storey of the place gave access to the roof-hugging walkways. Both looked out of the unglazed windows to see what was going on below. A few of the little white denizens of the strange community prowled about now, but most of the streets and alleys were empty.

"I hope you are right, Leda."

"How so, love?"

"You said before that we were likely to be within the central portion of the city — or what the ancient ones had managed to save of their capital. We must search this subterranean metropolis for the hiding place of the Final Key. It will be near the heart of it all."

The dark elf looked at him searchingly. "What makes you think that, Gord?"

"The one who instructed me told me that. I have no reason to doubt his wisdom or knowledge."

"I thought only we drow had such intelligence about the location of the last part," she added by way of explanation when she saw Gord looking at her with a strange expression.

"We *drow*? I thought you disclaimed the race, but you use that word more and more of late."

"What Eclavdra knew, I too know, though I like not to examine such memories," Leda told him seriously. "At any rate, tell more of what you know. Does the Final Key lie in plain sight?"

Gord nodded. "I am told it is plainly visible, the central object of worship in the great temple here. I am also informed that despite being in plain view, the Theorpart can neither be touched nor moved."

"Yes, so too my knowledge. In addition, I believe that it is set within the center of a huge sphere of some unbreakable stuff which is as transparent as water, yet hard as diamond."

Not wishing to be outdone by the dark elf, Gord added the rest of what he had been told. "The folk here hold it as their sole remaining treasure, their link to their lost greatness and empire. Their evil teachings state that one day the artifact will restore them to their former condition, and the Empire of Suel will rise to dominate all Oerik. Thus, the thing is a holy relic in their eyes, and any who profane their temple, let alone approach too near the Final Key, are subject to death."

"This seems a likely place to store our unneeded gear," Leda said, having nothing further to add to the other subject. "What do you think?"

"It will be easy enough to find this place again. I agree with you, girl. No sense in carrying unnecessary burdens on such a perilous mission as we now face. Speaking of which, I still need some good blade with which to arm myself. As puissant as this dagger is, it is no substitute for a sword when enemies must be fought."

By utilizing the long-deserted walkways high over the floor of the place, the two began a systematic exploration of the nearest buildings. Gord insisted on this, for he wanted to be sure of their base before plunging outward to search for the temple that housed the last portion of the Artifact of All Evil. It turned out that not one of the three buildings connected to the warehouse was inhabited. Once this fact was established, Gord and Leda oriented themselves and headed toward the buildings the albinos had gone into when the dark elf had detected the high-pitched sound.

None of the upper floors they traversed were occupied, although exploration discovered that the lowest levels were in use. The deep channel of the long-vanished river turned to their left far beneath where they traveled. No upper bridgeway spanned its great width, so they had to parallel the path of the deep stone bed.

There was virtually no activity in the city now, and this encouraged Gord. "I am going to venture below," he told Leda. "If the pygmies sleep now, it is the best time to discover what lies down there."

"If we can find a lone albino, Gord, we can force him to tell us all we need to know," the dark elf said. "My power will enable me to know if a lie is told, and a known falsehood is almost as good as an unknown truth."

"All right. Use that ring again, and let us see what can be found down there. These runts should be easy enough to take."

This ancient building, or more correctly remainder of a building, was four stories tall. When the two crept down the stairway to the third floor, they immediately encountered pygmies. A pair of the pale little men dozed on a landing of the very stairway they were descending, their backs to Gord and the invisible drow. Gord located her by touch, pointed, and made punching motions, his fist balled and hammering downward. Leda became visible, nodded, and drew her Yoli sword and held it over her head, blade curved away from her target. Its heavy pommel was a splendid addition to her small fist. Gord held his dagger the same way, and seconds later both of the pale pygmies were unconscious. Gord disarmed them and slipped their little swords into his belt for possible use later.

"Their mates below were not alerted, I think," Leda whispered. "I made too much noise when I struck, but you were absolutely silent, love. I wish I could operate as well as you do."

"You are no thief, Leda, that is certain. Nonetheless, don't worry. The rap of your blow and the thud of the little bastard's fall were not loud enough to alert anyone who was not nearby and concentrating on listening. These albinos are careless and sure of themselves. I don't suppose there have been intruders in this place for years — if ever."

"I hope you're right. Let's bind up both of them, then put a gag on one and toss him in an empty room somewhere nearby. Then we'll bring the other one around and begin our interrogation. Being alone and not knowing the fate of his comrade will frighten each of them and make them both more tractable."

They did as Leda suggested, and then prepared to start the questioning. These pygmy folk looked so much alike that Gord couldn't tell one from the other, but the one they selected to begin with appeared the more important of the pair; he had bits of silver set into his belt, while the other gray-garbed one had no such ornamentation. When the albino's big eyes finally came open from Leda's gentle slapping of his face, they nearly started from his head. Gord put on his most fearsome expression, showed the pygmy his blade, and then held the dagger over the little fellow's heart. That didn't seem to scare him as much as the sight of the girl did.

"A drow here!" the albino squeaked in a scratchy, disused-sounding voice.

"Make no other sound as loud as you just did, minimus," Gord warned, "else this blade will dine on your heart's blood in that same instant."

The albino glared defiantly at Gord with his pink-ish, pupil-less eyes. Then Leda bent low and fixed him with her own glare. "Listen to what he tells you, runt, or worse than that will befall you. I know a hungry demon who would find a morsel such as you an exciting little plaything — and tasty after-ward, too."

"I . . . I . . . can not speak as quietly as you seem to wish," he said in a near-whine, addressing him-self to the dark elf. "Have your servant untie my hands, and we will converse in silent speech."

Leda nodded, and Gord undid the binding that lashed the pygmy's wrists as he admonished their victim further. "At the least sign of treachery, runt, I'll skewer you. We can always put others of your sort to the question."

The little man began to move his arms, hands, and fingers in a complex series of signs and ges-tures. He appeared very desirous of supplying infor-mation, almost too much so. Leda signaled back more simply and briefly, and a series of such ex-changes took place over the next three or four min-utes. Then the dark elf spoke. "Now, little one, use your voice in answer to this question. Have you said nothing but truth to me?"

"Yes, drow. I have not lied," the pygmy answered in his squeaky tone.

"Bring in the second one," Leda said imperiously to Gord.

The young adventurer complied meekly. For this purpose, he was willing to be commanded. If these little bastards feared drow, he would not do or say anything to discourage their terror. The second fel-low was conscious and struggling against his bonds as Gord entered the chamber where he had been sequestered. For a second the little man actually re-doubled his efforts, boldly attempting to free him-self even with the human intruder looking on. When it became obvious to him that he would not succeed soon enough, the pygmy stopped his struggling and glared balefully at Gord.

Without a word, effortlessly, Gord picked up the captive, held him contemptuously under one arm, and strode back to the stairway where Leda stood over the other pygmy. In Gord's absence, she had tied him up again and shoved a gag in his mouth. After disdainfully dropping the second pygmy down upon the landing, the young thief stepped back and looked quizzically at the dark elf.

Leda did not give her full attention to the second captive right away. Instead, after making certain the other one was watching, she stepped up next to where the first pygmy was prone on the landing. She then made some gestures in the air, chanted softly for a few seconds, and reached down and grabbed the pygmy's head between her hands. The small body convulsed for a second as if a terrible force had shot through him, and then he was still. "He dared lie to a drow high priestess," she said, looking squarely at the second captive. The albino's eyes were about to pop from his head, and he quivered visibly in abject terror.

"Unbind his hands and remove his gag," Leda said to Gord. As he began to do this, she addressed the pitiful little figure again. "Now I am going to ask you questions too, and this time I will hear no lies."

The pale little man had grown paler still — or so it seemed to Gord, who had watched the whole episode with a mixture of fascination and horror. Never had he seen an execution performed in such cold-blooded fashion.

However, as he observed in the next few minutes, the tactic seemed to have the intended effect upon the second pygmy. The little man signed and gestured freely and frantically once his hands were unbound, occasionally using his voice if commanded by Leda to do so, and when the interrogation session was over the dark elf appeared satisfied.

"Bind and gag him again, Gord," she commanded. When that was done, she spoke again. "This one is far wiser than his dead comrade," she said with a small smile of triumph, "but he is still a comrade nonetheless." With that, she made the same gestures and sounds as before, then reached out and gripped his skull with one hand. The second pygmy died as the first one had, quickly but awfully.

Leda turned back to Gord, who made no attempt to hide the revulsion on his face. He thought he detected an evil gleam in her eyes, but perhaps it was just the way the reddish light struck them. "Tuck this one away in the same chamber he was before and meet me back here," she said coldly. He hoisted up the body and set off, somewhat in shock over what he had just witnessed. By the time he met Leda back on the stairway, the dark elf had disposed of the other corpse somewhere else.

"How could you murder those captives like that, girl? That was a very wicked thing you did," Gord accused.

Leda was anything but remorseful. "Really?" she said caustically. "Do you think so? Better, I suppose, to let them live and eventually escape their bonds. Then they and their lot could harry and hunt us through the city, capture us, enslave me in one of their filthy brothels, and use you as a beast of burden. Of course, sooner or later we would win release — by being butchered and served for supper when we were no longer useful other than as food. You soft fool!

"And besides all that, it is quite possible that these midges would learn or guess why we were here and take their precious relic elsewhere. Bad enough that it should fall into Eclavdra's clutches, and worse still if the pile of dung, Obmi, should gain the Final Key — but something even more awful could occur."

Even though her entire rebuttal was delivered in a voice just above a whisper, Gord was thoroughly humbled by the acidity of her words and the soundness of her logic. He felt that he had been stupid and judgmental, and was ashamed of what he had thought of her. As he finished turning all of this over in his mind, he realized that she had paused for a reaction or response from him. "What worse could occur, Leda?" he ventured softly.

"The pygmies could realize what they really possess in their temple," she explained, calmer now, and speaking as if to a naughty pupil. "These degenerate little ones are the kin of men above. If they understood the nature of the Final Key, and what they could gain, our little pygmy friends would carry it off to give to their own."

"Who are their kin?"

"The masters of the Scarlet Brotherhood, of course. Those devil-lovers disdain these degenerates, but they would grant them much in return for what the albino scum possess, for then those red-clad plotters would surely be able to unite all portions of the artifact, and . . . *he* . . . would awaken."

"I am sorry, Leda, for what I said to you — and more sorry still for what I thought."

"No matter, Gord. Time enough later for such talk, if we succeed. I learned much from that second minimus. Held on the floor below are many slaves. If we slip down and free them, these men will run amok and cause great trouble for their masters. Then, in the confusion, we will be free to seek out the temple."

Before they crept down the stairs to the slave barracks, Leda explained more of what she had discovered and formulated a plan of action for them. There were several other buildings used as slave quarters nearby. They would assist the captives on the floor beneath them, and then tell them how to go to release their fellows. The slaves were nearly all human and had little vision in the dim red light here, but they could be effective in numbers, and the few with elven blood among them could see in the darkness and serve as the leaders.

"On the other side of the riverbed is a museum," she said, "almost a holy place in itself to these lost degenerates. If the freed slaves can gain that place, they can arm themselves with man-sized weapons left from ancient times. That will encourage the men and enrage the albinos. In the chaos which follows, you and I will cross the riverbed farther up and find the temple of the albinos. It is made of snowy marble and gold, the only structure of its sort. We cannot miss it, I am sure."

"What about a weapon for me? I think I'll be needing a good sword before long, Leda. These toothpicks are better than nothing," he said, indicating the pygmy weapons he had claimed, "but they will not serve me well against the likes of Eclavdra or Obmi."

She nodded in vigorous agreement to that. "The old stuff which the slaves will gain — if luck is with us and them — will never suit your needs, Gord. But the second little lout told me something else of interest. These pale ones trade with others in the Sunless Realm. Over the years they have accumulated a storehouse of materials which are useless to them, for it is sized to large men, not runts such as these grubs are. You will surely find a good blade there, and with it an even better one can be gained."

"How so?"

"In their temple there are other objects of veneration. The arms and armor of their long-dead sovereigns are enshrined there, as well as who can guess what other things from the glory days of their empire. Could their ancestors but see these puny descendants now," the dark elf spat, "they would squash them in disgust like so many bugs!"

That ended Leda's briefing of Gord, so now the two proceeded cautiously down the stairs. A pair of drowsy guards flanking an open doorway proved no opposition at all, and once they were inside the slave quarters Gord used his enchanted, metal-slic-

ing dagger to quickly and quietly cleave through the
locks that held the two dozen humans, half-elves,
and elves in chains. Despite the poor physical condition of most of them, the slaves were alert and
smart. They had enough sense to make no outcry at
their deliverance, realizing they were far from safe
yet, and they got rid of their chains quickly and
silently when they were cut free.

After he freed them, Gord wordlessly offered the
slaves the four weapons that were immediately
available — the two swords from the dead guards
and the pair of little blades that Gord decided they
could use better than he.

Gord and Leda led the way to the lower floor,
finding a roomful of about a dozen sleeping pygmies.
They entered the chamber, accompanied by four
members of those few among the slaves who could
see in the dark and move soundlessly as well.
Dividing up the quarry to two pygmies apiece, this
group slaughtered all the albinos without waking a
single one.

Where they had been grateful but still grim
moments earlier, the slaves were now ebullient and
determined. They had gleaned nearly twenty more
pygmy-sized weapons from the assault just completed on the sleeping quarters, enough to virtually arm
every man in the band.

After allowing them a couple of minutes for a
subdued celebration of their freedom, Leda spoke
to the ex-slaves solemnly, pointing out that they
had much work to do if they hoped to survive and
return to the world above. The dark elf told the
others that they must arrange themselves to be led
by those who could see in the dark and gave them
all information on where the other slave barracks
were nearby, how to use the upper walkways to gain
these places, and where an arsenal was located
across the dry river course. Then Gord and Leda
bade them all good luck.

"Thanks to you, man, and you too, even if you are

a drow!" a lean, worn half-elf muttered as the band began to move out. "We have no sure course to escape this place, but dying free and in battle is preferable to slavery and consumption by these cursed ones. May we succeed, and may you gain success in whatever purpose you had in entering this miserable hole," he said over his shoulder. Then all of the ex-slaves were away, climbing into the floors overhead.

Gord and Leda waited a few minutes, watching outside all the while lest a wandering pygmy stumble upon the carnage of the slave barracks and sound an alarm prematurely. When they supposed the freed slaves were well on their way, the two dashed back upstairs themselves.

After they had passed through the interiors of three buildings and as many of the walkways, Leda thought it best to descend and find a place where they could gain the old riverbed, make a run across the wide way, and then get up to the other side of the city where the temple lay. The structure they were in was poised on the verge of the rocky channel, and Gord located a narrow flight of stairs that ended about twenty feet above the bottom of the old riverbed.

"This is the place where we disembark, Leda. Can you manage to climb down the rest of the distance after the stairs end?"

The dark elf examined the old stone carefully. "I think so — there are places to hang on and put my feet — but what if I slip and fall?"

"I'll catch you — no fear of that," he said hastily. Then the young man was over the edge of the little landing and down. It seemed to Leda that he almost slid rather than climbed, but the descent was not quite fast enough to be a fall. Then Gord was standing on the riverbed below, looking up at her, and motioning to the girl to follow. After she got about halfway down, Leda could not find her next foothold, and she panicked briefly. "The quickest way is to let go, my dear," he said. "I am right beneath you." She did as he suggested, and he had no trouble breaking her fall with his strong, outstretched arms.

"Right across the way is a ramp going up the far side of the riverbed. Let's run for it," Gord urged just after putting her down.

Leda suddenly froze. "Listen! I hear the piping note again, only this time there are quavers in it, and it is more intense. The little white things must have discovered there are slaves armed and in revolt."

Then the air was filled with a dim throbbing, a sound that even seemed to permeate the ancient stones of the place. Some monstrous iron gong was being beaten a long distance away, struck with repeated force every few seconds, so that the reverberations went in deep swells through not only the air but through the fabric of the rock beneath the city, causing the surface on which they were standing to vibrate beneath their feet.

"I think more than a slave revolt would be needed to make the pygmies resort to that sort of alarm," Gord said between tremors. "That sound makes my very bones shake."

Leda was about to reply when yet another sound joined the chorus of nearly inaudible horns and iron gong. This was a brassy shrieking, a wailing series of notes blown on some larger horn than that which made the thin piping.

"That sound I have heard — or, I should say, Eclavdra has heard," said Leda. "Her memories tell me it is the rallying horn of the pygmies. I don't know the significance, but it seems to come from up the river channel."

"Yes, I think so, Leda. And the gong sounds from that way," he added, pointing the opposite way. "The pygmies are under attack from two directions, I'll wager, and their slaves are in armed revolt even as their enemies come upon them. I hope those miserable little cannibals are about to get their just deserts!"

"Never mind justice right now, Gord. Let's find that temple while the pale ones are *really* busy." Chuckling grimly, Gord loped along beside her as Leda took off at a brisk run for the opposite side of the depression.

Chapter 17

THEY DASHED UP THE RAMP and stood panting in the gloom, sheltered from casual view by a portion of the building they leaned against. As they rested thus, a company of armed pygmy soldiers trotted past a short distance away, went down the ramp the two had just ascended, and were gone. Leda suggested that they find a way to enter this old mass they stood beside, saying that it matched the description of the place where too-large items were stored for trade with nonpygmy groups.

After a few minutes of searching, they found an alley door. It was locked, but Gord had no trouble opening the simple mechanism, using a bit of wire from the little pouch of tools kept on his belt for just such a need. A brief search through the welter of stuff strewn about inside the place uncovered all sorts of arms. Not one was of any great value, but finally Gord selected a light long sword, probably once the property of some woman or small man. It was longer and heavier than his old short sword, but not so different as to require hours of practice before he could use it properly. The weapon was stacked in a corner along with axes, a mace, several other swords, and a long-spiked morning star. Not wanting to waste still more time searching for a scabbard, Gord grabbed up a couple of the other weapons and hurried out. As he went, he dropped an axe just inside the door and a broadsword just outside the entry.

"What are you doing?" Leda asked.

"Leave the door wide open, girl. I hope that a band of roaming slaves — or ex-slaves, that is — will stumble upon this place. Now let's go find that bedamned temple and see what happens!"

As the two trotted out of the alley and along a street that they thought would lead to the pygmies' sacred shrine, a bright flash lit up the sky. It was followed by a fiery light that sent tawny shadows dancing along the underground thoroughfare for several beats, then died as quickly as it came. The display came from their right and was about a mile distant, Leda thought. "That was a magical sphere of fire, Gord. The others seeking the Final Key must be attacking at this moment. We must run!"

"Oh, hells! Look, Leda, to your left." As Gord spoke, pale spurts of glowing green energy zipped along a broad avenue that intersected the road they were following at a distance of about fifty yards. The darts were answered by a rolling cloud of some hellish vapors that gleamed with a grayish internal light as it boiled toward a group of albino soldiers who stood in its path. One of the pale little men in the front rank held a long wand, and from it issued more of the darting green spurts. Farther down the avenue, someone cried out; one of the wand-wielder's foes had apparently been struck by the force that came from the weapon. Then the vapors enveloped the squad of little soldiers, and only the lone, wand-using one staggered out of the cloud. He ran from the scene at a good clip, but made the mistake of heading for where Gord and Leda were hidden.

"Cut him down, Gord. We can use that wand he has."

Without hesitation, the young thief sprang out and angled so as to approach the little man from the side. The pygmy seemed disoriented, ill, and panicky, all of which made him an easy target for Gord's new blade. The long sword bit through flesh and bone before the little man even noticed Gord's presence. "Here, girl, is your toy," he said, taking the wand from the dead fingers of the pygmy and tossing it to the dark elf, who had trailed along behind him.

"Good. It shoots magical missiles, Gord. We'll need them, I think, for those who approach behind that poisonous cloud are drow — and that means Eclavdra. I felt she was near. . . ."

"Those other fireworks must be the dwarf and his henchmen, then," Gord said as he scanned the urban landscape. "There's a white building in the distance, midway between the two forces — see it? Run as if demons are on our heels, Leda."

"There *are* demons after us, Gord," she said, moving swiftly to show she meant it. Together, the two dashed through the dark streets without encountering any opposition; the albino forces were all off in other locations, trying to deal with two bands of invaders and a slave revolt all at the same time. A few minutes later they were bounding up a narrow stairway leading into a white, pillared edifice trimmed with red gold. This had to be the place they sought. At last, they had come to the shrine that housed the last portion of the artifact of great darkness. Without hesitation, they entered and prepared to confront whatever awaited them inside.

* * *

Not far away, Obmi, Bolt, and a group of Yoli warriors were finishing off the remnants of a company of pygmy soldiers who had thought to oppose them. The dwarf was rumbling a happy battle-song deep in his broad chest as he sent his deadly hammer flying to crack the skull of an albino priest trying to work up a spell against him. The martel was a handy thing to have, and he was glad for its presence in his right hand, but the hammer he had owned for a longer time, and it held a special place in his dark

heart. It was able to wreak horrible damage, even
when thrown, and the best part was that whenever
Obmi released it, the hammer would hit its target
and then circle around to return to the dwarf's
grasp — as it did now.

With his left hand Obmi caught the bloodied
weapon that came whirling back to him, and in the
same instant buried the long pick of his martel in
the side of a nearby pygmy. The force of this impact
drove the tiny man sideways into his fellow defenders. At the same time, the dwarf jerked the pick
sideways, freeing its bill and arcing the weapon to
his left, where it struck another of the pale soldiers
with its toothed hammer head, destroying the albino's face.

The dwarf felt wonderful. Here was a proper
perspective at last! He was fighting men over whom
he towered by a foot. And the magical boots bestowed upon him especially for this mission made
him quicker than any ordinary human anyway, regardless of size. The dwarf flashed through the
ranks of the desperate little albinos, a whirlwind of
destruction that left a trail of blood and death behind. The poisoned quarrels from the repeating
arbalests that the pygmy soldiers relied upon were
next to useless against Obmi and his lieutenant. Bolt
the wizard was protected from ordinary missiles by
an enchantment, and the dwarf was by nature virtually immune to venom. Obmi smiled as he recalled plucking a little projectile from where it had
stuck in his arm and using it on the fool who had
shot him with it at point-blank range. The expression on the white runt's face as he had driven the
still-envenomed quarrel into the very eye that had
aimed it was hilarious.

The wizard was quite useful. Bolt had cleared
away much of the opposition with a forked bolt of
lightning — a stroke much bigger and more deadly
than the defenders had supposed was possible. It
had crisped a pair of the pygmy folk's own magic-

workers before they knew what had hit them. Then
Bolt had used his power to fry many of the remaining pale little men with a fireball, so the avenue up
which Obmi marched was clear of opposition of serious sort, and he was able to amuse himself by
crushing several of the pygmies with his own weapons. After a few minutes of this close fighting, half
of the ten barbarian warriors accompanying the
dwarf had been lost, but one had to expect as much.
It didn't matter at any rate. One guide had been
kept behind in a safe place outside the city, and
that was all Obmi needed to get back to real civilization once the prize was his.

As Obmi came to an intersection of two avenues
and turned the corner, he first peered ahead and
caught sight of a commotion taking place in the distance. "Blast!" he roared. "Could it be that the filthy
drow yet survives?" Bolt, as mystified as his master
was angry, wisely let the question pass. Obmi stood
still, taking a few seconds to discern the path along
which the distant activity was moving, then let his
gaze continue to track along the same route. Suddenly he set eyes upon an imposing building a few
hundred yards away. "There!" he bellowed to the remainder of his assault group. "Look, you dogs! The
temple lies ahead, and we must get there first. Run
over any who stand in your way, now, and move for
that place!"

* * *

Gord and Leda had come into the pygmy shrine
from a secondary way, one reserved for the clerics
who were housed nearby. Of course, the two had no
idea that this was the case, for they couldn't see the
grand entrances on the other faces of the great
block that was the temple building. A large vestibule
with three passageways was the first thing they saw
upon entering. To either hand the reddish light
common in the undercity was apparent, for the tem-

ple was filled with the strange globes. Ahead, though, the corridor glowed with a golden illumination that was unique to the place.

"Straight on, Leda," Gord hissed to the dark elf. "That light must come from their most precious place of veneration." The pair ran on down the passage, a ten-foot width of polished alabaster with precious gold inlaid in the mosaic tiles of its walls.

"The light is mysterious to them, I think. They must make this place so bright to awe the commoners — a reminder of the time when their ancestors dwelled upon the surface," Leda panted as they hurried forward. "It gives us a great advantage, for the pygmies will be nearly blind in such conditions."

"And a drow?"

"Most will be, but not I," Leda replied. "Eclavdra was supplied with dweomered cusps that protect the eyes from radiation of most sorts — and I, as her physical duplicate, also wear a pair of them."

Before they could converse further, the two came into a huge, pillared hall. They looked out upon a curved end wall, columned side aisles, and a wide central way. Down the middle of the four broad main aisles stretched lines of displays, as if the place was a museum. Perhaps it once had been such. The displays were encased in clear material — glass, crystal, or whatever, Gord could not tell. Along the way they came, the exhibits were of priestly nature, it seemed. They dashed past ancient books and even older-looking scrolls, carved chairs, displayed vestments, ornate reliquaries and sacred offery and altar pieces, and clerical paraphernalia of gold and silver.

The central portion of the mighty chamber was domed in gold, and the floor beneath this dome was a disc of dark, polished onyx. Set around this circle was a rail of wood, inlaid with gold, and broken at only one spot, on the side from which they approached. Outside the rail were curved benches of a size suitable for the pygmy folk. Perhaps a hundred or so could be seated there. Naturally, the benches faced inward so that the greatest of the albinos' treasures could be venerated. From the apex of the dome, fully forty feet above the onyx floor, hung a massive chain of dull, greenish metal. About two-thirds of the way down from the roof on this upper chain was fastened a massive ring. Four slightly smaller chains radiated out beneath this ring, enclosing a globe of crystalline transparency. Each of these four lengths of greenish links was caught fast again below the sphere by another great ring, and this, in turn, was fastened to another stretch of thicker chain that extended down to the onyx floor, held fast by a massive staple of the same metal as itself.

"If I stretched, I think I could just about touch the lower ring," Leda said to the young thief.

"I have never seen anything quite so black," Gord said in wonderment as he stared at the transparent globe. He referred to the small object set inside the crystal, a vaguely cone-shaped thing with three protruding parts that vaguely resembled horns.

Leda tugged at his arm to break his trancelike state. "Don't stare at it — don't look directly at it at all! That thing gives onto a part of the multiverse which is the opposite of what we know. It seems so black because it devours light. Don't touch it, for it will drain your life as it withers your flesh."

"How in the hopping hells do you expect me to touch it, girl? No one can get at it!"

"We must, Gord — and stop calling me girl. I am far older than you are!"

Gord slapped the dark elf on her round posterior, chuckling as he did so to break the tension of the situation. "No, you aren't. You said yourself that you are only months old — I should call you child, not girl."

"Ass! My memories stretch back over centuries, so I am no girl. Stop this foolish behavior and get

moving. We have to loose that globe. crack it somehow, and gain the Final Key while the pygmies are
busy elsewhere."

What the dark elf said made sense. There should
have been dozens of guards and priests in the place,
yet the temple was seemingly deserted — for now
anyway, and there was no telling when the battles
going on outside would carry over to within this
chamber.

Gord glanced around to see if there was anything
nearby that might help him in what he meant to do.
His eye fell upon a nearby display case. It held a statue, a lifelike work that depicted a warrior of the ancient empire, arrayed for battle and holding an oval-
shaped shield and a surprisingly modern-looking
sword. The weapon fairly radiated excellence of
craftsmanship to the young adventurer. It was as
long as the blade he held now, and shaped very
much like it, yet there were differences that struck
Gord as indicating that some great artisan had
fashioned the weapon in the case. The blade was
not as heavy and thick as the one he held, and the
guard and quillons were far better. When he took a
step and looked closer, Gord saw that the sword
had a dish-shaped cutting edge and a ridged spine
along its length. All in all, an excellent tool.

"There is my new weapon!" he said with quiet
determination.

Leda's face contorted in anger. "Have you gone
daft?" she scolded. "Use that vaunted dagger of
yours to sever those chains. We must have the Final
Key now!"

Ignoring the dark elf entirely, Gord strode up to
the tall case of wood-framed glass and peered at the
incredibly realistic statue of the Suel knight therein. "Sorry, paragon of lost dreams of conquest, I
have greater need for that blade than you do," he
said, and with that he smote the case with the
sword he was carrying. Strips of wood snapped, and
thick panes of glass shivered into fragments that

chimed and tinkled as they split into slivers upon contact with the stone floor. At the same moment, a puff of smoke erupted within the sundered display. Gord jumped back to escape the foul-smelling emission, coughing and wiping away the tears that the stuff caused to stream from his eyes.

"What have you— Look out, Gord!"

Leda's warning was unnecessary, for Gord saw it too. There was a crunch of powdering glass as the statue of the Suel knight, complete with sword in hand, leaped down upon the shards and flinders of the wrecked case. "You seek this blade, sooty-haired subhuman? I shall give it to you!" The warrior set upon Gord with a rush as he spoke the last sentence. The so-called statue was alive!

The ancient knight was clad in armor of antique design, but the metal was as good as, or even better than, that of any cavalier who boasted of the latest plate today. He held a shield of good metal, too. All that plus his sword made him more than a match for the young thief, even though Gord wore a shirt of elfin chainmail and could use his enchanted dagger in addition to the unimpressive long sword. Gord met the warrior's rush, avoided his opening shield-smash, and parried an overhand stroke of the sword. The duel was on then, but the third time their weapons made contact, Gord's steel broke under the force of the blond knight's blow. At that, the young adventurer hurled the remnant of the old sword at the laughing Suel. As the knight jerked his shield up to ward off the missile, Gord did a back somersault followed by several rolls, and was clear of danger for a moment.

"Tumbler's antics won't save you, niggling," the tall man said as he strode forward to attack again.

At that pass, Leda sprang into the conflict. Her sudden rush surprised the haughty fellow, and the dark elf's flashing scimitar nearly went home. As it was, the knight barely had time to try to parry the vicious cut, while attempting to duck away at the same time. He succeeded only partially, for the tip of the curved blade drew a red line across his cheek. "Face a truly sooty foe, then, you yapping human cur!" she snarled. Her tone and posture demonstrated that Leda was very ready to fight this ancient minion of the Empire of Suel to the death.

Infuriated at the little wound, the challenge, and the fact that not only was this a female, but a black-skinned, nonhuman one at that, the knight roared some ancient oath and unleashed a storm of steel upon the drow. His attack was so swift and brutal that Leda had all she could manage to survive, blocking, parrying, and retreating without getting in another blow of her own. But she kept the knight busy, and that was all that was needed. In one instant, Leda saw Gord move across her field of vision with unhuman swiftness, springing from behind the knight's left flank with his dagger sweeping in a sideways arc.

The momentary distraction almost cost Leda her life, for at that very moment the Suel warrior planted his feet and sent a downward cut at her. She brought her scimitar up a split-second too late; by then, the knight's stroke had gathered sufficient momentum. His sword was deflected, but not before it had knocked Leda's weapon from her numbed hand and drove her to her knees with its force. Laughing in anticipation, the fair-skinned knight drew back his arm to sink the sword point first into the dark elf's breast, but his peal of laughter ended in a high-pitched howl of anguish.

Gord yanked the long-bladed dagger from where it had sunk through the knight's armor and into the flesh of his bicep. The young adventurer twisted the weapon as he pulled it free, mocking the laughter that the knight had voiced just an instant before. "Ah, ha, ha, hah! Now you think such work is mirthful?" The knight whirled and swung a cross-body cut at him, but Gord was too quick. He ducked under the blow, dived into the man's legs, and sent the knight sprawling. Again Gord's dagger struck, and again its magically sharp point penetrated metal and flesh, this time that of the haughty Suel warrior's left thigh.

"Wait! I cry a truce!" the knight said as he tried desperately to regain his feet.

Leda kicked at the arm he was using to lever himself up in such a way as to maintain his shield between himself and Gord. The boot knocked the arm so that it bent. Again the knight sprawled, and this time it was worse, for the sword spun from his grasp when Leda's foot impacted against his arm. "I'll show you a truce, pig!" she growled as she reached for her scimitar.

"Wait, Leda," said Gord quickly. "Perhaps this revivification of the ancients can help us."

"Don't be foolish," she shot back as she picked up her sword and advanced on the near-helpless man. "This one is like a scorpion. We must kill him."

"Listen to me, foreigner," the knight pleaded, addressing the more merciful of the pair. "I honorably ask for quarter now, not truce. I offer by proof of my surrender the sword you coveted. Take my blade, and this fine armor too, as is your right, but spare my life."

One long stride put Gord between the half-prone man and the advancing dark elf. "Leda, please get his sword and bring it to me," Gord said mildly. She hesitated, then with a look of disgust at the young man shrugged her shoulders and turned to do his bidding, keeping one eye on the enemy all the while. "As for you, warrior from the past," Gord continued, "don't you know that your empire and all like you are gone? The land above, and the bones of all your fellows too, blow as dust over a desert which has swallowed up your vaunted realm."

"Fagh! Just because you two forced my surrender does not mean I am deranged. Lies will not serve you at all. Spare me now, and when my companions come to slay you I will speak on your behalf. Your sort are useful in our auxiliary bands. Service might even earn you the right of citizenship."

"Your words make no sense," Gord said without anger. "What do you know about the sphere suspended yonder?"

The Suel stood up and looked where Gord pointed. "So they have encased the Cone of the Magi in resochist. . . . but what of Uattho?"

"Never mind," said Gord, not knowing how else to respond to this cryptic question. "You are on your parole, so stand quietly and do nothing until I say otherwise," he instructed the bemused warrior. Then Leda was beside him, handing him his newly won sword, and Gord smiled as he held it and felt its balance. "Thanks, love," he said to her. He walked over to one of the benches surrounding the globe and laid the sword there for safekeeping. "I'll see about the Final Key now, and then we can be away."

"High time," was all the dark elf replied. She took up a post where she could guard the Suel warrior as well as get a good view of the four wings of the temple, watching lest some unexpected arrival should take them unawares.

*　*　*

A little more than a bowshot distant from the temple, Eclavdra, high priestess and champion of the demon Graz'zt, drained the last trace of energy from a wailing albino spell-binder. The little man had failed to avoid the kiss of her demon-wrought staff, and the leering visages that were carved along its length seemed to gloat as the thing sucked the pale midget's life from his trembling body. Eclavdra and her guards, four drow males, had faced a great many of these same little men. The members of her escort, however, were skilled not only with weapons but also with magic. All who dared oppose their advance had died. She did not know, of course, that the albino force had been divided. Her contempt for the pygmies was great, and Eclavdra credited herself and her henchmen with being so puissant as to be able to virtually walk over such puny opponents.

"The temple we seek is just ahead, Chosen of Graz'zt," one of the males said to her. Just then there was a blue flash inside the big building the male was pointing toward.

"What was that?" Eclavdra demanded of the smaller drow.

"Some energy discharge — of what sort I cannot say."

"No matter," Eclavdra told the woolly-haired male. "Gather up your fellows and precede me. Kill any who oppose you. I will cover your advance."

"There are savage bands of wild-looking humans roaming around these streets, great one. Perhaps I should remain behind with you in case one of these groups should attack."

That triggered something in Eclavdra's mind. While she hated to think that their assault had been aided by such a lowly event, the situation did amuse her. "Nonsense, underling! The stupid albinos are beset with a revolt of their slaves, and just at the time we came to their filthy little hive to take what is rightfully ours. Obviously, this is the work of The Dark Lord of the Abyss. He smiles on us and gives us his aid! Get moving, dolt — I want the Theorpart now!"

Bowing his cotton-white head, the male hurried away to gather his comrades and obey Eclavdra's command, cursing her mentally as he went. Were it not for the mighty black demon who favored her, he would be able to dispose of the High Priestess unaided. How dare such a nothing order him around! No matter — he would have the other three take his instructions, and he would cover *their* assault upon the temple. If any of them were to survive, it would be him. . . .

*　*　*

It took some time, but the dagger did its job, and the lower chain fell to the polished onyx floor with a loud clatter. Gord grabbed the bit of chain that dangled from the bottom of the now free-swinging globe and was about to clamber up the thing when he heard a choking cry from behind. "What . . . ?" He turned, and there was Leda, red-smeared scimitar in hand, and the knight of the ancient empire lying at her feet in a spreading pool of blood. "The flaming hells! What have you done?"

"The sneaky bastard was preparing to steal up behind you, Gord, ready to kill you when your back was turned," Leda replied with an icy tone. Then she used her toe to roll the man over. As his corpse flopped into its back, the dagger he held gripped in his dead fingers was exposed. "As I told you, his kind are scorpions."

Angry but much abashed, Gord returned to his work. With a little spring, he was upon the strange globe, averting his gaze from what the glassy ball contained. It swung like a pendulum, but that didn't bother him in the least. In a moment Gord was on top of the globe and climbing up the long chain, but a little ways only. Then, holding fast with his left hand, the young thief began cutting the greenish metal of the heavy link just below the one he gripped. The enchanted blade of his dagger bit into the weird metal, but only so as to make the dull greenish cast a little brighter. It was not surprising to him, for this was the same as had occurred when he had attacked the lower binding of the globe. Several more such slashes and chops, however, made the metal gleam still more brightly as the cut widened and deepened.

"Beware below," he called softly to Leda.

"I'm watching, you child! Stop playing around and bring that thing down!"

Gritting his teeth in frustration, Gord gripped the dagger and prepared to smite the chain exceptionally hard. Then he heard shouts and clanging nearby.

"Damn!" Leda cried. "Our foes are coming, Gord! Stop this delaying and get the Theorpart down."

With a grunt of effort, Gord brought his long-bladed dagger's edge against the bright spot on the link. The force and the keen edge were sufficient. The strange, green-hued metal split apart at the point of impact. The broken link groaned as its form stretched and bent under the weight of the chain-bound sphere it held. Then it gave, suddenly, and the ball of transparent substance fell to the stone beneath, making the domed temple boom and clang with the force of its impact. The rail smashed and benches broke where it hit. That thing was heavy!

Gord started to shout with glee as the chain-enwrapped globe bounced and rolled across the temple floor. His gaze followed it as it weaved this way and that, then the young man's eyes widened and his delight was cut short. The careening sphere's course took it toward the wing to his left. Although Gord didn't know it, this was the northern entrance to the place, and one that had just been entered by another group of invaders. The globe veered and turned as it rolled unevenly on the chains, finally coming to a stop at the feet of a small figure, not much taller than the ball of translucent material itself, who had just stepped into the chamber. It was an armored little fellow with vast shoulders and huge beard — a dwarf with a huge hammer in his left hand and a bloodstained military pick in his right. Gord recognized him at once, and spat his name under his breath as if it were a curse.

"Obmi! You dirty toad! I'll—"

The dwarf did not hear that remark, but even if he had he could not have scowled any more blackly as he looked up at Gord. Figuring him to be one of

Eclavdra's minions, he did not hesitate in issuing an order to kill. "Bolt, bring down that monkey!" he commanded, pointing toward Gord as he spoke.

Leda took advantage of the moment to run as fast as she could back into the corridor she and Gord had used to get into the place. Her companion was in a bad spot, but she saw no way she could either help him or take on both the dwarf and his spellworker at the same time. She had no spells she could put to good use at the moment, and in her haste she forgot entirely about the wand she was carrying in the pocket of the cloak she wore beneath her robe. So, she fled for a short distance, until she was out of sight of Gord and the dwarf — and then she remembered the ring. . . .

"Yes, lord," the wizard replied, already holding the components he needed to cast his spell. Gord had a scant few seconds to form and execute a plan. He dared not to try leaping down hastily, for an uncontrolled drop from this height might injure him or at least hinder his mobility. The safer course was to remain hanging from the chain, at least for the time being, where he would have distance on his side. He tried to start his body swinging on the end of the chain so as to present a tougher target, but he did not have time to build up much momentum before a bolt of crackling energy shot from the spellcaster's fingertips.

Obmi watched with glee as the force of the spell crossed the distance between Bolt and the suspended figure faster than the eye could follow, a purplish-blue flash of electricity that hit the thick metal chain and made an eerie, fiery light play up and down its length. Was the man who had grasped the chain dropping off just as the lightning hit? No matter, it was too late. An aura of light surrounded the falling form, and the fellow fell like a stone, hitting the floor feet first and then collapsing with a dull plop. The victim lay burned and unmoving.

"That one will not trouble me now," Obmi said

with a cruel smile. "I congratulate you, Bolt. It is fortunate for you that you succeeded." The ugly dwarf was suddenly in an exceptionally good mood, since he had vanquished his opposition and the object of his quest lay literally at his feet.

"My thanks, great dwarf. I am here to serve capably, not misperform," the wizard responded ingratiatingly.

"Very well," said Obmi in a magnanimous tone. "In light of what you have accomplished since, I will overlook the fact that you misperformed when you supposedly killed Eclavdra and her party those many weeks ago. I know not who you victimized that time, but I do know that it was the drow bitch herself who disappeared down that hallway a minute ago." The dwarf turned to a pair of the Yoli warriors who stood behind him. "Go find her — but do not kill her. Bring her to me, and I will reward you well!"

The two nomads bowed hurriedly and sped away.

Chapter 18

THE VOICES CAME FROM FAR, far away. By listening intently, he could just make out what they were saying.

"Are you sure that is the right container?"

"Yes. . . . Be careful there!"

"I think this is a waste of our precious— "

"Do your work and keep silent. Our lives might depend on this. . . ."

Then there was a tingling all over the universe. The night sky changed. It had been lightless — no moons, no stars. A glow appeared, and then the whole canopy of darkness was suddenly peppered with tiny points of light. These motes twinkled, grew brighter, and then began to blaze and dance. Soon the velvety black sky was a mass of whizzing comets and little suns that seemed to spark and dance as the cosmos grew brighter and stranger with each passing moment. But as the comets streaked here and there, and the stars became larger and brighter, the tingling changed to sharp pain, and the whole universe shuddered.

"That's done it!"

"Ready with the draught, there."

"Must we add elixir to balm? It seems we expend the whole— "

"There would be no whole without this part."

Gord opened his eyes. He hurt all over, but the pain was fading even as it forced him into consciousness. Several faces swam into shape in the distance as he forced his eyes to focus. As his vision cleared, one of the faces came nearer and spoke to him.

"Drink this now, carefully. You mustn't spill a drop."

He was thirsty — parched, in fact — and did not need to be told twice. One hand supported the back of his head while another raised the cup to his lips. The liquid had a slightly effervescent quality, and it was sweet-tasting and felt soothing to his mouth, throat, and stomach as he drank. Gord was willing to drain every drop, no need to caution him about that! It was very tempting to try to gulp the stuff, but the young man repressed the urge and quaffed it slowly, allowing only a trickle at a time to pass his lips, wash over his tongue, and go down his gullet. He sighed with regret as the last drop was consumed. His outside still hurt, but his insides felt better than he could ever recall. The hand propping up his head lowered it gently back down to a pillow of rolled-up cloth.

"Can you speak?" It was the voice of the nearest face again.

Gord blinked his eyes and thought about that for a minute. The glow inside him was fading, moving outward. As it did so, the hurt that had pervaded him changed and shrank, squeezed out of existence between the cool tingling coming from the surface of his body and the wonderful warmth radiating out from his core. "Yes, and I can sit up too," he finally replied. Before anyone could speak or act, the young man pulled himself into a sitting position. The brisk movement made his head swim a bit, but he felt no more pain. "What is this?" he blurted out as he looked down at himself. Gord was stark naked, and his skin was a bright pink!

"We found you near death," a thin man with corded muscles and stubbled cheeks said. "I was not for it," the fellow explained, "but Smoker and the others insisted."

"What Post is trying to tell you, stranger, is that

279

we used healing balm and an elixir of much potency to bring you back from the gate of death," the one called Smoker added.

Gord was impressed and grateful, but being alive was not the most important thing on his mind right now. "Can I have a shirt and hose, even a tunic or robe? I have many more questions, but I prefer to converse in a more dignified condition." Gord was neither shy nor prudish, but when all others around him were clothed, the young thief saw nakedness as an extreme disadvantage. He quickly surveyed the room. He was still in the temple, but the place was a total shambles. The walls and floor were scarred and broken. Dead bodies were scattered around the chamber — three male drow, two men in nomad garb, and one corpse dressed in the robes of a spell-worker.

After a moment, someone had stripped one of the dead nomads and tossed a burnous of Yoli sort to him. It was only slightly torn, and he put it on without hesitation despite its pungent odor. "I thank you," he said, meaning it sincerely. "Now, what the dancing devils happened to me?"

"Dohojar here," the one named Smoker spoke up, "thinks you were hit by a bolt of lightning. That dead spell-binder over there was tossing all sorts of them around."

Gord looked at Dohojar, a small, brown-skinned fellow with blue-black hair and very white teeth that he showed as he smiled at the young adventurer. "I was studying magic, stranger, when the Death Pygmies took me as a slave," he said. "I was young then . . . had I only studied harder, perhaps I could have taught those little blasters a lesson or two."

The brown man didn't look very old now, scarcely into adulthood, except that his body was worn and his eyes looked very old and very hard. "So that's why I'm so pink. You healed my burns?"

"That is right, Zehaab," Dohojar chimed in again.

"We found a small store of medicines in the barracks of the pygmy chiefs and kept it with us for any great emergency. I thought you needed such help if you were to survive."

"Why did you bother with me? Your revolt appears to have succeeded. You — all of you — should be getting clear of this miniature version of the hells as quickly as you can. I don't want to see my work go to waste, after all," he finished with a thin smile.

Smoker looked hard at Post. "Didn't I tell you? He is the one!" Then, turning to Gord, the big, scar-faced man related more of his tale. "I was with the group that you and that drow female freed, stranger. How you managed to get to this city, and to bring those others from the outside to join in the attack, is a miracle. I am grateful, and all the rest of us are too. I — we — want you to be our leader as we fight our way out."

Instead of acknowledging the request, Gord sought more information. "Where are the others — the ones who began attacking when you men were freeing yourselves and finding weapons?"

Smoker turned to a thin ex-slave with the telltale signs of mixed elvish and human blood — pointed ears, slight stature, fine features with slanting eyes, fair and flawless complexion. "Shade, you know that answer best. Tell him."

The half-elf brushed back his long, black hair from his forehead. "I didn't see it all, but Mullen and Cockleburr did — both caught it, or I'd have them speak too. . . . Anyway, stranger, we'd all have been in it deep except for the others who were fighting the pygmy folk. We only had to contend with their baboons, mostly, and a few squads of their warriors. Most of the little white vermin were busy trying to stop the dwarf and his bunch coming at them from the north, and that little group of drow sliding up from the opposite direction. That took all of their spell-casters away, mostly, you know, . . ."

The young man nodded, still not sure what had happened in this place. "Call me Gord — or Farzeel, as the nomads have taken to naming me, if you like. It doesn't matter to me either way. What I need to know now, though, is what happened to the others when they got to the temple, here — especially the drow female and the . . . the . . . thing that was in the crystalline sphere."

"Sure thing, Gord — that's a good name," Shade continued. "There were groups of escapers all over the center of the city, most of them sticking to the areas around the red lights so the men could see to fight. Anyway, Mullen said that he and a group of three or four dozen were arming themselves from an arsenal the pygmies kept when the dwarf and his henchmen came on the scene. They had a spell-user with them who was tossing magic left and right, while the dwarf was cleaning up on those little white midgets like a fox goes after chickens."

"What other things did this Mullen tell you?" Gord prompted.

"That's about it," Shade replied, brushing away his long bangs again. "When the dwarf kept moving, he and his company followed, taking advantage of the confusion to wipe up pygmies. I met Mullen near here, and that's when he told me what he'd seen."

"What about the drow?" Gord asked.

"That wasn't Mullen, that came from Cockleburr — he was from the other side of the Crystalmists, you know, some sort of grugach, pure-blooded, he was. The sight of dark elves made him mad — he didn't know that a drow actually helped to set us all free. He and a handful of others thought these birds were fair game, and wanted to go after them instead of the pygmy bastards. Then they saw that the drow were really giving it to the little albinos, knocking the blasters off with all sorts of magic, and those nasty little crossbows of theirs, too — you know, the ones which are small enough to hold in your hand and—"

"Yes, Shade! But what happened?"

"Sorry, Gord. . . . Cockleburr and his friends gathered up a company along the way, just like we were all doing. They stripped dead pygmies and found arms wherever they could, all the while trailing the drow. Our group got here from another direction, coming up behind the dwarf with Mullen's group. We figured him for an ally, and wanted to join up with him, so we waited for him and his spell-worker to come out. That's when I met Cockleburr, and he told us about the dark elves. Then we figured we'd have lots of help when the dwarf and the drow came out. Problem was, the damned albinos decided to rally here, right outside this temple. We got in big trouble, because all of those little bastards tried to kill us to get at who was inside. Before it was over, the runts managed to get most of us — that's when Cockleburr and Mullen went down — but we got most of them at the same time, and the others scattered. Then I heard a big commotion inside here, so I took a few of the boys and came in to see what was going on. It was one hell of a sight, let me tell you."

At last this garrulous fellow was going to get to the point. "What was going on?" Gord asked impatiently, tempted to grab Shade and give him a shake to make the half-elf speak more quickly.

"Well, the dwarf was about to toss his hammer at a ball of glass or whatever it was that was sitting on the floor. We'd just come in, and he and the rest didn't even notice us, but we saw plenty. I guess he'd already thrown it once — that was the noise I heard from outside — 'cause this time he hollered 'It will not withstand another blow!' just before he let the thing go. The hammer hit the globe, and the thing rang, making a big sound just like earlier, but it didn't break — and the hammer came flying right back to him! The dwarf's magic-worker tried to say something, but the dwarf was cursing a streak, and I never heard so many demons' names as that one knew. That's when all of us got into the best cover we could find.

"Then big-shoulders shoved the mage off, and he *really* chucked the hammer this time. When it banged into the globe, the damned thing flew into fragments, and bits of steel buzzed in all directions, I'll tell you. The globe broke into pieces at the same time, exploding with a bang. Could be that was what busted the hammer. I saw pieces of chains go sailing off in all directions. The glass stuff just sort of disintegrated after it broke, and then I got a glimpse of this thing on the floor — a cone-shaped black thing, sitting right where the glass ball had been.

"The dwarf was dancing up and down. I think he was madder than a wet fire elemental about losing the hammer and pleased to have shattered the sphere, all at the same time. Before you could tell for sure, though, and before he or any of his pals made a move for where the black cone lay, three male drow appeared in the room as if by magic — and magic they began tossing! The guy with the dwarf was no slouch at the game, either. He sent some vicious stuff and took a lot in the process. The dwarf cleared out of the line of casting between the dark elves and his henchman — I'll bet he wanted that throwing hammer then! A whole storm of stuff came out of those spell-binders, and then it went as black as pitch in the temple. Even I was blind."

"It's plenty bright in here now," Gord said. "How did the light return?"

Shade bit his lip, pondering that. "I just don't know. We started crawling up toward the center when there was no more noise, only the pitch dark. Then these gold-light globes started to appear — almost like fireflies at first, real dim and faint. Then they popped back to full brightness, and I had to blink a couple of times to be able to see. I think I

saw one drow standing off alone over that way," the
half-elf told Gord, pointing to the way the young
thief had first come into the temple with Leda.
"And there were two others still in the room, a
male and a female. The male was carrying a sack
with something in it, and the black cone wasn't on
the floor where it used to be any more. These two
black elves were moving pretty quick already, but
when the lights came full on they took off together
as fast as they could run.

"There were three dead drow in the room — the
ones over there — and the human spell-binder was
a goner, too. The dwarf was on his feet, but didn't
seem to know where he was for a minute. Then
when he spotted the dark elves running away, he
let out a bellow that made my ears hurt. There were
a couple of his nomad warriors nearby, I know, because they came out from hiding at big-shoulders'
roar and tried to catch up with their master. The
dwarf had wings on his heels — magic boots for
sure, Gord. He ran after the drow like a courser in
full charge, this awful-looking weapon held over his
head with one hand, and the two men dressed in
Yoli garments were left way behind. That was a good
thing for them, too! I peeked around to see what
was going to happen, and just as the dwarf gets to
the doorway over there that the dark elves ran
through, I heard a pop and a fizzing sound. From
where I was I could see only partly, because the
dwarf was between me and whatever it was."

"I saw a little of it, too," the one named Edge interjected. "Shade's getting around to saying something appeared in the air."

"That's so," the half-elf affirmed. "I've never
seen black fire before, and I don't hope to ever
again. What suddenly appeared with the pop, and
burned with a fizzing sound, looked like black fire
done so as to create some sort of awful sign. The instant it started, the dwarf dropped his weapon and
began howling and beating at himself, as if he were

on fire. I thought he'd gone crazy because of the thing, but then I see that the fellow's beard is on fire — real flames, though, not the black stuff. Big-shoulders was in real trouble, because he couldn't seem to put out the flames. All he could do was howl and whack himself uselessly. Then the pair of nomads saved his ass. One knocked the dwarf down, the other flung something over him. Both had their backs to the black fire, and as soon as the dwarf went down I was careful not to look at it. When I did look again, one was carrying the awful weapon and the other was dragging the dwarf away, still not looking back, of course. We let them clear out, and then we came out from hiding and discovered you," Shade finished.

"Thanks," Gord said with a heavy sigh. Then he remembered something he wanted very much to check on. "Did you see the one drow, the lone one I mean, after that?"

"No."

"I've got the picture of what happened," Gord said, turning to the one called Smoker. "Now, what is it you want me to do?"

"You can see in the dark better than any of us — we know, because some of us have seen you in operation. We have scouts out now, rounding up everyone else we can find who has escaped."

"You are hereby appointed our captain," Post added with a tinge of challenge in his tone. "You lead the way, and the whole lot of us will follow — until we get above!"

Gord wasn't sure he wanted to be saddled with the responsibility. After all, he had a dwarf and a couple of drow to chase down. However, his chances of getting out were better if he had a group around him. . . . "What if I refuse?" he asked in a casual tone.

"That's what I thought you'd do," Post said grimly, "and that's why I was against wasting our medicines on you. Speaking for me, I'd say we should kill you for refusing, but that's up to Smoker, Edge, and Shade."

Not waiting to hear what those worthies had to say, Gord decided to take initiative in the matter. "Well, I hate to disappoint you, Post, but I do *not* refuse. Let's just say that I wanted to know who was fully behind me and who might be slow to assist."

The others laughed at that, and the lean man glowered. Gord had settled the matter to the apparent satisfaction of everyone, but had made an enemy in the process. "What are your orders, cap'n?" a burly man asked, a huge grin splitting his ugly but honest face. "I'm called Barrel, and we're all willing and able to do as you say — only get us *out!*"

"First I'll need my weapons and my armor. Where are my dagger and sword, and my mail shirt?"

Post grumbled for a second, then produced the dagger and its sheath, the sleeve slightly burn-damaged but intact. That little episode explained a lot, thought Gord. Then someone called Grubstepper handed forth the sword, saying honestly that he did not know Gord had possessed it. The young thief forgave this man, since Gord had not been wearing the weapon when he climbed the chain. Someone else produced the elfin mail from just a few paces away where it lay on the floor; it had simply been removed so that Gord's body could be covered with the healing balm. Now the young thief took charge, and giving orders seemed to come naturally to him.

"One of you go to that body over there, the man in old-fashioned armor," he said. "You'll find he wears the belt and scabbard for this sword, and I want both. Smoker, or anyone else, get some runners out and spread the word — we move out in half an hour, and not a second longer! The albinos seem to be in shock at the moment, but there must be plenty of them left. Maybe they've lost their sacred relic, but they surely will want their slaves back —

or, at least, revenge upon them — once they gather their senses and regain courage. All of us are goners unless we move quickly."

"I'll tell them a quarter-hour, Gord," Smoker said. Then he passed instructions to a trio of rugged-looking escapees and all four ran out.

"Get ready, men," Gord said to those who remained inside the chamber. "Scavenge what you can from these corpses, but don't burden yourselves with treasures — and by all means, stay away from the bodies that are standing." While the rest were occupied, Gord went to search the wing where Shade had said he'd seen the lone drow. If the half-elf was right, it could only have been Leda. He went to the vestibule and called her name softly once, then tried the same with more volume. No reply. There was no trace of her in either of the side passages or the rooms beyond — quarters and vestries for senior clergy and acolytes, from all appearances. Then, just as he was about to think the worst, he noticed a bundle in the corner by the door leading to the street. It turned out to be the short, black cloak that Leda had been wearing under her Yoli robe — and in the pocket sewn into the lower edge of the garment was the wand she had taken from the pygmy spell-caster!

Leda had deserted him, but not without reason; Gord could hardly blame her for trying to get away when they were taken by surprise. After all, as she had once said to him, their mission was more important than either of their lives. Gord assumed that she had fled in order to be able to take up the chase after Obmi and Eclavdra later, and he saw the wand as a token that she cared about him, something left behind for him in case he also managed to escape somehow. After replacing the wand and donning the cloak, Gord strode back to the central chamber.

He spent the next few minutes searching for more suitable garments and a case to protect the wand. He found both in a small side room, its contents apparently left over from when human-sized residents inhabited this city. As he returned to the central chamber, little brown Dohojar came smiling up to him. "Gord Zehaab, Smoker says that all is in readiness. Those that are able are gathered outside. You are to come now, please, and take charge."

That was it. No direction, no plan. He was to go out of the ancient building, "take charge," and find a short way out of the maze of this subterranean city just like that. The whole affair was crazy, but even as he thought that Gord had to grin a little. Didn't he still hope to somehow catch up with whomever possessed the Final Key before it was too late? Of course he did! What these ex-slaves expected of him was no more daft than what he expected of himself. . . . "Tell Smoker and the rest that I will be with them in a moment, Dohojar," said Gord, the smile still crossing his face. "Are they all well armed?"

"Oh, most assuredly, Zehaab!" The dark-brown fellow raised his right arm, holding aloft one of the pygmies' small arbalests that shot a half-dozen bolts before having to be reloaded. "See? And we have swords, spears, and glaives too. Each of us has a weapon or two."

Gord nodded, dismissing Dohojar, and then turned to the one man in the whole group that he was least sure of. "Post, get everyone in this place together, now! You and this bunch will be with me, understood?"

He had a black look on his face, but Post didn't argue. In a moment or two he had rounded up a score of others. "Let's go, then," Post said as he reported back, standing defiantly before the young thief.

Gord ignored the affront, and the one who delivered it, instead addressing the assemblage. "Boys, I'm happy to see that none of you broke the other cases — the ones with the lifelike statues inside them."

"Not likely, cap'n!" Barrel shouted back. "One look at the guy whose sword you got was enough. Those things come alive, don't they?"

"You bet your ass they do, Barrel," Gord called back with a laugh. "And that was good reasoning, too, by the way. You, and any of your mates who you know to have thought the same thing, are hereby promoted. Barrel, you're my serjeant, and it's up to you to say who are to be corporals — a half-dozen is fine."

The burly man began his selections, and Gord turned back to the truculent Post. "You," he told the lean man, "are to be at my side every moment. When there's something that needs doing, you'll be the one who gets the job if I say so. Clear?" The man nodded, a little less cocky now. "That's fine. Now get some help and see if you can pry loose a half-dozen of those globes," Gord ordered, pointing to the golden spheres that were each only as large as a small melon but shed sufficient light to make a big room as bright as day. Post walked away to speak with two others, even offering a half-hearted salute before he turned. Gord noticed but did not return the gesture, for he was already busy considering the next step in his plan.

"Barrel!" he hollered as his serjeant approached. "Find leather or cloth bags, heavy ones, for those lights Post is getting for us. If you can't find bags, gather dark cloth to wrap them in."

"Sure thing, Cap'n Gord," Barrel called back. Behind him, men were already gathering and contributing the needed materials. After a minute or so, Barrel said, "We got your globes covered as soon as Post brings them to you — and here he comes!"

The lean fellow had two of the shining spheres. Freeing them from the mesh of wire that held their power was evidently not harmful to their power, and Gord saw that they could be grasped without discomfort. Post's two assistants each brought a pair as well. Gord directed the three over to the waiting serjeant. "Now we go," he told the group after the globes had been contained and covered.

Gord led them outside to where a crowd was gathered. A rapid scan indicated about sixty men and a handful of women. He quickly noted a couple of gnomes and a dwarf. "Serjeant," he said loudly enough for all the men to hear, "hand three of the globes to that dwarf and those two gnomes over there. I'll need some volunteers to carry the other three," he said to the crowd as he looked from face to face in the reddish dimness. "These bundles contain the golden lights from inside the temple," he explained. "Those carrying them will be in the front, at the rear, and on each flank. If we're attacked, they'll move away and uncover them. Then the humans here will be able to see and fight — and the hateful pygmies will be hindered at the same time, since they can not stand bright light."

"Good enough," Smoker affirmed. "This is our leader — and I say he's the best we've got, just in case anyone has doubts. His name's Gord — only the lot of you will call him captain. He'll get us to the surface, and then everyone's on their own."

"Smoker said it," Gord told the throng. "I'm captain, and Smoker and his mates Edge and Shade are lieutenants. Dohojar, I'm making you a serjeant, just the same as Barrel there is. Agreed?"

"Very good, Captain Gord Zehaab!"

"Smoker, you three lieutenants have to decide on other corporals. Barrel will tell you who his choices are — about six, I think. I want to divide this bunch up into fighting groups before we set out. One corporal to a group, and each squad no bigger than ten, no smaller than five. Let the men decide who is in each squad — but the ones with the globes are not in any unit. They operate alone, so they can move when needed."

"What about the ones who can see well in this gloom?" Smoker asked.

"Divide them between the squads," Gord said,

"so there's at least one up in the lead with me, one back in the rear, and the rest spread out along the flanks, I'd say. Are there enough?"

The newly made lieutenant scratched his mat of hair. "We got Shade for sure, and maybe another seven or eight — although it won't surprise me a bit if some others of elvish sort happen to join up along the way. Some of them we approached didn't like our chances, you might say. But when they see you leading, that'll change."

"Bull," Gord mumbled wryly, pleased at what the man said. "Organize on the march, Smoker. I was the one whining about time, and I've been dithering around ever since. There's enough of the reddish lights on our line of march for everyone to manage for the time being. Let's get on with it."

After making certain that Post was right behind him, Gord walked quickly to get to a position ahead of the others. He was headed down the avenue the drow had taken in getting to the temple, figuring that where the dark elves had entered, they could leave this little, cystlike nest of albino cannibals and sunless horror. He thought it should be a fairly simple matter to trace the path the invaders followed, for there would be signs of fighting along most of the route. The young man went slowly, missile-shooting wand in hand.

After Gord had traveled away from the temple for five minutes, he told Post to locate a lieutenant and find out if everyone was now formed in a fighting team. In a bit the lean man returned; all was according to Gord's wishes. So far they had encountered no opposition nor seen any of the little albinos, other than the dead bodies of those slain by the drow advance.

The company was passing through a large plaza littered with pale corpses when the first attack came. It turned out that not all of the bodies scattered about were dead ones, and for that Gord had to give the runts credit for being clever. Almost a dozen of the ex-slaves fell after the initial discharge of the pygmies' crossbows, the poisoned bolts giving any normal man hit virtually no chance of surviving. The revolutionaries were tough and determined, however. As soon as the attack was apparent, everyone dropped prone. Those able to find a target shot back, using the albinos' own weapons and poison to retaliate. Then golden light sprang up on both flanks and ahead. There were shrill screams at that, for as Gord had said the little men couldn't abide such illumination so suddenly.

A pair of violet streaks caught Gord full in the chest. They hurt dreadfully, and his heart skipped a beat as each nerve-searing hit scored. Vowing to fry the nasty little bugger who did that to him, the young thief darted into a place of concealment and watched. The albino revealed himself a moment later, seeing an opportunity to kill one of the men nearby with another pair of glowing missiles from the wand he pointed.

"Got you, grub," Gord muttered with content as he aimed his own wand and pressed his thumb into a hollow in the shaft. Sure enough, as he suspected, that was the way to trigger the thing. But his aim was off; he was not instinctively good at using the wand, especially since he was holding it in his left hand while grasping his sword in his right. The shot of energy zipped past the pygmy harmlessly, and the little fellow ducked and sought to locate the source of the potshot. Gord could see him despite the crouch his target had assumed.

The next streak from the wand caught the fellow just as Gord had hoped. With a screech, the pygmy dropped his own wand and hopped around for an instant. Then he disappeared from view, probably searching for the object. While the little man was thus engaged, Gord darted to a nearer position and again waited. The pygmy's head reappeared, scant feet from where Gord was hiding, and then the hand with the wand crept out from behind the cover the little man was employing. The albino saw a figure crawling toward him in the distance, assumed it was the one who had used a wand to attack him, and straightened out his arm to aim at the prone shape.

"Gotcha!" Gord shouted in triumph, as loudly as he could to paralyze his foe for the split-second he needed to strike. The albino froze in shock and horror at the proximity of his foe. Gord's longsword came down, and the pygmy's hand and wand were both on the cobbles as the pale cannibal ran howling away, gripping the bloody stump of his arm. After pulling the wand free from the now-useless hand that still gripped it, Gord scurried back to where his fellows were holding off the pygmy assault.

"Who knows how to employ a missile-shooting wand?" he whispered loudly.

Shade suddenly appeared, swiping away his hair as usual as he said, "I do. What's up?"

Gord pressed the device he had just acquired into the half-elf's hand. "Use this on those little bastards, and don't spare a single opportunity, either." Shade took off without a word, and in a few moments Gord saw little darts of violet striking the attackers on his left. At that, Gord began firing his wand toward the other flank to give the pygmies something to think about. With every shot, he felt better about his ability to use the wand — and more often than not, one of the albino scum screamed and fell.

After Gord had gotten off five or six blasts with the wand, his mind had had enough time to figure out what to do next. "Post!" he cried out. "Where the hell are you, man?"

"Here," a voice said from just behind him.

Gord whirled, and there was Post all right — with an arbalest pointed at the young man's chest. Gord didn't react at all, giving the surly man the benefit of the doubt.

"Go find Smoker," he ordered, "and tell him that he should have most of the men concentrate their shots ahead. I want all the pygmies directly in our path dead. We'll move up that way, bit by bit, until we're sure that only a few of the little bastards are alive. Then we'll charge the survivors on my signal, cut 'em down, and get the hell out of here. Can you remember all that?"

"Sure, I'm not stupid," Post muttered in reply. "But what if I can't find Smoker?"

"Tell Edge, then — and don't ask the same question about finding him. I'll cut your godsdamned head off if you screw this up, Post!"

The man turned and headed off resolutely, apparently believing what Gord had said. Within a couple of minutes, Gord saw motion among the company, men working their way up, running in a crouch or crawling on their bellies, moving toward the blocking force of pygmies ahead. The movement was slow at first, then gathered speed. Gord went forward too, using the wand more selectively now, sending glowing missiles at any of the albinos who acted like he might be a spell-caster. A voice, it sounded like that of Edge, shouted, and a score of men leaped up and ran toward a central position where the pygmies still fought from. The little albinos ran away, hid inside the buildings, or died where they stood.

"Run up the street like blazes, boys!" Gord called as loudly as he could, then stepped aside to allow the company to do just that. Near the tail end of the column were the gnomes and the dwarf, all huffing and puffing to keep up with the faster walking pace of the longer-legged humans. As the dwarf noticed Gord standing off to one side, he grinned and held up the bundle he had been given to show that his duty as light-bearer in the rear was still being carried out.

After the troop had passed him by, Gord turned and waited for a few seconds, serving as a one-man rear guard. A lone pygmy appeared, and Gord sent a missile of burning energy into him. Then the young adventurer turned back again and ran to catch up with the company. As he came up with the tail of the advancing column, he took the bundle from the dwarf and carried it himself. A bowshot's distance from where they had been ambushed, he unwrapped the bright globe and trotted on, leaving it resting in their rear. "Let's see what those little farts do about that!" he muttered. As he intended, the light served as a barrier to pursuit by the few pygmies that still remained in the area, and the group's passage back along the rest of the dark elves' trail was swift and devoid of any more major incidents.

Gord worked his way briskly back toward the head of the group, taking time along the way to congratulate and encourage his charges. After less than an hour of steady trekking, the group arrived at the place where Gord was sure the drow had fought their way into the underground city. There were many dead, including a dark elf, in front of the entrance to a fortresslike structure, and the building's iron door had been blown off its hinges from the inside.

"Everyone, take shelter in here," Gord commanded, stepping past the crumpled door and into the lowest level of the place. "Lieutenants, post men at doors and windows — those who can see in the dark. Make sure they have plenty of bolts. Shade, back them up with your wand."

After making sure that this was being done properly, Gord then took Post and three other men upstairs to scout for the existence of enemies. The place was obviously a pygmy barracks or stronghold, and one that was used frequently from the look of things. There were dead albinos all over on the second and third levels of the building, many of them felled in their cots, throats slit. These floors also had partially stocked pantries containing sacks of edible fungi, plants that somehow must have been brought down from the surface, and skins of water. If nothing else, thought Gord, this place would serve as a means for all of the escapees, numbering about a hundred, to lay their hands and mouths on an ample supply of provisions.

By the time they had investigated the third floor and found no evidence of activity, Gord became quite convinced that the rest of the place would be free of albinos, except perhaps for dead ones. "Go back and tell Smoker to have some of the boys get that door back up and barricade it. Then move everyone up here, and show them where the food and water are. I'm going to see what's above," he told Post and the others. "If you don't see me again in half an hour, send a small squad up to investigate," he shouted after the retreating men.

The fourth floor level was all but empty; the windows were blocked with stone and mortar, and the floor had a thin layer of dust and ash on it. The next floor was just as dusty, but the room was littered with crates and boxes containing large, strange-looking saddles, harnesses, and other leather gear, and a strange smell pervaded the air. The young thief went higher, and the odor grew stronger with each step he took up the stairway. By the time he was halfway up the stairs to the sixth floor, he could clearly hear hisses and snapping sounds. He proceeded slowly, but need not have been so careful.

He discovered that the whole of the sixth story was given over to cagelike stalls, and each of these pens held a giant lizard — obviously the beasts for which the saddles and other gear were used. At the far end of the room was a pair of large double doors. By peering through the crack between the portals, Gord saw a sight that relieved him and excited him at the same time. He never thought he would be happy to see it, but there it was — the surface of the Ashen Desert, with ash blowing gently along the ground and sunlight, real sunlight, bathing the gently rolling terrain. Gord had all he needed to know, and he ran back down to tell the others the good news.

"Everybody follow me!" he shouted from the top of the steps on the third floor. "We are leaving the albinos to their city!"

Chapter 19

WIND WHISTLED AND MOANED through the old stones, roofs and towers, domes and turrets that stuck up from the ashes and dust like broken teeth and bones. It was not a strong wind, nor was it cruel. It sprayed only fine powder in its gusts, and the dust devils it sent among the deserted structures were small and playful. The movement of air was actually kind, for it cooled the dark stuff of this waste, material that baked under the merciless sun every day to become as hot as a griddle.

It had been three hours since sunset, and roughly the same length of time since the last of the escaped slaves stepped tentatively through the doorway out onto the Ashen Desert. The heat of the air and ground was below human body temperature, barely. It would drop much faster soon, and then the heat of the day might be longed for . . . almost.

"It is so bright here!" said a woman standing near Gord as she shielded her eyes from the full moons of Midsummer. She was a human, and thus should not have had light-sensitive eyes, but her long captivity underground had changed that.

"Remember the sun, Falina?" said the man next to her. "In a few hours it will soar in the sky above, and then we will know real brightness. I only hope that we can again become accustomed to normal light before too long, for we have a long way to travel."

Gord watched the man lead the woman away,

heading for a cluster of other humans who all meant to take a northwesterly route away from this place. When everyone reached the surface, they celebrated, but only briefly. They had escaped their subterranean prison, but there was still the desert to contend with, and none of them could claim to be truly free until they had reached their homelands again, or at least made it to a place where they could resume normal lives.

How many former slaves had died? Gord could only guess, but the toll was certainly in the hundreds. This estimation saddened him, but then he recalled the essence of the words of one of the slaves he had personally helped to free: Better a death killing the pygmies than enslavement and eventual slaughter as a source of food for the little cannibals. The inhabitants of the underground cyst beneath the City Out of Mind would long remember this incident, he thought with a smile of grim satisfaction. He figured that the slaves, the drow, and the rest must have done for around a thousand of them — and at least as many more of their degenerate hounds, the mute baboons that must once have been the soldiers and slaves of the shrunken descendants of Suel.

Gord saw Dohojar moving toward him from the side, and turned to face the smiling, brown-skinned man just as he spoke. "The gwahasti are ready to set out, Gord Zehaab." The man referred to the lizards by the name they were known by among his people, the tribesmen of Changar.

"I guess I'm ready, too, Dohojar. How are the others doing?"

"Some have already set off, heading for the north and west. I think the rest will be going their own ways soon."

"Aren't you going west yourself? You said that's where your home lies."

"How can I see the wonders of the unknown east, Zehaab, if I run for my village like a peasant?"

Dohojar replied, his smile widening. "If you do not mind, I will make the long journey eastward with you."

Gord shrugged. "As you wish, Dohojar. I warn you, though — to accompany me could mean your death. Probably will, in fact."

Now it was Dohojar's turn to shrug. "Who can dispute with fate, Gord Zehaab? What is written will be. Poor Dohojar merely follows the course laid down for him."

"Liar! You steer your own way, and that's a fact," Gord said to him with a clasp of the man's shoulder to accent the statement. "You owe me nothing! Don't risk your newly won chance for liberty and life by coming with me because you feel obligated, Dohojar. I got here fine, and I'll leave and get where I'm heading the same way."

"I do not question that, Zehaab. I have as much faith in you as you have in yourself, and I wish to accompany you for my sake, not for yours." Dohojar finished this statement with another grin. Gord couldn't tell if he was speaking the whole truth or not — but after all, he thought, it doesn't really matter either way.

"Bah! You're hopeless," Gord said to the smiling fellow. "But if you are determined to follow me, you might as well make yourself useful. Bring the lizards — the gwahasti, I mean. We should be on our way quickly." One of the last decisions that Gord made as leader of the group concerned the animals he had found caged inside the tower. He decreed that the surviving officers should get first choice in the disposition of the lizards, and most of the lieutenants and serjeants had eagerly staked their claims. Many others in the group actually preferred to set out on foot, mostly because they were afraid of the animals, or unfamiliar with them, and did not want to have to use some of their food and water to keep a lizard alive. As a result, there were more than enough of the creatures to go around.

"On our way, Gord Zehaab, yes. I hurry now to bring our mounts," the mahogany-hued man said with a little bow.

Left to his own thoughts again, Gord had one last chance to survey the area and reflect upon where he had just been. What a place, he thought to himself. As it turned out, the City Out of Mind was only half buried by dust and ash. Its bones thrust up stark and weathered from the desert around, a reminder that glory is fleeting indeed. Judging from the extent of the ruins and the size of the structures, the metropolis must have been the largest ever known. The young adventurer supposed that it must have housed a million people once. Now it sheltered a fraction of that number — degenerate pygmy descendants of its builders — in a subterranean portion of itself. "And they exist in that darkness and disgusting condition by *choice*. . . ." he mused aloud.

"Who do, cap'n?"

"Oy! Barrel, you gave me a start. What are you doing sneaking around like that?"

The ugly man smiled good-naturedly. "Guess I just move sort of quietly, sir," he replied with ill-concealed pride at not having been heard by the redoubtable Gord, even though the burly fellow knew his captain had been lost in thought. "The others will be here in a jigger."

"Jigger? What do you mean? What others?"

"Oh, Dohojar, Shade, Delver the dwarf, and a couple of the others."

"Just a damned minute now," Gord said with some heat. "I didn't invite a party to come along with me, and I'm not going to play nursemaid to a bunch of . . . of . . . you know what I mean!"

Dohojar had approached Gord again during this brief conversation and overheard his last remark. The small Changa smiled, bowed, and hastened to reassure the young thief. "Oh, no, Zehaab. We are only going along in your direction. You need not fear, for soon we will undoubtedly veer off on another course. And meanwhile, you must not concern yourself with such insignificant ones as we."

Gord could not help but be impressed with the desire of these men to travel with him, regardless of what their true motivation might be. "Stop chattering," he said to hide his appreciation and embarrassment, "and bring me my liz— gwahasti. You'll have me out here talking all night at this rate."

Barrel nodded to Dohojar. "You heard the cap'n! I thought you were bringing them *lizards* a long time ago!" The ugly fellow winked at Gord as he emphasized the word, inferring that Gord had no need to use the Changar term for such beasts if he didn't like, or couldn't remember, such a strange and foreign term.

Within the next couple of minutes, a small group of men gathered around Gord, all of them familiar faces. They were six in number, but were leading a group of ten of the strange, paddle-footed lizards. Gord frowned and was about to demand an explanation for the excess of mounts when Post and Smoker stepped up and coughed to get the young thief's attention. It was Post who spoke.

"No sense in mincing words, Captain Gord. You don't like me much, and I had no love for you. That's changed — on my part, anyway. You brought us out of that mess below in a way I never would have expected, and risked yourself plenty in the process. You are all right, and I was wrong. That said, I decided that I'd like to throw in with you a bit more, and I talked Smoker into joining me. We'll pull our own weight and get out when you say so." The others all nodded and voiced their assent to this last statement. Gord looked into their eyes, one after the other beginning with Post, and saw nothing but sincerity in each return gaze.

"No harm in us setting out together," he said solemnly, "but if you stay with me I hope you realize what you may be getting yourselves into. And now, will someone explain to me why we need these extra lizards?"

Smoker replied. "We have a long way to go, and though we don't know much about what you must do, we know that your mission is important and dangerous. The extra beasts are carrying all the food and water we could heap upon them, and they will serve as mounts in case we lose a creature or two in the wastes."

Obviously, these men had thought things out well, and had prepared for a large expedition even before they knew for sure that Gord wanted company. He didn't want to get close to them, but Gord could not entirely suppress the affinity he was beginning to feel for this ragtag bunch.

"I give up," he said warmly. "It seems that the lot of you are determined to lead your leader no matter what he may want to do. Dohojar, show me how the dancing devils these beasts are controlled, and then I'm riding. The rest of you can come if you can keep up with me!"

"Yes, Gord Zehaab. First you must put on your leggings and robe — they are of gwahasti hide, you know, very useful, like the hood and mask you must also wear. The storms are terrible out there, you can be assured." Despite Gord's protests and fidgeting, the Changa helped him to don the leather garb, complete with strange face mask. Dohojar was smiling as usual as he did this, but Gord thought he detected a trace of slyness in this grin, as though the dark-skinned man knew some things he wasn't talking about.

"Now you look a proper gwahastoo!" Dohojar said after Gord was fully outfitted. The young thief sprang up and landed on the back of his mount, and at this the others in the group did the same. "Nothing to the rest, Zehaab, nothing at all," continued the Changa. "See how the hooks on the reins fit into the holes on either side of this big beast's jaw? Tug, and it turns one way or the other — or it stops if you pull on both reins at once.

"This is your *angwas*," said Dohojar, indicating a wooden pole with a thorn lashed to its end that was stored in a sleeve on the side of the saddle. "To make a gwahasti run fast, you just poke it with this thing at the dark place you see behind its skull. Don't bother to try anyplace else, I tell you now, for the thick scales of these brutes allow the gwahasti to laugh at such pinpricks."

"I know all I need to know," said Gord. "Let's be off, so we can cover some ground before the sun comes up and cooks us inside these leather prisons!" Dohojar had more he wanted to say, but happily deferred to his leader's desires, and the group headed east.

The lizards traveled slowly at night, no faster than a man might trot, and a slow trot at that. Still, Gord thought, it was faster than walking. The reptiles' feet weren't webbed, as was the case with others of their ilk that Gord had seen. Instead, their feet looked as if what once had been normal extremities had been thickened and cooked in the desert, so that now these members were hard, spongy-looking, and platterlike — much like dustwalkers, in the way they allowed the beasts to traverse the dust and ash without sinking in too far.

Sunrise, from their vantage point on the high plateau they rode across, was a spectacular sight — especially to the six of them who had not viewed such a scene for a long, long time. Even more fascinating to Gord was what happened to the dark, sooty hide of the creature he rode as the sun's rays struck it. As he watched, the reptile's scales gradually turned from black to dark gray. Then they seemed to stand up slightly from its skin, and as this occurred the dark gray turned to a dull metallic color.

This was unusual enough, but then Gord happened to glance down at his own arm, and found that the garment he wore was also of the same metallic luster! Last night when he put it on, it had been as dark as the lizards around him. He understood that the lighter color reflected heat more readily, so that this characteristic of gwahasti hide offered some protection for him and his mount from the ravages of the desert sun.

"Now I can see why the pygmy folk cultivate these beasts for riding and dress," he remarked to Dohojar, who was traveling alongside him.

"No, no, Gord Zehaab," Dohojar said politely. "The little white cannibals got the idea from Changar — even though the Jahindi claim they were the first to use gwahasti. In fact, these beasts were those maintained by the pygmies for use by traders from both Changar and Jahind. You see, Zehaab—"

Gord interrupted him with a smile and a wave. "Enough said, little man." Dohojar fell silent, wearing his everpresent smile, and Gord concentrated on riding. The saddle strapped to the lizard was small for him and not too comfortable. It made him feel insecure, especially now that the creature was picking up its pace. The sun felt hot, even inside the leather robe that reflected most of its rays. Yet the warmer it grew, the faster the gwahasti ran. By mid-morning the beast was speeding along like the wind, seemingly tireless and willing to run forever.

Of course, the huge reptiles had no such ability — as Gord abruptly found out some time later. He was actually beginning to feel relaxed atop the beast, despite its speed, when all of a sudden the lizard stopped dead in its tracks. Gord went sailing over his mount's saurian snout and sprawled ungracefully in the dust. As the young adventurer floundered around in the powder, sending a billowing cloud of it into the breeze, and tried to wade back to where the big lizard stood like a statue, peals of laughter resounded from the others, who were all still astride their stationary mounts.

"What's so friggin' funny?" he demanded from behind his mask. Even to Gord the angry statement sounded muffled and ridiculous. He jerked the leather face covering off, and another little cloud of the powdery stuff floated away in the wind. Spitting and wiping dust from himself, Gord looked around at all the others. All were dismounting now, and Post was assiduously concentrating on unloading one of the lizards carrying their extra gear and provisions. Smoker was there too, his back to Gord. Both men's shoulders were moving as if they were laughing. Delver Oldcavern was doing his best to help Barrel unload another of the pack reptiles.

"It is time for the gwahasti to hunt, Zehaab," Dohojar said with an expressionless face. "Was not the Zehaab aware of that, perhaps?"

"No, confound you! Is that why the blasted lizard stopped and pitched me off?"

Somehow, for once, the Changa managed to keep his face absolutely bland. "Before we set out last night, I told all the others that as the sun reached its zenith, and the scales of the gwahasti grew silvery, then they must be prepared for the beasts to halt. But you, Gord Zehaab, told me that you had heard all you needed to know, so I did not disturb you by sharing knowledge that you already had."

Gord squinted at the fellow, but there wasn't a hint of mirth in the plain, brown face. Still, it was very difficult to tell if the little man was actually being serious, for he customarily made very earnest statements while grinning from ear to ear. Gord was confused and more than a little embarrassed. If he had been the object of a prank, then so be it. Let them have their fun now, for things would certainly get worse before they got better.

"It appears, Dohojar, that what I had heard about these lizards was not complete or accurate," Gord lied. "So tell me, what do we do during this rest period?"

The Changa's face broke out in a big smile again; now they had each had their little joke. "It is not all rest, oh no, Zehaab," he said. "The gwahasti must be allowed to run free and hunt. When they have fed, they will come back and sleep for a time. Then we ride on."

The others were already busy pitching a sort of tent, a lean-to affair set so that it kept the wind from them. The fabric was of the same lizard skin as their garments, and it gleamed with a silvery light now as the stuff reflected the rays of the burning sun. Were there observers within miles, Gord thought, their garments and tents would be beacons. But observers were most unlikely — at least ones able to reason. Gord assumed it quite unlikely that there would be creatures who sought the giant lizards as prey, not with the beasts' speed and teeth. Not even the biggest of dustfish would care to tangle with a pack of gwahasti, although the reptiles might hunt the dustfish.

"What do the gwahasti eat, Dohojar?"

"Anything they can catch," the Changa replied with his white-toothed smile. "The beasts like big insects, though, like the ants and beetles of this place. No matter what they find, they come back afterwards to get the salty water we have for them. That's why they return quickly."

"Would they eat us?"

"Never, Zehaab — as long as we wear these lizard garments, anyway. If we had no such clothing on, the stupid things would then think us to be food, and we would be in trouble."

Gord had been about to strip off the very garb Dohojar spoke of and relax in the shade of the tent. At hearing the Changa's words, he decided a bit of discomfort was acceptable after all. It was hot even in the shade of the tent, but it was better than being in the sun. After about an hour the giant reptiles came racing back, all ten in a pack. Dohojar greeted the lizards with a skin of salted water, giving each of the creatures in turn, largest to smallest, a squirt of the stuff from the container. Immediately thereafter, the gwahasti settled into the dust with much scattering of the stuff into the air. When they were done with their work, only their backs and noses were visible. The group of travelers managed to doze too in the meantime, resting for about three hours. In mid-afternoon the lizards erupted to life, and the noise of their hissing and mock fighting with each other roused the group.

"I'll be fried!" Gord muttered as he helped to load one of the pack beasts.

"What is it, Gord Zehaab?" Dohojar asked in a concerned tone.

"I just realized that the wind has been blowing from the west since we set out!"

All of them were surprised at that, especially Barrel. "Will you ram me if that ain't so, cap'n," the burly fellow exclaimed. "I been a seafarer a bit in my time, I'll tell you, and I should have noticed that for sure. The wind most always comes easterly in this forsaken waste, don't it?"

Gord nodded, puzzled. "You know it. Besides its direction, the force of it is pretty strange, too. It's been nothing more than a gentle breeze, with nary a gust above that. I wonder what caused the shift."

The dwarf spoke up at that. "It's a gift, whatever the reason. Having the damned dust at our backs is a whole lot better than th' other way round."

The group mounted and moved on again. Shade brought up the rear, with Post seeing to the three pack lizards that bore the two tents, food, and extra water on their backs. All except Gord were armed with the pygmy arbalests and a miscellany of other weapons. Of course, each one also held one of the sharp prods used to control the gwahasti. Dohojar mentioned to Gord that he was a terrible shot with the little crossbow and suggested that 'Gord Zehaab' might wish to take his, for the Changa felt he could never hit anything with it anyway. That gave the young thief an idea.

"You say you studied magic once, Dohojar?"

"Very true, Zehaab, very true. For many years I was the apprentice of a wise and powerful worker of illusions and spells. But that was a time ago, Gord Zehaab. I have forgotten much, and I have no books or the stuff with which to try even a simple cantrip — if that is what the Zehaab was suggesting. . . ."

Gord shook his head. "No, that isn't what I was thinking, Dohojar. But I do have an idea. I'll take the arbalest. Even though I'm not much with such a weapon myself, I have used crossbows a few times in my days sailing with the Rhennee on the Nyr Dyv.

"I've used this thing with fair success," he continued, drawing forth his wand from beneath his robe, "but I'm not as comfortable with it in hand as I am with a normal weapon. You take it in place of the arbalest. Perhaps you'll be able to employ it better than I."

"You are most gracious and generous, Zehaab! Use this I can! Now I begin to feel much, much more better."

Smiling at the small fellow from behind his mask, Gord managed to keep his tone neutral. "I expect you to be ready for action with it from now on then, Dohojar. You're hereby appointed to remain in the lead — except after dark, when Shade or I will have to take the point."

"Thank you, captain. It is honorable duty I will not fail in," the fellow replied with obvious pride.

By a couple of hours after sunset the lizards had slowed to walking speed again. Then they slowed even more. It was time for another of their sleep periods. The party got about six hours of rest this time, arising about two hours before sunrise to begin their journey once again. The reptiles would have preferred to sleep until the sun came up, but Dohojar got them awake and moving, despite their dreadful hissing and snapping at the prospect of having to work again. He explained that by pushing the gwahasti they could travel twenty leagues or more a day, while if they allowed the lizards to go at their own pace, fifteen or so would be the best distance they would make.

Whatever had caused the wind to blow from the west hadn't kept it there today. Around sunup the breeze shifted to a northerly one, sending the powdery stuff of the Ashen Desert dancing and swirling off to their right, still a little ahead. Barrel said he reckoned this to be a slow shift from west-north-west to north-northwest by sunset, and he thought perhaps a storm was brewing. Dohojar didn't agree with this, for the lizards weren't behaving strangely. Just before the usual hunting time, however, the lizards did begin to act up. The party was near the place where the high plateaus of the central portion of the Ashen Desert plunged down in a stark line. The Changa managed to get the reptiles in line sufficiently for them to make the descent, but thereafter the beasts would not move. Instead of hunting, the gwahasti found shelter and buried themselves as if for sleep. That was sufficient warning — time enough for the seven travelers to also dig in and wait.

The storm came less than an hour later and struck from almost due north. What it would have been like to be exposed to its full fury was unthinkable. The force of the winds was terrible, and visibility was no more than a foot or two. But the whole group was at the base of the cliff where the plateau rose suddenly from the wastes, and with an arm of that high table of land sheltering them from the north, men and lizards suffered little — except perhaps mentally, as the humans, the half-elf, and the dwarf reflected on what would have happened to them had they not chanced to be here at the time the storm brought its fury upon the dusty wastes around them.

"I think it is weather magic, Zehaab," Dohojar shouted to Gord between howling blasts of wind.

"If so, Dohojar, I don't want to confront the one who worked it up!" Gord called back.

At one point, a drift avalanched down the cliff, entirely burying the dwarf and the young thief. Post

311

pulled Gord free from the suffocating stuff, for the young adventurer had been stunned by a rock that fell amid the dust and was unable to save himself. Delver, calling upon his dwarvish talents, managed to burrow out single-handedly. The others were more fortunate, happening to be in places where their heads and faces did not get covered by the whirling, falling dust and ash.

Within minutes after this near-calamity, the wind began to die, and the seven dug out their equipment and took stock of things. One of the lizards had been killed, its head crushed by a large boulder that accompanied the dust slide, but the nine remaining reptiles were unharmed and in good shape. Gord thought it disgusting, but the creatures devoured their dead comrade without hesitation, using their saw-edged teeth to bite through its tough hide and get at the pale flesh beneath.

"It is cannibalism, Gord Zehaab, I know," Dohojar said to the young man as he stood watching the fight between the lizards for the next mouthful of their dead kin. "Still, we are very, very fortunate because of it, too. The beasts are now rested, you know, and with this feeding they will not need to hunt. In an hour we can be riding again!"

Because there were still occasional blasts of wind from the north, the travelers headed southwest, keeping the plateau between themselves and the dying storm. Near sundown they discovered a partially buried oasis. Its spring still sent water forth, and the clean liquid was cutting a new channel to the half-filled pool. They all took time to bathe, even the lizards. After being unloaded of their gear, the gwahasti went into the ashy places to soak in the near-mud, while men, half-elf, and dwarf rinsed themselves off in the clear jet and got rid of the fine dust that covered every portion of their bodies. Waterskins were emptied, rinsed, and refilled with much splashing and squirt`ng of one another. Everyone drank until they could hold no more. While the gwahasti browsed on knife cacti and bed-of-nails plants, with an occasional nip from a young rolling-spikes bush still too immature to tumble freely, Dohojar caught snake weeds for the party to eat.

The Changa held up one of the thin, writhing plants proudly. They were a vegetable imitation of a worm more than a snake, although their mottled skin and their tapered shape suggested the latter. The plants moved quite quickly, slithering along beneath the top few inches of dust and ash to feed on other vegetation, ash worms, and anything else small enough for them to ingest. Dohojar told Gord that they were found near moisture only, and were always around an oasis. They were poisonous, and the rootlets near the mouthlike openings on their front ends oozed the nasty stuff heavily. The Changa had simply caught them, shaved the rootlets off with his dagger, and then showed the others how the remainder of the thing could be cleaned and eaten without fear of harm. The flesh, which Gord eventually consented to try, was firm and rich, and tasted a little like crabmeat. Somehow he managed to eat quite a bit of the stuff thereafter. Full and refreshed, the party mounted up and headed eastward again into a desert of ash that was, for the moment, absolutely calm.

* * *

A hundred miles to the southeast, Eclavdra was cursing and threatening her remaining servitors. The sudden storm had blown her fishlike vehicle before it, despite all efforts to keep that from happening. Finally, to keep from being overturned, the crew had been forced to allow the vehicle to run before the gale. Now the craft was lodged among rocks, stuck fast in the outcropping stone. It would take a long time to free it, if they could. The drow high priestess was in a fury, but that couldn't change the situation.

About the same distance away from Gord's group to the northeast, Obmi was in a similar state. His sailing ship of the desert was motionless, the masts broken and sails torn to shreds. It would be a difficult task to clear the pile of fine dust and ash that had drifted against it so the thing could move again. There were spare sails, of course, and a new mast could be raised. Now the favorable wind was gone, though, so at best his progress would be slow . . . perhaps too slow.

"Where is the filthy bitch?" the dwarf growled to his companion, who was intently staring out across the desolation.

"I sense her location to be about three hundred miles south, Obmi, and she is getting neither farther from us nor closer to us."

The dwarf grinned in satisfaction. "She is not moving either. Is she dead?"

"If she were dead, I would not be able to perceive her location as I do, and I would have other ways of discerning her lifeless condition, too — believe me. She is stationary, but alive — of that I am very sure."

"You had better be, Leda, or else I'll make you—"

The dark elf whirled toward Obmi, an icy glare fixed on her face. "Don't bother threatening me in any way, *dwarf*. I joined you willingly, and I serve you in the same fashion. Our bargain stands — you get the Final Key, I kill Eclavdra. If you seek trouble, look no farther than here. I have only one desire, and I will see it realized — with you or without you."

At that Obmi laughed, reached out, and slapped Leda on her round bottom. "You're cool-headed and tough, drow. That I admire!"

* * *

"Give the gwahasti their heads," Dohojar suggested. "These old dust runners know where water can be found. They can smell it for miles." The men were thirstier than the lizards, for when it came to a choice, the water was salted and given to the mounts and the men went dry — or with scant ration, more accurately. It was more than seven days now since they had bathed and drank at the oasis near the plateau. Since that time, they had plunged east into the desert of dust and ash and had seen no sight of even a damp spot. Dohojar's suggestion brought no better result either, at least as far as they could tell. The big reptiles just continued going in the direction they were headed anyway, directly toward the morning sun.

"We cut our water ration by half again, tonight, unless we find a spring or oasis," Gord told the others. Not even Delver bothered to answer. He was too dry, and grumbling did no good. The lizards ran on, and the men dreamed of deep, blue lakes. All this time there had been but little wind. It was as if the skies had exhausted themselves in the fury of the storm a week ago and were now recouping strength. Mere zephyrs blew from the north, eddying and shifting all around the compass at times. When it was time to make camp for the night rest, each of the seven got a mouthful of water only. Even the gwahasti were on half rations. Men and reptiles were growing thin and weaker all the time.

Hunting had been bad for the lizards; that was evident from their increasingly gaunt flanks. Only eight returned from the noon foray the next day, and Gord was uncertain about what had caused the loss. Either the others had eaten their comrade, or else it had been too slow and some predatory lurker in the dusts had gobbled it up. It wasn't much of a loss, for with their water nearly exhausted and food down to a couple of days' worth for each of them, two pack beasts weren't needed. The remaining extra animal was loaded down with the tents, and the water and food were distributed among the seven members of the little band.

Even though the gwahasti ran more slowly these days, they still made good speed, and the miles fell behind. The next day was much the same, only they noticed little specks circling in the sky above them. When they dipped closer to the ground, all could see that they were some sort of vultures, with wing-spreads of ten or twelve feet. The birds didn't come especially close, but it was impossible for the travelers to ignore their presence or what their appearance portended. Gord wasn't worried for himself just yet, but he wondered how the others were taking this ominous turn of events. Then he overheard a short exchange that put his mind at ease.

"I think we're in big trouble now," Smoker remarked laconically to Post.

"Yep," the lean fellow replied. "Unless those damn things come a little nearer, we're never going to get fresh meat."

Shortly thereafter, dust-striders started to appear — strange, long-legged arachnids with beak-like mandibles. These things were as big as jackrabbits in the body, and their legs were two feet long. They were carrion eaters, too, but according to Dohojar they were not edible. The dust-striders paralleled the little band at a distance, just as the huge vultures flew high above. When dusk came, the vultures disappeared, and with full darkness the striders were gone too. The party halted for their nighttime rest period. As soon as the gwahasti were unsaddled and unloaded, all eight managed to hit a fair run as they sped off to the northeast instead of settling down to sleep. Even Dohojar was at a loss. "Never have I heard of such behavior," the Changa said. "It is unheard of, Zehaab — unthinkable!"

In the course of further conversation about what had just happened, the brown-skinned man admitted that he was not really an expert on the lizards. He had ridden them a few times, seen the big reptiles handled, and talked with those who were familiar with gwahasti, but that was the sum of his experience until their recent escape. Dohojar was ashamed and morose. "Never mind, serjeant," Gord said to him with a hearty slap on his narrow back. "You've helped us all to get this far. That itself was one fine piece of work, and all of us are in your debt. Cheer up, now, and let's see what we can do to put our band back on the trail tomorrow!"

Despite this encouragement, Dohojar was glum and looked ready to wander away into the dust to escape his failure. Just then, Shade intervened with a shout from about a hundred feet away, where he stood on sentry duty. "Hey! Look sharp there in camp!" he hollered. "Ridgebacks cutting through the dust toward you — from the north!"

Just as fins cutting the surface of the water signal the approach of sharks, so do ridgebacks above the ash herald the arrival of the dreaded dustfish. Gord had heard about them from his fellow travelers, and knew enough to be sure that he never wanted to meet one — but there was nothing to be done for that now.

"Grab your weapons and look for any bit of rock you can find!" Gord shouted to the rest of the men as he snatched up his own arbalest. There was a waning half moon in the sky, that being Luna, and Celene was just above the horizon. The two satellites shed a fair amount of light — hopefully enough to enable Smoker, Post, Barrel, and Dohojar to see well enough to aim and hit their targets. Gord clambered atop the leather tents to get a height advantage, such as it was. Just then a streak of light darted forth from where Dohojar had run to. He was at the edge of the camp, in a position nearest the approaching monsters, and the dart of violet-hued light revealed a monstrous, finlike ridge for a split-second as it splattered upon the extruding back of the approaching dustfish.

"There's a whole bloody school of the bastards comin'," Delver muttered as he jumped up beside Gord and loosed a bolt from his crossbow. "We just might be in trouble, captain."

After making his courageous but futile attack with
the wand, Dohojar was trying to bound through the
powdery dust back toward the others, and a huge
fin was close behind him. It must have been the
dustfish he'd hit with a missile from the wand —
enough to attract its attention, but insufficient to injure the monster seriously. Gord and Delver saw the
situation at the same time, both realizing that the
Changa would never make it. The dwarf was growling oaths of his folk as he triggered off a quarrel,
despite the fact that the running man partially
blocked his line of fire. Gord likewise loosed a bolt
from his own arbalest, silently praying that he'd hit
the dustfish and not Dohojar. The small man gave a
great leap just then, and the dust at his heels erupted in a geyser that obscured the rest of what happened from the sight of both onlookers.

Chapter 20

SHE COULD DO NOTHING but watch, invisible but helpless, as Eclavdra brought forth a heavy bag and slipped the Theorpart within it. The male with her was certainly a magic-user as well as a sword-wielder. She would become visible if she attacked, and she could not risk that. Leda could do nothing except grit her teeth in anger and despair as her parent and counterpart made off with the Final Key. Then, when she saw Obmi collapse before the doorway and watched his two servants carry him and his weapon from the chamber, she acted, for she had realized that there was something to be done about it after all.

Still invisible thanks to the ring she wore, Leda crept across the main chamber and out the same doorway that Obmi and the nomads had exited. As she went, she noticed a group of slaves huddled together around the place where Gord had fallen to the ground. In the back of her mind, she wished him well, but she did not pause, for there was a far more important matter to be tended to now. It was easy for her to circle around to where she was in the nomads' path as they left the temple. Then she removed the ring and put her plan into action.

"Put him down!" Leda commanded as she appeared suddenly in front of the Yoli warriors. They needed no further urging, promptly dropping the dwarf and his weapon and fleeing. They had seen enough of drow to know what they could expect from such a one as Leda was. Obmi was groggy, and she could have used his own martel to kill him on the spot. Instead, she first confiscated his weapon and his magical boots and then conjured up a spell to heal the dwarf and bring him into full awareness. She stood a couple of paces away from him as Obmi slowly opened his eyes and shook his head.

"Eclavdra!" muttered the dwarf as he regained his senses. He lunged at her, trying to get to his feet and grab the martel as his mouth began to spew forth the foulest of curses. Leda let him rant and rave for a few seconds, realizing that he was still too weak to present any real threat to her.

"Stop your foolish prattling, Obmi," she said condescendingly. "You have neither your pick nor your magical boots, so you may as well not try to either fight or escape. Relax a moment and take a close look at me."

"Fuck yourself, drow whore!" Obmi glared at her with a baleful expression, resigned to die defiantly. Then the dwarf's eyes narrowed, and his stare of hatred changed to a puzzled frown. "What is different about you, bitch of the black dogs? Has the Theorpart affected you already?"

"Don't be stupid, Obmi. I have no artifact. Look hard at me — you've seen me before, in the chamber just a short time ago."

"There is no doubt about who you are, Eclavdra. What is the point—"

"Eclavdra and her servants even now make their way out of here with the Final Key. She has duped you all along, dwarf. I am her clone — one meant to fall into your grasp while she stole the prize from under your nose! You see me changed, as you seem to notice, because something in the magic which engendered me from her flesh went awry. I am not her exact duplicate."

The dwarf put his head in his hands and moaned. "Outwitted — tricked by that nighted bag of offal! I am finished, finished! How will I avoid the wrath of the demoness? Oh, my poor Obmi! We were so near—"

"Stop that sniveling, you stupid little *nothing*," she spat. "Eclavdra hasn't won yet, has she? There is a long way for her to go yet before the game is over. I am here to give you the victory — if you are not too weak and spineless to grab it."

"What is this you say? Victory? Do not think to play some demon's game upon me now, drow, for unarmed and hopeless as I am, I can still break your scrawny neck with my bare hands," and as he said the latter words, the dwarf flexed his thick fingers.

"No game, Obmi, just simple fact. Accept the fact that I am a clone of Eclavdra. Then the fact that I desire her death — even more than you do — is apparent. With those things evident, why should I care about the last bit of that cursed artifact? You may sit on it, for all I am concerned. I would see my progenitor die, slowly, before my eyes — that is all I desire. Give me that, dwarf, and I will gladly yield the Final Key to you."

Obmi stared at her then, hard, searchingly. "Why do you seek my aid in this matter?"

"Simple. Eclavdra has guards, a means of traveling across the Ashen Desert, and the Theorpart. I am alone now and without any mode of transport. You have henchmen, and I assume you also possess the means to pursue that wretched bitch."

"So? Why should I take you if I have all that?"

"Because I have clerical powers, just as she does, and am an expert with weapons too. Yet, all of that aside, there is a principal reason which you cannot disregard for any cause."

The dwarf looked dubious at that claim. "Just what can that be, drow?"

"The link I have with she from whose flesh I sprang grows stronger each day, Obmi. I know what direction she lies in, and I can closely estimate the distance between us. Better still, the aberration which occurred during my formation has another

321

most delightful consequence."

"Which is?"

"Eclavdra hasn't the foggiest idea that I exist!"

They struck a bargain then and there. The dwarf realized that Leda had used her spells to help him, and after she voluntarily returned his dweomered weapon and boots, there was actually a modicum of trust for her in the dwarf's black heart. Together they made off for the place where Obmi's vehicle was kept. The few yellow-maned baboons and the creatures' masters who sought to have them attack the two were dealt with in summary fashion. Before going far, they came upon four Yoli — the two who had failed to locate Leda when they were sent after her, and the two whom she had surprised while they were dragging their leader away from the temple. Leda was surprised by the dwarf's generosity in accepting them back without more than a few light blows and heavy curses. "I need those big rats to work my craft," he confided to her. "When they outlive their usefulness, I shall show them that failure to protect one's master is a crime to regret — sorely indeed!"

It was a clumsy thing, Obmi's vaunted ship, but the shift in wind enabled them to make fair speed in the direction they desired. Leda had warned the dwarf about the precipitous drop that divided the plateau upon which the City Out of Mind rested. He had known about the existence of the cliffs to the north, because he had come from that direction, but those to the east were a surprise. Forewarned, he found the edge and skirted along it for a score of miles. This course delayed them somewhat, but the alternative was far worse. Finally they came upon a steep incline, and the vessel rolled down at breakneck speed but survived the descent.

Then they encountered a line of hills that forced a detour northward. They were zigzagging, but all the while the direction and distance of she whom they both sought was clear to Leda. The wind remained favorable, something that pleased and disturbed the dark elf at the same time. Perhaps, she conjectured silently, some being was taking a hand, one who dared to meddle where demons and devils, even deities, dared not. . . . Then the storm struck from the north, almost as if Leda's very thoughts had triggered retribution. They survived, barely. It required several days of work to make the craft usable again and free of the dust and ash that had nearly buried it and them in a powdery tomb.

Now they rolled south and east, with a soft wind pushing out the makeshift sail of the vessel. The Yoli were haggard and worn from having to work constantly with little sleep, but Obmi was unrelenting. If they failed, they would die, he said plainly. To succeed was a dream that they would enjoy, with rewards uncountable. The four men worked without a word of complaint.

While the ship sailed smoothly along again there was much free time to talk, and now that Leda and Obmi had become fairly comfortable in each other's presence they learned some things about one another. After the dwarf revealed to her his earlier plan to have Eclavdra killed, Leda explained that it was her party, not Eclavdra's, whom the bandits came after. "The sorcerer got a lot of my group with his work," she told him. "But I managed to find cover before his blasts went off, and when the spell-binder saw none left who could fight, he left the scene in a hurry. But the nomad bandits were thorough — and greedy. They discovered me in my hiding place and were able to grab me because I had not yet matured to the point where I could use spells or weapons against them. Instead of killing me, they took me prisoner, headed south, and joined a caravan, thinking to sell me in Karnoosh for yet more loot," she said with a laugh.

"Did you then learn to use your spells, drow? How did you escape those fools?"

"The Arroden attacked the caravan. The men of

Yoll were many and determined. For once, if what I hear is true, the veiled riders were hard pressed to prevail. More Arroden came, though, and I thought the Yoli were finished. It was a lone man who brought the whole battle to an end, with both sides running off with their tails between their legs."

Obmi was puzzled. "A lone man? What do you mean by that?"

Leda laughed again. "The lout rescued me from where I was pinned beneath my mount. I'd never have escaped otherwise. He is — or, more probably, was — an adventurer from City Greyhawk bent on stealing the Theorpart from both you and Eclavdra. I convinced him that I would aid his mission, thus getting his aid while I journeyed safely all the way to the City Out of Mind."

"Describe this man, and spare no details," Obmi said.

When Leda completed her description, the dwarf was scowling and livid. "I thought that one to be long gone," he growled. "One time before this Gord crossed my path, and the result was not pleasant for him; yet it turned out worse for me. The gray-eyed niggling must bear a charmed life. What makes you think him dead now?"

"When I left the temple to seek you out, Obmi, he was lying charred on the floor. Gord was the one on the chain which your wizard hit with that great stroke of lightning."

Now Obmi smiled. "Yes, yes . . ." he almost purred, stroking his huge beard. "At first, I saw him as a servant of Eclavdra — but that was when I thought that you were she. And just as Bolt sent that charge at him, I thought there was something famil-iar about that human — something I detested. In the heat of the affair, though, the issue slipped my mind. It is most gratifying to imagine that gray-eyed pig being frazzled and fried as the last true service that overweening wizard ever performed on my be-half. . . . But enough of this maundering stuff, Leda.

There are far more important things now at hand."

"Now what could they be, I wonder?" Leda said innocently.

"Humph! First of all, where is that bitch Eclavdra now?"

The dark elf concentrated for a few seconds and then had an answer. "On the move again, and coming closer all the time. There can be no doubt that she makes for the same pass through the Inferno Peaks as we are heading toward."

Obmi rubbed his horny hands with anticipation. "We should see the mountains by tomorrow, and make the pass by nightfall. If we ambush—"

"Don't be stupid," Leda said without passion, cutting the dwarf off in his gloating anticipation. "With her spell-binders alert, we would not have a chance of besting Eclavdra, surprise or no. We need to precede her across the mountains and gather a force on the far side. We can find marshmen there more than willing to serve for such a purpose."

After some growling and grumbling, Obmi finally agreed to accept the dark elf's counsel. After all, why not let a horde of wild humans take the brunt of the thing? Eclavdra would surely have considerable resources for defense. When the marshfolk had worn down the drow, then he'd send in one of their own kind to finish the work. If there was any resistance left beyond that, he would personally take care of it. "I accept your plan, Leda. Now, however, I have a few suggestions of my own. . . ."

"Is there any of that wine remaining?" the dark elf interrupted coyly. "This parching heat will destroy me entirely if I do not get some respite. Let us go into the back of this vessel, find a shady place, and refresh ourselves. Then you can detail what you have on your mind."

Chapter 21

THE SOUND OF THE IMPACT could have been heard for a quarter-mile or even farther, despite the smothering effect of the dust. The metalled head of the creature struck the long wedge of rock with such force that splinters of stone flew in all directions. It had seemed to the onlookers that the man was dead, certain prey for the hungry, onrushing dustfish, but Dohojar had fooled them and it.

The brown-skinned Changa knew exactly where the upthrust of shale was, and as the huge thing came for him, Dohojar floundered through the powdery ash and dust as quickly as he could. At the last moment he dived up and onto the shelf of rock, placing the wall of rock between himself and his pursuer. Because of the height he had to attain with his leap, all he could do was sprawl flat upon the surface, instead of being able to maintain his footing and keep running. This fact helped to save his life, because none of the flying slivers and chunks of shale could hit him when he was prone. But the dustfish had hit the wall with full force and it was in stunned agony, its writhings and thrashings spewing dust and ash up and around in a cloud. The Changa scrambled to his feet, turned back toward the injured creature, and aimed. Spurts of energy shot from the wand he still held. The convulsions of the monstrous thing doubled in intensity when the glowing streaks struck its soft hind portion.

What the western folk called a dustfish, or sometimes a dustdemon, depending on their nationality, was actually an adaptation of a millipede. The creature had grown and changed to suit its new habitat and prey. The head and first segments of the body had become more chitinous, the eyes set high upon this exoskeleton on a sort of ridge, or fin, that cut through the powdery surface of the Ashen Desert. This anatomical oddity allowed the monster good vision while it moved through the dust, even though most of its body remained beneath the surface. The remainder of its many-segmented body flattened even more along the belly portion, then humped upward along the rear area in another fin-shape that helped the creature cleave through the dust. Its many legs had become broadened and paddlelike through evolution, so that the elongated thing now "swam" through the ashy powder rather than ran upon the ground.

These mutated millipedes seldom hunted alone, instead usually traveling in packs — called schools, of course, by those who used the name "dustfish" for the creatures. When lying still, these monsters were indistinguishable from bits of rock jutting up from the floor of the wasteland. In motion, they vaguely resembled sharks cutting the surface of the sea. Anything, or almost anything, that went on the surface or dwelled just beneath it was fair game for these hungry myriapods. Certain creatures were too fierce for the dustdemons, or weren't considered tasty, but humans didn't fall into either category. The one that sought to dine upon Dohojar was a large specimen, even among the giants of its species, and as the multi-segmented body heaved upward in pain, the Changa could see much of its length — fifty or sixty feet at least.

"Poor beggar!" muttered Gord as he witnessed the splintering of the shale and the explosion of dust and ash that followed. Because of the dust that was already swirling about as Dohojar dove for safety, Gord did not see what really happened to the man, and he assumed the worst. He knew that the creature had impacted with the rock, but figured that as an indication that Dohojar had been caught and crushed at the same time and did not realize that the beast had been seriously hurt. When the dustfish began thrashing, Gord squinted to try to catch a glimpse of the Changa's body caught in the monster's jaws and being tossed around. Then he saw some faint streaks of light through the gloom of the dust cloud, but failed to see them for what they were, and the commotion became greater where the young adventurer thought his friend must be dying horribly. There was nothing he could do about it, so Gord swung his small crossbow in search of some target he could see.

"That's done for one of them!" Delver boomed as his bolt sank into the multifaceted eye of an approaching dustfish. That his words were true was obvious from the effect of the missile. The creature made a screaming noise, its mandibles clattering loudly as it did so. The whole forepart of its body reared up from the dust, its legs beating the air frantically as the poison coating the shaft imbedded in its eye coursed through the monster's brain and body. As it curled upon itself in its death agony, still more dust arose to cloud the area, and the whole camp became obscured. Although two of the things had fallen, the remainder of the school was now free to attack without hindrance, for none of the beings who were the prey of these strange creatures could see to defend themselves.

Gord understood the situation immediately and tried to shout an order. "Everyone for himself! Try to—" Then his words were gone, knocked with the breath from his body. A dustfish had struck the mound of stuff he was upon, and Gord sailed through the air to fall stunned into the dust, his arbalest gone. He could just barely see the thing that had attacked him, now shaking its head to free itself from the tangles of the ruined tents. That kept the monster busy long enough for the young man to regain his footing and draw his sword and dagger — puny-looking weapons against a monster of thirty or more feet in length.

"If that ugly bastard is goin' t' eat *me*, I'll make sure he has a headache before I give 'im indigestion!" Delver's threat was rumbled forth amid spitting and coughing as the dwarf hauled himself up from the ashes to stand near Gord. The dwarf freed his long-handled, beak-backed hammer from his belt and gripped it with both hands. His face was grim and determined, for he knew that death was certainly imminent.

Acrobatics and agility were useless in the deep powder. Gord could do nothing more than prepare for doom as Delver did beside him. "Oh, shit, here it comes," he called to the dwarf without taking his eyes from the dustfish. The thing had thrown off the remains of the tents and was coming toward the two. The huge millipede raised its head a little to get a better view of its motionless prey, for such a static condition was unusual to the creature. Food ran, crawled, flopped, or wriggled. Things that remained motionless were either inedible or enemies . . . usually. The monster, instinctively cautious or perhaps confused, paused less than ten yards away from where Gord and Delver stood.

Suddenly screechings and hissings came through the air from somewhere near. The dustfish must have recognized the noises, for it began to turn toward the sounds. The movement exposed a joint between its armored segments. Gord saw the opening and took the opportunity to strike. In two quick, leaping strides, he got to a place within a few feet of the millipede's huge body — near enough to bring the longsword down upon the center of the six-foot-wide back. Aided by the momentum of his leap, Gord brought the blade down, the steel just missing two plates of thick chitin and cleaving through the tough flesh between them. The sharp edge cut through the cord of nerves that stretched from the millipede's tiny brain to the distant tip of its body. The creature's head drooped immediately, and the half-severed front part of its body flopped crazily as the tail lashed from side to side in helpless frenzy.

"Yarrgh!" Delver snarled as he too moved forward and swung his weapon. The beak of his hammer penetrated the tough exoskeleton of the dustfish's sloping head, the six-inch point imbedding itself in the brain that was already in a turmoil of confusion because its nerve link had been chopped through. The dwarf held on for dear life as the monster tried its best to cut him to ribbons with its scissoring mandibles. The haft of the hammer he clung to was just long enough to save Delver from the retaliation of the creature's death throes. The hind portion of the millipede kept jerking and twitching for a short time after the forepart was still, but this activity presented no threat.

Even as the creature's lifeless head sank into the dust, Gord was looking around anxiously in hopes of detecting another of the things before it struck by surprise. The cloud of dust and ashes was too thick to allow him to really prepare for another attack, but fortunately none came. "Delver, can you tell what's going on?" he shouted as the dwarf tugged his beaked hammer free from the now-still head.

"Like I can tell what's goin' on behind a wall o' gneiss," he called back. "Let's see what this'll do to improve my view," the dwarf added as he crawled upon the back of the dead dustfish.

"Well?" said Gord after a couple of seconds. When the dwarf ignored him, he got more emphatic. "Well, what do you see, damn it?"

"Dip me in boiling batshit!"

"I just might do that!" Gord shouted to the dwarf.

Delver turned around and grinned down at Gord, feeling good because he towered over the young man by several feet at the moment. "Those filthy great lizards — they've come back, bless 'em! I can see two or three tearin' one of those insects apart, and the rest o' the bastards seem to have swum off!"

Gord waded through shin-deep powder in the direction Delver was gazing. In a minute he could indeed see that there were several of the gwahasti intent on feeding upon a dustfish, and he thought the dark, moving shapes just beyond his clear range of sight were probably more of the reptiles at work on another of the huge millipedes. Then, as the shape of a man plodded into view on his left, Gord got an even bigger surprise.

"Gord Zehaab! You are alive!" squealed Dohojar as he closed the distance between them.

"You bet your brown ass I am, you little Changa monkey! How in the hells did you manage to survive, though?" he cried, actually hugging Dohojar as he spoke.

"Easy, Zehaab. The stupid creature smashed his head upon a big rock, and while he was trying to clear his brain, I shot him full of magic missiles from this wand . . . which now seems to be depleted, I am sad to report."

"Bugger the bit of bone," Gord said, grabbing the wand and tossing it into the dust. "That sort of stuff we can always get, but good men like you are irreplaceable."

Dohojar was embarrassed and delighted all at once. "Oh, no. I am of no importance at all, but I am very glad the Zehaab Captain thinks well of me."

Barrel, Post, and Smoker appeared on the scene, looking left and right in amazement. Now that the dust had mostly settled again, they could see the shapes of a pair of dead dustfish in the vicinity and two others being eaten by the hungry lizards farther off. All three of them spoke virtually at once, asking what had happened. Then Dohojar, Delver, and Gord chimed in simultaneously, each trying to tell his version of the events. Seconds later Shade came up as well and immediately began demanding to know the details.

The others didn't seem to mind the cacophony of voices, but it was too much for Gord. "As captain of this band," he shouted, "I call for *silence!*" The clamor subsided. "That's better. Dohojar, tell what happened to you. When he's finished, boys, Delver and I will fill you in on the action we fought. Then it'll be your turn to account — Smoker, Barrel, Post, and then Shade because he came in last."

The retelling of the fight with the dustfish was becoming a contest of exaggeration when a waddling, hissing gwahasti intervened. The big lizard was coming for its ration of salted water, and behind it were six more. One of the lizards had been killed by the dustfish as it attacked the things, but that was a part of life — and death — in the Ashen Desert. Dohojar, grinning, went to care for the reptiles, and the other six travelers watched in happy amazement as the gwahasti in order from largest to smallest opened their toothy maws to receive a squirt of the saline solution they craved. "Is *that* what brought them back?" Shade asked.

"Sure thing, fellow," the Changa replied, "but don't you have any curiosity about why they left us?"

"Damn lizards ran off to get water, o' course," Delver growled. It was a guess on the dwarf's part, but an accurate one — as Dohojar, his mystery spoiled, confirmed in a grumpy tone.

"Let's get going, then," said Gord. "We could all use a drink ourselves, eh, boys?"

"Not yet, Zehaab," Dohojar cautioned. "The gwahasti will want to sleep now." And sleep they did, refusing to be roused until the sun was an hour high on the horizon. That gave the group time to get their camp equipment in order, and Gord was happy to find that the tough, gwahasti-hide tents were relatively undamaged from their encounter with the dustfish.

The lizards, watered and satiated with enough food to last them for days, were slow and moved with a lot of hissing and grumbling as they carried their riders to the place where they had found water. None of the travelers minded the delay, though. These creatures had done far more than simply return to lead them to water — the gwahasti had most assuredly saved men, half-elf, and dwarf from being eaten by the monstrous millipedes.

"I don't suppose I'll ever be able to love those musty-smelling blasters," Smoker said with feeling, "but I'll sure as hell have a fond spot in my heart for all gwahasti from now on!" Everyone laughed at that and chimed in with their own expressions of appreciation, and the trek to the waterhole was a cheerful ride.

The place was a deep pool that had formed in a rocky pocket. It was fed from a spring that bubbled up from the strata of stone below, keeping the water clear and fresh despite constant infusions of dust and ash. The latter came from a huge volcano, just dimly visible on the far horizon, scores of miles distant but still close enough. The travelers knew then that they had finally come within sight of the Inferno Peaks, and the worst of their journey was over. By riding directly toward the smoking cone for all of the next day, the seven were at the foothills of the range of volcanic peaks and jagged ridges before dark. The next morning they turned the lizards to the north, skirting the worst ground as they sought a likely-looking way to get through the rugged mountains.

"There!" boomed Delver after a few hours of searching. "That defile is the way we must take." The others were willing to trust the dwarf's instincts, and besides that they were very anxious to leave the Ashen Desert behind. Gord was as hopeful and excited as any of them, but decided they could all spare a couple of hours in the interest of caution and safety. He directed Delver and Smoker to try the pass, traveling into the mountains for an hour and then returning. In the meantime, everyone else unloaded the gwahasti and, since it was close to midday, allowed them to burrow in for their customary slumber.

The lizards were still resting when Smoker and the dwarf returned. "It looks like a good route, captain, at least as far as we could see," reported Smoker. "Believe me, you're going to like walking on solid ground again. The dwarf seems to know his stuff."

"You don't have to tell me that," said Gord with a sidelong glance and a smile in Delver's direction, remembering the way the stocky little warrior had helped him handle the dustfish. "Well, let's pack ourselves up and be gone from this hellish place."

Taking all they could carry and leaving non-essentials such as their riding gear behind, the seven of them bade the still-sleeping lizards a fond farewell and hiked up the good, hard stone of the pass. Only Dohojar seemed moist of eye at parting with the reptiles, and that lasted only briefly. Soon, however, the rock became less wonderful to tread upon, and the wind off the peaks above blew cold. The nature of their difficulties had changed, but their hardship was far from over. Everyone was quite exhausted by sunset, when they came across a good-sized rock overhang and made camp for the night. The main topic of talk around the fire, of course, was how hard it had been to trudge up the slopes with all their gear on their backs.

"I'll admit it wasn't easy," said Gord, "but you all talk as though your packs were filled with lead. Are you sure you left all your unneeded stuff behind?"

That was the sort of remark the others had been waiting to hear. Barrel looked at Gord with a sly grin and said, "Cap'n, with due respect, it's high time you started carryin' your share of the load!"

Gord could hardly believe his ears. "What are you talking about?" he asked, too amazed at the statement to be angry.

Post stood nearby, grinning, and the others gathered round upon overhearing the exchange. Barrel dug into his makeshift pack and took out a small but obviously heavy bundle. "Drag your stuff out too, boys," he called, "and we'll make Cap'n Gord tote his lot from now on!" As the others began rummaging in sacks and backpacks, not one of them spoke a word to the young man. At a signal from Barrel, everyone opened their parcels and displayed the contents . . . and then Gord understood.

"You pack of pilferers looted the temple!" he said with a mixture of surprise and relief.

"This is nothing to compare with the stuff we actually hauled out, Gord," Smoker confided. "We had to leave behind the bulkier things bit by bit as we lost the pack beasts. Still, I suppose it isn't a bad bit of pay for our slave labor — and your freeing us. If you'll divvy it into ten equal shares, we'll be honored, sir."

After voicing a moderate protest, Gord got to work. The haul included almost a hundred of the golden wheels that were the coin of the lost realm of Suel, some loose gems, some ornate jewelry, and a variety of small things such as statuettes, carved ivory seals, little boxes, and so on. It was difficult to be exact, but the young thief felt comfortable with the result when he finished a few minutes later. "That's the lot of it. And here I thought you were accusing me of dereliction of duty. . . ."

"Oh, no, Gord Zehaab," said Dohojar between chuckles. "All we ever said was that it was fair for you to carry what rightfully belongs to you."

"And now," offered Smoker, "sit back, and we'll see just what that amounts to."

By virtue of the others' prearranged agreement, Dohojar got first pick of the piles, Post second, and then Shade, Delver, and Barrel chose their shares of the loot in that order. Then Smoker scooped two of the remaining heaps into a little mound for himself, winked at Gord, and said, "Sorry you got last dibs, cap'n, but to make up for the slight we voted you three shares."

By tucking some of the big coins here and there on his person and stuffing his rucksack to near bursting, Gord was able to load all of his loot. When they set out again the next morning, Gord quickly got accustomed to the added weight — no doubt due in part to the nature of the burden, which he did not at all mind carrying. The other six seemed in highest spirits too, as if the division and sharing out had wiped the old slate clean and new vistas beckoned them all.

Several days afterward, the seven came out of the highlands and into a warm, subtropical area with the smell of the sea clearly evident on the breeze. The trials and dangers of the climb over the mountains had been hard and harrowing, but they had endured, overcome, and reaped a fair reward for all their difficulties.

"No mistakin' this strip o' land, cap'n," said Barrel. "I've been here many a time afore. We're on the west coast of Jade Bay, part o' the Azure Sea. Me and my mates used to put in along this shore for water and food when we sailed from Dolle Port to trade with the savages of the Western Jungle."

"That being the case, Barrel, what do you suggest we do?"

"Seems a good bet that if we hike up on the coast, we'll encounter some ship or other bound for the Seakings' Lands," the burly fellow replied after some thought. "If we're not in luck, why, we're still heading on the right tack — even though it's quite a haul from here to the cities of the Princes."

It was indeed a long march north up the coast. But the going was easier, for the savannah land they traveled across was well-watered, full of edible vegetation and game. Almost sixty leagues they went, generally following the coast, skirting salt marshes, and once in a while taking to the high ground so they could sight well out over the waters of Jade Bay. They did spot sails in the distance occasionally, but no ship came close enough to even signal by smoke, let alone hail.

At last the seven, tattered and tired wanderers all, came to a point where they had a choice. The shore turned sharply to the east, and before them were the low, tree-covered sides of an arm of the Inferno Peaks that towered to their left. A dispute arose then.

Delver, backed by Shade, thought the group should again take to the high ground. The dwarf asserted that getting over the low ridges of this extension of the Inferno Peaks was child's play — an obviously slanted view, for Delver was born and raised in such terrain. That the half-elf concurred was surprising, but Shade explained that he had heard that an area of tidal marshes lay to the east of their location, making progress afoot that way an impossibility. "We'll have to retrace our steps," Shade told the others, "as sure as I'm standing here talking to you, and come back to this spot. Why waste time in all that when we can do the right thing now?"

Barrel and his friends were of a contrary view. The burly fellow admitted that he'd even seen the tidewater marshes the half-elf had merely heard of, but he was of the opinion that they could skirt this inhospitable area and make for Ocherfort thereafter without climbing mountains again. "I'm in with Barrel," Smoker told Gord. "No more mountaineering for me if it can be avoided."

Gord called a vote then. "Mountains!" said Delver, and both Shade and Dohojar agreed with him. "Coast!" Barrel said loudly, with Post and Smoker nodding their assent to that. It was up to Gord, not as leader, but as the deciding vote. Biting his lip, the young man considered the alternatives, keeping in mind his actual purpose. Both sides watched him anxiously. That made him nervous, so Gord thought about it some more.

"I am unable to decide for the group," he said

finally, speaking each word slowly. "Going into the rugged mountains again is not my idea of a pleasant stroll, and the path along the shore is possibly usable, certainly more to my liking." At that, Barrel grinned. "But — and this is important," and now the dwarf looked pleased, "the quickest, most direct way for *me* is over those peaks yonder."

"So? What do we do, cap'n?"

"It comes down for each of you to determine for himself, I guess," the young adventurer admitted. "I feel I must continue north, mountains or no. You three can head along the shore if you feel so inclined. I don't believe you are obligated to follow the course I must take."

The matter was settled. Delver, Shade, and Dohojar took a few steps northward, separating themselves from the three who preferred the coast route. Before any of them could start to say their farewells to the other three, Barrel cut loose with a stream of obscenities that practically made the air shimmer with their force. He shouldered his pack, grabbed his crossbow, and suggested that Smoker and Post do the same. Then the trio held a brief conference, exchanging quick words in low voices.

Gord didn't bother to try to overhear. He simply turned away to face the mountains and went down on his haunches, too saddened to speak. There was no going back on his decision, but he couldn't help feeling dejected over the loss of three such staunch fellows. Then Barrel's voice boomed out again from behind him.

"Well, godsblast it, cap'n! Are you just going to hunker there, or are we headin' up into those futterin' mountains?" Without waiting for a reply, Barrel, Smoker, and Post stumped by, their backs stiff, heading for where Delver and the others were standing. Gord got to his feet, caught up with the three of them, and wordlessly expressed his feelings by clasping each man around the shoulders.

It was an easy trek, as hikes over mountains go,

and the seven were down on rolling ground again in a couple of days, none the worse for the passage. "Just like I told you," Delver said smugly. "Bat-crap!" was the burly seafarer's only retort.

"Enough of those little pleasantries, you two," Gord said — although he didn't really care if they insulted each other, because that meant they were in good spirits. "I think we should angle away from the mountains a bit, so that we can travel on level ground if possible. The land ahead appears very hilly, but off to the west a bit it seems to grow level — and that glint looks to be a big lake."

"Must be Emerald Lake," Barrel volunteered. "The headwaters of the Ocher River, so I've been told, though I've never seen it."

"What makes you think that?" the dwarf asked curtly.

"The Seakings' Lands are my country, shorty," Barrel shot back. "You might know your stuff when it comes to heaps of granite, but don't think I don't know what's in my own land."

They trudged across the steep hills, going west and slightly south along the route that seemed the least taxing. When the seven reached the low, level land beyond the steep foothills, night was falling. The last rays of the sun showed a toothy northern horizon — certainly more mountains, but they sunk away just a little to the west of due north. Gord's desire to gain the plain had been well founded. After an uneventful night, the party moved on, maintaining the northwesterly course. There was water ahead — the Ocher River, Barrel again asserted. Its valley enabled the seven to bypass the little spur of mountains and slog on into the heart of the hinterlands of the territory ruled by the Seakings. Fish from the river fed them that evening, and the waters of the Ocher washed bodies and clothing equally clean.

Gord was more relaxed that night than he had been in a long time. His turn at the watch was not scheduled until the hours just before sunrise, and as he ate his evening meal he was looking forward almost obsessively to getting six straight hours of sleep on a mattress of soft, grassy ground. He quickly fell into a deep, dreamless sleep.

It seemed like minutes later, but was actually several hours into the night, when Gord heard a whispered "Zehaab!" and then felt Dohojar's hand shaking his shoulder as his eyes flew open. "Shade says come quick! All hell's breaking loose across the river, and all of us should come and see in a hurry!"

Gord was up and ready in a moment. Dohojar was still rousing the others as he ran off in answer to the half-elf's summons.

Chapter 22

A GLOBE OF RADIANCE washed over a dell plainly visible from their vantage point across the river and not more than a half-mile distant from the scene. As the light blossomed and made several figures near its center plainly visible, two things happened almost at the same time. Something dark spread itself over the glow, and the light was gone, leaving the depression in darkness again. At nearly the same instant, a group of capering little figures glowed greenly, outlined by some mystical means where they stood between river and dell.

"What's going on?" Gord asked as he came up beside the half-elf.

"This is mild compared to what happened before you got here," Shade hissed. He spoke as if he was afraid to be heard by those across the Ocher despite the distance between them.

"Sure, sure, but what happened before?"

Post thumped up and flopped down beside the two. Then Smoker and Dohojar came up, the Changa winded and gasping for breath from the hasty round trip he had just negotiated. Just as Gord was about to ask the half-elf again, Barrel came trotting up, his rolling gait unmistakable even in the gloom, and not far behind was the bandy-legged Delver bringing up the rear. "No talking, any of you — except Shade, I mean," the young adventurer ordered. "Now, Shade, what's been going on over there?"

341

It seemed that a big audience encouraged the half-elf to be more explicit. "I happened to be looking out that way at what must have been the start of a surprise attack. There wasn't much noise — isn't now, for that matter. All of a sudden there's a half-dozen pale blue balls of light in the dell. At first I thought they were will-o-wisps, but then those things winked out and a bright light floated in the air in our direction. That showed a bunch of folks."

"I thought you said you witnessed an attack, not a show of lights."

"As soon as those figures were exposed, Gord, damned if a bunch of big, black tentacles didn't come up right out of the ground and grab the men nearby. You could hear the yelling from here!"

"Oh, I see. Sorry, Shade."

The half-elf was mollified at that. "No need for apology. I guess I was trying to be too dramatic. The defenders took some losses. I heard screams from their camp too, when the dancing lights were floating through their area. Could the attackers use will-o-wisps as allies?"

"No," Gord said softly. "The spheres of blue light were cast from a spell, Shade."

"It is a simple one, too," Dohojar added.

After the half-elf told them the rest of what he had seen, Gord realized that they still knew nothing about who was being attacked by whom. The seven held a hurried council. The others said the group should simply move on, slipping off in the night to avoid encountering either of the parties involved in the fighting, but Gord thought differently. For one thing, as he pointed out to them, this could be advance elements of two armies skirmishing, and to try to move off blindly might place them directly in the path of opposing hosts.

Also possible in Gord's mind, although he didn't articulate it, was a hunch he had formulated. Leda, in revealing to him what she knew of the contest, had inferred that while the contestants could go to either place, Obmi had preferred a return to Yola-kand, while Eclavdra was intent on making for Ocherfort. If half of what Leda had said and what Gord knew was true, the drow high priestess had the Final Key and the dwarf was hot on her heels. If by some miracle he and his comrades had actually gotten ahead of both of the demoniacal contestants, then the altercation they were witnessing could be Obmi and Eclavdra battling for possession of the prize. It was a slim chance, but it couldn't be over-looked.

"To remain here is to invite disaster," Smoker said with finality. "If, when light breaks, we find our-selves between two armies, each adversary will think us scouts or spies for the other." To that point there was general agreement.

Gord still dissented, however. "I must see just what is going on. I will do my work alone, though," he added quickly as both Delver and Shade started to volunteer themselves for the mission. "I have night-sight myself — and better than either of you have, if you recall," he told the pair dryly. "You help the rest to gather their things and conceal the traces of our camp. At the first paling in the east, move off toward the high ground behind us. Don't worry — I'm experienced at tracking, so I'll find your trail no matter how carefully you hide it . . . and do be careful!"

"What will we do then, Gord Zehaab?" said Do-hojar, bewildered and a bit apprehensive at this strange turn of events.

"If I'm not back right after dawn, I'm not coming back at all. In that case, my friends, you six will just have to take my share of things, divide it among yourselves, and look to yourselves thereafter."

"But we can't just leave a comrade — our cap'n at that! — stranded, can we?"

Gord gripped Barrel by his thick arm and peered into the ugly, honest face of the fellow. "Believe me, comrade, you had better. If I can't return, then

343

there's nothing the whole lot of you can do to aid
me. Without meaning to sound a braggart, I can
fend for myself in such situations far better than all
the rest of you combined. Trouble which prevents
my returning to you, good folk, means that you'll be
dead if you try to rescue me. . . . Besides, I'll probably be beyond saving anyway. Now, heed the orders
of your captain and move out," the young man finished with a softness in his voice he wished wasn't
there.

Whispering their wishes for safety and success,
the six adventurers headed back toward their
camp, leaving Gord alone with his thoughts.

*   *   *

The night was alive with sounds and smells, each
blade of grass starkly outlined against the glowing
sky, shadows making only slightly deeper pools of
dimness. Insects scuttled and leaped from his path.
Little mammals and big ones too crouched down
and froze, hearts thudding, hoping not to be the
ones sought. Without sound, barely discernible even
to the keen senses of the wild creatures around, he
paced along the verge of the river's marshy banks,
avoiding the wet ground whenever possible. A male
leopard out on his night's hunt saw him and considered disputing the passage of this stranger, but
only for a moment. The big cat's brain wasn't a marvel of intelligence, but even so dim an intellect as
the leopard possessed could note the size and power displayed by the intruder. The cat slunk off in
the opposite direction, trusting that tomorrow the
stranger would be gone from its territory. Besides,
the reek of men was strong in the direction in
which the intruder went, and the leopard knew
from experience that many men meant danger,
even if this one seemed unaware of it.

Crouched in the weeds and tall grass of a low
ridge, Gord surveyed the night. The illumination of

the waning moon and the stars were all he needed
to make the sky seem bright as day to his cat's eyes.
The young thief was, of course, in the form of a
huge, coal-black panther. None he might possibly
encounter this night knew that he could take such
shape. He growled softly to himself, and his long
tail twitched as he viewed the scene before his
eyes.

Nearly four score men, wild tribesmen from marshy regions judging from the smell of them, were
scattered in a crescent between the dell and the river bank. Gord had crept on his belly to a point near
them. These men had come by boat, probably from
downstream, to attack. Their enemies were a
mixture of humans and dark elves. His cat's nose
related that to him clearly, recalling odors earlier
detected by the far less efficient human nose he
normally used.

The defenders were encamped in a hidden glen,
and the men had apparently been there for several
days. The odor of horses and humans was much
stronger than would be the case if they had come
but recently. There were a dozen men and mounts
to begin with, but the attacking marshfolk had
killed some of each. The odor of blood and death
was clear. The dark elves and their human associates had not suffered alone, certainly. Gord had
counted two or three dozen dead marshfolk with
his own eyes, so their casualties were undoubtedly
greater than that.

Both sides were quiet now. The defenders were
alert, and any movement by the tribesmen was sure
to draw an unpleasant response from the elves and
men they beleaguered. Spell-casting had been used
by both forces — the drow having more such power,
he supposed, for the more numerous attackers had
been kept at bay.

A sour, earthy-smelling scent suddenly came
wafting to his black nose. His whiskers twitched
and, uncontrollably, his cat's ears flattened along

345

his broad skull. His panther lips drew back, and
Gord bared his massive fangs in a snarl. The smell
was of dwarf, and an odor both human and feline
brain recognized well indeed — Obmi's distinctive
scent and none other! Suppressing a nearly overwhelming urge to voice a coughing roar of challenge, Gord brought his cat's body belly-down and
slunk forward. He wanted to see the broad-shouldered dwarf with his own eyes.

Keeping to the lowest places and using every bit
of vegetation he could find along the way to conceal
himself, Gord-panther made his way closer to the
river before moving toward the place his nose told
him the dwarf was. Something was nagging at his
brain; his nose was telling him something else. He
shook his great head, tossing the other impression
aside. First the dwarf, then he'd concentrate on other things.

It was quite easy to proceed. The warriors were
all watching ahead of themselves toward the drow
encampment while the big panther-form stole
along behind them unnoticed. A few men were
guarding the dugout canoes, but they were only half-
alert, listening mainly, and watching the water for
signs of attack coming from there. Ahead, in line
with the center of the crescent of marshmen, a bowshot behind their advanced line, was a long, bush-
covered swale. To this place Gord went, his padded
paws making only tiny sounds.

He froze about fifty feet away from the line of
men. The dwarf was there all right, accompanied by
three tribesmen evidently conferring with him as to
what strategy they would follow next. What made
Gord's head swim was the other figure sitting with
Obmi and the marshfolk leaders. It was a female
drow — and both his nose and eyes told Gord that it
was Leda!

Gord trusted his senses, even though logical
thought screamed at him that this could not be so.
It was Leda he saw and smelled, and she was not a

captive, either. The dark elf was actually assisting
Obmi and the other three in planning. His black
form pressed to the ground, Gord-panther inched
closer to hear what was being said.

"Those filth have depleted their powers," Obmi
said to one of the marshmen. "Why aren't your warriors attacking?"

Another of the tribesmen leaned over and whispered something to the one the dwarf had addressed, and then the first man spoke. "Ostarth, our sorcerer, says the dark elves are more powerful than
you led us to think, lord. He points out that many of
our men have been killed already, and both of his
assistants have likewise been slain by drow spells.
He joins our priest in advising that we withdraw
before the sunrise so that no more Wenhulii will
fall."

"What do *you* say, chief of the Wenhulii?" Leda
asked the question with scorn evident.

"Why should my people die uselessly?" the leader responded.

Obmi raised a clenched fist to the marshman.
"You are an old woman — and you forget our bargain
in your cowardice! I paid you much gold to overcome my enemy — what of that?"

The chief of the marshmen tilted his head back
and looked down his nose at the dwarf. "You spoke
of a handful of near-helpless ones, easy killing,
much loot. Perhaps it was a simple mistake . . . perhaps not. What does matter is that the few coins you
paid are insufficient to compensate the families of
those who have died, let alone make the surviving
warriors eager to fight on. The drow use strong magic, and their soldiers are well armed and armored
too. I think the Wenhulii will go home now."

Obmi cursed and threatened, but the marshmen
sat immobile and silent. "All right, you filthy brig-
and!" roared the dwarf. "I will agree to pay you
more, much more! Order your warriors to attack!"

"Show me — us — exactly how much more you

will pay. No more will we trust your word."

Leda was expressionless, but the dwarf was scowling darkly as he pulled forth a leather bag from under a pile of cloth nearby. "Here," he said with anger in his voice, "is so much wealth that even the faintest of hearts and palest of livers will be emboldened." With that, the broad-shouldered dwarf spilled the contents of the bag onto the ground in front of the tribal leaders. Coins and gems glittered in the moonlight. The chief made a low whistling noise at the sight.

"I . . . we . . . can take this now?"

"If your warriors attack the enemy, yes," Obmi growled in reply. "If you do not, then I will personally flay you alive."

"Think on this, too," Leda added in a low, evil tone. "I too am a drow, and the very magic you fear I also wield. My powers will support you when you attack, or harry you should you think to turn tail and run. Take your payment and go now. I will come with you . . . magically. I will hear your words and watch your actions, even though you see me not. Treachery will earn only death."

The chief, his cleric, and his spell-binder stood up in that order. No expressions showed on their faces. "Bah!" the leader said. "Stop these foolish threats and prepare to join the Wenhulii in a dance of victory over the dead in the camp of the dark elves. I will order a rush upon the enemy just before the dawn. First, however, we must take this just payment to a place of safety." At those words, the marshfolk leaders cast dignity aside and stooped to gather up the gold and precious gems as quickly as they could while Obmi and Leda looked on with foreboding expressions.

As this last bit of activity occurred, Gord's feline shape was backing away as cautiously and silently as it had come. In a minute the dark form was bounding along the river, heading upstream, then across the grassland to approach the dell from the rear.

Gord was bent on seeing what was happening in the drow encampment, and there was only a little time left for him to do it. In a little more than an hour, he estimated, the eastern sky would show a streak of milky white, and then that would disappear for a few minutes and the night would be darker still. It was during that brief time just before dawn when the marshmen would come. Gord wished to be well away when the attack took place, for he thought that the dark elves and their remaining troops would put up one devil of a defense. Contrary to Obmi's words, and despite their leader's assurance of victory, the young adventurer knew that the tribesmen were likely to be slaughtered.

Remaining undetected by the horses in the drow camp was a problem, but the wind enabled Gordpanther to come close without these animals panicking at the scent of a carnivore. If there was a wind shift, he would be in trouble, for the fright of the horses would alert the drow defenders. Otherwise, he felt confident of things. There was a possibility he would remain near the dell, poised to strike when the defenders were busy with the onslaught of marshmen. If he could manage to enter the camp then and carry off the Theorpart, nothing else was important. Let Eclavdra fight with the vile dwarf and the unspeakable Leda, all killing each other for all he cared — while the last portion of the artifact, the prize they fought for, was taken from under their very noses!

There were mailed men in the encampment, but Gord had no eyes for them. He counted three drow as well, but he gazed through his gray panther's orbs at only one of them. Only the edge in her voice and the mannerisms she displayed differentiated Eclavdra from Leda. Even those small things would not have been noticeable to Gord, had he not just come from watching her clone dealing with the marshfolk headmen. So this was the original, the terrible high priestess, the feared Eclavdra. She virtually radiated evilness but was gorgeous nonetheless, just as Leda was. But beauty meant nothing — if he could sink his fangs into her throat, and gut her with his hind claws, Gord would feel fierce joy. . . . No! Those were animal thoughts, and he was here for more than such work. He listened and could hear Eclavdra issuing orders to the pair of small males who had evidently just come to her.

"Nighthand, return to the perimeter. See that these blind humans use what little of hearing and sight they possess to best advantage. We want no surprise inrush from front, flanks, or rear until I am ready."

"As you command, my lady," the cotton-topped male said. "I will take the two men still nearby out with me when I go."

"Do just so . . . now!"

The drow male flitted away like a wraith, and Eclavdra then addressed herself to the second one. "You, my dear Wickert, are not so expendable as he," she told the fellow, with a small gesture to indicate clearly that she referred to the departed Nighthand. "While he serves to sound an alarm, you must hasten to restore what you can of your magical prowess. If the enemy should prevail, you and I, Wickert, must be ready to escape with the . . . object. The others do not matter, of course, if we have that safely away."

"Of course, high priestess, but are we not in grave danger of being ringed and unable to make good such an escape?"

"Do not be a fool! Would I waste My breath with words which I could not support with actions?" She stared hard as she spoke, and the male lowered his eyes quickly, not daring to answer. Satisfied, Eclavdra spoke on, hurriedly now. "Then do as I've ordered, but come to Me at the first sign of trouble. I withdraw to make certain that no man — or foul dwarf — can interpose between our path and this place. In but two days we will have companies of soldiers. . . . Roast Obmi's shriveled gonads!"

Wickert was backing away as Eclavdra spoke. The dark elf had no desire to be around if Eclavdra worked herself into a fury. That was how it seemed to Gord as he watched the tableau unseen in the undergrowth and shadows in which he crouched. When the little dark elf male had gone to his own campsite twenty yards distant, Eclavdra chuckled softly to herself as she unknowingly walked toward the place Gord-panther was hidden. The beautiful drow moved to where a few small trees and shrubs screened her from view by others — except Gord. As she glided to her sanctuary, he watched and followed her cautiously, making sure that her elven senses did not pick up a trace of his nearness. As soon as he was in position to see whatever she did, Gord sank down to watch as Eclavdra went to work.

The high priestess was traveling light, or at least it seemed that way at first. But then her small backpack began to yield a surprising amount of gear as she busied herself pulling things from it. It was quickly evident to Gord that Eclavdra had some kind of dweomered bag. Clothing, weapons, and many other things came forth from inside the pack. Then the drow breathed an audible sigh as she reached inside once more and grasped something. "There you are, dear Theorpart, object of My success!" she murmured aloud as she drew forth an oblong case of metal.

Eclavdra placed the metal box on the ground before her and sat cross-legged before it. She then took a number of other objects she had drawn from her magically commodious pack and arrayed them about, surrounding herself and the rectangular coffer as she placed each little object down with care. There was some order to her activity, for the things each seemed to have a desired location. What she was setting down in the grass, though, and why she was doing all this Gord was unable to determine.

A crooning, wavering sound began to issue from

deep inside the drow. Eclavdra had completed her placement of the little things, and now she sat motionless and brought forth the soft, barely discernible sound. It made Gord drowsy, and he had to blink to keep his eyes focused. He tensed his cat muscles, flexed his claws, and forced his mind to remain alert. The high priestess began faint body movements then, little swayings and noddings of her head. At that, Gord looked quickly down, concentrating on the metal box. It had a grayish color in the moonlight, but so did everything else under this light that did not give off its own illumination. Could it be copper? No, it was too light a hue. Silver? No, too dark. Tin? Eclavdra had seemed to move it more carefully than a chest of tin would be handled. Brass? Possibly, or maybe gold. . . .

His feline hearing noted a change in the sound coming from Eclavdra even as he kept his eyes and thoughts elsewhere. Now the drow high priestess had ceased making the noise that had almost mesmerized Gord and was whisper-singing some weird chant, a paean of a ghastly sort that made Gord-panther's flesh crawl. He thought the dark elf was now in the process of weaving some evil spell, and he dared not move, for that would surely alert Eclavdra to his presence. Why, Gord was not sure, but every one of his instincts, human and feline, screamed to him to remain undetected.

Little points of light seemed to appear in the air, dancing like minute fireflies above the strange ring of objects the high priestess had so carefully placed. Then the metal coffer began to glow with a dim, purplish luminosity. The faint chanting became more rapid but no louder, and then the movements of Eclavdra's body and arms became faster and more contorted, seemingly defying human, or elven, physiology.

Then suddenly the ritual ceased. Eclavdra halted all movement, and only a thin, sweet note came from her perfect throat. When Gord thought the note could be held no longer, he saw the dark elven cleric move slowly, so slowly, reaching toward the glowing box, the note incredibly sustained all the while. As her hands neared the coffer, the purple hue that it gave off changed, deepened, and became totally black.

Now every hair on Gord's sleek, muscular body was standing straight up. He knew that at any instant his cat-part would break through, and a growl of rage and fear would come from him at the same instant. An all-pervasive horror enveloped him. Awful, malign horror was about to be exposed, evil was about to come pouring out, for Eclavdra was intent upon opening the coffer and releasing that which she had summoned.

Inch by careful inch, Gord moved his cat body back, his panther-nerves screaming to stop delaying and bound away as fast as his four strong legs would carry him. Fighting for control, the human part of his mind forced his muscles to obey. As the drow's hands touched the metal chest, he was moving with utmost care, fully in control of himself both as man and cat. Then Eclavdra's extended hands did something, and the box came open, its lid flying back of its own volition — or due to some force from within the container.

When the scratchy, metallic sound of the lid's opening came to his ears, Gord could retain control of his cat-body no longer. Feline instincts took over, and his panther body obeyed them. With a spring and a contortion in mid-air, Gord-panther was facing the opposite direction from the terrible scene and racing away at full speed.

The human portion of his mind realized that there was obviously no chance to steal the Final Key from the wicked elf now. His cat brain did not care about such a consideration, simply wishing to put as much distance between itself and Eclavdra as it could. Gord streaked through the night in ebony bounds, making away from the dell faster than any normal leopard could have run.

Then, in mid-stride when he was quite some distance away from Eclavdra, something stopped him. A wave of purest evil swept over Gord-panther, traveling as fast as thought — far, far more quickly than even he could run. He collapsed and rolled, his momentum taking him onward as his muscles contracted in agony at the impact of the wave. Then his body stopped rolling, shuddered, and twitched. As Gord lost consciousness, he felt himself changing, altering form again, but this time painfully. He was returning once more to his man-shape, and he had no control. Then blackness as deep as that of the Theorpart overcame him, and the young adventurer could think no more.

Chapter 23

"OBMI! DO YOU SENSE IT?"

"What are you blathering of, drow bitch?"

"Stop being an asshole for once, you dwarven dunderhead, and try to think rationally," Leda told him acidly. "It just could be that I have a real brain inside my skull."

The dwarf started to retort, then made a face and said only, "All right, I'll play along. What are you saying I should magically sense?"

"I don't think it's anything magical at all, you shithead! Something is happening over there in Eclavdra's camp. Can't you just *feel* that she's up to something?"

"No."

"Well, I can! Take my word for it and be prepared — alert the marshmen if you have a mind to. She's working up something very, very bad and powerful. If we don't do something quickly to counter her, you can kiss your precious ass goodbye."

That made Obmi uneasy. He had scant respect for females, less for elven females, and least of all for dark elven bitches. Still, this Leda seemed above her type, and she was somehow attuned to the machinations of Eclavdra. With those thoughts in mind, Obmi decided to violate his strict orders and seek guidance from the one whose cause he championed. If his adversary dared to break the pact, then why should he not do the same?

"I call upon the power of Zuggtmoy," the dwarf

intoned softly. When nothing happened after a few heartbeats, he repeated the call a second time, this time more loudly and at more length, adding the name of her kin: "I, Obmi, champion of Queen Zuggtmoy, beseech her in the name of Szhublox to come to My aid!" His gut felt awful after he spoke, but no tangible manifestation of the demoness appeared.

"Let me try," Leda suggested.

Groaning, Obmi muttered, "Go ahead, but once only. As soon as these pangs reside, I shall bring the Mighty Queen of the—"

"Right. Just shut up a moment and give me one try, then." The dwarf clamped his teeth shut with a snap, and the dark elf began her conjuration. "I call upon the Power of the Abyss, on its Six Hundred and Sixty-Six Planes and Forbidden Names. Oh, Zuggtmoy, Queen of Fungi, She of Chaos, Zuggtmoy, whose very name strikes terror into the hearts of all, Your humble servants urge—"

An ear-splitting screech cut through the air. Leda halted her incantation, but even if she had not, the shrill noise would have drowned it out, to all listeners on this plane . . . and perhaps other planes as well. Then the atmosphere around Obmi and Leda began to grow thick, and they became aware of a foul stench emanating from some other place.

"Bah!" growled Obmi when the screech subsided. "My call got no results, but yours was worse. What have you wrought, black bitch?"

"Shut your mouth and gather your senses, if that is possible," Leda shot back at him. "The uproar comes from Eclavdra's camp, you fool. She is up to something big, and you had better gather your puny forces and attack before things get any worse."

* * *

The screech, originating from a point in the air only feet away from where Eclavdra sat, would have deafened any normal being from that distance. And the awful odor that accompanied the sound would have sickened anyone else who got the full force of it . . . but Eclavdra was no ordinary being. She sat quietly, watching as the events she had set in motion unfolded.

As the shrill sound dissipated, it was replaced by a tearing noise. Monstrous, taloned hands appeared in mid-air a few feet off the ground, their fingers gripping something unseen as if by the edges. The ripping sound continued, and more of the creature owning the disembodied, clawed hands became clearly visible through a rent, literally a tear in the fabric of space, plainly discernible in the air.

A hideous, evil head thrust itself through the unnatural opening, and then a massive arm poked out, its huge hand reaching toward the drow as the face leered and said, "Wanna fool around?" The fiend's exact intentions were unclear, perhaps even to itself. Eclavdra merely rested her left hand on the brass box and pointed her right index finger. A purple-black spark jumped from the outstretched digit to the creature's forehead, and it stopped grinning and howled.

"Little lizard-daemon! Listen carefully, or I shall allow the force to wholly devour you," Eclavdra said in a low, threatening voice. "Leave the gate I have readied and get your ilk together. You know by what power I summon you all, so do not delay an instant longer."

The daemon disappeared, leaving the strange hole in the air empty. The dark elven priestess sang another brief, hideous chant, and something else appeared in the opening — another daemon, this one having five arms and an insectlike head. The creature clicked its mandibles hungrily at the sight of her, and Eclavdra treated this creature to a taste of the fell power drawn from the Theorpart, just as she had done with the previous one. The insect-daemon then received its instructions and disappeared. After a few minutes, daemons began coming through the unusual gate in a steady flow.

Without saying a word, both types of daemons knew by what they had been summoned and what they were to do. The giant-sized lizard-daemons ambled off toward the center of the enemy line, while the three-legged insect-daemons trooped toward either side. Eclavdra meant to encircle and crush her attackers with an overwhelming force of daemons — monsters from Hades conjured through the power of the Theorpart. Despite her knowledge that she was acting in a fashion that would attract all powers watching for even minor occurrences of such sort, the drow high priestess drew upon the awful nature of the Final Key to wreak havoc on those who dared to challenge her.

Obmi, meanwhile, had proceeded with his assault — too late. The hapless marshmen, expecting to encounter a force many times smaller in number than they were, instead found themselves charging into the arms of the waiting daemons.

Yells and screams of terror and pain from the marshmen alerted the dwarf, who lurked far to the rear of the battleground, and in moments he was aware of the general circumstances. He did not know what his mercenary force had encountered, but clearly it was more formidable than a small group of humans and a couple of drow spell-users. Leda had darted off in the confusion, and was nowhere to be found. The dwarf considered beseeching his mistress for aid once again, but did not know if the call would be answered — and besides, he didn't have the time to make another attempt. Growling curses under his breath, Obmi did the only thing he could.

The broad-shouldered dwarf brought forth a tiny bronze figurine that Zuggtmoy had secretly given him, with instructions to employ it only if he found himself alone and threatened by ultimate failure. With a powerful twist, he snapped the head off the figure's body. Although Obmi did not know this at the time, the statuette was formed in the likeness of the demon Uliel, one of the most powerful who served Zuggtmoy. With the snapping of the old bronze, flames shot forth from the body of the little idol, and the metal grew scorchingly hot. The dwarf uttered a sharp sound of pain and flung the thing a few feet away from him. As the statuette was consumed, Uliel took shape in the air above, a solid form composed of blackest shadow and licking fingers of flame.

The huge demon glared at Obmi only briefly, then turned so as to magically perceive what was happening on the battleground beyond. "You have not erred, dwarf!" the demon said in a voice that made the very air vibrate. The shadows deepened around the creature, and the flames grew bigger and brighter. A booming sound echoed in the air above the demon's head, and in the next instant another monster from the Abyss was beside Uliel. "Boar-demon," the bigger demon grated to the lesser one, "in the name of She you serve, summon the thralls of our Queen!"

The smaller demon appeared to be a mixture of the worst features of a ravening boar, a carnivorous gorilla, and a human. It grunted, a snarling yet obedient sound, and squealing, gibbering notes issued from the air in front of its huge chest. Then a popping sound issued forth, and on the ground before the boar-ape-human demon was a batrachian thing, its gaping mouth filled with a hundred needlelike teeth. "Toad-demon, bring those of your sort who serve you!" the boar-demon commanded.

Croaking in reply, the ugly beast hunkered down on its bent legs and began to make sounds such as a bullfrog of monstrous sort might give off during spring courtship. The greatest of the three demons present, Uliel, nodded his horned head, a head that was above that of the ten-foot-high boar-demon beside him. "You obey and live! See that the toad-demons propagate thus until I say otherwise. Send them forth immediately upon their bringing forth a companion of theirs — they are needed to contend with the spawn of Hades who swarm toward us now!" With that, the demon of flame and shadow stalked toward the daemons, and the first toad-demon hopped and croaked at his heels as he went, for already that creature had brought forth another, and the second was summoning a third.

Soon demons fought with daemons, while the few remaining men sought to hide, trembling in fear at the struggle that was now being waged in the remote grassland beside the Ocher River.

Meanwhile, Leda had not been idle. When the dwarf rushed off at her urging to spur the marsh-men to action, she had held back and then em-ployed her ring to invisibly slip away from him. Her first invocation had gone unfinished and thus unful-filled, but Leda still had hope that she could success-fully call upon assistance from beyond — if she could get to a secluded place and begin the process anew, this time carrying it to completion.

When she came upon a small clearing from which the ongoing struggle could be heard but not seen, Leda knelt and began to utter as elaborate a plea as she could formulate. She actually fell into a trance-like state while continuing to call for aid — and final-ly, after an indeterminate amount of time had passed, she got what she was asking for. Or, per-haps the maelstrom of daemons and demons being brought to the Material Plane by other forces was the trigger; for whatever reason, the Queen of De-mons finally brought her attention to the place where Leda invoked her. In the first instant that her form appeared, Zuggtmoy was livid.

"How dare you, bitch of Graz'zt . . ." she said in her growling, burbling tone — and then Zuggtmoy paused, for her assessment of Leda made her aware of the fact that this was not Eclavdra herself, but a clone-not-clone of the drow who served the six-fingered lord. In the next instant, as Leda came back to full awareness, Zuggtmoy transformed herself from human form to a towering, fungoid thing with vegetable eyes that saw in all directions around the copse.

"This is madness! We are undone!" the Queen of Fungi said in her strange, hollow tone in a voice that seemed to issue from inside a rotten log and sent a pungent odor of mold and decay wafting toward the little dark elf cowering nearby. Leda could not know exactly what caused the demoness to exclaim so, but the problem was evident to her. Zuggtmoy and all the other demons involved in the contest had wanted total and complete secrecy. Now, all of the beings in the multiverse who sought the last portion of the Artifact of Evil were alerted to its location and were certain to react swiftly and with all their might.

This supposition on Leda's part was swiftly borne out. A wave of hordlings came into the open, and with them were winged devils. A pack of toad-demons and a flock of vulture-demons flying above were instantly engaged with the servants of the Nine Hells in a life-and-death fight. To this combat streamed the soldiers of Law and the equally weird warriors of Chaos, while around and above them swirled shining, powerful presences that exuded an aura of Good — evidence that those of the Upper Planes were now also alerted to the goings-on.

Leda, once she realized that Zuggtmoy was paying no attention to her, gained her feet and ran off in a panic. She still cared about destroying Eclavdra, but right now the most important thing was to find a place of refuge, if any such existed in the midst of this cataclysm. Shortly thereafter Zuggtmoy vanished, but from where she had been came a tide of poisonous fungi, moving, growing, a deadly carpet that rolled toward the dell wherein the Theorpart rested.

More and more beings from all planes of the multiverse were appearing and joining in the fight. There could be no doubt that unless something happened soon, the very fabric of the material world would be unable to support this collection, and not even the deities who commanded these forces and brought them forth could be sure of controlling what would occur then. Perhaps all of the stuff that made the whole of the multiverse would be pulled into the maelstrom that this concentration of creatures and powers would soon bring about, and the parts of the terrible artifact would conjoin willy-nilly then. If deities and devils agonized over such an occurrence, they were not deterred from their purposes, either. For one reason or another, all of those who fought and directed the fight desired more than anything to possess the Final Key. So the air was alive with fighting creatures, and the ground beneath likewise swarmed with combatants, while the fabric of all that existed strained and trembled at what was occurring.

Chapter 24

THE LITTLE WOODEN QUARREL struck the ravening, four-armed monster full in its beady, red eye. Fortunately, the target was a demon, not one of the other horrors that were swarming across the field. Had it been a daemon, for instance, the venom would have been of no consequence, and a wounded, enraged creature of such sort would surely have torn its attacker to shreds in a second. Instead, as the quarrel lodged in the demon's head, the thing bellowed in terrible agony, its pincer-tipped outer arms worked frantically, and then it fell dead at Barrel's feet.

"Skunar's pearly pizzle!" the burly man exclaimed at the close call, naming the one said to rule salt waters. The oath, ancient and time-honored among seafarers as it was, would not have annoyed the deity even if Skunar himself had been on hand.

"Keep your head down!" Post shouted. Barrel ducked as a winged servant of huge size flew only a couple of yards above the ground, pursuing some monstrosity from the Lower Planes. The lean Post had by now exhausted all of the bolts he had possessed for his small crossbow and was clenching a weapon he had scavenged from the battlefield, a short-hafted fauchard with a keen-edged hook backing it, making the weapon similar to fauchard-fork-bill with an abbreviated shaft — a strange pole arm indeed, but one that the sinewy Post seemed to ply with vigor and considerable effect upon any who came near. He and four of his comrades were formed in a tight ring, facing outward to provide defense all around their perimeter.

Whether because of the posture they maintained, or for some other reason, the five forming the ring seemed to be miraculously keeping the two within it safe as they held at bay the denizens of other planes, a riotous host of which abounded now. Inside the circle, Dohojar was virtually screaming, both from distress and so as to make himself heard above the tumult. "Gord! Gord! You must wake up, please!" In his anxiety the brown-skinned Changa had forgotten about his usual honorific, Zehaab.

"Who? . . . What? . . . Where am I? . . ."

Grinning happily at the response, Dohojar said, "Gord! Oh, Gord Zehaab! You live! It was most terrible, I'll tell you — you were so blue you looked black just a few minutes ago, but now it is all right!"

"Dohojar? I . . . I must have been dreaming. Are we at camp still?"

"No, no, Zehaab. We are in the middle of a great battle with devas and devils all around!" the Changa told him.

The young adventurer managed to sit up with Dohojar's assistance. "I'm weak as a kitten," Gord said apologetically. "Wait. If we aren't at the camp, what are you doing here? All of you," he added, "are supposed to be making tracks away from here!" Gord said as he looked around and noticed the comrades who ringed him.

"Friends must take care of each other, Captain Zehaab, and we are but here in obedience to duty, for soldiers must see to the safety of their commander."

"That's a crock of crap, Dohojar, and you know it. Troops obey their leader."

The brown man gave Gord his white, toothy smile. "And leave him abandoned to die? Not so, Zehaab. We are not a pack of jackals, you know."

"I guess you're not! More like crazy men, I'd

say." The Changa smiled more broadly still at that, and Gord stopped his tirade. They were here, saving his hide, and it was high time he did something to merit their loyalty. "Help me up. If I can get some of this stiffness out of me, perhaps I can help to fight off this weird collection of creatures that are swarming all over here."

Dohojar helped him to his feet, saying, "We don't think to win, Zehaab. Mortal men cannot survive such a struggle as this. We fought only to save you. Now perhaps we will all die — or we will die and you will escape."

"Batshit! These monsters are so busy taking care of each other that they'll never notice a few folk slipping out of their confrontation."

By this time the two had struggled to take positions in the circle, the Changa assisting the still-woozy Gord to stand and walk slowly. There was a lull in the confused melee around them, so the others greeted him warmly and took a minute to breathe and rest. "How did you lot come to rescue me — again?" Gord demanded, trying to be stern.

Smoker replied. "We were going to get away, I'll tell you, when Post here saw a funny cloud gathering over the place we thought you were. It was low, and seemed to glow with a purple-black fire inside of it. We watched, and the damned thing spread outward, just like a smoke ring."

"The Changa started to go and investigate," Delver put in, "and I, for one, wasn't about to be outdone by some human. I guess Shade wasn't either, were you, Shade?" the dwarf said with a nod toward the half-elf. "Being like you are — humans — these lads were left with nothing else, so they joined in."

Gord was still bemused. "So, I understand how you decided not to get away. How you discovered me here, though, is another thing altogether."

"That was pretty easy, too," Smoker said, regaining the lead in telling what had happened. "We knew you well enough to figure you'd go to the rear of the place, so it wasn't hard to do that ourselves — all the fuss was between the two camps."

"It's Dohojar who deserves the credit, Gord," the half-elf interjected, and then corrected himself by adding, "Captain Gord Zehaab, I mean." The others managed a short round of forced laughter. "He kept an eye on you for as long as he could, and we managed to track you quite a ways. Some damned big cat — probably a leopard — got onto your trail then. He was big, and he must have been hungry. We followed his prints for a bit, then circled this way and found you."

The young thief was nearly himself now. He looked at the six and shook his head ruefully. "Now you've managed to bring me around, all right, and all you'll earn for it is a bloody end. You should have followed instructions." They all held their heads high at that, each conveying a staunch rejection of the thought of abandoning him. It made Gord feel happy and sad at the same time. "Well, the fat's in the fire, as they say, so let's see if we can get away in the smoke. Do any of you see a place where the fighting's less intense?"

"You must be jesting," Delver rumbled, and gave his beard a tug by way of emphasis. "Look around. It's getting thicker and worse. Maybe those shining fliers are champions of Good, but I think that right now they're attacking anything moving. What I'd like to find is a good, deep cave to hole up in until this fray is over."

A knot of fighting things suddenly approached them, and the seven prepared for the worst as a tall, pin-headed monster detached itself from the group and came toward them. Whether or not the thing thought they would be easier opponents, a shower of bolts discouraged it. As it hesitated, a six-legged, six-armed cylinder spun near and the pair of weird creatures fell to fighting furiously with each other. "That was too close," Smoker said as the group moved cautiously away. "Anyone have extras for the crossbows?" A fast inventory came up with only a pair of quarrels left in the group. "Well, now we have to go hand to hand," Gord observed grimly, "and the odds are good that we'll not survive that."

Streaks of fire, jets of energy, and flashes of electricity flickered and darted in all directions. Although none of these discharges seemed to be aimed in their direction, the seven had to remain alert and wary at all times. And these were not the only manifestations of magic evident around the growing melee. Rocks and logs arose from the ground, seemingly of their own volition, gathered speed, and flew through the air. Telekinesis was being used by devils and demons and who knew what else to attack their opponents. So too unseen spells and powers were in play. Light, dark, dazzling beams, fog, disembodied hands, snapping jaws, and things that couldn't be described in words were appearing and disappearing throughout the field of confrontation.

The din of roars, stentorian voices singing battle hymns, yells, shrieks, clashing metal, blaring horns, and thundering of spells sounded in ever-growing waves. Occasionally the sounds would be muffled or changed as the tide of combat shifted, but the cacophony was growing to such a pitch that the ears of men and demi-humans alike would soon no longer be able to bear it.

They all clasped hands. "Good bein' with you, cap'n," Barrel shouted, trying to demonstrate a cheerful air. Just as the others were about to bid their farewells to each other, a strange thing happened. A hush fell over the tumultuous battlefield. A strange, icy wind whispered over them, and the hush turned to dead silence. Amazingly, one by one the mighty creatures from planes of existence other than Oerth began to disappear, winking out like candle flames being extinguished. All the while the odd wind blew and a faint, cold chiming accompanied its chill.

The seven of them could still move and speak, but the otherworldly things around them were frozen by something. Whether in the air or on the ground, the creatures continued to simply wink out of existence — at least as far as the seven startled folk could tell. For a second, Gord wondered when their time would come, and then he gathered his wits about him and decided to take matters into his own hands. He pointed toward a glen not far away. "The noise of chiming comes from over there, and I'd rather see what's causing it than stand here and wait for it to take us. Follow me!" he said, and with that the young adventurer broke into a run.

When he got to a ridge from where he could see what was in the glen, Gord froze in his tracks. Post, who was following closely but had looked behind to see how the others were coming, gave a yelp of pain as he ran into Gord's back. But then, when the lean fellow saw what was directly in front of Gord in the distance, he forgot about his discomfort and also stood transfixed in surprise and shock.

An eerie tableau was laid out before them in the little glen. A female dark elf was prone upon the grass. It looked like Leda, but Gord sensed right away that it was the high priestess Eclavdra herself. Standing upright nearby, its arms raised, was a very tall, very thin figure that might have been carved from a column of snowy alabaster. The form was sexless. This was evident, for it wore not a shred of clothing. The drow seemed to be prostrate before it, in an attitude of adoration or supplication.

The dazzling white being was no statue — that was evident from the sound that came from its throat. The noise was the same faint, silvery chiming sound the group of seven had first heard a moment or two ago. Somehow, as if the being contained a hundred little bells inside it, the tinkling and chiming issued from its throat, swelling and becoming louder as it issued forth. At the same time, the being held some object above its head with both hands, and this seemed to be the source of the cold wind that whirled through the area.

Only two other figures were visible aside from dead bodies. Off to Gord's right, fifty or sixty paces distant from the white figure and the dark elf, was a male drow — a spell-binder by the looks of him, for he was frozen seemingly in the act of casting some dweomer. The wind rippled his garments, giving the dark elf a semblance of motion. Perhaps he still lived, perhaps not. On the other side of the dell equidistant from the two central figures, a blood-smeared man in battered armor leaned on his sword, staring around in a state of dazed wonder. A few of his comrades were lying nearby, dead. No enemies were in sight.

His eyes fixed on the object the willowy creature of dazzling white held above its androgynous head, Gord came down the gentle slope toward the central pair. After taking only a few steps, he could recognize the object as the Theorpart itself. While part of his mind told him to turn and run, the more sensible portion of his brain won out; certainly, this white . . . thing . . . could kill him effortlessly any time it chose to do so. But with every step he took forward, his life became that much longer, so he elected to keep advancing . . . or was it really his choice?

Gord had closed to within a few paces of the white figure when he chose to, or was caused to, halt. At the same moment, the chiming stopped. The long, thin arms moved, and the Theorpart descended from overhead to waist height. Then the being turned to one side and lowered the object into a coffer of brass as the young thief watched, transfixed by the sight. Without looking at him, the alabaster being spoke.

"You have come as is fated, Gord of Greyhawk," a clear, cold voice said. "Take your ease now, while you may, for soon you will be in trial for your life."

"Who are you that claims to know such?" Gord asked.

"Claims?" The white creature turned, looking directly at Gord for the first time with mirthless, red eyes as it laughed. "I, Vuron, make no claims at all. I simply tell you what I know."

At this point Gord first became aware that his six comrades had followed him down the slope into the glen, because he detected a sudden, collective intake of breath from behind him. They, like Gord, had just met the figure's gaze for the first time, and this was sufficient to strike awe, if not terror, into the stoutest of hearts. With great effort of will, Gord managed to prevent any visible display of fear on his part, but could not suppress a feeling of dread that rose up inside him. If this creature before him was not a mockery of goodness, a thing of evil, then no such jape could ever be thus. Handsome in its strange and sexless way, the snowy form exuded a power that made the very marrow of the bones cold. The force it radiated was of malign, frigid evil. So too the face, for despite all its handsome aspects, it embodied the demoniacal in near-human form.

As if reading his very thoughts, the alabaster demon lord Vuron looked down at Gord and said, "There is evil, as your sort name it, and there is *Evil.* I pose you no physical threat, Gord of Greyhawk, nor any mental one either — unless you believe that reason is baneful. . . ."

"Demon-talk, Vuron, is just that. Yet I confess," Gord went on, "that your actions and words . . . puzzle me."

"They trouble you. You wonder why I simply do not take up the Final Key, slay you and your associates for the pleasure of seeing you die, and transport myself and the Theorpart to the safety of the Abyss."

At this, the young adventurer knew that the tall demon was indeed reading his thoughts. "And?"

was all Gord said.

"We must speak with no reservations, and our time is brief. I do read your thoughts, but the amulet around your neck allows me only to scan the very surface of your mind. I tell you this in order to gain your trust — sufficient trust to consider what I have to tell you now. You are thereafter, of course, free to make whatever decision you choose. What I have just done is—"

"Shut your perverted mouth!" This screeching demand came from Eclavdra. The High Priestess of Graz'zt had sprung up at Vuron's last words, her beautiful face contorted in rage. She pointed a finger and glared up into the red eyes of the towering, thin demon without the slightest trace of deference, let alone fear. "You have done too much already, you pale snake, and I will make you answer to My king for what you seek to tell this mortal now!"

Vuron never blinked, but he did smile a cold, dead smile. "My liege *and* yours, too, and I have served him for eons. . . . Yet this is not the time for such petty matters. You too have to face the prescribed conclusion of your trial, as it were."

"My trial is you, Vuron," Eclavdra shot back with acidity, hatred still written on her every feature. "I have powers too, and I name you a traitor now and always. The human you seek to treat with is not of the Abyss, and you would give over to him that which is Mine by right!"

"Yours?" the alabaster demon lord said expressionlessly. "If you claimed it our king's, I must acquiesce in spirit if not avow it a fact. No matter. You have spent the time allowed you uselessly, it would seem. The moment is gone, and they come. . . . Prepare now, drow — and you too, Gord of Greyhawk — to face your opponents in combat. You see? The two come now, and with them are their supporters."

Both Eclavdra and Gord looked to where the

thin, white demon was pointing. At the edge of the dell was the broad-shouldered Obmi, martel in hand, and with him were Leda and a dozen fierce-looking marshmen.

"Eclavdra, you dark bitch!" the dwarf boomed out. "You have put yourself into My hands by violating the rules of the contest, and I'll close my fists and crush you for it!"

The dwarf rushed forward, accelerating at an unbelievable pace thanks to his magical boots. "Gord," said Vuron as Obmi began his charge, "you must face that one. The life of Eclavdra is not his to take or die trying — that opportunity belongs to her clone, the one you named Leda."

Without pausing to consider the veracity of the statement, Gord drew his sword and leaped to intercept Obmi's rush. Behind him, his six friends moved to defend him from any other foe who sought to interfere in the duel. The wild brigands from the Hool marshes gladly went to meet these opponents.

As for Eclavdra, as soon as she laid eyes upon her clone, she paid no attention to any other, even the onrushing dwarf. In fact, had Gord not intervened, Obmi could have struck the dark elf down with a single blow. Their eyes locked, Eclavdra and Leda closed with each other and squared off.

"I should have known!" spat the high priestess.

Leda smiled at the outcry, shouting back, "Yes, you should have, mother, sister, and self," and she laughed at that even as Eclavdra scowled.

"How could it be? You had a telepathic link — I know that now! — and I had none . . . or did I?"

"You didn't, for all I know," Leda said as the two stood only a few feet apart. It was as if a mirror cast the reflection of the other — they were identical twins, cloned and clone. "You failed because of me. That I *do* know!"

The triumph evident in Leda's expression was too much for Eclavdra. Her mouth set in a grimace of fury, eyes blazing violet evil, she flew at her twin with nothing more than clawed hands and bared teeth. It was not surprising to any onlooker knowing the circumstances that Leda responded in the same manner. The two dark elves collided, locked, and fell to roll on the ground in a parody of how females battled when they sought to scratch and claw until one or the other surrendered. This fight, however, was not likely to end until one of the combatants was dead.

When the young thief interposed himself between Obmi and the original object of the dwarf's ire, the broad-shouldered servant of the demoness checked his attack. He faced Gord with his pick held ready in both hands. His face bore a sneer of contempt, but there was a crafty gleam in the dwarf's eyes. "I once supposed you a pile of stone, but then I heard you had returned — just as a wart does," rumbled the dwarf, allowing himself a small chuckle at his own joke. "Miracles of that sort don't often happen, lightweight little human. Stand aside and let Me slay the drow, or better still for you, join Me in the killing of that whore, and I will reward you—"

Gord's longsword flicked out in a lunge, and the dwarf had to bite off his sentence and dance backward. "No, you lying and crooked dungheap!" Gord spat back. "No demon-serving dwarf will make bargains with me. After you overcome me, the field is clear to do as you will — but you'll find me no easy foe!"

The reply was too long — just what Obmi had hoped would happen. As the young adventurer was uttering the last two words, Obmi rushed suddenly to his right, darted in, and swung a two-handed, backhand blow with the martel's hammer head. It was aimed at Gord's left kneecap, but it went high and landed with a meaty thud upon his thigh instead. The young thief was unable to stifle a gasp of pain as the force of the blow buckled his leg, but it was because he toppled that he was able to avoid the next stroke.

As Gord was going down, Obmi pivoted on his left heel, executing a full circle with incredible speed and wheeling the martel around as he did so. The long pick was aimed at the left side of the young adventurer's chest. If he had simply dropped in his tracks from the effect of the first wound, the point of the martel would have taken Gord just under the ribs and struck his heart as it hooked upward. However, instead of trying to stand his ground, Gord had used the momentum of the leg-blow to help him move to his right in a motion that turned to a roll and a recovery slightly behind and to the right of where he had been struck. The pick missed its mark by inches, but that was enough. The upswing caught and tore his already tattered smock, exposing the fine mesh of steel he wore beneath it.

"Quick as a mouse," Obmi snarled, "but this cat's claw of mine will pin you down yet!"

Gord had to grit his teeth to stand on his wounded leg and appear unhurt. Not only was the dwarf terribly strong, but the martel's hammer head had small spikes upon it, and the blow it had delivered was very painful. Blood trickled down his leg, and this made Gord both wary and angry. "You are not a cat, dwarf, but a rat! That little nosepicker of yours is no cat's claw — it's just your ratty little teeth!" Then, his longsword ready, Gord came slowly forward. "This is a weapon more fitted to a cat, dungpile, and I'll let you feel it in a moment."

Obmi edged away just as cautiously as his foe approached. He was confident of ultimate victory, especially as he saw the effects of his blow upon the dark-haired, lean human. The fellow might be small and quick, a superb swordsman possibly, but his strength and skill would prove no match for the dwarf if Obmi but took his time and used his vast store of experience to fullest advantage. The human would lunge at him soon, using the length of his arm and sword in hopes of gaining a hit that the shorter martel would be unable to reply to. But he would be unpleasantly surprised when he tried the attack, for Obmi was ready and planning a quick lunge himself. He'd move under the sword and bring the hammer head up from beneath, using it against the arm this time. Then Gord's attack came, and as the lunge began toward his chest, Obmi ducked and began his countermove.

A smaller opponent with a shorter, non-thrusting weapon has limited resources in a duel, and Gord understood this well. His lunge was a feint, in a way. He began the strike high, but as he shot his arm forth he also thrust out his right leg, which lowered his body. The point of the blade went down as it sped out, and the dwarf couldn't duck low enough to escape it. The sword went home cleanly, imbedding six inches of its bright metal in Obmi's right shoulder. Then it darted out, withdrawn in the next instant as Gord managed to back off quickly despite his painfully wounded left thigh. Naturally, the dwarf's countering strike never came off.

"Damn you, man!" Obmi snarled, his huge beard seeming to bristle in fury as he spoke. His left hand clasped over the place where the sword had struck, the dwarf backed away from his opponent, swinging the martel loosely before him with his right hand to guard his retreat.

By concentrating on not yielding to the pain, Gord was slowly bringing his leg back to the point where he could utilize it fully in acrobatic attack maneuvers. The deep wound he had inflicted on Obmi would begin to tell soon in any case, he told himself, so there was no need to hurry. He made careful thrusts that did not land, parried swipes of the martel in turn, and readied for a final series to bring the battle to a close. In preparation for this last rush, Gord drew his dagger. As he moved in, he would use the shorter blade to catch the pick, turn it, and leave the way clear for telling work with the sword.

Upon seeing this second weapon, Obmi merely snorted, grabbed the martel with both hands once again, and stood rock-still with the pick cocked above his big head. Gord's eyes widened, and he drew back a step as he noticed something shocking — no blood came from the place where he had impaled the dwarf!

"You see, do you?" Obmi laughed. "Time is on My side, mouse, not yours. Even as I tell you this, the last of the harm done by your sword is healing itself magically. Lay down your weapons now, and I will give you a swift and clean death!"

As the dwarf should well have known, a swift and clean death was not part of Gord's plan for himself. In fact, he preferred no death at all, if he had anything to say about it. Instead of shrinking back or lowering his weapons, Gord burst forward in a flurry of motion, his body and his sword whirling at blurring speed. Obmi backed away only slowly, deflecting each sword strike with his hammer held before him while he waited for an opening through which to strike a killing blow. Impatience got the better of the dwarf, and he decided to end things with an overhead stroke despite two important facts: he needed a second to bring the hammer up before he could use it, and he stood a good two feet shorter than his foe.

As Obmi raised the martel over his head, Gord brought his dagger to the fore. When the hammer came back down, the long-bladed dagger rang against the latten of the pick, and the dagger's quillon caught and held the curved spike high as if it were frozen there. Obmi was strong, stronger by far than Gord, but leverage because of his greater height was in favor of the gray-eyed thief for the moment — and a moment was all he needed.

Before Obmi could utilize his demon-bestowed strength to fully counter the leverage, Gord brought the long blade of his sword in a sweeping blow that struck low. Its half-circle of travel before impact lent it terrible force, and the edge bit through flesh and bone despite the metal and leather that protected it. Obmi managed, somehow, to shove Gord away, for his power was that of a giant despite his small stature. But as Gord tumbled and sprawled backward from the desperate shove, so too fell the dwarf. His left leg had been severed just below the knee.

"Tit for tat, rat! Will your magic grow that back?" Gord mocked. Even as he spoke, though, the young thief saw that the stump stopped bleeding almost instantly, and by the time Gord had regained his feet the pain-wracked visage of the dwarf had begun to clear. The young thief stared in amazement as Obmi scrambled back to a standing position, using his hammer to help his still-intact leg support his body — while the leg that Gord had severed seemed to grow longer by the minute.

Gord was not afraid, but quite confused. Was this Obmi some sort of troll? What if the severed leg grew into a second dwarf to fight with him? While he involuntarily considered these questions for a second or two, Gord failed to follow up on his advantage. As he hesitated, Obmi tore an ebon crystal from around his neck and hurled it at Gord. Instinctively, the young man sought to deflect the missile with his sword. The black object struck the blade and shattered, and Gord was engulfed in night.

Gord lunged and struck then at the place where his foe had been but a moment before. It was too late, of course. In the cloaking darkness, Obmi had moved elsewhere. Gord's blade stabbed grass and soil, not flesh. He could hear no sound from the dwarf, but this was not because the blackness surrounding them cloaked noise; there were noises aplenty in the air as men fought and yelled and died nearby. Unfortunately, those sounds masked any noise that the desperate dwarf might make while doing whatever he was doing. Not wishing to be taken by some other trick of Obmi's, Gord stepped backward as rapidly as he dared, feeling the ground as he did so to avoid a misstep. After ten such moves the blackness thinned, and another crabwise step carried him into sunlight.

Paying no heed to the melee around him, Gord began to circle the blot that covered the dwarf. The darkness lay on the land in a hemisphere at least thirty feet across and half as high. As he proceeded to search the perimeter, looking for Obmi if he attempted to escape, Gord's eye happened to fall upon his sword blade. The length of its metal no longer gleamed. The whole was deepest black, and the inky stain was even now spreading downward over the guard and onto the grip toward his hand. With an oath, Gord hurled the weapon from him, fearful that the sooty hue would somehow harm him. As he watched the blackness creep over his weapon, an idea came to him — a way that he could pursue and find Obmi even within the lightless dome he had conjured up. . . .

The odor was strong. Dwarf, dwarven blood, dwarven sweat, dwarven breath too. The huge black leopard waited not an instant to attack. Little motes of light were dancing within the ebony of the blot now, but whether the darkness was somehow evaporating or some other dweomer was transforming it, only one matter was important: Obmi must be slain. The dwarf was taken completely by surprise when Gord-panther pounced upon him from the side. Somehow the broad-shouldered demi-human managed to bring his martel to bear, and the weapon inflicted a few wounds upon the sleek, black-furred cat's body. But the panther's long fangs sank deep, and its claws tore and raked the dwarf.

Then, after absorbing a particularly vicious blow, Gord-panther managed to seize Obmi's shoulder with his teeth, hold the dwarf's torso fast in his forepaws, and draw the unnatural demi-human into an inescapable embrace — an embrace of death. The rear legs of his leopard body drew up and kicked downward once, twice, thrice as the foreclaws dug deep and Gord-panther's jaws closed tighter and tighter. Obmi screamed in agony and attempted to use his magical strength to dislodge the feline attacker. The dwarf had his arms free, so he seized the great cat by its throat and tried to throttle it. Gord held his teeth fast upon Obmi's shoulder, hardened his muscular cat's throat, and continued to rake with his hind legs. Flesh tore to ribbons. The thick little fingers, fingers that had felt like steel bars sinking into his windpipe and jugular, suddenly went limp. Gord-panther relaxed the grip he had held with forepaws and jaws, but the raking of his rear claws continued on instinct. Obmi's throat rattled, and then his gutted body flew a few feet through the air, propelled by the cat's still-kicking back legs.

In a bound, Gord was atop the seemingly lifeless body. It was a limp thing, a collection of bloody rags and a mutilated, eviscerated shambles of what had been a mighty champion of Evil. That made no difference to Gord, for even in his feline killing fury one thing remained clear in his mind — the dead dwarf had *two* legs.

Gord-panther picked up the corpse in his jaws and shook it as a terrier shakes a rat. He used claws too, tearing and rending the lifeless body until it was no longer an integral unit but lay in several pieces. Only then did Gord allow his panther self to cease its furious assault and slink a short distance away. The darkness was nearly gone now, nothing more than a haze of black motes that were slowly dissolving. As the last of the motes vanished and the sun again shed its light upon the torn circle where Obmi had fought his last fight, Gord stood again as a man.

"Gord! I thought I saw a great black panther in that— By the Great Horn Spoon!" Barrel's ugly face, marred still further by a long cut across his cheek, lost its grin as he spoke. The burly man's eyes were riveted on the shambles before him.

Following Barrel's gaze, Gord too muttered a shocked oath. The torn bits of the dwarf were pulsing, moving, creeping toward each other. "That vile bastard still lives!" Gord shouted. The cry brought Delver and Shade on the run. It was the dwarf who spoke first.

"That one is like a troll, Gord. Keep those hunks o' flesh apart from one another, and I'll build a fire quickly. Then when it's going, we toss in all the pieces. Burning is the only way to finish such a thing as that." Delver set about his task while the other three kept busy at the strange and grisly business of prodding and pushing the pieces so that they could not come together.

"The other three are in bad shape, cap'n," Barrel said to Gord as they worked. "We've got 'em restin' on the other side of that little hillock."

"We'll tend to them soon," said Gord sincerely, "but much as I hate to say it, what we're doing right now is more important than all three of their lives — or ours either, for that matter."

"Aye, cap'n," said Barrel, who did not really need to be impressed with the seriousness of the situation as he contended with the scuttling bits of flesh and bone.

Minutes later the fire was ready, and they all took up pieces one by one and threw them in the flames. Dark, pungent smoke plumed skyward, and it was over. Obmi the dwarf, servant of Evil, champion of demons, was no more. Gord imagined he heard a wailing, the nearly inaudible sound of an evil life force lamenting as it went off to its end in the lowest of the lower planes.

Barrel had gone back to check on their three injured comrades while Gord witnessed the dwarf's final undoing. The burly seaman trudged back up to his captain with tears glistening in his eyes. "Dohojar an' Smoker seem like they'll be okay . . ." he said, putting his hand upon the young thief's shoulder, "but poor Post is a goner."

"When does this end?" Gord said to himself more than anyone else. Then shaking his head to clear away the depression, it occurred to him that the battleground was more empty than it should have been. "Where are the others?" he asked. "What's happened to the white demon? Leda? Eclavdra?"

"Those three were right over there," Shade answered, pointing to the spot where Gord had first laid eyes on Vuron and Eclavdra. "I happened to be looking there, because a pair of Obmi's wild men were headed for the two females — the dark elves."

"Leda and Eclavdra," Gord supplied.

"I went for the men, thinking to take 'em both on, but the pale demon did something, and he . . . it . . . and both of the drow just vanished!" Then the half-elf added as an afterthought, "Those lousy marshers were so startled at that that I did for them both without much trouble at all. I guess they were the last left alive."

"Let's see to the wounded," Gord replied after a few seconds of contemplation, "and then we'll worry about what's happened to the rest."

As the four started toward the place where Dohojar and Smoker lay unconscious, the earth shook and rumbled. Steam spurted up through a fissure that opened at their feet, and the group jumped back as quickly as they could. Then the ground erupted in a gout of smoke and flames, the blaze of the fire and blackness of the fumes obscuring the vision of all four.

Chapter 25

THE ALABASTER DEMON LORD stood on a circle of ground that appeared as bright and fresh as a morning meadow. The grass was green and sparkling with dew; little flowers tipped their faces toward the sun overhead. No sign of struggle, blood, or death was visible upon this unspoiled disc. Beside the tall, thin being from the Abyss stood Leda. At least it appeared to Gord to be her, for her garments were those that Eclavdra's clone had worn just today, and her sword was the very one she had taken from the dead Yoli warrior what seemed like an age ago. The demon merely regarded the four warriors with his red-pink eyes, and the dark elf spoke.

"Gord! You live! You have actually slain Obmi?" she cried, smiling and coming toward him as she spoke, her arms opening and then embracing him as she got close.

Gord was tempted to return her embrace. But instead, he remained stiff and unresponsive. "Yes," he said without emotion. "I killed the dwarf." At his cold reaction and toneless words, Leda released her grip on his torso and stepped back from him, her face showing hurt. Gord disregarded that. "What of Eclavdra?" he inquired in the same emotionless voice.

"Eclavdra is gone — finished! Only Leda lives."

"Is there a difference?"

Now the dark elf's beautiful face showed both

hurt and anger. "How can you, of all who know me, ask such a question?"

"Much has occurred since last I thought I knew you . . . Leda. How am I, a poor, simple man, to know the truth of anything?"

Vuron laughed a musical, silvery-cold laugh at that. "Well put, Gord of Greyhawk. Yet even demons must often labor under the same burden which you claim. Allow Me to assure you that this is indeed Leda, not the one from whom she sprang — and there *is* a difference."

"Truth from the mouth of a demon?"

Again Vuron laughed. "Yes. Stranger things occur frequently. And there is yet more. . . ."

Delver, Shade, and Barrel had been close to their friend when the strange appearance of demon and drow occurred. Each was clasping his weapon, prepared to fight a hopeless fight to the last against this supernatural enemy. Now they were confused and uncertain, just as Gord was. Delver growled a warning, which was supported by Barrel's advice to "Beware the words of demons, cap'n!" Shade merely shook his long-haired head and took a step closer to the young thief, his weapon pointing at the snow-white Vuron.

Without any apparent offense taken at the reactions of the four, the demon lord slowly lowered his head to gaze at the sward at his feet. With a slight gesture and a soft series of sounds, Vuron caused a chest of beaten brass to appear at his feet, out of thin air. "The Final Key, Gord, lies therein," the demon said, indicating the container. "Perhaps you will allow Me to explain what has happened before you decide to do what you must do."

"Explain? Or do you mean, tell me what I am to do?" Gord shot back with contempt.

"Oh, no. I can by no means tell you what to do, Gord of Greyhawk. Your course is very much your own, and even a demon lord of My power is unable to alter that fact. Still, I can alter a few things," and as he spoke this the alabaster being looked away from the four who stood staring at him to the place a few paces away where the body of Post lay.

"I heal you, man," the demon pronounced. Post's chest heaved, he groaned, and then the lean man sat up, rubbing his eyes as if just awakening from a night's sleep. Vuron turned his glance to the injured pair, Smoker and Dohojar. "You two have likewise fought bravely. Be whole." Smoker rolled over on his side and began snoring peacefully, while the brown-skinned Changa sat up and looked at his friends with a white-toothed smile, not knowing what to say.

Gord did have a reply to these acts. "You use demon-powers to bribe me, to bemuse and befuddle my mind. I am unmoved, Vuron."

"That is exactly as I thought," the pale creature said. "The gesture was simply meant to take concern for your comrades from your mind. It must be free of such worries, Gord of Greyhawk, if it is to properly absorb what I now ask your permission to relate."

After a few seconds of consideration, Gord nodded. "I will hear your words, Vuron, with as much disinterest as is possible for one such as I."

"That is considerable, I assure you, but your attention is all I ask. Now I will relate what has transpired," the demon lord said, sinking to a sitting position on the long grass. The four disliked doing so, but they too sat warily when Leda followed Vuron's example, taking a position between the demon and the group of men and demi-humans. "Now, pay full attention," said Vuron in a contented tone. "What I have to say is rather lengthy.

"When the contest for the Theorpart commenced, I brought Leda into being. She is not and never was a true clone of Eclavdra, for never would I replicate such a one as that drow was. If ever a mortal creature could have visited ruin upon My liege lord, that one could have. I altered Leda — as

384

you named her, Gord — and did what I could to aid her. Being as I am, a demon, I could not place any goodness within her, not even any balance or neutrality. She now possesses some modicum of both, and that is because of you, Gord of Greyhawk."

"Do you state blame or proffer some credit toward me, Vuron? Your words make no sense."

"Oh, but they do! As for blame, I just might harbor that against you for many reasons, but I also balance that with much credit for what you did, Gord. The clay of the almost-clone was molded by you — even if just a little. This version of Eclavdra, this Leda, can never act as the original did. There is no longer any threat to My lord."

"Perhaps I rue those words, demon! Why should I be interested in what benefits the denizens of the Abyss?"

"Rest assured that the influence of the departed drow would have been baneful in many ways, Gord of Greyhawk. She would have brought destruction to your world, ruin to Mine own realm, and all the others of demonkind too."

"Yes, Gord," Leda interjected urgently. "It was Vuron's work which gave me the telepathic power to influence Eclavdra without her knowing it. Without such an advantage, she would have taken the Final Key but for a brief time, only to lose it to Obmi and his mistress."

"One demon or another, what does it matter? All humanity loses either way."

"Be not so quick to decide, Gord of Greyhawk," Vuron said in his clear, sexless voice. "What I tell you now centers on that very matter, on the Final Key, and certainly on the fate of all we know as the multiverse."

"I am to decide this?" Gord uttered a mocking laugh in disbelief.

"When I intervened in Eclavdra's actions," Vuron said without commenting on Gord's utterance, "she had violated the compact regarding the Theorpart, and I could take it from her. Once this was done, I could use its power for but a moment to undo what the foolish drow had wrought. Despite those facts, I have no power to claim the Final Key. You, or Leda, must decide what is to be done with it."

"You mean—"

"Yes. You could take it now and in an instant present it to the Demiurge. Basiliv might even accept it. . . ."

Leda spoke then, her voice heavy with emotion. "One thing is sure, Gord. I will not be the arbiter of this. I yield my right to you."

"What she is saying, Gord of Greyhawk," the pale demon explained, "is that she could challenge you for the Final Key. Whichever of you survived would then possess the right to dispose of it. But Leda gives you her right. She will not fight against you, and that is evidence of the effect you have made upon her persona."

This placed Gord in a terrible quandary. Basiliv, and Rexfelis the Catlord as well, had charged him with the very same responsibility. Long, long ago, at the time Gord had first set out on the quest for the last portion of the artifact, both of his mentors had said that the ultimate decision would be his, should he actually succeed in gaining possession of the Final Key. Now Leda, once his beloved, now a distrusted uncertainty, and Vuron, a hated foe, a demon lord of unknown power and certain evil, both placed the same decision squarely upon his head.

"I could give the thing over to Basiliv?" Gord said. Vuron nodded affirmatively. "Mordenkainen? The Cabal? Iuz? The Brotherhood? Anyone?" To each question the alabaster demon indicated a positive answer. Finally the young thief asked, "Myself? I could keep and wield its power for myself?"

"You could hold the Theorpart for as long as fate allowed, Gord of Greyhawk. Whether you could employ it is unknown to Me, but I think that somehow you would manage. . . ."

"What *am* I to do with the cursed thing?"

"Being nothing more nor less than a demon lord," Vuron said without force, "I cannot say."

Gord looked at Leda. Now she seemed again like the beautiful dark elf he had grown to love as they adventured across the Barren Plains and onto the Ashen Desert — no longer a stranger, a drow, and a priestess of demons. Her return gaze was warm. Her violet eyes were deep pools of emotion that he could only interpret as love for him. "And you, Leda? Have you any words for me on this matter?"

"If you will truly hear them, Gord — with your heart as well as your mind."

He gave a tiny shrug, a little gesture of hopelessness. "I am what I am. I can hear only as I can, but I will try, Leda, to listen with all of my being."

"Then I will speak to you, love, even though what I must say is so painful that I would rather die now than say what I believe. . . . Good can never possess the artifact — no part of it, not even its essence. Should those who stand between Good and Evil and between Law and Chaos obtain the Theorpart, it will at least corrupt and change them to suit its nature. The possessor of such a thing must surely come to be like the one to whom it is linked — or else, the Theorpart will bring ruin."

Gord cocked his head at that. "Ruin? How so?"

"The power of the artifact flows through each of its parts. Each calls to the other, each seeks to place itself into the hands of those attuned to its nullity. It will be united, or it will bring destruction on any being preventing its conjoining."

"Then either whomever I bestow the Final Key upon is doomed, or I bring doom to all the world!"

Vuron responded to that. "Not exactly, but Leda's words and your understanding are almost perfect in this matter. The artifact must always exist, and if it remains in its separate parts, there must always be tension and conflict as the portions exert their influence. Only one force can now be used to keep them from being joined, Gord of Greyhawk, but the selection must be yours. More cannot be said."

"Quite a lure — the temptation to employ evil to overthrow evil," Gord murmured in observation.

Vuron said nothing to that, but Leda came close to him and placed her arm around his hunched shoulders. "Even the greatest and wisest of the minions of Good would fall to such a lure, Gord."

"So if any faction of Good or Evil holds two parts, the third part would be subject to the other two, and the whole artifact would conjoin. . . . But yet is there not the force of Concordance?"

"Is there?" Leda asked softly.

"No . . . I am not reasoning properly," Gord admitted. "Those who hold to the necessity of all and seek balance are too weak to oppose the others. They would be assailed from all sides, by Good and Evil alike. The key would fall into other hands soon enough, and the inevitable would then result."

"I think you should destroy the blasted thing, cap'n," Barrel ventured weakly.

"Would that such an option existed," Vuron said with such emotion that it amazed all. "Not even the greatest of deities could safely do that. To try is to bring ruin, for the thing would then unite as all other forces became disrupted in sympathy, and He-Who-Must-Sleep-Forever would then awaken!"

"Evil alone can possess these Theorparts," Gord said in amazement, realizing the final truth of the matter. "Each of the keys had been resting with those of malign sort, although none knew it . . . at that time."

"That is correct, Gord of Greyhawk," Vuron said, again without expression in his voice.

"But only the chaos of the Abyss seeks to keep the artifact disjoined, for the proud and independent rulers of demonkind would not willingly bow to any."

"Again, you relate the facts as they exist," Vuron observed unemotionally.

"Then you, Vuron, must accept the Final Key!" It was a demand, not a request or statement.

"Perhaps," the alabaster-hued demon lord said slowly. Vuron nodded, looking squarely at Gord with his red eyes. "Yes, perhaps. But even one who wields the might of a Theorpart cannot force that object upon another if that one is unwilling."

"You're telling me that you — and your master too — are unwilling to possess the thing?"

"I am willing only under certain conditions, Gord of Greyhawk. As for My liege, I must serve him as best I am able. . . ."

"But the devil-serving Brotherhood holds one, and Iuz the other! If either of them should gain this portion, then all are doomed!"

"That is correct — but what difference if My acceptance spells eventual doom anyway?"

Gord stared at the pale being in bewilderment for a moment, then asked, "The conditions. What are they?"

"Leda must accompany the Final Key. She must go with it as Eclavdra, High Priestess of Graz'zt. You must agree to this first. Then you must willingly give over the Theorpart to her. And then she and I will depart with it," Vuron said slowly and clearly.

"Never! I will never, never consign the one I love to the Abyss!"

Leda embraced him, kissing him tenderly, holding him as she murmured words of endearment. The pleasure lasted all too brief a time; then she spoke. "But you must, my love. I am willing, for if I were not, then all of Oerth would be ruined! Think of all, not of me or yourself. The price we each must pay is nothing in the balance of all."

Gord pushed her away in a fury of disbelief. "What is this demon's trick, Vuron?"

"No deception, Gord of Greyhawk. Leda speaks as must be spoken. As Eclavdra — an Eclavdra with more than selfishness and lust for power within herself — she alone can mitigate against the force that the Final Key will assert. My liege will accept such influence, I think, if any help is possible in this matter. Possession of the Final Key will bring woe upon us, but My rede is that it will not ultimately destroy him or the whole of the Abyss if this drow is there to assist Me. She must come, or else I must refuse the Theorpart."

For minutes Gord sat in stunned silence, his mind reeling, frantically seeking some different solution. Leda seemed to realize the instant when he finally gave in.

"You know what you must do, my dearest one."

"Yes, I know, Leda," Gord answered. "There is an inescapable conclusion, and I understand I must now face it."

"I will love you always, Gord, even when I must become more and more Eclavdra and less and less myself."

"I know. . . ."

"Then you must do as Vuron says."

"But I am not ready to give you up yet! Can we have time for a proper farewell, at least?"

"There is no time, love. Even the power of the Final Key cannot maintain this static condition for long. Unless it passes to me soon, and I to the deeps of the Abyss, there will be what was here before — all alignments contending in a struggle of doom."

Gord bent and kissed her then, a long, lingering kiss of farewell. It had to last him forever, and he knew it. Then he stepped back, holding her shoulders at arms' length. "You are free to act, Leda, my loved one. Do as you must. I do not resist your decision, be it as it may. I freely give you the Final Key." There was no feeling in his voice as he uttered those words, no light in his eyes as he spoke.

Leda took his hands briefly, then allowed hers to trail slowly from his grasp in a last, unspoken goodbye. "I am ready now, Vuron," she told the pale demon lord as she picked up the brass coffer.

"Eclavdra, High Priestess and Champion of Graz'zt, declares victory in his name and commands you to carry Me and the prize I have won to him!"

Vuron said not a word, but he looked at Gord with what might have been sympathy. His gaze moved aside, fixing on a spot not far from where the young adventurer sat. Then Leda-Eclavdra stepped to a position beside the demon, and the two disappeared without a sound.

His friends looked at him in stunned silence, none daring to speak. Gord didn't notice. He sat slowly, bowed his head, and remained that way in silence, eyes open but not looking at anything. He sat this way for so long that the ones who waited for him might have thought him dead, except for the shallow breathing that was barely discernible to those closest to him. Finally, Shade sat down next to him and spoke.

"You did as a hero would do, Gord. I speak for all when I tell you that none of us would have had the wit or the will to do so brave a thing as you have done."

The young man lifted his head and turned his gray eyes toward the half-elf, but Shade could detect nothing within their depths. The gaze was flat and bore no hint of what lay beyond the windows of his mind.

Then Barrel approached deferentially. "Your sword, cap'n. . . . I found it just layin' in the grass and figured you'd be wantin' it soon."

Gord accepted the proffered weapon without comment. Then he looked down again, his eyes still dead and his face a mask. Everyone else simply waited as the sky turned a leaden gray and a drizzle of cold rain began to fall. Gord didn't seem to notice. It would be a long afternoon . . . and a longer night.

Chapter 26

"AIN'T MUCH OF A PLACE!" Barrel said disdainfully, gesturing to indicate that the remark referred to the whole of Dolle Port.

"I thought, big-bellied one, that you came from this place," Dohojar said with mock wonder at the burly man's expression of distaste.

"Sure, sure," Barrel agreed. "The Seakings' Lands is where I was born as all babes must be birthed, but I was raised aboard a ship — and it's the smell of salt air and the sound of wind in the rigging that I long for now, you sun-baked lubber!" He made a mock gesture of anger that even the Changa could not fail to interpret as jesting.

"Barrel's right," Smoker agreed. "This town is about as dirty and dull as any I've ever seen. What say, Gord? I'm ready to see the last of this place if you are."

Delver rumbled his affirmation of that. "We dwarven folk aren't known as seafarers, captain, but as far as I'm concerned, Barrel said it. Even a sea voyage is better than spending another night in Dolle Port."

At that Shade laughed, and Post too chuckled. "That's unanimous, Gord, for the two of us can't disagree," Post said for the half-elf and himself. "It's up to you, though, because you're the one we elected as leader, and nobody's taken that back yet."

"Yet? What does that mean, Post?"

"Hell's flaming floors, captain!" the lean man exclaimed. "You don't really expect us to agree to elect you *permanent* captain, do you?"

Even Gord had a laugh at that. "Well, I just don't know what to do next," he then said with a serious tone. "There are a number of possibilities. . . ."

"Not at all!" Barrel was adamant. "There's a vessel leavin' for a cruise along the coast o' the Western Jungle tomorrow — just the ticket for us, and there's places left we can take. Why, with a bit o' luck, we'll all come out as rich as the potentates of them places Dohojar keeps talkin' about. Even if we don't make it big, exactly, the master of that ship — the Slobberin' Sea Lion, or somethin' like that — tells me he's headed for the Ulek Prince's state to trade when he's done with the jungle savages. With the wealth we pick up there, we can—"

"Enough," Gord said with a sigh of resignation. "I guess a little sailing on the seas of Oerth is bound to do me some good. Seeing as how the rest of you seem to have already made up your minds, I'll go along with the decision. First thing in the morning, we sign up with the Sovereign Sea Lion," he said, casting a sly glance at Barrel as he corrected the man's pronunciation. "For better or worse, we'll be sailing the sea as free traders by tomorrow afternoon."

For a second, Barrel considered pointing out that true sailors didn't consider Jade Bay part of the sea, though it was a good-sized body of water. "Then we'd better be prepared, boys!" he caroled happily to the others. "Settin' sail tomorrow means we've a heap o' funnin' to do tonight. It just won't do to board a new ship without an achin' head and a flat purse, you know."

All six managed to get a grasp on some portion of Gord. By pulling and pushing, the laughing band directed their leader toward the line of taverns that stood near the wharf. Barrel was the most experienced sailor of the lot, and there was no profit in disagreeing with such learned opinion.

"Soon I will see the true wonders of the east," Dohojar said to Gord. The young thief couldn't tell for sure if the dark-eyed Changa was serious or pulling his leg. Somehow, it didn't really matter. In a few minutes there would be beakers of wine and lusty songs to fill his mind with meaninglessness. Tomorrow was tomorrow, and there was no merit in knowing either it, or truth, right now.

The light of dawn made the waters of Dolle Port's deep pool a bright mirror, and for a short time the winds were calm, keeping the big ship motionless upon the surface of the bay. Then the heat of the rising sun brought a breeze from the land. The sails flapped idly at first, then filled and grew taut. The wind pushed the Sovereign Sea Lion southward, and in its stout-timbered hull its crew and officers raised a cheer. Even the ship seemed to leap at that, as glad in its own way as the life aboard it was to be making for distant ports and far places.

A solitary, muffled figure stood watching from the docks as the ship's creamy sails grew smaller and soon were but a black speck disappearing on the horizon. The figure stayed until the ship vanished entirely. Then it turned, mingled with the passing throng, and was lost.

LOOK FOR MORE

GORD the ROGUE™

BOOKS SOON!

City of Hawks

The next GORD THE ROGUE™ novel takes a giant step
backward in time, chronicling the major events in Gord's life prior to
Sea of Death. You'll learn about his childhood and his early adult
years, find out more about his relationship with the mysterious
Rexfelis, and witness the excitement and suspense as he faces nine
tests that will determine how the rest of his life will unfold.

Come Endless Darkness

In the sequel to *Sea of Death*, Gord grows older and wiser, and the
challenges he must face also magnify in power to the point where no
one can be sure whether the world as Gord knows it will continue to
exist. Can he prevent the destruction of his world, or should he be
content to merely survive the events that unfold — and if he does
survive, what will life afterward be like?

Night Arrant

Of course, Gord's life has not always revolved around issues where
the fate of the world is at stake. Sometimes his adventures are
small ones, and not all of them are serious. In *Night Arrant*, the first
GORD THE ROGUE short story collection, you'll travel with Gord
through the streets of the city where he grew up, you'll meet some
of the interesting characters he has played with and fought against,
and you'll see how he copes with both triumph and tragedy.

ALL GORD THE ROGUE books are written by Gary Gygax, the pioneering creative
force in the role-playing game industry. The spirit and excitement of a fantasy role-
playing adventure are captured in all the books and stories — yet they can be enjoyed
by people who are not involved in the hobby of gaming as well as by those who are.

**Look for GORD THE ROGUE books wherever quality
literature is sold!**

MANKIND'S LAST HOPE . . .

. . . AND OUR FIRST GAME!

CYBORG COMMANDO™

It is the near future, and Planet Earth is on the verge of an
unprecedented era of peace and prosperity. Then, one day, unusual . . .
things . . . begin appearing in the sky, and everything is changed. Our
world is under attack by despicable aliens who don't even have the
guts to fight their battles themselves! Instead, they attack with
Xenoborgs, strange constructs of metal and flesh, grown in their vile
starship laboratories.

The Xenoborgs spread destruction and terror, and man's conventional
methods of attack and defense are all but useless against them. The
human race may be down, but it's not out. Scientists and technicians
have been laboring in underground complexes since the invasion, and
just when things look bleakest, they unleash the fruits of their labors:
the CYBORG COMMANDO fighting men/machines.

Every CYBORG COMMANDO character is a combination of man's
best feature — his intellect — and the latest advances in technology.
Sophisticated weapons systems, defense mechanisms, and sensory
devices are contained in a manufactured body that looks like a human
being, and all of the technology is controlled by the finest computer
known to man — the human brain!

Each player character in the CYBORG COMMANDO role-playing
game is part of an elite group whose goal is as simple as it is
challenging: Turn back the alien invasion force and save the Earth!
Using their individual special talents and abilities, player characters
perform singly or in groups — with the fate of the world in their hands
every time they set out.

The initial CYBORG COMMANDO game set, published by New
Infinities Productions, Inc., will be supported by scenarios and other
accessories, and will be supplemented by additional complete games
that augment the CYBORG COMMANDO game. Designed by Gary
Gygax, Frank Mentzer, and Kim Mohan, the CYBORG COMMANDO
game will revolutionize the role-playing game hobby. Watch for the first
boxed set in a game or hobby store near you, and get in on the
excitement — save the world and have fun at the same time!

CYBORG COMMANDO is a trademark owned by Trigee Enterprises Corporation.

THE PATH TO FUN

FOLLOWS THE

LINE!

Nothing but the best — that's what the FANTASY MASTER™ game accessory line is all about!

For too long, players of fantasy role-playing games have been frustrated by the abundance of adventures, scenarios, and accessories that can only be enjoyed by the people who play a *particular* game. New Infinities Productions, Inc., in cooperation with Gary Gygax, is out to change all that.

Every FANTASY MASTER adventure or accessory is designed and written by one of the top creative talents in the field, and each product in the line carries Gary's personal seal of approval. Best of all, each of them can be played or used with *any* fantasy role-playing game — even those yet to be published! Other companies have tried to produce so-called "generic" accessories before, but no one has done it the way New Infinities is doing it. Try one, and you'll be back for more!

The Convert, an adventure for mid-level characters written by Frank Mentzer, is the first product in the FANTASY MASTER line. It will be followed by *Baldemar: A Town*, a setting description created by Bob Blake. When you see the craftsmanship and creativity that went into these accessories, you won't want to wait for the others in the series. And fortunately, you won't have to wait long; New Infinities plans frequent and regular releases in the FANTASY MASTER series. Ask for them at your favorite game store or hobby store, or wherever role-playing game products are sold.

FANTASY MASTER is a trademark owned by New Infinities Productions, Inc.